Teacher Resource System

Short Vowels
and Consonants

Benchmark Education Company

145 Huguenot Street • New Rochelle, NY 10801

ISBN: 978-1-4509-3300-1
For ordering information, call **Toll-Free 1-877-236-2465** or visit our Web site at **www.benchmarkeducation.com.**

Table of Contents

StartUp PHONICS Introduction

Introduction

Components at a Glance

Getting Started

Using the Components

Managing Instruction in the Phonics Block

Phonics Instruction in a Balanced Literacy Program

StartUp™ Skills

Core Kit Materials Correlated to Units

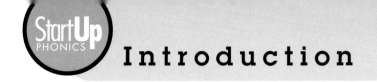

Introduction

StartUp™ Phonics is a complete kit designed for use in the phonics block within the Benchmark Literacy balanced core reading program. It presents a research-based, explicit, and systematic approach to teaching the phonics skills students need when learning to read.

Welcome to *BENCHMARK PHONICS™ StartUp™ Levels 1 and 2*

Thank you for selecting *StartUp™ Phonics* from Benchmark Education Company. *StartUp™ Phonics* supplies all the lesson resources, books, posters, and support tools needed to provide whole-group instruction, guided practice, and support in small groups, as well as independent practice opportunities. Teachers and students alike will find the lessons and materials engaging, hands-on, and motivating. Level 1 begins with phonological awareness and letter awareness, and Level 2 expands to cover short vowels and consonants, and introduces the concept of long vowels.

Why Teach Explicit Phonemic Awareness and Phonics?

A good reader is like a builder who is able to reach into a toolbox of familiar tools and pull out the right tool at the right moment. Like tools, each reading skill or strategy has an important use in the complex cognitive process of reading.

Think about a young student who is in the beginning stages of learning to read. He meets a large number of unfamiliar words in his environment. His brain is very busy trying to categorize, integrate, compare, and analyze the graphophonic information about letters, sounds, and words. Without the keys to this decoding process, the student cannot move quickly to other reading skills.

The Goals of *StartUp™ Phonics*

In order to shape young students' development of phonemic knowledge, *StartUp™ Phonics* creates opportunities to provide students at different stages of literacy growth with varied experiences that promote automatic and flexible control of letters and words. The systematic lessons will:

- **Build a foundation for successful phonemic awareness and phonics instruction**
  Most students are expected to begin phonics instruction in kindergarten, but many of these students still need reinforcement in readiness skills to ensure success. *StartUp™ Phonics* provides explicit lessons to teach and review phonological awareness skills. There is also explicit hands-on instruction to teach and/or review letter recognition and formation.

- **Explicitly teach short vowels and consonants**
  Once students have developed the readiness skills for phonics, each five-day unit focuses on a single phonetic element and its sound. Instruction over the five days moves from direct whole-group modeling and guided practice to real reading of decodable books, and skill review through independent literacy center activities. Each day includes explicit instruction for phonemic or phonological awareness, sound/symbol relationships, blending, spelling, and sight words.

- **Support and motivate all learners**
  Some students grasp phonics skills quickly and easily. Others need more time to practice each new skill. Every *StartUp™ Phonics* unit helps teachers tailor instruction to their students' needs with hands-on small-group activities for additional practice; independent extension activities; support tips for English Language Learners; motivating, multisensory manipulatives; and take-home practice activities.

- **Make systematic phonics instruction manageable in a comprehensive literacy classroom**
  Phonics is only one of the many daily literacy events in a comprehensive literacy classroom. *StartUp™ Phonics* is designed to help teachers maximize their time in the phonics block. The explicit teacher's guides in this book can support teachers who have little or no phonics experience. This program provides all the information teachers need to be successful.

The Research Behind *StartUp*™ *Phonics*

StartUp™ *Phonics* reflects the most current research on how to teach phonemic awareness and phonics effectively. The bibliography on page xlvi summarizes this research.

Phonological and Phonemic Awareness

Phonological awareness is the ability to hear and orally manipulate sounds in spoken language. It includes the recognition of words within sentences, the ability to hear rhyming units within words, the ability to hear syllables within words, and the ability to hear and manipulate phonemes, or individual sounds, within words, which is known as phonemic awareness. Phonemic awareness is the understanding that the sounds of spoken language work together to make words.

What the Research Says About Phonological and Phonemic Awareness Instruction	What *StartUp*™ *Phonics* Provides
• Before children learn to read print, they need to become aware of how the sounds in words work.	• Fifty Level 1 lessons reinforce students' awareness of sounds so that they can more easily move to sound/symbol relationships.
• If children do not know letter names and shapes, they need to be taught them along with phonemic awareness.	• The Level 1 lessons also reinforce letter recognition and formation through explicit modeling and guided practice.
• Children who have phonemic awareness skills are likely to have an easier time learning to read and spell.	• As short vowel and consonant phonics instruction begin with Level 2, Unit 1, phonemic awareness instruction continues on a daily basis.
• Blending and segmenting phonemes in words is likely to produce greater benefits to students' reading than teaching several types of manipulation.	• Students practice orally blending and segmenting sounds in every phonics unit.

Phonics Instruction

Phonics instruction focuses on teaching students the relationships between the sounds of the letters and the written symbols. In phonics instruction, students are taught to use these relationships to read and write words. Phonics instruction assumes that these sound/symbol relationships are systematic and predictable and that knowing these relationships will help students read words that are new to them.

What the Research Says About Phonics Instruction	What StartUp™ Phonics Provides
• Systematic and explicit phonics instruction is more effective than nonsystematic or no phonics instruction.	• StartUp™ Phonics units provide direct, explicit teaching of letter/sound relationships in a clearly defined sequence that schedules high-utility letter sounds early in the sequence.
• Students need frequent and cumulative review of taught letter sounds.	• Every StartUp™ Phonics unit incorporates review of previously taught letters and sounds.
• Effective phonics programs provide ample opportunities for students to apply their knowledge of letters and sounds to the reading of words, sentences, and stories.	• Within each unit, students progress from blending individual words to reading word lists to reading decodable texts that contain only words built on the phonics elements students have been taught. A carefully controlled number of sight words are introduced in each unit, as needed to read meaningful decodable texts.
• Approximately two years of phonics instruction is sufficient for most students.	• For most students, StartUp™ Phonics provides a year of beginning phonics instruction. BuildUp™ Phonics, for extending phonics instruction, also provides a year's worth of instruction. However, both kits can be paced to speed up or slow down instruction as needed.

Components at a Glance

Lesson Resources

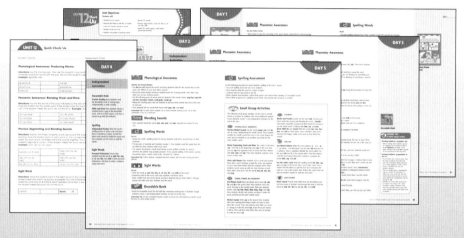

50 Lessons for Phonological and Letter Awareness. Engaging activities for the classroom and at home.

25 Units for Short Vowels and Consonants. Explicit instruction to motivate students in the classroom and take-home activities to increase success.

Books and Posters

Front

BUDDY

Under my umbrella
is my pug pup, Buddy.
I must soak him in the tub.
Buddy is all muddy!

26 Start Up™ Poetry Posters
(double-sided; 17"x 23")

Back

**26 Decodable Titles
(6-packs)
(8 pages; 5 7/8" x 6")**

**Take-Home Books
(available on the resource site)**

Support Tools

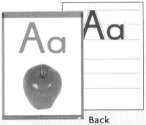

Front   Back

Alphabet Frieze Cards/ Letter Formation Cards
(set of 26; 8¹/₂" x 11")

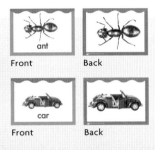

Front   Back

Front   Back

StartUp™ Picture Word Cards
(set of 129; 5" x 7")

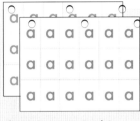

Phonetic Letter Card Set

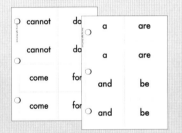

StartUp™ Sight Word Card Set
(set of 42; 8¹/₂" x 11")

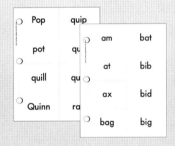

StartUp™ Decodable Word Card Set
(set of 153; 8¹/₂" x 11")

Alphabet Charts
(one 17¹/₂"x 23")

Student Alphabet Strips
(set of 20; 17¹/₂" x 23")

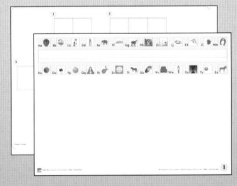

Student Workmats
(set of 20; 14" x 19¹/₂")

- **StartUp™ Song and Rhyme CD**
- **StartUp™ Poetry CD**

Getting Started Checklist

Use the following checklist to help you get ready to use *StartUp™ Phonics.*

❑ **Unpack your program components.** Use the *StartUp™ Phonics* Components at a Glance on pages viii–ix to make sure you have everything.

❑ **Organize your classroom.**

❑ **Familiarize yourself with how to use the program.** Read Using the Components on pages xii–xxi and review the *StartUp™* skills on pages xxiv-xxvii. Visit http://phonicsresources. benchmarkeducation.com to familiarize yourself with the digital tools available.

❑ **Study the teacher's guides.** Examine the posters, decodable texts, support tools, and assessments.

❑ **Prepare for assessment.**

• Download and print one copy of each student assessment page (laminate, if desired).

• Make one copy per student of the teacher record forms.

❑ **Prepare for instruction.**

• Create the spelling transparency (using the blackline master on page xli).

• Make copies of the parent letter (on pages xlii–xliii) if you wish to establish a home connection at the beginning of the year.

• Make student copies of lesson activities for upcoming lessons (using the downloadable blackline masters on the resource site).

❑ **Administer the pre-assessment** and analyze the results to determine your students' starting point in the *StartUp™ Phonics* skill sequence and how to group students for small-group instruction.

Setting Up Your Classroom

StartUp™ Phonics instruction accommodates whole-group and small-group instruction as well as center activities. Use the model below to help you prepare your classroom.

Whole Group Center

Classroom Resources
- Easel
- Overhead projector
- Pocket chart
- CD player
- Chalkboard or chart paper

***StartUp™ Phonics* Materials**
- Lesson resources and support tools as needed
- Poetry Posters

Small Group Center

Classroom Resources
- Pocket chart
- Chart paper

***StartUp™ Phonics* Materials**
- Lesson resources and support tools as needed
- Decodable texts
- Poetry Posters

Independent Centers

Classroom Resources
- CD player and headphones

***StartUp™ Phonics* Materials**
- Lesson resources and support tools as needed

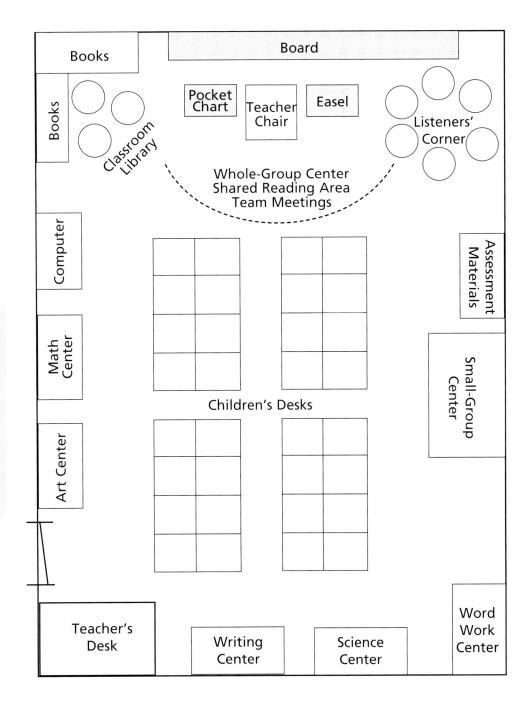

StartUp Level 1 Teacher's Guides for Phonological and Letter Awareness

Fifty Level 1 lessons begin the instructional sequence in *StartUp™ Phonics*. These explicit lessons are intended for students who need beginning-of-the-year instruction or review in phonological and letter awareness before they move to phonemic awareness and phonics instruction. Use the pre/post assessments to determine whether or not to use these lessons with your students.

Phonological awareness instruction follows a systematic sequence that moves from simple to more complex phonological tasks.

Two explicit phonological awareness activities are provided in each lesson using the Song and Rhyme CD, picture cards, and other support tools.

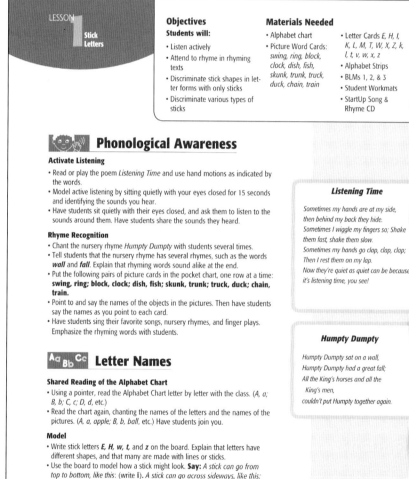

LESSON 1
Stick Letters

Objectives
Students will:
- Listen actively
- Attend to rhyme in rhyming texts
- Discriminate stick shapes in letter forms with only sticks
- Discriminate various types of sticks

Materials Needed
- Alphabet chart
- Picture Word Cards: *swing, ring, block, clock, dish, fish, skunk, trunk, truck, duck, chain, train*
- Letter Cards *E, H, I, K, L, M, T, W, X, Z, k, l, t, v, w, x, z*
- Alphabet Strips
- BLMs 1, 2, & 3
- Student Workmats
- StartUp Song & Rhyme CD

Phonological Awareness

Activate Listening
- Read or play the poem *Listening Time* and use hand motions as indicated by the words.
- Model active listening by sitting quietly with your eyes closed for 15 seconds and identifying the sounds you hear.
- Have students sit quietly with their eyes closed, and ask them to listen to the sounds around them. Have students share the sounds they heard.

Rhyme Recognition
- Chant the nursery rhyme *Humpty Dumpty* with students several times.
- Tell students that the nursery rhyme has several rhymes, such as the words *wall* and *fall*. Explain that rhyming words sound alike at the end.
- Put the following pairs of picture cards in the pocket chart, one row at a time: **swing, ring; block, clock; dish, fish; skunk, trunk; truck, duck; chain, train.**
- Point to and say the names of the objects in the pictures. Then have students say the names as you point to each card.
- Have students sing their favorite songs, nursery rhymes, and finger plays. Emphasize the rhyming words with students.

Letter Names

Shared Reading of the Alphabet Chart
- Using a pointer, read the Alphabet Chart letter by letter with the class. (*A, a; B, b; C, c; D, d,* etc.)
- Read the chart again, chanting the names of the letters and the names of the pictures. (*A, a, apple; B, b, ball,* etc.) Have students join you.

Model
- Write stick letters *E, H, w, t,* and *z* on the board. Explain that letters have different shapes, and that many are made with lines or sticks.
- Use the board to model how a stick might look. **Say:** *A stick can go from top to bottom, like this:* (write I). *A stick can go across sideways, like this:* (write _). *A stick can go across in a slant, like this:* (/) *or like this:* (\). *Some letters are made with more than one stick, like these.* (Say the name of each letter as you write it *M, E, H, K, T, Z, x, z, w,* and **v.**)
- Place letter cards *T, I, K, V, E, H, L, M, W, X, Z k, l, t, v, w,* and *x* in a pocket chart.
- Select a letter card and model how to trace the sticks. For example, say: *The name of this letter is* **T.** *Straight stick down, straight stick across the top.*

✓ **QUICK-CHECK** Distribute blackline master 1 and instruct students to cut out each picture and say its name. Have them match the rhyming pairs and glue them on their papers.

Listening Time

Sometimes my hands are at my side,
then behind my back they hide.
Sometimes I wiggle my fingers so; Shake
them fast, shake them slow.
Sometimes my hands go clap, clap, clap;
Then I rest them on my lap.
Now they're quiet as quiet can be because
it's listening time, you see!

Humpty Dumpty

Humpty Dumpty sat on a wall,
Humpty Dumpty had a great fall;
All the King's horses and all the
King's men,
couldn't put Humpty together again.

©2012 Benchmark Education Company, LLC

Benchmark Phonics • StartUp Level 1 • Phonological Awareness and Letter Awareness

To provide students with a quick beginning-of-the-year review of previously taught skills, complete each lesson in one day. To provide more intensive instruction and practice, spread the lessons over more than one day by slowing the pace, repeating some of the activities, and incorporating the small-group and independent activities.

Letter lessons begin with letter discrimination and then move through the alphabet from A to Z. All lessons include modeling, guided practice, and writing.

Small-group and independent activities help you support students at a range of levels.

Independent Activities

Phonological Awareness

Place the following picture cards in the literacy center: **swing, ring, block, clock, dish, fish, skunk, trunk, truck, duck, chain, train.** Have students say the name of each picture card and match the picture cards that rhyme.

Letter Discrimination

Instruct students to sort individual sets of stick-letter cards according to their various attributes: long sticks, short sticks, and long and short sticks.

Provide models of the various types of sticks, as well as various stick letters, on a large sheet of butcher paper. Students can practice writing sticks and stick letters.

Guided Practice

- Ask individual students to select a letter card from the pocket chart, trace the sticks, and say the name of the letter. Provide support as needed.
- Provide additional support for students who need it by guiding their fingers over the sticks in the letter and telling them the letter name.
- Repeat the task until all the letter names have been identified and the students understand that all the letters are alike because they have sticks.
- Distribute individual sets of letter cards **H, K, L, M, t, v,** and **z.** Have students line up the cards on their workmats.
- Instruct students to pull down each stick letter.
- Ask them to trace the sticks of each letter and say the name of the letter if they can.
- Help individual students use a finger to trace the sticks in the letters or give them the name of the letter, if necessary.

Write

- Have students practice writing the different types of sticks on their workmats. Model each type of stick again on the board. Say: *Make some straight sticks on your workmats. Make them like this:* (l, l, l ,l). *Make some slanted sticks like this:* (/, /, /, /). *Make some slanted sticks like this:* (\, \, \, \, \). *Make some sticks like this:* (_, _, _, _, _).
- Distribute blackline master 2 and ask students to trace the different types of sticks. (The blackline master may be completed at this time or in a literacy center.)

 QUICK-CHECK Use blackline master 3. Instruct students to cut out each letter card and sort the letters into those that have short sticks and those that have long sticks.

 ## Small Group Activities

Select from the following small group activities to provide hands-on practice for students who need extra support.

LISTENING

Have students sit quietly with their eyes closed. Ask them to listen to the sounds around them for 15 seconds. Encourage students to discuss the sounds they heard. Then have students listen for an additional 15 seconds with their eyes open. Discuss the difference between what they heard with their eyes open and closed.

RHYME RECOGNITION

Recite *Humpty Dumpty* to students, emphasizing the rhyming words by whispering them, saying them louder, or using crescendo. Recite the poem again. As you come to some of the rhyming couplets, stop and say each word of the couplet. Tell students to use a signal if the words rhyme. For example, ask: *Do the words* **wall** *and* **fall** *rhyme? If they do, show me by giving me a "thumbs up" signal.*

LETTER DISCRIMINATION

Use the board to show the different types of sticks and that some letters are made with more that one stick. Say the name of each letter as you form it. Distribute letter cards that have only sticks to students. Choose from **E, H, I, K, L, M, T, V, W, X, Z, k, l, t, v, w, x,** and **z.** As you model the task with letter cards in the pocket chart, have each student trace the sticks and say the letter name.

2   Benchmark Phonics • StartUp Level 1 • Phonological Awareness and Letter Awareness   ©2012 Benchmark Education Company, LLC

StartUp Level 2 Teacher's Guides for Phonemic Awareness and Phonics

The twenty-five Level 2 units in *StartUp™ Phonics* teach short vowels and consonants in a systematic sequence that supports current research on best practices. All teacher's guides follow a consistent sequence that provides five days of instruction targeting one phonetic element and its sound.

Start with phonological and phonemic awareness. (Days 1–4)

Move to quick sound/symbol relationship activities with word and picture sorts. (Days 1–2)

Provide blending practice daily with decodable word lists. (Days 1–4)

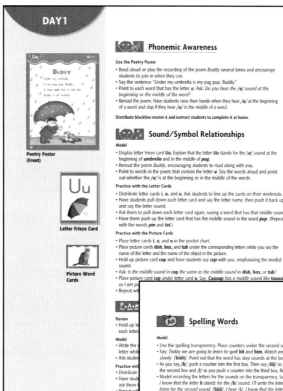

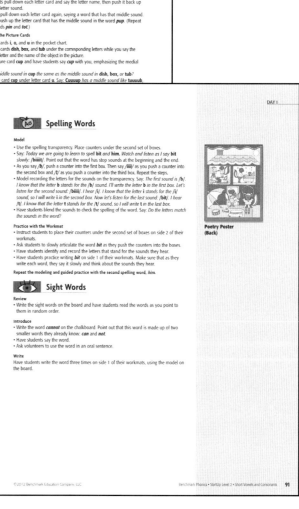

Introduce and practice six spelling words per unit. (Days 1-4)

Beginning with Unit 6, introduce and practice sight words. (Days 1–4)

Work with small groups of students to read decodable texts. (Days 3–4) Students who are not reading the text complete a blackline master and independent activities.

Use the quick-checks provided on the last page of each unit to assess students' progress. Work with small groups of students who need extra support. (Day 5) Students who are not in the small group complete a blackline master and independent activities.

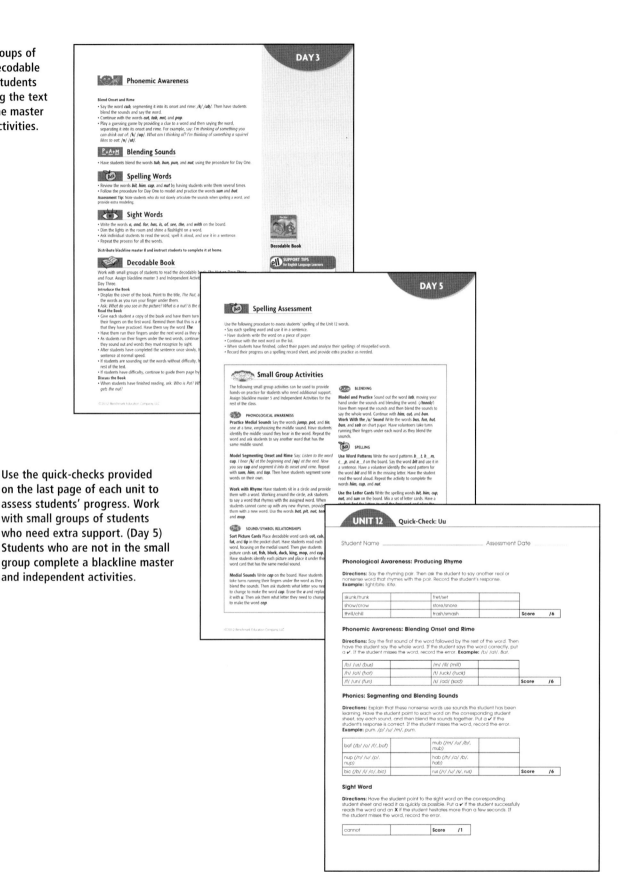

StartUp™ **Poetry Posters**

Twenty-six Poetry Posters—one for each letter of the alphabet—can be folded for easy storage. (Unit 1 has two Poetry Posters.) The posters are used for whole-group instruction as well as small-group activities to provide additional support.

The front of each poster features a playful, alliterative poem that emphasizes the target letter and sound. It is used to develop phonemic awareness and sound/symbol relationships.

The back of each poster features a playful, wordless illustration with many objects whose names reflect the target sound. Students practice phonemic awareness as they locate objects with the sound.

Decodable Texts

StartUp™ Phonics follows best-practice research that recommends students have frequent opportunities to apply phonics skills in authentic reading contexts.

The *StartUp™ Phonics* decodable texts have been carefully written so that only phonics elements that students have learned and practiced appear in the books. A very limited number of sight words are also used in the decodable texts. New sight words are always explicitly taught before they appear in students' decodable text reading. Previously taught sight words are also reviewed.

20 Fiction Titles

Twenty engaging fiction titles introduce the new skills. Beginning in Level 2, Unit 6, one of these decodable titles is provided for each phonetic element that is introduced. Students will respond to the playful illustrations and the cast of characters they encounter from story to story.

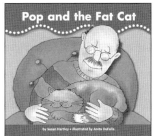

6 Nonfiction Titles

Six nonfiction, photo-illustrated decodable titles provide additional practice after all twenty-five Level 2 units of the StartUp™ Phonics skill sequence have been completed.

Take-Home Books

allow you to send students home with a real book to share with family members. Available for download and printing on the resource site.

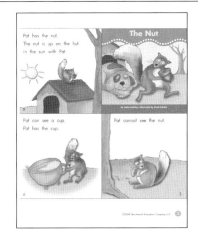

Support Tools

High-quality, durable, and motivating manipulatives are provided to support the instruction throughout *StartUp™ Phonics*.

StartUp™ Song and Rhyme CD
Twelve playful, familiar rhymes and twelve well-loved children's songs support the Level 1 phonological awareness lessons.

StartUp™ Poetry CD
Lively readings of all twenty-six *StartUp™ Phonics* Poetry Posters support the phonological awareness lessons and literacy center/independent activities in the Level 2 units.

26 Alphabet Frieze Cards/Letter Formation Cards
The uppercase and lowercase letters are displayed on the front of each laminated frieze card, along with a photo illustrating the target sound. The card fronts are used in Level 1 lessons and Level 2 units to teach letter recognition and sound/symbol relationships. On the back of each card are letter formation guides and writing lines. The card backs are used to model and provide practice with letter formation in the Level 1 lessons.

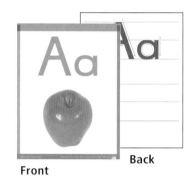

Front   Back

StartUp™ Picture Word Cards
All picture cards used in the Level 1 lessons and Level 2 units are provided in an alphabetically indexed box within the *StartUp™ Phonics* storage box. Because you will use these cards in many lessons, it is recommended that you store them alphabetically for easy reference. The cards have pictures on one side, for phonological awareness practice, and pictures with labels on the other side for picture and word sorts.

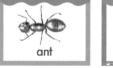
Front   Back

Front   Back

StartUp™ Sight Word Card Set
Two copies of every sight word explicitly taught in *StartUp™ Phonics* are provided on card stock to support whole-group instruction and small-group and independent activities. These cards are used in multiple lessons. Keep in mind that blackline master versions of these cards, organized by lesson, are also provided on the resource site.

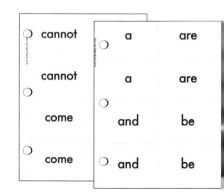

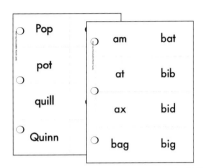

StartUp™ Decodable Word Card Set

One copy each of every decodable word used in *StartUp*™ *Phonics* lessons is also provided on card stock. These cards are also used in multiple lessons. Blackline master versions of these cards are provided on the resource site for each Level 2 unit.

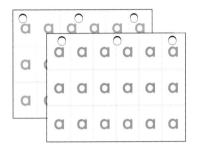

Phonetic Letter Card Set

Multiple copies of each letter of the alphabet are provided on card stock for use in pocket chart, small-group, literacy center, and independent activities with Level 1 lessons and Level 2 units. Blackline master versions of these cards are also provided on the resource site for each Level 1 lesson and Level 2 unit.

Student Alphabet Strips

Twenty alphabet strips, sized for student use, support learning the alphabet and sound/symbol relationships.

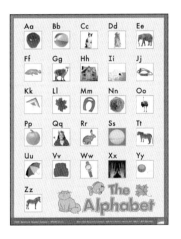

Alphabet Charts

A large alphabet chart is included in the kit. It is a useful resource for the Level 1 letter-awareness lessons.

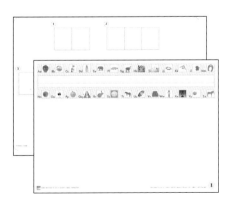

Student Workmats

The twenty laminated Student Workmats are double-sided. Side one has an alphabet strip at the top and a blank space on the bottom for practice in writing letters and words with a dry-erase marker. Side two has elkonian boxes for two-, three-, four-, five-, and six-letter words. Students can practice hearing and recording sounds with counters or by writing letters in the boxes.

Reproducible Tools, Activities, and Home Connections Resources

Every Level 1 lesson and Level 2 unit has corresponding reproducibles needed for instruction. They are all available for download and printing at http://phonicsresources.benchmarkeducation.com. You may also choose to display these resources on your whiteboard.

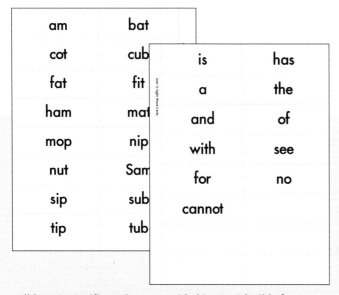

All lesson-specific tools are provided in reproducible form for literacy center and independent activities. Once you make reproducible versions, save them in envelopes.

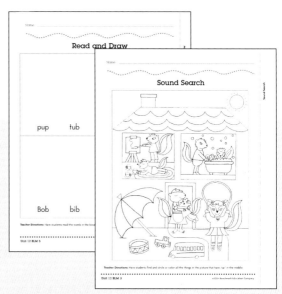

Activity blackline masters, referenced in each lesson or unit, are available.

Level 1 lessons have one take-home activity.

Level 2 units have three take-home activities.

Use the parent letter in English or Spanish on pages xlii–xliii to establish a home connection at the beginning of the year.

All assessments have teacher records for documenting individual student progress.

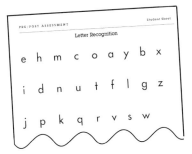

Letter, phonics, and sight word assessments have student pages. You may wish to laminate these for reuse.

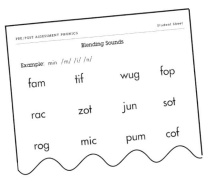

Phonics assessments require students to decode nonsense words in order to truly assess their knowledge of sound/symbol relationships.

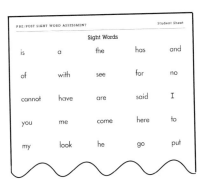

A sight word assessment measures all the words that are not decodable.

Assessment

This *StartUp™ Phonics* Teacher Resource System provides a variety of methods for you to gather, record, and evaluate information about your students' knowledge of sound/symbol relationships. Based on this information, you can decide what skill instruction your students need and whether they would benefit from small-group instruction.

Pre/Post Assessments

Pre/Post Assessments cover all skills taught in the kit. All assessments are administered on a one-to-one basis. They are located behind the Assessment tab in this TRS.

Quick-Checks

Quick-Check Assessments, included after each week of instruction, include phonological awareness, segmenting and blending, and sight-word recognition. As you analyze student responses, note which sounds or sight words give students difficulty. You may decide to provide further practice in the skill by using the small-group activities in each unit. The student sheets are available on the resource site.

Informal Observation

It is recommended that in addition to the Pre/Post and Quick-Check Assessments, you use informal observation to note whether students are mastering the skills. If you are uncertain about how a student is performing on a skill, call on that student to perform the task during the lesson and observe what he/she does. If you feel the student requires more practice, use the small-group mini-lessons provided within each unit. Throughout the unit, teacher assessment tips are provided to help you make observations about student progress.

Quick-Check Teacher Record

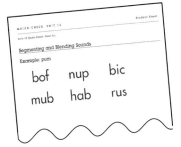

Quick-Check Student Sheet

Grouping Students

Use the pre-test to determine where in the kit you will begin instruction (Level 1 lessons or Level 1 units). The pre-test will also help you determine whether or not you need to do all sections of the unit lessons, and it will help you identify students who will need more support in learning the sounds. The independent activities for each unit allow you to provide meaningful learning for the larger group while you work with a small group or individual students who have not mastered the skills.

Most of the Level 2 unit instruction can be done with a whole class, using a pocket chart or chalkboard for demonstration purposes. Assessment tips throughout the unit help you determine whether students need further support in a small group. It is recommended that decodable texts be read with small groups of students so that you can more easily monitor students' reading.

Pacing the Instruction

StartUp™ Phonics has been designed for use with a whole group during the phonics block of your comprehensive literacy program. Each day's lesson is designed to fit within a 20–30 minute instructional block of time. During this time, students will practice sounding out words in a controlled, decodable format. They should have the opportunity to apply their decoding skills, along with other reading strategies, during the small-group reading block of your literacy program.

Each unit spans a five-day period. In other words, you will introduce one skill per week. You can choose to use some or all of the activities, depending on the needs of your students. For example, you may find that you want students to work more quickly and learn a new skill every three days. If this is the case, you may select from any of the activities that you feel will most benefit your students.

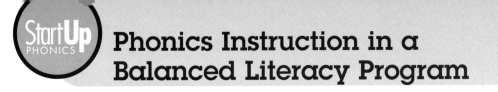

Phonics Instruction in a Balanced Literacy Program

Introducing Benchmark Literacy for Grades K–6

Benchmark Education Company is known for its pedagogically sound, research-proven literacy solutions. Now Benchmark Education is proud to put these carefully developed, scientifically tested components into one comprehensive, easy-to-implement reading program for Grades K–6. Benchmark Literacy supports all the daily components of high-quality reading instruction, including the research-based, systematic approach found in StartUp Phonics.
You will find:

- **Assessment** to drive instruction and help teachers monitor progress

- **Interactive read-alouds** to model good-reader strategies with award-winning trade literature

- **Shared reading mini-lessons** to explicitly model comprehension, vocabulary, and fluency

- **Differentiated small-group reading** that builds seamlessly on shared-reading instruction and addresses the needs of above-, on-, and below-level readers, as well as English learners and special-needs students

- **Independent reading** to encourage the transfer of skills and strategies

- **Phonemic awareness, phonics, and word study** to build strong decoding and word-solving strategies

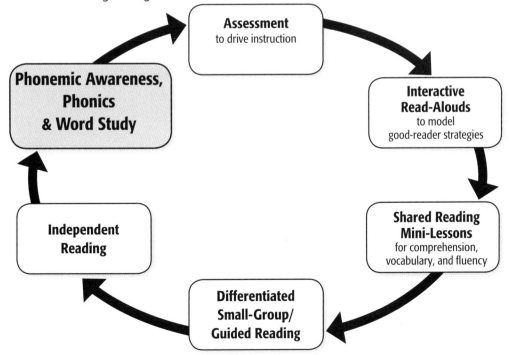

LEVEL 1 Phonological and Letter Awareness Lessons

Week 1	Day 1	Day 2	Day 3	Day 4	Day 5
Phonological Awareness Skill	• Listening • Rhyme recognition	• Listening • Rhyme recognition	• Listening • Rhyme recognition	• Listening • Rhyme recognition	• Listening • Rhyme recognition
Letter Recognition and Formation	Letter Discrimination • Stick letters	Letter Discrimination • Straight sticks	Letter Discrimination • Slanted Sticks	Letter Discrimination • Straight and slanted sticks	Letter Discrimination • Review stick letters
Week 2	**Day 1**	**Day 2**	**Day 3**	**Day 4**	**Day 5**
Phonological Awareness Skill	• Listening • Rhyme recognition	• Listening • Rhyme recognition	• Listening • Rhyme recognition	• Listening • Rhyme recognition	• Listening • Rhyme recognition
Letter Recognition and Formation	Letter Discrimination • Circles and curves	Letter Discrimination • Sticks and curves	Letter Discrimination • Sticks and circles	Letter Discrimination • Letters that look alike	• Review letter discrimination
Week 3	**Day 1**	**Day 2**	**Day 3**	**Day 4**	**Day 5**
Phonological Awareness Skill	• Word discrimination • Rhyme recognition	• Word discrimination • Concept of words	• Listening • Rhyme recognition	• Word discrimination • Concept of words	• Word discrimination • Rhyme recognition
Letter Recognition and Formation	A	a	B	b	Cc
Week 4	**Day 1**	**Day 2**	**Day 3**	**Day 4**	**Day 5**
Phonological Awareness Skill	• Word discrimination • Rhyme recognition	• Listening • Concept of words	• Word discrimination • Concept of words	• Word discrimination • Concept of words	• Word discrimination • Concept of words
Letter Recognition and Formation	D	d	E	e	F
Week 5	**Day 1**	**Day 2** .	**Day 3**	**Day 4**	**Day 5**
Phonological Awareness Skill	• Rhyme recognition • Concept of words	• Word discrimination • Concept of sentences	• Listening • Concept of sentences	• Rhyme recognition • Concept of words	• Listening • Producing rhyme
Letter Recognition and Formation	f	G	g	H	h

Week 6	Day 1	Day 2	Day 3	Day 4	Day 5
Phonological Awareness Skill	• Producing rhyme • Segmenting words by syllables	• Identifying rhyme • Segmenting words by syllables	• Listening • Segmenting words by syllables	• Segmenting initial sounds • Identifying repeated sounds	• Segmenting initial sounds • Segmenting compound words
Letter Recognition and Formation	Ii	J	j	Kk	L
Week 7	**Day 1**	**Day 2**	**Day 3**	**Day 4**	**Day 5**
Phonological Awareness Skill	• Producing rhyme • Segmenting compound words	• Producing rhyme • Segmenting initial sounds	• Listening • Producing rhyme	• Identifying rhyme • Segmenting initial sounds	• Sound discrimination • Segmenting words by syllables
Letter Recognition and Formation	I	M	m	N	n
Week 8	**Day 1**	**Day 2**	**Day 3**	**Day 4**	**Day 5**
Phonological Awareness Skill	• Producing rhyme • Segmenting initial sounds	• Sound discrimination • Segmenting words into syllables	• Performing steps in a sequence • Identifying rhyme	• Segmenting initial sounds • Segmenting words by syllables	• Segmenting initial sounds • Segmenting words into syllables
Letter Recognition and Formation	Oo	Pp	Q	q	R
Week 9	**Day 1**	**Day 2**	**Day 3**	**Day 4**	**Day 5**
Phonological Awareness Skill	• Producing rhyme • Segmenting words into syllables	• Blending syllables • Segmenting initial sounds	• Blending syllables • Segmenting words into syllables	• Sound discrimination • Blending syllables	• Segmenting initial sounds • Segmenting words into syllables
Letter Recognition and Formation	r	Ss	T	t	Uu
Week 10	**Day 1**	**Day 2**	**Day 3**	**Day 4**	**Day 5**
Phonological Awareness Skill	• Producing rhyme • Segmenting initial sounds	• Blending syllables • Segmenting initial sounds	• Blending syllables • Segmenting initial sounds	• Blending syllables • Segmenting initial sounds	• Segmenting initial sounds • Segmenting words by syllables
Letter Recognition and Formation	Vv	Ww	Xx	Yy	Zz

LEVEL 2 Phonemic Awareness and Phonics Units

Unit/ Phonics Skill	Phonological Awareness Skill	Phonemic Awareness Skill	Sight Words	Spelling Words
1/Mm and Short Aa	listening for rhyme	• initial /m/ • medial /a/	N/A	am
2/Ss	listening for rhyme	• initial /s/ • listening for initial sounds	N/A	am, Sam
3/Tt	listening for rhyme	• initial /t/ • listening for initial consonant sounds	N/A	am, Sam, mat, sat, Tam
4/Nn	listening for rhyme	• initial /n/ • differentiating consonant sounds	N/A	man, Nat, mat, sat, Tam, tan
5/ Short Ii	listening for rhyme	• medial /i/ • differentiating medial sounds	N/A	man, Nat, tan, am, in, sit
6/Ff	listening for rhyme	• initial /f/ • listening for initial consonants	is	man, mat, fan, fit, if, fin
7/Pp	identifying and producing rhyme	• initial /p/ • blending and segmenting onset and rime	a, has	tin, fat, tap, pat, pin, sip
8/ Short Oo	identifying and producing rhyme	• medial /o/ • discriminating medial sounds	the	nap, fit, on, pot, mop, not
9/Cc	identifying and producing rhyme	• initial /k/ • discriminating sounds	and, of	pit, top, cat, can, cot, cap
10/Hh	identifying and producing rhyme	• initial /h/ • blending and segmenting onset and rime	with, see	nip, can, hat, him, hit, hop
11/Bb	identifying and producing rhyme	• initial /b/ • identifying final consonants	for, no	hat, sap, bat, bib, bin, bit
12/ Short Uu	identifying and producing rhyme	• initial and medial /u/ • blending onset and rime	cannot	bit, him, cup, nut, sun, but
13/Rr	identifying and producing rhyme	• initial /r/ • differentiating final consonants	have, are	cup, hop, run, rub, rip
14/ Short Ee	identifying and producing rhyme	• initial and medial /e/ • segmenting and blending onset and rime	said	rap, cab, met, pen, let, ten
15/Gg	identifying and producing rhyme	• initial /g/ • segmenting and blending onset and rime	I, you, me	men, bin, tag, get, beg, rug

Unit/ Phonics Skill	Phonological Awareness Skill	Phonemic Awareness Skill	Sight Words	Spelling Words
16/Dd	identifying and producing rhyme	• initial /d/ • blending phonemes	come, here, to	bag, pen, dig, had, red, did
17/Ww		• initial /w/ • blending phonemes • blending and segmenting onset and rime	my, look, he	bed, pat, wet, win, wig, wed
18/Ll		• initial /l/ • differentiating final consonants • blending and segmenting onset and rime	go	bag, dad, let, lap, lid, lip
19/Jj		• initial /j/ • initial sound substitution • blending and segmenting phonemes	put, want	lab, bin, job, jam, Jim, Jen
20/Kk		• initial /k/ • initial sound substitution • blending and segmenting sounds	this, she, saw	led, bad, kiss, Kit, jam, Kim
21/Yy		• initial /y/ • vowel substitution • blending and segmenting sounds	now, like, do	jog, but, yes, yap, yell, yet
22/Vv		• initial /v/ • vowel substitution • blending and segmenting sounds	home, they, went	yet, tip, vet, van, Val, hug
23/Qq		• initial /kw/ • initial sound substitution • blending and segmenting sounds	good	jam, bad, quit, yet, quip, quill
24/Xx		• final /ks/ • vowel substitution • blending and segmenting sounds	was, be, we	sip, did, mix, box, fox, wax
25/Zz		• initial and final /z/ • final sound substitution • blending and segmenting sounds	there, then, out	fox, quiz, zip, buzz, zap, fuzz

Core Kit Materials Correlated to Units

Level 2 Unit	Decodable Title	Poetry Posters	Alphabet Frieze Cards
1	N/A	Melons and Muffins; Apple Pie	Mm; Aa
2	N/A	Seven Silly Sailors	Ss
3	N/A	Turtles	Tt
4	N/A	Nip the Newt	Nn
5	N/A	Baking	Ii
6	Fit	Fuzzy Fox and Fiddle	Ff
7	Pam Has a Map	Pet Parade	Pp
8	Pop	Oliver and Dot	Oo
9	Pop and the Fat Cat	Camping	Cc
10	The Hot Pan	Happy Thoughts	Hh
11	The Bib	Baby Bird	Bb
12	The Nut	Buddy	Uu
13	Rob	The Race	Rr
14	Mem the Hen	The Red Hen	Ee
15	Get the Gum	By the Garden Gate	Gg
16	The Red Pen	Dot	Dd
17	The Wig	Worm	Ww
18	Pop and Len	Lenny Lion	Ll
19	The Job	Jumping	Jj
20	Kit and Kim	King Karl's Kangaroo	Kk
21	Yip and Yap	Yellow	Yy
22	The Vet	Violins and Violets	Vv
23	Quinn	The Queen's Nap	Qq
24	The Sax	Max	Xx
25	Buzz, Buzz	Baby Zigzag	Zz

UNIT **1**

Short Aa
and Mm

UNIT **1**
Short Aa
and Mm

Unit Objectives

Students will:

- Identify the sound /m/
- Associate the letter Mm with the sound /m/
- Listen for words that rhyme
- Identify the sound /a/
- Associate the letter Aa with the sound /a/
- Blend sounds to read the word am
- Spell the word am

Day 1

BLM 4

Letter Card:
m

Day 2

BLM 2

BLM 3

BLM 5

Letter Card:
m

Day 3

BLM 2

BLM 3

Spelling
Transparency

Letter Card:
a

Picture Word Cards: **ant, antelope, apple, ax, magnet, mitten, mop**

Day 4

BLM 3

Letter Cards:
a, m,

Day 5

BLM 1

Quick-Check
Student Sheet

Picture Word Cards: **ant, antelope, apple, ax, magnet, map, mitten, mop**

Poetry Posters

Student Workmat

Letter Frieze Cards

Poetry CD

Core Materials

All print resources can be downloaded from http://phonicsresources.benchmarkeducation.com

**Poetry Poster
(Front)**

Letter Frieze Card

Phonemic Awareness

Use the Poetry Poster

- Read aloud or play the recording of the poem *Melons and Muffins.*
- Ask students to listen for the */m/* sound while you read the sentence "'Melons and muffins are yummy!' said Monkey merrily."
- Reread the poem and have students clap each time they hear */m/* at the beginning of a word.

Distribute blackline master 4 and instruct students to complete it at home.

Sound/Symbol Relationships

Model

- Display letter frieze card **Mm**. Explain that the letter **Mm** stands for the */m/* sound in the word **magnet**.
- Reread the poem *Melons and Muffins,* and invite students to read along with you.
- Point to words in the poem that begin with the letter **m**. Say each word aloud and ask students to say the words with you. Emphasize the */m/* sound in each word.
- List students' names that start with */m/*. Ask students if they can think of other names that start with */m/*, and add these to the list.
- Ask students to brainstorm a list of words that contain the */m/* sound. Write these words on a chart. Underline the letter **m** in each word.

Practice with the Letter Cards

- Distribute letter card **m,** four per student. Have students line up the cards on their workmats.
- Have students pull down each letter card and say the letter name, then push the card back up and say the letter sound.
- Ask students to pull down each letter card again, saying a word that starts with the */m/* sound.
- Have them push up the letter card that starts the word **man**. (Repeat with the words **map, Michael,** and **miss.**)

Phonemic Awareness

Use the Poetry Poster
- Show students the picture on the back of the poetry poster and have them name all the objects in the picture.
- Point to the monkey in the picture and say the word **monkey**.
  Ask: *What sound do you hear at the beginning of the word?*
- Ask volunteers to point to something in the picture whose name starts with **/m/**.
  Have them say the name of the object, emphasizing the sound at the beginning.

Distribute blackline master 5 and instruct students to complete it at home.

Assessment Tip: Assess individual students by pointing to something in the picture, saying its name, and asking whether they hear the **/m/** sound in the word.

 # Sound/Symbol Relationships

Review
- Display letter frieze card **Mm**. Say: *This is the letter* **Mm**. *It stands for the* /**m**/ *sound, as in the word* **magnet**.
- Reread the poem *Melons and Muffins,* and invite students to read along with you.
- Point to words in the poem that begin with the letter **m**. Say the words aloud and ask students to say the words with you.

Practice with the Letter Cards
- Distribute letter card **m**, four per student. Have students line up the cards on their workmats.
- Have students pull down each letter card and say the letter name, then push the card back up and say the letter sound.
- Ask students to pull down each letter card again, saying a word that starts with the **/m/** sound.
- Have them push up the letter card that starts the word **mad**. (Repeat with the words **mop, Mary,** and **mat.**)

**Poetry Poster
(Back)**

Independent Activities

Phonological Awareness

Picture Cards Provide picture cards in the learning center. Students can:
• separate the cards that start with **/m/**
• separate the cards that have the **/a/** sound

Listen Have students listen to the recordings of the poems *Melons and Muffins* and *Apple Pie* in the listening center.

Poetry Poster 1 Provide copies of blackline master 2 in the learning center. Instruct students to circle all the objects that begin with **/m/**.

Poetry Poster 2 Provide copies of blackline master 3 in the learning center. Instruct students to circle all the objects that begin with **/a/** or have medial **/a/**.

Draw Pictures Have students fold a large piece of paper in half. Have them draw pictures of things that begin like *man* in one section and pictures of things that have short *a* in the second section.

Sound/Symbol Relationships

Spell the Word Place letter cards **a** and **m** in the center. Students can use the letters to spell the word *am*.

Letter/Picture Match Place picture cards **mop, map, mitten, magnet, apple, ax, ant,** and **antelope** in one pile and letter cards **a** and **m** in another pile. Have students match the picture card with the letter that stands for the beginning sound of the picture name.

Phonemic Awareness

Model
• Say: */Maaaan/. I hear the /a/ sound in the middle of the word* **man**. *Listen very carefully to the sound in the middle of these words:* **man, mat, cap.**
• Have students repeat the words and identify which sound is the same in all three words.
• Say the following words slowly, one at a time: *map, sat, run, sit, fat, let, ran, hot, fan, cat.* Students are to put their hands on top of their heads if a word has the /a/ sound in the middle, and shake their heads if it does not.

Practice with the Poetry Poster
• Show students the picture on the back of the poetry poster *Apple Pie* and have them name all the objects in the picture.
• Point to the cat in the picture and say the word **cat.** Ask: *What sound do you hear in the middle of the word?*
• Ask volunteers to point to something in the picture that has the /a/ sound in the middle of its name. Have them say the name of the object, emphasizing the medial sound.

Listen for Long Vowel Sounds
• Say: *Listen as I say the sounds that make up the word* **fame.** */f/ /ā/ /m/. The word* **fame** *has the long vowel sound. Listen again to the vowel sound. /f/ /ā/ /m/.*
• Repeat with the word **rain**.

Sound/Symbol Relationships

Model
• Display letter frieze card **Aa**. Explain that the letter **Aa** stands for the /a/ sound in the word **apple**.
• Read the poem *Apple Pie*, emphasizing the /a/ sound, and invite students to read along with you.
• Point to the words that have /a/ at the beginning. Have students say the words with you.
• Point to the words that have medial /a/. Say the words aloud and ask students to say the words with you.
• Ask students to brainstorm a list of words that contain the /a/ sound. Write the words on the board and underline the letter *a* in each word.

Practice with the Letter Cards
• Distribute letter card **a,** four cards per student. Have them line up the cards on their workmats.
• Have students pull down each letter card and say the letter name, then push the letter card back up and say the letter sound.
• Ask them to pull down each letter card again, saying a word that has the /a/ sound.
• Have them push up the letter card that stands for the sound in the middle of **man.** (Repeat with the words **map, cat,** and **pan.**)

Compare/Contrast Long and Short Vowel Sounds
• Ask students to brainstorm a list of words that have the long *a* sound. Next, ask students to brainstorm another list of words that have the short *a* sound.
• Discuss the two different sounds of the vowels.

Blending Sounds

Model

- Write the word *am* on the board.
- Demonstrate how to sound out the word by moving your hand under the letters and blending the sounds, holding each sound for one second (/*aaaammmm*/). Then say the word at normal speed.
- Ask students to sound out the word with you. Repeat sounding out the word several times.

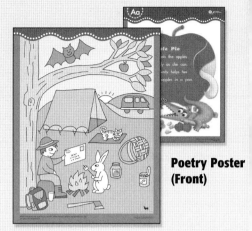

**Poetry Poster
(Front)**

**Poetry Poster
(Back)**

Spelling Words

Review

- Use the spelling transparency. Place counters under the second set of boxes on the transparency.
- Say: *Today we are going to learn to spell the word* **am***. Watch and listen as I say it slowly:* /**aaaammmm**/.
- As you say /**aaaa**/, push a counter into the first box. As you say /**mmmm**/, push a counter into the second box. Repeat the steps.
- Model recording the letters for the sounds on the transparency. Say: *The first sound is* /**aaaa**/*. I know that the letter* **a** *stands for the* /**aaaa**/ *sound. I'll write the letter* **a** *in the first box. Let's listen for the second sound:* /**ammmm**/*. I hear* /**m**/*. I know that the letter* **m** *stands for the* /**m**/ *sound, so I will write* **m** *in the second box.*
- Have students blend the sounds to check the spelling of the word. Say: *Let's blend the word* **am** *slowly:* /**aaaammmm**/*. Do the letters match the sounds in the word?*

Letter Frieze Card

Practice with the Workmat

- Instruct students to place counters under the first set of boxes on side 2 of their workmats.
- Ask students to slowly articulate the word *am* as they push the counters into the boxes.
- Have them identify and record the letters that stand for the sounds they hear.
- Have students practice writing the word *am* on side 1 of their workmats.
- Make sure that as they write the word, they say it slowly and think about the sounds they hear.

Assessment Tip: Note students who do not slowly articulate the sounds when spelling a word, and provide extra modeling.

Independent Activities

Spelling

As words are introduced, write them on index cards and place them in the literacy center. (Students will only have the word *am* to spell in this first week.) Ensure that the letter cards needed to build the words are also in the center. The students will follow the procedure to spell words:
• Choose a word card.
• Use their fingers and eyes to read the word.
• Turn over the card so that they don't see the word.
• Build the word using the letter cards.
• Turn over the card to check the word.
• Write the word.

 ## Phonological Awareness

Listening for Rhyme
• Say the words *cat* and *mat*. Tell students that these words rhyme because they have the same sound at the end.
• Repeat the words and have students tell you the sounds at the end of the words.
• Say the following word pairs, and have students tell you what sound they hear at the end of each pair: ***run/fun, ice/mice, hand/and, fan/man, treat/seat***.
• Reread the poem *Apple Pie* and have students listen for rhyming words. Have them clap when they hear two rhyming words.

Assessment Tip: Note students who do not clap at the appropriate times. Provide more practice in listening for rhyme. Assign Independent Activities for the rest of the class.

 ## Sound/Symbol Relationships

Practice with the Letter Cards
• Distribute letter cards **a** and **m**. Have students line up the cards on their workmats.
• Ask students to pull down each letter card and say its name, then push it back up and say its sound.
• Have students use the cards to build the word *am*. Encourage them to articulate the word slowly as they build it.
• Ask a student who built the word correctly to use the letter cards to make the word in the pocket chart.
• Have students use the pocket chart model to self-check.

 ## Blending Sounds

• Have students blend the word *am*, using the procedure for Day Three.

Spelling Words

• Review the word *am* by having students write it several times on their workmats.

Spelling Assessment

Use the following procedure to assess students' spelling of the Unit 1 words.
• Say the word *am* and use it in a sentence.
• Have students write the word on a piece of paper.
• When students have finished, collect their papers and analyze their spelling.
• Record their progress on a spelling record sheet, and provide extra practice as needed.

 Small Group Activities

The following small group activities can be used to provide hands-on practice for students who need additional support. Assign blackline master 1 and Independent Activities for the rest of the class.

 PHONOLOGICAL AWARENESS

Initial Sounds Instruct students to raise their hands when they hear the */m/* sound as you say the sentence "Millie Monkey made mushroom soup."

Poetry Poster 1 Display the picture on the back of the poetry poster for *Melons and Muffins*. Ask questions about the poster, reinforcing the */m/* sound. For example, ask: *Does a monkey like melon at a movie?* Have students take turns asking similar questions about the poster.

Poetry Poster 2 Display the picture on the back of the poetry poster for *Apple Pie*. Tell students that you want to put things into the van that have the */a/* sound. Say: *I'm going to put a glass in the van*. Then ask a student to put something else that has the */a/* sound in the van.

Rhyme Emphasize the medial sound in the word *cat*. Have each student repeat the word and the medial sound. Say pairs of words for students and ask them to stamp their feet when they hear a word pair that rhymes. Use the word pairs *hat/mat, fun/sun, rob/hot, make/ cake, in/bin, dig/sat, hand/can, blob/glob, pick/pack,* and *car/star*.

 SOUND/SYMBOL RELATIONSHIPS

Frieze Cards Hold up letter frieze card **Mm** for varying lengths of time. Students are to hold the */m/* sound for as long as you hold up the card. Then read the poem *Melons and Muffins,* and have students stand when they hear a word that starts with */m/*. Repeat with letter frieze card **Aa** and the poem *Apple Pie*.

Picture Match Provide picture cards **magnet, mitten, mop, map, apple, ax, ant**, and **antelope**. Place letter cards **a** and **m** in the pocket chart. Hold up each picture, and have students say its name and tell you what sound they hear at the beginning of the word. Have them place the picture card under letter card **a** or letter card **m**.

 BLENDING

Write the word *am* on chart paper. Have each student take a turn running their fingers under the word as the group sounds it out.

 SPELLING

Guided Practice Use letter cards **a** and **m** to make the scrambled word **ma**. Tell students that this word is *am* but that the letters are mixed up. Ask them what the word *am* starts with, then pull down the letter *a*. Then pull down the final letter and have students read the word. Then give students letter cards **a** and **m** and have them make the word on their workmats.

Missing Letter Write the word *am* on the board and read it with students. Without students seeing, erase a letter. Ask which letter is missing, then replace the letter.

Review Encourage students to look at the spelling word, say it, cover it, write it, and check their spelling.

Student Name _____ Assessment Date _____

Phonological Awareness: Listening for Rhyme

Directions: Say the pair of words and ask the student if the words rhyme. If the student answers correctly, put a ✔. If the student's response is incorrect, put an **X**.
Example: box/fox. *Yes.*

cat/hat *(yes)*		leg/peg *(yes)*			
man/let *(no)*		tab/top *(no)*			
Sam/ram *(yes)*		hit/sit *(yes)*		**Score**	**/6**

Phonemic Awareness: Listening for Initial Sounds

Directions: Say the word and ask the student to tell you if the word begins with /m/. If the student answers correctly, put a ✔. If the student's response is incorrect, put an **X**.
Example: moon. *Yes.*

mittens *(yes)*		tape *(no)*			
ball *(no)*		mushroom *(yes)*			
mat *(yes)*		mask *(yes)*		**Score**	**/6**

Phonemic Awareness: Listening for Medial Sounds

Directions: Say the word and ask the student to tell you if the middle sound in the word is /a/. If the student answers correctly, put a ✔. If the student's response is incorrect, put an **X**. **Example:** hat. *Yes.*

sag *(yes)*		pan *(yes)*			
bat *(yes)*		lip *(no)*			
met *(no)*		tap *(yes)*		**Score**	**/6**

Phonics: Segmenting and Blending Sounds

Directions: Explain that this word uses sounds the student has been learning. Have the student point to the word on the corresponding student sheet, say each sound, and then blend the sounds together. Put a ✔ if the student's response is correct. If the student misses the word, record the error.

am *(/a/ /m/, am)*		**Score**	**/1**

UNIT 2 Ss

Unit Objectives

Students will:

- Review the sounds of /m/ and /a/
- Identify the sound /s/
- Associate the letter Ss with the sound /s/
- Listen for rhyme
- Blend sounds to read the words am, Sam
- Spell the words am, Sam

Day 1

BLM 4

Letter Cards:
a, m, s

Letter Frieze
Cards: **Aa, Mm**

Picture Word Cards: **magnet, map, mitten, mop, sandwich, sock, sub, sun**

Day 2

BLM 3

BLM 5

Letter Cards:
a, m, s

Letter Frieze
Cards: **Aa, Mm**

Spelling
Transparency

Picture Word Cards: **ant, antelope, apple, ax, cat, magnet, map, mitten, mop, pan, sandwich, sock, sub, sun**

Day 3

BLM 6

Letter Frieze
Cards: **Aa, Mm**

Picture Word Cards: **ant, antelope, apple, ax, bat, cat, magnet, map, mitten, mop, pan, sandwich, sock, sub, sun**

Day 4

BLM 1

Letter Cards:
a, m, S

Day 5

BLM 2

Letter Cards:
a, m, s, S

Letter Frieze
Cards: **Aa, Mm**

Quick-Check
Student Sheet

Poetry Poster

Student Workmat

Letter Frieze Cards

Poetry CD

Core Materials

All print resources can be downloaded from http://phonicsresources.benchmarkeducation.com.

**Poetry Poster
(Front)**

**Letter Frieze
Cards**

**Picture Word
Cards**

 Phonemic Awareness

Use the Poetry Poster

- Read aloud or play the recording of the poem *Seven Silly Sailors*.
- Ask students to listen for the */s/* sound as you say the sentence "Seven Silly Sailors sat beside the sea."
- Reread the poem and have students tap their feet each time they hear */s/* at the beginning of a word.
- Reread the poem and have students clap each time they hear */s/* at the beginning of a word.

Distribute blackline master 4 and instruct students to complete it at home.

Sound/Symbol Relationships

Model

- Display letter frieze card **Ss.** Explain that the letter **Ss** stands for the */s/* sound in the word **sun**.
- Reread the poem *Seven Silly Sailors*, and invite students to read along with you.
- Point to words in the poem that begin with the letter **s**. Say each word aloud.

Practice with the Letter Cards

- Distribute letter cards **s, s, m,** and **m**. Have students line up the cards on their workmats.
- Ask students to pull down each letter card and say the letter name, then push it back up and say the letter sound.
- Have them pull down each letter card, saying a word that starts with that sound.
- Have them push up the letter card that starts the word **match**. (Repeat with the words **sun, silly,** and **monkey**.)

Practice with the Picture Cards

- Place letter cards **m** and **s** in the pocket chart.
- Place picture cards **magnet** and **sun** under the corresponding letters while you say the name of the letter and the picture.
- Hold up picture card **sub**. Have students say **sub** with you.
- Ask: *Does* **sub** *begin like* **magnet** *or* **sun**?
- Place picture card **sub** under letter card **s**. Say: **Ssssub** *begins like* **ssssun**, *so I am putting picture card* **sub** *under the letter* **s**.
- Repeat with picture cards **sandwich, sock, mop, map,** and **mitten**.

P+A+M Blending Sounds

Review

- Hold up letter frieze cards **Aa** and **Mm** and ask students to say the sound each letter stands for.

Model

- Write the word **Sam** on the board. Sound out the word by moving your hand under the letters and blending the sounds (*/SSSSaaaammmm/*).
- Say the word at normal speed, then ask students to sound out the word with you.
- Repeat the steps for the word **am**.

 Spelling Words

Review

- Give students letter cards **a** and **m**. Have them use the cards to build the word **am**.
- Have students practice spelling the word **am** several times on their workmats.

Phonemic Awareness

Use the Poetry Poster

- Show students the picture on the back of the poetry poster, and have them name all the objects in the picture.
- Point to the sun in the picture and say the word **sun**. Ask: *What sound do you hear at the beginning of the word?*
- Ask volunteers to point to something in the picture whose name starts with /**s**/.

Distribute blackline master 5 and instruct students to complete it at home.

Assessment Tip: Assess individual students by pointing to something in the picture, saying its name, and asking whether they hear the /**s**/ sound in the word.

 ## Sound/Symbol Relationships

**Poetry Poster
(Back)**

Review

- Hold up letter frieze cards **Mm** and **Aa** one at a time, and have students tell you the sounds the letter stand for.
- Encourage students to think of words that start with /**m**/. Record the words on the board, underlining the letter **m**.
- Have students think of words that have the /**a**/ sound in the middle. Write these words on the board and circle the medial **a**.
- Hold up letter frieze card **Ss**, and have students articulate the letter name and the letter sound.
- Reread the poem *Seven Silly Sailors*, emphasizing initial /**s**/ sounds. Have volunteers find words that begin with /**s**/.

Practice with the Letter Cards

- Distribute letter cards **s, m,** and **a**. Have students line them up on their workmats.
- Have students pull down each letter card and say the letter name, then push it back up and say the letter sound.
- Ask them to pull down letter card **m**, saying a word that starts with the /**m**/ sound.
- Ask them to pull down letter card **s**, saying a word that starts with the /**s**/ sound.
- Ask them to pull down letter card **a**, saying a word that has /**a**/ in the middle.
- Have them push up the letter that makes the sound in the middle of the word **fat**.
- Have them push up the letter that starts the word **six**.
- Have them push up the letter card that starts the word **many**.

Independent Activities

Phonemic Awareness

Picture Cards Provide picture cards in the literacy center. Students can:
• separate the cards that start with /s/
• sort the pictures according to their beginning sounds.

Collage Students can cut pictures from magazines of things that start with /s/. Have them paste the pictures on a sheet of paper to make a collage.

Listen Have students listen to the recording of the poem *Seven Silly Sailors* in the listening center.

Poetry Poster Provide copies of blackline master 3. Instruct students to color the objects that start with /s/.

Sound/Symbol Relationships

Letter/Picture Match Place picture cards **mop**, **map**, **mitten**, **magnet**, **apple**, **ax**, **ant**, **antelope**, **sandwich**, **sock**, **sub**, and **sun** in one pile and letter cards **a**, **s**, and **m** in another pile. Have students match a picture card with the letter that stands for the beginning sound of the picture name.

Word Match Provide decodable word cards **am** and **Sam** and picture cards **pan**, **cat**, **ax**, **sub**, **sun**, and **sandwich**. Have students match the picture cards that have /a/ to the card **am** and the picture cards with /s/ to the card **Sam**.

P+A+M Blending Sounds

• Have students blend the words *am* and *Sam*, using the procedure for Day One.

Assessment Tip: The goal is to have students sound out the words in three seconds or less. Note which students need more practice in blending.

 ## Spelling Words

Model

• Use the spelling transparency. Place counters under the second set of boxes on the transparency.
• Say: *Today we are going to learn to spell the words* **Sam** *and* **am**. *Watch and listen as I say* **Sam** *slowly:* /Ssssaaaammmm/.
• As you say */ssss/*, push a counter into the first box. Then say */aaaa/* as you push a counter into the second box, and */mmmm/* as you push a counter into the third box. Repeat the steps.
• Model recording the letters for the sounds on the transparency. Say: *The first sound is* /ssss/. *I know that the letter* **s** *stands for the* /ssss/ *sound.* **Sam** *is someone's name. It needs a capital* **S**. *I'm going to write a capital* **S** *in the first box. Let's listen for the second sound:* /saaaa/. *I hear* /a/. *I know that the letter* **a** *stands for the* /a/ *sound, so I will write* **a** *in the second box. Let's listen for the last sound:* /sammmm/. *I hear* /m/. *I know that the letter* **m** *stands for the* /m/ *sound, so I will write* **m** *in the last box.*
• Have students blend the sounds to check the spelling of the word.

Practice with the Workmat

• Instruct students to place counters under the second set of boxes on side 2 of their workmats.
• Ask students to slowly articulate the word **Sam** as they push the counters into the boxes.
• Have them identify and record the letters that stand for the sounds they hear.
• Have students practice writing **Sam** on side 1 of their workmats.

Repeat the modeling and guided practice for the second spelling word, *am*.

Assessment Tip: Note students who do not slowly articulate the sounds when spelling a word, and provide extra modeling. Assign Independent Activities for the rest of the class.

Phonemic Awareness

Listen for Initial Sounds

- Say the words *man, mitt,* and *sit*. Have students repeat the words.
- Ask students if they hear the same sound at the beginning of each word. Then ask them to identify the word that starts with a different sound.
- Say the words *silly, sun,* and *sink*. Have students repeat the words.
- Ask students if they hear the same sound at the beginning of each word. Then ask what sound is the same in all three words.
- Repeat this process with the words *sit/save/Sarah, mind/find/map, table/top/ten, mask/man/mint,* and *see/sick/sat.*

Assessment Tip: Call on individual students to assess whether they can identify the beginning sounds.

 Sound/Symbol Relationships

Review

- Place picture cards **apple**, **sun**, and **magnet** in the pocket chart. Have students say the names of the pictures and the sound at the beginning of each name.
- Show students picture card **ax** and ask them what sound they hear at the beginning of the word. Place picture card **ax** under picture card **apple**.
- Repeat with picture cards **ant**, **antelope**, **mop**, **map**, **mitten**, **sock**, **sub**, and **sandwich**.
- Replace picture cards **sun** and **magnet** with picture card **pan**. Place letter card **a** under each picture card.
- Ask students where they hear the /*a*/ sound in the words *apple* and *pan*.
- Show students picture cards **map**, **bat**, **cat**, **pan**, **ax**, **ant**, and **antelope**. Have them sort the pictures according to the beginning or medial /*a*/ sound.

P + A + M **Blending Sounds**

- Have students blend the words *am* and *Sam,* using the procedure for Day One.

Distribute blackline master 6 and instruct students to complete it at home.

 Spelling Words

- Review the words *Sam* and *am* by having students write them several times on their workmats.

DAY 4

Independent Activities

Spelling

As words are introduced each day, write them on index cards and place them in the literacy center. Ensure that the letter cards needed to build the words are in the center. Students can use the following procedure to spell words.
• Choose a word card.
• Use their fingers and eyes to read the word.
• Turn over the card so that they can't see the word.
• Build the word using the letter cards.
• Turn over the card to check the word.
• Write the word.

 ## Phonological Awareness

Listening for Rhyme

• Say the words *cat* and *mat*. Tell students that these words rhyme because they have the same sound at the end.
• Say: *Listen to these words:* **cat, mat**. *I hear* /**at**/ *at the end of* **cat**, *and* /**at**/ *at the end of* **mat**. *Say the words with me and listen to the ending sounds.*
• Reread the poem *Seven Silly Sailors* and have students listen for rhyming words. Have them clap each time you say a rhyming word.
• Say pairs of words and have students clap if the pairs rhyme.

Assessment Tip: Note students who do not clap at the appropriate time, and provide them with extra practice in listening for rhyme.

 ## Sound/Symbol Relationships

Word Building

• Distribute letter cards **a, S,** and **m.** Have students line up the cards on their workmats.
• Ask students to pull down each letter card and say its name, then push it back up and say its sound.
• Have students use two letter cards to make the word **am**. Encourage them to say the word slowly as they make it.
• Make the word in the pocket chart. Have students use the pocket chart model to self-check.
• Ask students to add a letter to the beginning of the word **am** to make the word **Sam**. Encourage them to say the word slowly as they build it.

 ## Blending Sounds

• Have students blend the words **am** and **Sam**, using the procedure for Day One.

Spelling Words

• Review the week's words by having students write them several times on side 1 of the workmat.
• Provide pairs of students with blackline master 1. While one student reads the words, the other student should write the words.
• The partner should put a check mark beside words spelled correctly. If a word is incorrect, the partner may provide prompts. If the second spelling of the word is correct, the partner places a check mark in the "Second Try" column.

Assessment Tip: Collect students' completed blackline masters and note which words gave them difficulty.

Spelling Assessment

Use the following procedure to assess students' spelling of the Unit 2 words.
• Say the word **am** and use it in a sentence.
• Have students write the word on a piece of paper.
• Continue with the word **Sam**.
• When students have finished, collect their papers and analyze their spelling.
• Record their progress on a spelling record sheet, and provide extra practice as needed.

 # Small Group Activities

The following small group activities can be used to provide hands-on practice for students who need extra support. Assign blackline master 2 and Independent Activities for the rest of the class.

 ### PHONOLOGICAL AWARENESS

Initial /s/ Have students close their eyes. Then tell them that you are going to say a sentence, and if they hear the /s/ sound in a word, they should raise their hands. Say: *Sally sells seashells by the sea.*

Poetry Poster Ask questions using words from the poetry poster that have the /s/ sound. Ask: *Does a sailor like sardines? Can a sea serpent sail? Does a seal wear socks? Will a seaplane land on the sand?* Have students clap when they hear /s/.

Model Rhyme Say two words that rhyme and tell students the ending sounds. Have students say the words with you and repeat the ending sounds. Use the following pairs for modeling: **hen/pen, man/pan, door/store, mitt/fit, ice/ nice, big/jig.**

Read the Poem Reread the poem with students. Have students stand when they hear a word that starts with /s/.

 ### SOUND/SYMBOL RELATIONSHIPS

Poem Emphasize the /s/ at the beginning of the words in the poem. Give each student the opportunity to find several words in the poem that start with /s/.

Frieze Cards Hold up letter frieze card **Ss** for varying lengths of time. Students are to hold the /s/ sound for as long as you hold up the card. Repeat with letter frieze cards **Aa** and **Mm.**

Letter Cards Place letter cards **a, m,** and **s** in a pocket chart. One at a time, show students the pictures for *m, a,* and *s.* Have them say the name of the object and the sound at the beginning, and place the picture under the correct letter according to its beginning sound.

 ### BLENDING

Model and Practice Use letter cards **S, a,** and **m** to build the word **Sam** on a workmat. Model how to sound out the word **Sam**. Then say the word. One at a time, give a student letter cards **S, a,** and **m.** Have him or her build the word on their workmats. Repeat with the word **am.**

 ### SPELLING

Workmat Give students letter cards **S, a,** and **m.** Have them make the words **Sam** and **am** on their workmats. Have them say each sound in the word and then pull down the letter that stands for the sound they hear. Then have them read the word.

Missing Letter Write the words **Sam** and **am** on the board. Have students read each word and say the sounds in each. Without students seeing, erase a letter in one of the words. Say the word and ask students which letter is missing. Repeat with the next word.

Letter Cards Place letter cards **s, m,** and **a** on a table. Say the word **am**. Ask a student to select the letter that begins the word **am**. Have him or her place it on a workmat. Then ask a different student what sound he or she hears at the end of the word **am** and what letter stands for that sound. Have the student place the letter next to the **a** on the workmat to spell the word. Repeat with the word **Sam**.

Student Name _____ Assessment Date _____

Phonological Awareness: Listening for Rhyme

Directions: Say the pair of words and ask the student if the words rhyme. If the student answers correctly, put a ✔. If the student's response is incorrect, put an **X**.
Example: box/fox. *Yes.*

make/take *(yes)*		luck/stuck *(yes)*			
fist/list *(yes)*		top/clip *(no)*			
pen/jam *(no)*		file/style *(yes)*		**Score**	**/6**

Phonemic Awareness: Listening for Initial Sounds

Directions: Say the word and ask the student to tell you the beginning sound. If the student answers correctly, put a ✔. If the student misses the sound, record the error. **Example:** sack. */s/.*

seed *(/s/)*		meat *(/m/)*			
mark *(/m/)*		medicine *(/m/)*			
save *(/s/)*		second *(/s/)*		**Score**	**/6**

Phonics: Segmenting and Blending Sounds

Directions: Explain that these real and nonsense words use sounds the student has been learning. Have the student point to each word on the corresponding student sheet, say each sound, and then blend the sounds together. Put a ✔ if the student's response is correct. If the student misses the word, record the error.
Example: Sam. */s/ /a/ /m/, Sam.*

sas *(/s/ /a/ /s/, sas)*			
mam *(/m/ /a/ /m/, mam)*			
mas *(/m/ /a/ /s/, mas)*		**Score**	**/3**

UNIT 3Tt

Unit Objectives

Students will:

- Review the sounds /a/, /m/, and /s/
- Identify the sound /t/
- Associate the letter Tt with the sound /t/
- Blend sounds to read the words am, at, mat, Sam, sat, Tam
- Spell the words mat, sat, Tam

Day 1

BLM 4

Letter Cards: **a, m, S, s, t**

Letter Frieze Cards: **Aa, Mm, Ss**

Picture Word Cards: **magnet, map, mitten, sandwich, sock, sub, tent, tiger, top, tub**

Day 2

BLM 3

BLM 5

Letter Cards: **a, m, s, t**

Letter Frieze Cards: **Aa, Mm, Ss**

Spelling Transparency

Day 3

BLM 6

Letter Frieze Cards: **Aa, Mm, Ss**

Spelling Transparency

Picture Word Card: **cap**

Day 4

BLM 1

Letter Cards: **a, m, s, t**

Day 5

BLM 2

Letter Cards: **a, m, S, s, t**

Quick-Check Student Sheet

Picture Word Cards: **magnet, map, mitten, mop, sandwich, sock, sub, sun, tent, tiger, tub**

Poetry Poster

Student Workmat

Letter Frieze Card

Decodable Book

Poetry CD

Core Materials

All print resources can be downloaded from http://phonicsresources.benchmarkeducation.com.

**Poetry Poster
(Front)**

**Letter Frieze
Cards**

**Picture Word
Cards**

 # Phonemic Awareness

Use the Poetry Poster

- Read aloud or play the recording of the poem *Turtles*.
- Say the sentence "Ten tiny turtles sit on a tabletop." Have students listen for /t/.
- Reread the poem. Have students tap their feet each time they hear /t/ at the beginning of a word.

Distribute blackline master 4 and instruct students to complete it at home.

Sound/Symbol Relationships

Model

- Display letter frieze card **Tt**. Explain that the letter **Tt** stands for the /t/ sound in *tiger* and *turtle*.
- Reread the poem *Turtles*, inviting students to read along with you.
- Point to words in the poem that begin with the letter *t*. Say the words aloud and ask students to say the words with you.

Practice with the Letter Cards

- Distribute letter cards **t, s,** and **m**. Have students line up the cards on their workmats.
- Ask students to pull down each letter card and say the letter name, then push it back up and say the letter sound.
- Have them pull down letter card **t** again, saying a word that starts with the /t/ sound. Repeat with letter cards **s** and **m**.
- Ask them to push up the letter card that starts the word *top*. (Repeat with the words *sock* and *man*.)

Practice with the Picture Cards

- Place letter cards **t, s,** and **m** in the pocket chart.
- Place picture cards **tiger, sandwich,** and **map** under the corresponding letters while you say the name of the letter and the object in the picture.
- Hold up picture card **top**. Have students say *top* with you.
- Ask: *Does* **top** *begin like* **tiger, sandwich,** *or* **map**?
- Place picture card **top** under letter card **t**. Say: **Top** *begins like* **tiger,** *so I am putting picture card* **top** *under the letter* **t**.
- Repeat with picture cards **magnet, mitten, sub, sock, tent,** and **tub**.

Blending Sounds

Review

- Hold up letter frieze cards **Aa, Mm, Ss,** and **Tt** one at a time.
- Have students say the sound each letter stands for.

Model

- Write the word *am* on the board. Sound out the word by moving your hand under each letter while blending the sounds. Hold each sound for one second. (/aaaammmm/) Then say the word at normal speed.
- Ask students to sound out the word with you several times.
- Repeat the steps for the words *at* and *Sam*. Point out that the word *at* has a stop sound at the end.

 # Spelling Words

Review

- Give students letter cards **a, m,** and **S**. Have them spell *am* and *Sam*.
- Have students practice writing the words *am* and *Sam* on their workmats.

Phonemic Awareness

Use the Poetry Poster

• Show students the picture on the back of the poetry poster and have them name all the objects in the picture.
• Point to the tent in the picture and say the word *tent*, segmenting the /t/. Ask: *What sound do you hear at the beginning of the word?*
• Ask volunteers to point to something in the picture that starts with /t/.

Distribute blackline master 5 and instruct students to complete it at home.

 # Sound/Symbol Relationships

**Poetry Poster
(Back)**

Review

• Hold up letter frieze cards **Aa, Mm,** and **Ss** one at a time and have students tell you the sounds the letters stand for.
• Encourage students to think of words that start with /m/ or /s/. Then have them think of words that have /a/ in the middle. Write these words on the board.
• Hold up letter frieze card **Tt.** Have students say *tiger* with you.
• Reread the poem *Turtles* with students, emphasizing the /t/ sound where it occurs at the beginning of words. Have volunteers find words that begin with /t/.

Practice with the Letter Cards

• Distribute letter cards **a, m, s,** and **t.** Have students line up the cards on their workmats.
• Have students pull down each letter card and say the letter name, then push it back up and say the letter sound.
• Ask them to pull down letter card **t,** saying the letter sound, and then push it back up, saying a word that starts with the /t/ sound. Repeat with letter cards **m** and **s.**
• Have students pull down letter card **a,** saying the letter sound, and then push it back up, saying a word that has /a/ in the middle.

Independent Activities

Phonemic Awareness

Picture Cards Provide picture cards in the literacy center. Students can:
• take two picture cards, name the pictures, and tell if the words rhyme
• sort the picture cards into those that start with /*t*/ and those that don't
• match a card with another card that has the same beginning sound

Listen Have students listen to the recording of the poem *Turtles* in the listening center.

Poetry Poster Provide copies of blackline master 3. Instruct students to color the objects that start with /*t*/.

Sound/Symbol Relationships

Letter/Picture Match Place picture cards **map, mitten, sock, sun, tent,** and **tub** in one pile and letter cards **m, s,** and **t** in another pile. Have students match the picture card with the letter that stands for the beginning sound.

Letter Toss Write the letters *m, s,* and *t* on large paper squares. Put the squares on the floor. Students can:
• toss a beanbag onto a square and say the sound the letter stands for
• toss a beanbag onto a square and say a word that has the beginning sound the letter stands for

Draw Display letter cards **m, s,** and **t.** Have students draw a picture of something that begins with each letter.

 # Blending Sounds

• Have students blend the words *mat, sat,* and *Tam,* using the procedure for Day One.

Spelling Words

Model
• Use the spelling transparency. Place counters under the second set of boxes on the transparency.
• Say: *Today we are going to learn to spell* **mat** *and* **sat.** *Watch and listen as I say* **mat** *slowly:* /**mmmmaaaat/.** Point out that the word has a stop sound at the end.
• As you say /***mmmm/,*** push a counter into the first box. Then say /***aaaa/*** as you push a counter into the second box and /***t/*** as you push a counter into the third box. Repeat the steps.
• Model recording the letters for the sounds on the transparency. Say: *The first sound is* /**mmmm/.** *I know that the letter* **m** *stands for the* /**m/** *sound. I'll write the letter* **m** *in the first box. Let's listen for the second sound:* /**maaaa/.** *I hear* /**a/.** *I know that the letter* **a** *stands for the* /**a/** *sound, so I will write* **a** *in the second box. Let's listen for the last sound:* /**mat/.** *I hear* /**t/.** *I know that the letter* **t** *stands for the* /**t/** *sound, so I will write* **t** *in the last box.*
• Have students blend the sounds to check the spelling of the word.

Practice with the Workmat
• Have students place their counters under the second set of boxes on side 2 of their workmats.
• Ask students to slowly articulate the word ***mat*** as they push the counters into the boxes.
• Have them identify and record the letters that stand for the sounds they hear.
• Have students practice writing ***mat*** on side 1 of their workmats.

Repeat the modeling and guided practice with the second spelling word, *sat.*

Assessment Tip: Note students who do not slowly articulate the sounds when spelling a word, and provide extra modeling. Assign Independent Activities for the rest of the class.

Phonemic Awareness

Listen for Initial Consonant Sounds

- Say: **Tiger, table. Tiger** and **table** *start with the same sound:* /**t**/. *Now listen to these words:* **tiger, man**. *These words start with different sounds.* **Tiger** *starts with* /**t**/, *and* **man** *starts with* /**m**/.
- Say the word pairs **sip/mat, tub/table, turtle/lamp, marble/monkey, silly/soap, make/take,** and **tiny/toe**. If the words start with the same sound, students are to raise their hands.
- Say each pair of words again. Ask students to identify the sounds they hear at the beginning of the words.
- If the two words start with the same sound, ask students to say another word that has that same beginning sound.

Assessment Tip: Note students who do not raise their hands at the appropriate time, and provide more practice.

 ## Sound/Symbol Relationships

Review

- Display letter frieze cards **Mm, Ss,** and **Tt**. Ask students to tell you the sound each letter stands for.
- Have students brainstorm words that start with /**t**/. As each student suggests a word, have the rest of the class repeat it. Repeat with **s** and **m**.
- Display picture card **cap**. Ask: *What sound do you hear in the middle of the word?*
- Hold up letter frieze card **Aa**. Say: *The letter* **a** *stands for the* /**a**/ *sound.*

 ## Blending Sounds

- Follow the procedures for Day One to blend the words **at, Sam,** and **Tam**.

Distribute blackline master 6 and instruct students to complete it at home.

Spelling Words

- Review the words **mat** and **sat** by having students write the words several times on side 1 of their workmats.
- Follow the procedure for Day One to model and practice the word **Tam**.

DAY 4

Independent Activities

Spelling

As words are introduced each day, write them on index cards and place them in the literacy center. Ensure that the letter cards needed to build the words are in the center. Students can use the following procedure to spell words.

- Choose a word card.
- Use their fingers and eyes to read the word.
- Turn over the card so that they can't see the word.
- Build the word using the letter cards.
- Turn over the card to check the word.
- Write the word.

 ## Phonological Awareness

Listening for Rhyme

- Say the words *big* and *fig*. Tell students that these words rhyme because they have the same sound at the end. Repeat the words and have students say the sound they hear at the end of the words.
- Say the following word groups. Students should clap if the words rhyme: *jam/jar, link/pink, mop/top, bike/hike, pat/pot, duck/dog, sail/pail.*

Assessment Tip: Note which students are not clapping at the appropriate times, and provide more practice in listening for rhyme.

 ## Sound/Symbol Relationships

Word Building

- Give students letter cards **a, s, m,** and **t.** Have them line up the cards at the top of their workmats.
- Ask them to pull down each letter card and say its name, then push it back up and say its sound.
- Have students use two letter cards to make the word *at.* Encourage them to articulate the word slowly as they make it.
- Ask a student who made the word correctly to make the word in the pocket chart. Have students use the pocket chart model to self-check.
- Have students blend the word *at.*
- Ask students to add a letter to the beginning of *at* to make *sat.* Encourage them to say the word slowly as they build it. Have students say what they had to do to make the word *sat* out of the word *at.* Blend the word *sat.*
- Repeat the steps to make and blend the word *mat.*

 ## Blending Sounds

- Have students blend the words *at, sat,* and *mat,* using the procedure for Day One.

Spelling Words

- Review the week's words by having students write them several times on side 1 of their workmats.
- Provide pairs of students with blackline master 1.
- While one student reads the words, the other student writes each word. If a word is spelled correctly, the student puts a check mark beside it. If a word is incorrect, the partner may provide prompts. If the second spelling of the word is correct, the partner places a check mark in the "Second Try" column.

Assessment Tip: Collect students' completed blackline masters and note which words gave them difficulty.

Spelling Assessment

Use the following procedure to assess students' spelling of the Unit 3 words.
• Say each spelling word and use it in a sentence.
• Have students write the word on a piece of paper.
• Continue with the next word on the list.
• When students have finished, collect their papers and analyze their spellings of misspelled words.
• Record their progress on a spelling record sheet, and provide extra practice as needed.

 ## Small Group Activities

The following small group activities can be used to provide hands-on practice for students who need extra support. Assign blackline master 2 and Independent Activities for the rest of the class.

 PHONOLOGICAL AWARENESS

Initial Sounds 1 Say: *Listen as I say the word* **tap**. *I hear* /t/ *at the beginning of the word. Now you say the word and tell me the sound you hear at the beginning.* Tell students that you will say some more words. They are to tap their fingers on the floor when they hear a word that begins with /t/. Use the words **tab, man, Tim, Sam, teach, toast, milk, sat, tune, tire, laugh,** and **town**.

Initial Sounds 2 Distribute picture cards **mitten, sub,** and **tent** to three students. Have them say the name of the picture and then say another word that has the same beginning sound. Then have those students pass the picture cards to other students.

Rhyme Ask students to identify the rhyming words in the word pairs **jam/jar, link/pink, mop/top, bike/hike, pat/pot, duck/dog,** and **sail/pail**.

 SOUND/SYMBOL RELATIONSHIPS

Letter Match Place three sets of letter cards **a, m, s,** and **t** facedown. Have a student turn over two cards and say the sounds the letters stand for. If the letters stand for the same sound, the student keeps the cards and turns over two more. If the letters do not stand for the same sound, the student turns the cards facedown and the next student has a turn.

Picture Match Place picture cards **mop, mitten, sandwich, saw, tiger,** and **tub** in the pocket chart. Give three students letter cards **m, s,** and **t**. Have them name the letter, say the sound, and match it to the picture. Repeat the activity until all students have had the opportunity to match picture and letter cards.

Poem Distribute letter card **t**. Read the poem. Tell students to hold up the letter card each time you say a word that begins with /t/.

Picture Match Distribute picture cards **mop, map, sun, sock, tiger,** and **tub,** one to a student. The first student says the name of the object on his or her card, then collects the other card that begins with the same sound.

Decodable Words Have students sort decodable word cards according to ending sounds. Then have them tell you what sound is the same in all the words. Ask students where they hear the /a/ sound in each of the words.

 BLENDING

Model and Practice Use letter cards **S, a,** and **m** to build the word **Sam** on the workmat. Sound out the word, then say the word. Give a student letter cards **S, a,** and **m**. Have him or her build the word **Sam** on the workmat, then segment and blend the word. Repeat with **mat, Tam,** and **sat**.

 SPELLING

Guided Practice Using letter cards **a, s,** and **t**, make the scrambled word **ast** on a workmat. Tell students that this word is **sat** but that the letters are mixed up. Ask them what letter starts the word **sat**. Then ask them what letter they need to make the middle sound. Finally, pull down the final letter and have them read the word. Repeat with **Tam** and **mat**.

Missing Letter Write spelling words on the board, with one letter missing in each word. Say each word and have students name the missing letter.

Workmat Using letter cards, model making the word **mat**. Say each sound as you make the word. Give students letter cards **a, m, s,** and **t**. Ask them to build the word **mat** on their workmats. Have them say the sounds as they build the word. Repeat with the word **sat**.

Guess the Word Write the spelling words on the board. Give clues and have students guess which word you are thinking of. For example, say: *I'm thinking of a word that starts with the same sound as* **sub**.

Student Name _____ Assessment Date _____

Phonological Awareness: Listening for Rhyme

Directions: Say the pair of words and ask the student if the words rhyme. If the student answers correctly, put a ✔. If the student's response is incorrect, put an **X**. **Example:** box/fox. *Yes.*

must/dust (*yes*)		eat/feet (*yes*)			
hope/joke (*no*)		pack/last (*no*)			
kit/mitt (*yes*)		sent/bent (*yes*)		**Score**	**/6**

Phonemic Awareness: Listening for Initial Sounds

Directions: Say the word and ask the student to tell you the beginning sound. If the student answers correctly, put a ✔. If the student misses the sound, record the error. **Example:** table. */t/*

surprise (*/s/*)		toy (*/t/*)			
talk (*/t/*)		soft (*/s/*)			
mouth (*/m/*)		tomorrow (*/t/*)		**Score**	**/6**

Phonics: Segmenting and Blending Sounds

Directions: Explain that these real and nonsense words use sounds the student has been learning. Have the student point to each word on the corresponding student sheet, say each sound, and then blend the sounds together. Put a ✔ if the student's response is correct. If the student misses the word, record the error. **Example:** tam. */t/ /a/ /m/, Tam.*

tat (*/t/ /a/ /t/, tat*)		tas (*/t/ /a/ /s/, tas*)			
sat (*/s/ /a/ /t/, sat*)		mat (*/m/ /a/ /t/, mat*)		**Score**	**/4**

UNIT 4 Nn

Unit Objectives

Students will:

- Review the sounds /a/, /m/, /s/, and /t/
- Identify the sound /n/
- Associate the letter Nn with the sound /n/
- Listen for initial sound /n/
- Differentiate initial consonant sounds
- Listen for rhyme

Day 1

BLM 4

Letter Cards:
a, m, n, s, T, t

Picture Word Cards: **napkin, nest, notebook, nut, sandwich, sub, sun, tent, top, tub**

Day 2

BLM 3

BLM 5

Letter Cards: **a, m, n, s, t**

Letter Frieze Cards: **Aa, Mm, Ss, Tt**

Spelling Transparency

Day 3

BLM 6

Letter Cards:
a, m, n, s, t

Day 4

BLM 1

Letter Cards:
a, m, N, n, s, t

Picture Word Cards: **map, mitten, nest, nut, sock, sun, tent, tiger**

Day 5

BLM 2

Letter Cards:
a, i, m, N, n, s, t

Quick-Check Student Sheet

Decodable Word Cards for Unit 4

Picture Word Cards: **napkin, nest, notebook, nut, sock, sub, sun, tent, top, tub**

Poetry Poster

Student Workmat

Letter Frieze Card

Poetry CD

Core Materials

All print resources can be downloaded from http://phonicsresources.benchmarkeducation.com.

**Poetry Poster
(Front)**

**Letter Frieze
Cards**

**Picture Word
Cards**

 ## Phonemic Awareness

Use the Poetry Poster

- Read aloud or play the recording of the poem *Nip the Newt.*
- Repeat the sentence "Nip the Newt is nice and neat." Ask students to listen for the **/n/** sound.
- Reread the poem and have students clap each time they hear **/n/** in a word.

Distribute blackline master 4 and instruct students to complete it at home.

Sound/Symbol Relationships

Model

- Display letter frieze card **Nn**. Explain to students that the letter **Nn** stands for the **/n/** sound in the word **nest**.
- Display the poem *Nip the Newt*, and read the poem aloud, emphasizing the **/n/** sound. Invite students to read along with you.
- Point to words in the poem that have the **/n/** sound. Say the words aloud and ask students to say the words with you. Emphasize the **/n/** sound in each word.

Practice with the Letter Cards

- Distribute letter cards **n**, **t**, and **s**. Have students line them up on their workmats.
- Have students pull down each letter card and say the letter name, then push it back up and say the letter sound.
- Ask them to pull down each letter card again, saying a word that starts with that sound.
- Have them push up the letter card that starts the word **nap**. (Repeat with **turtle** and **sun**.)

Practice with the Picture Cards

- Place letter cards **n**, **s**, and **t** in the pocket chart.
- Place picture cards **notebook**, **sub**, and **tent** under the corresponding letters while you say the name of the letter and the object in the picture.
- Hold up picture card **napkin**. Have students say **napkin** with you, emphasizing the initial sound.
- Ask: *Does* **napkin** *begin like* **notebook**, **sub**, *or* **tent**?
- Place picture card **napkin** under letter card **n**. Say: *Nnnnapkin begins like* **nnnnotebook**, *so I am putting picture card* **napkin** *under the letter* **n**.
- Repeat with picture cards **nest**, **nut**, **sandwich**, **sun**, **top**, and **tub.**

P+A+M ## Blending Sounds

Review

- Hold up letter frieze cards from previously taught lessons one at a time. Ask students to say the sound each letter stands for.

Model

- Write the word **man** on the board. Sound out the word by moving your hand under each letter and blending the sounds. Hold each sound for one second. (**/mmmmaaaannnn/**) Then say the word at normal speed.
- Ask students to repeat sounding out the word with you several times.
- Repeat the steps for the words **sat** and **tan**.

 ## Spelling Words

Review

- Give students letter cards **a**, **m**, **s**, **t**, and **T**. Have them use the cards to spell the words **mat**, **sat**, and **Tam**.
- Have students practice spelling the words **mat**, **sat**, and **Tam** on side 1 of their workmats.

Phonemic Awareness

Use the Poetry Poster

- Show students the picture on the back of the poetry poster and have them name all the objects in the picture.
- Point to the net in the picture and say the word *net*, emphasizing the /*n*/. Ask: *What sound do you hear at the beginning of* net?
- Ask volunteers to point to something in the picture that starts with /*n*/.

Distribute blackline master 5 and instruct students to complete it at home.

 # Sound/Symbol Relationships

Review

- Hold up letter frieze cards **Aa**, **Mm**, **Ss**, and **Tt** one at a time. Have students tell you the sounds the letters stand for.
- Have students think of words that start with /*m*/, /*s*/, and /*t*/. Then have them think of words that have /*a*/ in the middle. Write these words on the board.
- Display letter frieze card **Nn**. Then reread the poem with students, emphasizing the /*n*/ sound where it occurs at the beginning of words. Have volunteers find words that begin with /*n*/.

Practice with the Letter Cards

- Distribute letter cards **a**, **m**, **n**, **s**, and **t**. Have students line up the cards on their workmats.
- Have students pull down each letter card and say the letter name, then push it back up and say the letter sound.
- Ask them to pull down each letter card, saying that letter sound, then push each card back up, saying a word that starts with that sound.
- Instruct students to pull down the letter whose sound they hear in the middle of the word *sat*, then push up the letters that start the words *sat*, *milk*, *tiger*, and *nod*.

**Poetry Poster
(Back)**

Independent Activities

Phonemic Awareness

Picture Cards Provide picture cards in the literacy center. Students can:
• match a picture card with a letter frieze card that has the same beginning sound
• separate the cards that start with /**n**/
• take two cards, name the pictures, and tell if the words rhyme

Letter Collage Tape a sheet of chart paper to a wall. Have students draw or cut from old magazines pictures of things that begin with /**n**/.

Listen Have students listen to the recording of the poem *Nip the Newt* in the listening center.

Poetry Poster Provide copies of blackline master 3. Instruct students to color the objects that begin with /**n**/.

Sound/Symbol Relationships

Say the Word Write **m**, **n**, **s**, and **t** on cards, one letter per card. Attach the cards to a bulletin board. Students can:
• put a check mark by a letter and say the sound the letter stands for
• put a check mark by a letter and say a word that has the beginning sound the letter stands for

Sound Collage Provide letter cards **m**, **n**, **s**, and **t**. Have students cut from old magazines pictures whose names begin with **m**, **n**, **s**, and **t**. Then have them sort pictures according to their beginning sounds and place the letter card for the beginning sound with each group of pictures.

P+A+M Blending Sounds

• Have students blend the words *mat*, *Nat*, and *sat*, using the procedure for Day One.

Assessment Tip: The goal is to have students sound out the words in three seconds or less. Note which students need more practice in blending. Assign Independent Activities for the rest of the class.

 ## Spelling Words

Model

• Use the spelling transparency. Place counters under the second set of boxes on the transparency. Say: *Today we are going to learn to spell* **man** *and* **Nat**. *Watch and listen as I say* **man** *slowly:* /**mmmmaaaannnn**/.
• As you say /**m**/, push a counter into the first box. Then say /**a**/ as you push a counter into the second box and /**n**/ as you push a counter into the third box. Repeat the steps.
• Model recording the letters for the sounds on the transparency. Say: *The first sound is* /**mmmm**/. *I know the letter* **m** *stands for the* /**m**/ *sound. I'll write the letter* **m** *in the first box. Let's listen for the second sound:* /**maaaa**/. *I hear* /**a**/. *I know the letter* **a** *stands for the* /**a**/ *sound, so I will write* **a** *in the second box. Let's listen for the last sound:* /**mannnn**/. *I hear* /**n**/. *I know that the letter* **n** *stands for the* /**n**/ *sound, so I will write* **n** *in the last box.*
• Have students blend the sounds to check the spelling of the word.

Practice with the Workmat

• Have students place their counters under the second set of boxes on side 2 of their workmats.
• Ask students to slowly articulate the word *man* as they push the counters into the boxes.
• Have them identify and record the letters that stand for the sounds they hear.
• Have students practice writing *man* on side 1 of their workmats.

Repeat the modeling and guided practice with the second spelling word, *Nat*. Point out the use of the capital letter in the name.

Assessment Tip: Note students who do not slowly articulate the sounds when spelling a word, and provide extra modeling.

Phonological Awareness

Listen for Rhyme

• Say the words *mat* and *sat*. Tell students that these words rhyme because they have the same ending sounds.
• Say the words again and have students say the sounds they hear at the end of each word.
• Reread the poem *Nip the Newt* and have students listen for rhyming words. Have them clap each time they hear a rhyming word.
• Tell students that you are packing a box of things that rhyme with *mat*. Say: *Can I put a house [ham, cat, cup, bat] in the box?* Have students tell which things you can put into the box.
• Repeat with things that rhyme with *big* (use *fig*, *gift*, *wig*, *twig*, *chimp*); things that rhyme with *fog* (use *dog*, *fox*, *lock*, *log*, *frog*); and things that rhyme with *jug* (use *buck*, *plug*, *bug*, *mutt*, *mug*).

Assessment Tip: Note students who are not able to say which words rhyme, and provide more practice in listening for rhyme.

 ## Sound/Symbol Relationships

Review

• Display letter cards **a**, **m**, **n**, **s**, and **t** in the pocket chart. Ask students to tell you the sound each letter stands for.
• Have volunteers arrange the letter cards to make the words *man*, *mat*, *Sam*, *sat*, *Nat*, and *tan*. As each word is completed, read the word aloud with students.

 ## Blending Sounds

• Have students blend the words *at*, *mat*, and *tan*, using the procedure for Day One.

Distribute blackline master 6 and instruct students to complete it at home.

Spelling Words

• Review the words *man* and *Nat* by having students write the words several times on side 1 of their workmats.
• Follow the procedure for Day One to model and practice the word *tan*.

DAY 4

Independent Activities

Spelling

As words are introduced each day, write them on index cards and place them in the literacy center. Ensure that the letter cards needed to build the words are in the center. Students can use the following procedure to spell words.

- Choose a word card.
- Use their fingers and eyes to read the word.
- Turn over the card so that they can't see the word.
- Build the word using the letter cards.
- Turn over the card to check the word.
- Write the word.

 ## Phonemic Awareness

Differentiate Consonant Sounds

- Place picture cards **map**, **mitten**, **nest**, **nut**, **sock**, **sun**, **tent**, and **tiger** in the pocket chart.
- Ask a volunteer to pick two cards whose picture names begin with the same sound. Have the student say the picture names and tell what sound is at the beginning of the picture names.
- Continue with the other picture cards.
- Hold up two cards. Ask students to say the two picture names and tell you if the two words begin with the same sound. Have them identify the beginning sound(s) of the picture names.

 ## Sound/Symbol Relationships

Word Building

- Distribute letter cards **a**, **s**, **m**, **N**, **n**, and **t**. Have students line them up on their workmats.
- Ask students to pull down each letter card and say its name, then push it back up and say its sound.
- Have students use three letter cards to make the word **Nan**. Ask a student who made the word correctly to make the word in the pocket chart. Have students use the pocket chart model to self-check.
- Ask students to change the **N** at the beginning of the word to make **tan**. Have students tell what they did to make the word **tan**.
- Repeat the steps to make the word **man**.
- Have students use the letters to make the words **at**, **Nat**, **sat**, and **Sam**.

P+A+M Blending Sounds

- Have students blend the words **at**, **Nan**, and **tan**, using the procedure for Day One.

Aa Spelling Words

- Review the week's words by having students write them several times on side 1 of the workmat.
- Provide pairs of students with blackline master 1. While one student reads the word, the other student writes each word. The partner should put a check mark beside words spelled correctly. If a word is incorrect, the partner may provide prompts. If the second spelling of the word is correct, the partner places a check mark in the "Second Try" column.

Assessment Tip: Collect students' completed blackline masters and note which words gave them difficulty.

Spelling Assessment

Use the following procedure to assess students' spelling of the Unit 4 words.
- Say each spelling word and use it in a sentence.
- Have students write the word on a piece of paper.
- Continue with the next word on the list.
- When students have finished, collect their papers and analyze their spellings of misspelled words.
- Record their progress on a spelling record sheet, and provide extra practice as needed.

 Small Group Activities

The following small group activities can be used to provide hands-on practice for students who need extra support. Assign blackline master 2 and Independent Activities for the rest of the class.

 PHONOLOGICAL AWARENESS

Model and Practice Initial /n/ Say: *Listen as I say this word: nag. I can segment this into sounds: /n/ /a/ /g/. The sound at the beginning of the word is /nnn/*. Then ask a volunteer to hold picture card **nut**. Say the following words slowly: *note, pop, soap, need, name, moose, nice, nip, sad, no, night*. If students hear the /n/ sound in a word, they are to line up behind the student holding the card.

Initial Sounds Say the following words clearly and slowly: *mitt, hat, man, fun, his, pen, tip,* and *sit*. Then ask students to tell you the beginning sound.

Rhyming Provide more practice with rhyming words. Say: **Bad, lad, sag.** *Which words have the same ending sounds? I hear /ad/ at the end of* **bad** *and* **lad**, *but I don't hear /ad/ at the end of* **sag**. **Bad** *and* **lad** *rhyme, but* **sag** *does not.* Have students identify the nonrhyming word in these sets: *bell/bet/tell, bag/ram/rag, hem/gem/gum*.

 SOUND/SYMBOL RELATIONSHIPS

Picture Practice Have students sort picture cards **napkin, nest, notebook, sock, sun, sub, tent, top,** and **tub** according to their beginning sounds. Then have students identify the letter that stands for the beginning sound in each group of pictures.

Word Sort Distribute the decodable word cards. Have students sort them into groups according to beginning sounds, then by ending sounds.

Letter Cards Display letter cards **m, n, s,** and **t** in the pocket chart. Ask students to listen to this set of words: *nine, nurse, nut*. Point out that these words start with the same sound, /n/. Point to the letter **n** and remind students that **n** stands

for the /n/ sound. Have students listen to the following sets of words and identify the beginning sound and the letter that stands for the sound: **mad/march/men, seal/seven/sink, tube/team/tack.**

 BLENDING

Model and Practice Use letter cards **s, i,** and **t** to build the word **sit** on the workmat. Model how to sound out the word **sit**. Then say the word. One at a time, give a student letter cards **m, a,** and **n**. Have him or her build the word **man** on their workmats. Then have another student make the word and blend it. Change the **m** to **t** to make **tan**, and repeat the process. Repeat the steps to blend the words **Sam** and **sat**.

 SPELLING

Guided Practice Use letter cards **m, a,** and **t** to make the scrambled word **atm** on a workmat. Tell students that this word is **mat** but that the letters are mixed up. Ask them what letter is at the beginning of the word and pull down the letter **m**. Then ask them what letter they need to make the middle sound. Finally, pull down the last letter and have students read the word.

Review Encourage students to look at a spelling word, say it, cover it, write it, and check their spelling.

What's Missing? On the board, write **man, Nat,** and **tan**, then draw three blank lines. Fill in two letters. Ask volunteers to fill in the missing letter and say the word.

What's the Word? Write the spelling words on the board. Give a clue to the spelling words and have students guess which word or words go with the clue. Say: *I'm thinking of two spelling words that rhyme. I'm thinking of a spelling word that starts with the same sound as* **nest.**

Student Name _____   Assessment Date _____

Phonological Awareness: Listening for Rhyme

Directions: Say the pair of words and ask the student if the words rhyme. If the student answers correctly, put a ✔. If the student's response is incorrect, put an **X**. **Example:** box/fox. *Yes.*

desk/pet *(no)*		loft/lock *(no)*			
crib/fib *(yes)*		bump/sung *(no)*			
want/jaunt *(yes)*		smoke/folk *(yes)*		**Score**	**/6**

Phonemic Awareness: Differentiating Initial Sounds

Directions: Say each set of words. Then have the student say the two words that begin with the same sound. Put a ✔ if the student's response is correct. If not, record the words the student chooses. **Example:** milk/toe/money. *Milk, money.*

new/number/tall *(new, number)*		
teacher/south/soup *(south, soup)*		
take/mother/tail *(take, tail)*		
today/north/tool *(today, tool)*		
many/monster/soft *(many, monster)*		
minute/name/nap *(name, nap)*		**Score** **/6**

Phonics: Segmenting and Blending Sounds

Directions: Explain that these real and nonsense words use sounds the student has been learning. Have the student point to each word on the corresponding student sheet, say each sound, and then blend the sounds together. Put a ✔ if the student's response is correct. If the student misses the word, record the error. **Example:** Nan. /n/ /a/ /n/, *Nan.*

man *(/m/ /a/ /n/, man)*		
Nat *(/n/ /a/ /t/, Nat)*		
nas *(/n/ /a/ /s/, nas)*		
tan *(/t/ /a/ /n/, tan)*		
nam *(/n/ /a/ /m/, nam)*		**Score** **/5**

UNIT **5** Short **Ii**

Unit Objectives
Students will:

- Identify the sound /i/
- Associate the letter Ii with the sound /i/
- Listen for medial sounds
- Listen for rhyming words
- Blend sounds to read the words am, man, mat, in, it, sat, sit, Tam, Tim
- Spell the words am, in, sit

Day 1

BLM 4

Letter Frieze Card: **Ii**

Picture Word Cards: **cat, dish, fan, fish, map, ring**

Day 2

BLM 3

BLM 5

Letter Cards: **a, i, m, n, s, t**

Letter Frieze Cards: **Aa, Mm, Ss, Tt**

Spelling Transparency

Day 3

BLM 6

Letter Frieze Cards: **Aa, Mm, Nn, Ss, Tt**

Decodable Word Cards: **man, mat, sat, sit, tan, tin**

Spelling Transparency

Day 4

BLM 1

Letter Cards: **a, i, m, n, s, t, T**

Day 5

BLM 2

Quick-Check Student Sheet

Letter Cards: **a, a, a, i, i, i, m, n, s, t**

Picture Cards: **cat, dish, fan, fish, igloo, iguana, inch, ink, map, mop, nut, ring, sun, tent**

Poetry Poster

Student Workmat

Letter Frieze Cards

Poetry CD

Core Materials

All print resources can be downloaded from http://phonicsresources.benchmarkeducation.com.

Poetry Poster (Front)

Baking

"Will you wear a bib?"
Ink the Cat asked his pal Tig.
"This mix will make a mess.
It may be rather big!"

Letter Frieze Cards

Picture Word Cards

Phonemic Awareness

Use the Poetry Poster

- Read aloud or play the recording of the poem *Baking*.
- Say the sentence "'Will you wear a bib?' Ink the Cat asked his pal Tig." Ask students to listen for the /i/ sound.
- Reread the poem and have students clap each time they hear /i/.

Distribute blackline master 4 and instruct students to complete it at home.

Sound/Symbol Relationships

Model

- Display letter frieze card **Ii**. Explain that the letter **Ii** stands for the /i/ sound at the beginning of the word *igloo*.
- Reread the poem *Baking*, emphasizing the /i/ sounds. Invite students to read along with you.
- Point to words in the poem that have the /i/ sound. Say the words aloud and ask students to say the words with you.

Practice with the Letter Cards

- Distribute letter cards **a, a, i,** and **i,** and have students line them up on their workmats.
- Have students pull down each letter card and say the letter name, then push it back up and say the letter sound.
- Ask students to pull down each letter card, saying a word that has that sound in the middle.
- Have students push up the letter card that stands for the middle sound in the word **big.** (Repeat with the words **fill, bat,** and **tap.**)

Practice with the Picture Cards

- Place letter cards **a** and **i** in the pocket chart.
- Place picture cards **cat** and **ring** under the corresponding letters while you say the name of the letter and the object in the picture.
- Hold up the picture card **fish.** Have students say **fish** with you, emphasizing the medial sound.
- Ask: *Is the middle sound in* **fish** *like the middle sound in* **cat** *or* **ring**?
- Place picture card **fish** under letter card **i** and picture card **ring.** Say: **Fiiish** *has the same middle sound as* **riiiing,** *so I am putting picture card* **fish** *under the letter* **i.**
- Repeat with picture cards **dish, fan,** and **map.**

Blending Sounds

Review

- Hold up letter frieze cards of previously taught sounds one at a time and ask students to say the sound each letter stands for.

Model

- Write the word **sit** on the board. Sound out the word by moving your hand under each letter while blending the sounds. (/ssssiiiit/) Point out that the word has a stop sound at the end so students don't hold the sound. Then say the word at normal speed.
- Ask students to sound out the word with you. Repeat sounding out the word several times. Repeat the steps for the words **am** and **mat.**

Spelling Words

Review

- Distribute letter cards **a, m, n, N,** and **t.** Have students use the cards to spell the words **man, Nat,** and **tan.**
- Have students practice spelling the words **man, Nat,** and **tan** on their workmats.

Phonemic Awareness

Use the Poetry Poster

- Show students the picture on the back of the poetry poster, and have them name all the objects in the picture.
- Point to the chimp in the picture and say the word **chimp,** emphasizing the /**i**/. Ask: *What sound do you hear in the middle of the word?*
- Ask students to point to something in the picture that has /**i**/ in the middle.

Distribute blackline master 5 and instruct students to complete it at home.
Assessment Tip: Assess individual students by pointing to something in the picture, saying its name, and asking whether they hear the /**i**/ sound in the word.

Listen for Long Vowel Sounds

- Say: *Listen as I say the sounds that make up the word* **pie.** */p/ /ī/. The word* **pie** *has the long vowel sound. Listen again to the vowel sound. /p/ /ī/.*
- Repeat with the word *tie*.

**Poetry Poster
(Back)**

 # Sound/Symbol Relationships

Review

- Hold up letter frieze cards **Aa, Mm, Ss,** and **Tt,** one at a time, and have students tell you the sounds the letters stand for.
- Encourage students to think of words that start with /**m**/, /**n**/, /**s**/, and /**t**/. Then have them think of words that have /**a**/ in the middle. Write these words on the board.
- Hold up letter frieze card **Ii.** Then reread the poem *Baking,* emphasizing the medial /**i**/ sound. Have volunteers find words that have the /**i**/ sound in the middle.

Practice with the Letter Cards

- Distribute letter cards **a, i, m, n, s,** and **t.** Have students line up the cards on their workmats.
- Ask students to pull down each letter card and say the letter name, then push it back up and say the letter sound.
- Have them pull down a letter card, saying the letter sound, then push it back up, saying a word that has the sound.
- Ask them to pull down the letters they hear in the middle of the words *tin* and *tan*.
- Ask them to pull down the letters that start the words *mop, nose, six,* and *top*.

Assessment Tip: Observe students as they manipulate the letters cards. Note which students have difficulty finding the right card or saying a word for each letter. Provide these students with extra modeling and practice in a small group setting.

Compare/Contrast Long and Short Vowel Sounds

- Ask students to brainstorm a list of words that have the long *i* sound. Next, ask students to brainstorm another list of words that have the short *i* sound.
- Discuss the two different sounds of the vowels.

Independent Activities

Phonological Awareness

Picture Cards Provide picture cards in the literacy center. Students can:
- match a picture card with another card that has the same beginning sound
- take a picture card, name the picture, and say another word that has the same medial sound
- separate the cards that have the /i/ sound

Listen Have students listen to the recording of the poem *Baking* in the listening center.

Poetry Poster Provide copies of blackline master 3. Instruct students to color all the objects that have short *i*.

Sound/Symbol Relationships

Draw Display letter cards **a** and **i**. Have students draw pictures of something that has /a/ in the middle and something that has /i/ in the middle.

Word Patterns Display letter cards **m, n, s,** and **t**. Write the word patterns __*an,* __*in,* and __*at* on cards. Have students add letters to make words, then write the words.

Scrambled Words Write the words *am, at, in, mat, Sam, sat, sit,* and *tan* in scrambled form on index cards. Have students write the words in their correct form.

Tongue Twisters Place letter cards **m, n, s,** and **t** facedown and have students pick a letter. Then have them make up a tongue twister using as many words as possible that begin with that letter.

 Blending Sounds

- Have students blend the words *in, sat,* and *sit,* using the procedure for Day One.

Assessment Tip: The goal is to have students sound out the words in three seconds or less. Note which students need more practice in blending.

Spelling Words

Model

- Use the spelling transparency. Place counters under the second set of boxes on the transparency.
- Say: *Today we are going to learn to spell* **sit** *and* **am.** *Watch and listen as I say* **sit** *slowly:* **ssssiiiit.** Point out that *sit* has a stop sound at the end.
- As you say */ssss/,* push a counter into the first box. Then say */iiii/* as you push a counter into the second box and */t/* as you push a counter into the third box. Repeat the steps.
- Model recording the letters for the sounds on the transparency. Say: *The first sound is* /ssss/. *I know that the letter* **s** *stands for the* /s/ *sound. I'll write the letter* **s** *in the first box. Let's listen for the second sound:* /siiii/. *I hear* /i/. *I know that the letter* **i** *stands for the* /i/ *sound, so I will write* **i** *in the second box. Let's listen for the last sound:* /sit/. *I hear* /t/. *I know that the letter* **t** *stands for the* /t/ *sound, so I will write* **t** *in the last box.*
- Have students blend the sounds to check the spelling of the word.

Practice with the Workmat

- Instruct students to place their counters under the second set of boxes on side 2 of their workmats.
- Ask students to slowly articulate the word *sit* as they push the counters into the boxes.
- Have them identify and record the letters that stand for the sounds they hear.
- Have students practice writing *sit* on side 1 of their workmats. Make sure that, as they write the word, they say it slowly and think about the sounds they hear.

Repeat the modeling and guided practice with the second spelling word, *am.*

Assessment Tip: Note students who do not slowly articulate the sounds when spelling a word and provide extra modeling. Assign Independent Activities for the rest of the class.

Phonemic Awareness

Differentiate Medial Sounds

- Say the words *pill* and *with*. Have students repeat the words. Instruct them to stand if the words have the same middle sound.
- Repeat with the word pairs *can/kid, Nat/man, fin/swim, Sam/Tim, brick/back, bib/wig,* and *tip/pat.*
- Repeat the pairs of words, one pair at a time. Ask students to identify the middle sound in each word.

 Sound/Symbol Relationships

Review

- Display letter frieze cards **Aa, Ii, Mm, Nn, Ss,** and **Tt** in the pocket chart. Ask students to tell you the sound each letter stands for.
- Give students decodable word cards **mat, man, sat, tan, tin,** and **sit.** Have students read each word, focusing on the beginning sound, and sort the words according to their beginning sounds.
- Mix up the word cards, and have students read each word, focusing on the middle sound, and sort the words according to their medial sounds.

Distribute blackline master 6 and instruct students to complete it at home.

 Blending Sounds

- Have students blend the words *am, it,* and *man,* using the procedure for Day One.

Aa **Spelling Words**

- Review the words *am* and *sit* by having students write the words several times on side 1 of their workmats.
- Follow the procedure for Day 1 to model and practice the word *in.*

DAY 4

Independent Activities

Spelling

As words are introduced each day, write them on index cards and place them in the literacy center. Ensure that the letter cards needed to build the words are in the center. Students can use the following procedure to spell words.

- Choose a word card.
- Use their fingers and eyes to read the word.
- Turn over the card so they can't see the word.
- Build the word using the letter cards.
- Turn over the card to check the word.
- Write the word.

 Phonological Awareness

Listening for Rhyme

- Say the words *chick* and *stick*. Say: **Chick** and **stick** *have the same ending sound,* /ik/, *so we say they rhyme.*
- Say the words *chick* and *chimp*. Say: **Chick** *ends with* **-ick** *and* **chimp** *ends with* **-imp**. *These words do not rhyme, because they do not have the same ending sounds.*
- Say the following word pairs and have students clap if the two words rhyme: *luck/tuck, box/bun, clip/drip, hill/bill, neck/knock, camp/lamp, nose/hose, kite/king*.

Assessment Tip: Note which students are not clapping at the appropriate times and provide more practice in listening for rhyme.

 Sound/Symbol Relationships

Word Building

- Place letter cards **a, i, m, n, s, t,** and **T** in a pocket chart, and give students copies of the letters.
- Have students line up the letters on their workmats. Ask them to pull down each letter card and say its name, then push it back up and say its sound.
- Have students use the letter cards to make the word *Tim*. Encourage them to articulate the word slowly as they make it.
- Ask a student who made the word correctly to build the word in the pocket chart. Have students use the pocket chart model to self-check.
- Have students blend the word *Tim* together.
- Repeat the steps to make and blend the words *Tam, in, am, man, mat, sat,* and *sit*.

P+A+M **Blending Sounds**

- Have students blend the words *in, Tam,* and *Tim,* using the procedure for Day One.

Aa **Spelling Words**

- Review the week's words by having students write them several times on side 1 of the workmat.
- Provide pairs of students with blackline master 1. While one student reads the words, the other student writes the words.
- The partner should put a check mark beside words spelled correctly. If a word is incorrect, the student may prompt his partner. If the second spelling of the word is correct, the partner places a check mark in the "Second Try" column.

Assessment Tip: Collect students' completed blackline masters and note which words gave them difficulty.

Spelling Assessment

Use the following procedure to assess students' spelling of the Unit 5 words.
• Say each spelling word and use it in a sentence.
• Have students write the word on a piece of paper.
• Continue with the next word on the list.
• When students have finished, collect their papers and analyze their spellings of misspelled words.
• Record their progress on a spelling record sheet, and provide extra practice as needed.

 # Small Group Activities

The following small group activities can be used to provide hands-on practice for students who need additional support. Assign blackline master 2 and Independent Activities for the rest of the class.

 PHONOLOGICAL AWARENESS

Model and Practice Say: *Listen as I say this word:* **big**. *I can segment this into sounds: /b/ /i/ /g/. The middle sound is /i/.* Using the following words, have students practice identifying middle sounds: *mitt, hat, man, fun, his, pen, tip, sit.*

Differentiating Medial Sounds Say the following groups of words and ask students to repeat the words that have the same medial sound: *pit/fin/pal, kiss/sap/sip, pat/lad/win, Sam/tip/pan.*

Model Rhyme Say two words that rhyme and tell students the ending sounds. Have students say the words with you and repeat the ending sounds. Then repeat with another pair. Use the following pairs: *hen/pen, man/pan, door/store, mitt/fit, ice/nice, big/jig.*

 SOUND/SYMBOL RELATIONSHIPS

Medial Sounds 1 Place picture cards **cat, fan, map, fish, dish,** and **ring** in the pocket chart. Say the name of each picture as you place it in the chart. Place letter cards **a, a, a, i, i,** and **i** in a bag. Have students take turns choosing a letter card from the bag, then saying the letter name and the sound it stands for. Then have them place the letter card with the picture card that has that letter sound.

Medial Sounds 2 Write the letters *a* and *i* on the board and review the sounds the letters stand for. Tell students that you will say some words and that they are to listen for the middle sounds. Have volunteers place a check mark next to the letter that stands for the middle sound they hear in a word. Say these words, emphasizing the medial sound: *brick, bat, hill, hall, fin, fat, sack, sick, tap, tip.*

Initial Sounds Place letter cards **a, i, m, n, s,** and **t** in the pocket chart. Have students say each letter and the sound it stands for. Then show picture cards **igloo, iguana, ink, inch, mop, nut, sun,** and **tent.** Have students name each picture and place it with the letter card that stands for the beginning sound in the word.

 BLENDING

Model and Practice Use letter cards **s, i,** and **t** to build the word *sit* on a workmat. Model how to sound out the word *sit*. Then say the word. One at a time, give a student letter cards **s, I,** and **t,** and have him or her build the word on a workmat. Repeat with the words *am* and *mat*.

 SPELLING

Guided Practice Use letter cards **a, m,** and **n** to make the scrambled word *amn*. Tell students that this word is *man* but the letters are mixed up. Ask them what letter the word starts with and have them pull down the letter. Then ask what letter they need to make the middle sound. Finally, pull down the last letter and have them read the word.

Letter Lineup Give each student one of these letter cards: **a, i, m, s, t.** Ask students to line up to make the words *am* and *sit*. Have each student say the name of their letter and the sound the letter stands for. Then have students spell and say the whole word.

Missing Letter Write the spelling words *am, in,* and *sit* on the board. Together say and spell the words. Then erase one letter from each word. Ask volunteers to tell what letter is missing.

Student Name _____   Assessment Date _____

Phonological Awareness: Listening for Rhyme

Directions: Say the pair of words and ask the student if the words rhyme. If the student answers correctly, put a ✔. If the student's response is incorrect, put an **X**.
Example: box/fox. *Yes.*

crank/bank *(yes)*		clock/smock *(yes)*			
beg/fog *(no)*		suit/boot *(yes)*			
floor/flow *(no)*		buy/bay *(no)*		**Score**	/6

Phonemic Awareness: Differentiating Medial Sounds

Directions: Say the pair of words and ask the student if the words have the same middle sound. If the student answers correctly, put a ✔. If the student misses the sound, record the error. **Example:** table. */t/*

rinse/mist *(yes)*		sit/sat *(no)*			
smack/gift *(no)*		slip/crib *(yes)*			
pack/snap *(yes)*		fax/fix *(no)*		**Score**	/6

Phonics: Segmenting and Blending Sounds

Directions: Explain that these real and nonsense words use sounds the student has been learning. Have the student point to each word on the corresponding student sheet, say each sound, and then blend the sounds together. Put a ✔ if the student's response is correct. If the student misses the word, record the error.
Example: min. */m/ /i/ /n/, Min.*

nis *(/n/ /i/ /s/, nis)*		tis *(/t/ /i/ /s/, tis)*			
sim *(/s/ /i/ /m/, sim)*		sit *(/s/ /i/ /t/, sit)*			
mit *(/m/ /i/ /t/, mit)*		mis *(/m/ /i/ /s/)*		**Score**	/6

UNIT 6 Ff

Unit Objectives

Students will:

- Identify the sound /f/
- Associate the letter Ff with the /f/ sound
- Blend CVC words
- Read the sight word is
- Spell CVC words using f and letters previously learned

UNIT 6 Ff

Day 1

| BLM 1 | BLM 6 | Letter Cards: **f, m, s, t** | Spelling Transparency | Picture Word Cards: **fan, fish, fork, fox, magnet, map, mitten mop, tent, tiger, top, tub** |

Day 2

| BLM 1 | BLM 7 | Sight Word Card: **is** | Decodable Word Cards: **fat, fit, man, sat, sit, tan, tin** | Spelling Transparency | Picture Word Cards: **fork, map, sock, tiger** |

Day 3

| BLM 1 | BLM 3 | BLM 8 | Spelling Transparency |

Day 4

| BLM 1 | BLM 2 | BLM 4 | Sight Word Card: **is** | Letter Cards for Unit 6 |

Day 5

| BLM 5 | Letter Cards for Unit 6 | Decodable Word Cards for Unit 6 | Quick-Check Student Sheet |

Poetry Poster

Student Workmat

Letter Frieze Card

Decodable Book

Poetry CD

Core Materials

All print resources can be downloaded from http://phonicsresources.benchmarkeducation.com.

DAY 1

Poetry Poster
(Front)

Letter Frieze Card

Picture Word
Cards

Phonemic Awareness

Use the Poetry Poster

- Read aloud or play the recording of the poem *Fuzzy Fox and Fiddle.*
- Ask students if they can hear the */ffff/* sound in the sentence "But Fuzzy Fox has four."
- Have students say the sentence with you. Before each of the words that start with */f/*, say the phoneme first in isolation. Say: *But /f/ Fuzzy /f/ fox has /f/ four.*

Distribute blackline master 6 and instruct students to complete it at home.

Sound/Symbol Relationships

Model

- Display letter frieze card **Ff**. Explain that the letter *Ff* stands for the */f/* sound, as in the word *fish*.
- Reread the poem *Fuzzy Fox and Fiddle.* Invite students to read along with you.
- Point to words in the poem that begin with the letter *f.* Say the words aloud.

Practice with the Letter Cards

- Distribute letter cards **f, s,** and **t**. Ask students to line up the cards on their workmats.
- Have them pull down each letter card and say the letter name, then push it back up and say the letter sound.
- Ask them to pull down each letter card again, saying a word that starts with that sound.
- Have them push up the letter card that starts the word *fan*. (Repeat with the words *Tim* and *sit*.)

Practice with the Picture Cards

- Place letter cards **f, m,** and **t** in the pocket chart.
- Place picture cards **fish, magnet,** and **tiger** under the corresponding letters while you say the name of the letter and the object in the picture.
- Hold up picture card **map**. Have students say *map* with you.
- Ask: *Does* **map** *begin like* **fish, magnet,** *or* **turtle**?
- Place picture card **map** under letter card **m**. Say: **Mmmmap** *begins like* **mmmmagnet,** *so I am putting picture card* **map** *under the letter* **m**.
- Repeat with picture cards **fork, fox, fan, mitten, mop, top, tub,** and **tent**.

Blending Sounds

Review

- Hold up letter frieze cards of previously taught sounds. Ask students to say the sound each letter stands for.

Model

- Write the word *Sam* on the board. Sound out the word by moving your hand under each letter while blending the sounds. (*/SSSSaaaammm/*) Then say the word.
- Say the word at normal speed, then ask students to sound out the word with you.

Practice with the Word Lists

- Distribute blackline master 1.
- Have students point to the word *Sam*. Ask them to sound out the word with you, holding each sound for at least one second. Then ask them to say the word at regular speed.
- Repeat with the words *it, at,* and *sit*. Then have students sound out the words in random order.

Spelling Words

Model

- Use the spelling transparency. Place counters under the second row of boxes.
- Say: *Today we are going to learn to spell* **man** *and* **mat**. *Watch and listen as I say* **man** *slowly:* /**mmmmaaaannnn**/.
- As you say /**mmmm**/, push a counter into the first box. Then say /**aaaa**/ as you push a counter into the second box and /**nnnn**/ as you push a counter into the third box. Repeat the steps.
- Model recording the letters for the sounds on the transparency. Say: *The first sound is* /**mmmm**/. *I know that the letter* **m** *stands for the* /**mmmm**/ *sound. I'll write the letter* **m** *in the first box. Let's listen for the second sound:* /**maaaa**/. *I hear* /**a**/. *I know that the letter* **a** *stands for the* /**a**/ *sound, so I will write* **a** *in the second box. Let's listen for the last sound:* /**mannnn**/. *I hear* /**n**/. *I know that the letter* **n** *stands for the* /**n**/ *sound, so I will write* **n** *in the last box.*
- Have students blend the sounds to check the spelling of the word.

Practice with the Workmat

- Instruct students to place counters under the second set of boxes on side 2 of the workmat.
- Ask students to slowly articulate the word ***man*** as they push the counters into the boxes.
- Have students identify and record the letters that stand for the sounds they hear.
- Have students practice writing ***man*** on their workmats. Make sure that as they write the word, they articulate it slowly and think about the sounds they hear.

Repeat the modeling and guided practice with the second spelling word, *mat*.

Sight Words

Introduce

- Use the pocket chart and letter cards to model how the new word, ***is***, looks in print. Say: *This is the word* **is**. *It is made up of the letters* **i** *and* **s**.
- Point to the word and say it. Then have students say it as you point to it.
- Have students say the letter names as they trace the word ***is*** with their finger on their palms.
- Write the sentence "The mat is tan." Underline the word ***is*** and read the sentence with students.

Write

- Have students write the word is three times, using the model in the pocket chart.

DAY 2

Independent Activities

Phonemic Awareness

Picture Cards Provide picture cards in the literacy center. Students can:
• separate the cards that start with **/f/**
• match the words on picture cards that rhyme
• match the picture card under the letter frieze card that has the same beginning sound

Collage Students can cut out pictures from old magazines of things that start with **/f/**.

Listen Have students listen to the recording of the poem *Fuzzy Fox and Fiddle* in the listening center.

Sound/Symbol Relationships

Word Sort 1 Provide decodable word cards and have students sort the cards into groups according to the medial sound.

Word Sort 2 Have students use decodable word cards and picture cards to sort for beginning sounds. Have students match a word card under the object in a picture card that has the same beginning sound.

Letter Toss Write each letter that has been taught on separate cups. Provide the frieze card for support. Students can:
• toss a button into a cup and say the sound
• toss a button into a cup and say a word that begins with that letter sound

Build Words Provide the letter cards and decodable word cards. Have students select three word cards and build the words using the letters.

 ## Phonemic Awareness

Use the Poetry Poster
• Show students the picture on the back of the poetry poster, and have them name all the objects in the picture.
• Point to the fork in the picture and say the word **fork**, emphasizing the **/f/** sound. Ask: *What sound do you hear at the beginning of the word?*
• Ask students to point to something in the picture whose name starts with the **/f/** sound.

Distribute blackline master 7 and instruct students to complete it at home.

 ## Sound/Symbol Relationships

Sort the Decodable Word Cards
• Place picture cards **fork, tiger, sock,** and **map** in the pocket chart. Have students say the name of the object on each card.
• Show students decodable word card **man** and have them blend the word.
• Ask students if **man** begins like **fork, tiger, sock,** or **map.** Then place decodable word card **man** under picture card **map.**
• Repeat with decodable word cards **tin, sat, tan, fit, fat,** and **sit.**

Assessment Tip: Observe which students have difficulty associating the sound with the appropriate letter. Provide them with extra practice. Assign Independent Activities for the rest of the class.

 ## Blending Sounds

• Have students blend the words *tan, fit, fat,* and *fin.*

 ## Spelling Words

• Review the words *man* and *mat* by having students write the words several times.
• Follow the procedure for Day One to model and practice the words *fan* and *fit.*

 ## Sight Words

Review
• Place sight word card **is** in the pocket chart and have students read the word.
• Take away the card and ask students to write the word *is* three times on their workmats. Make sure students read the word each time they write it.
• Place the model in the pocket chart so that students can self-check and correct if needed.

Phonemic Awareness

Listen for Initial Consonants
• Say the words *fan, fit,* and *man,* and have students repeat the words.
• Ask: *Do you hear the same sound at the beginning of each word? Which word starts with a different sound?*
• Repeat with the words *time, tick,* and *tell.* This time, after students have determined that the words start with the same sound, ask them to tell you what sound is the same in all three words.
• Repeat with the words *sit, fish, sand; fig, find, fish; make, man, more; fit, finger, fast.*

**Poetry Poster
(Back)**

P+A+M **Blending Sounds**

• Have students sound out the words *fan, it, Sam,* and *fin.*

Distribute blackline master 8 and instruct students to complete it at home.
Assessment Tip: The goal is to have students sound out the words in three seconds or less. Note which students need more practice in blending.

 Spelling Words

• Review the words *man, mat, fan,* and *fit* by having students write them several times on side 2 of their workmats.
• Follow the procedure for Day One to model and practice the words *if* and *fin.*

 Sight Words

• Write the word *is* on the board and have students read the word several times
• Ask volunteers to make up oral sentences using the word *is.*

 Decodable Book

Work with small groups of students to read the decodable book *Fit* on Days Three and Four. Assign blackline master 3 and Independent Activities for the rest of the class on Day Three.

Decodable Book

Introduce the Book
• Show students the cover of the book. Point to the title, *Fit,* and have them sound out the word as you run your finger under it.
• Ask: *What do you see in the picture? What does it mean to be fit?*

Read the Book
• Give each student a copy of the book. Have them turn to page 2 and put their finger on the first word. Have them run their finger under the word as they sound it out: */SSSSaaaammmm/.*
• Have students point to the next word. Remind them that this is a word they don't sound out and that they have been practicing during the week. Have them say the word *is.*
• Have students point to the last word and sound it out as they run their finger under the word: */ffffiiiitttt/.*
• Have students read the whole sentence at normal speed.
• If students can sound out the words without difficulty, have them whisper-read the rest of the text.
• If students have difficulty, continue to guide them page by page.

Discuss the Book
• When students have finished reading, ask: *Why did Sam and Tim feel fat at the end of the meal? What did they do to feel better?*

**SUPPORT TIPS
for English Language Learners**

Develop: Concept and Vocabulary for fit

• Before reading, have students work in pairs or small groups to create collages showing people who are (physically) fit and people who are not.

• Introduce the vocabulary word *fit,* and encourage groups to use the word *fit* while they are working on the collages and when they share their collages with the other groups.

• Enlist the aid of the physical education teacher to reinforce the vocabulary word.

DAY 4

Independent Activities

Decodable Book

When students have had a chance to read the decodable book in the small group setting, have them read the book independently or with a buddy for practice.

Spelling

As words are introduced each day, write them on index cards and place them in the literacy center. Ensure that the letter cards needed to build the words are in the center. Students will use the following procedure to spell words.
- Choose a word card.
- Use their fingers and eyes to read the word.
- Turn over the card.
- Build the word with the letter cards.
- Turn over the card to check the spelling.
- Write the word.

Sight Words

Word Search Have students find examples of the word *is* around the classroom.

Build the Word Have students build the word *is* using the letter cards in the center.

Write Ask students to practice writing the word *is* several times.

Personal Dictionary Have students place the word *is* in their personal dictionaries.

Find the Word Have students circle the word *is* in a familiar poem and write it several times on their workmats.

Phonological Awareness

Listen for Rhyme
- Say the words *fan* and *man*. Remind students that these words rhyme because they have the same sounds at the end. Repeat the words.
- Reread the poem *Fuzzy Fox and Fiddle* and have students listen for rhyming words. Have them clap each time you say a rhyming word.
- Say the following groups of words and ask students if the words rhyme: *up/cup, man/tan, bed/bat, jump/pump, laugh/calf, make/mind*.
- Repeat the rhyming pairs and ask students to tell you what sounds they hear at the end of the words. (*man/tan = /an/*)

Assessment Tip: Note which students are clapping when they hear a pair that rhymes.

 ## Blending Sounds

- Have students blend the words *man, it, at,* and *mat*.

Spelling Words

Review
- Review the spelling words by having students write them several times on their workmats.
- Provide pairs of students with blackline master 2. While one student reads the spelling words, the other student writes the words.
- If a student spells a word correctly, the partner puts a check mark beside the word. If the student spells a word incorrectly, the partner may prompt the student while the student tries to spell the word a second time. If the second spelling is correct, the partner places a check mark in the "Second Try" column.

Assessment Tip: Collect students' competed blackline masters and note which words gave them difficulty.

 ## Sight Words

Review
- Hold up sight word card *is* and call on individual students to quickly read the word.
- Ask volunteers to use the word in an oral sentence. The other students should clap when they hear the word *is*.

 ## Decodable Book

- Read the decodable book *Fit* with the remaining small groups of students. Assign blackline master 4 and Independent Activities for the rest of the class.

Assessment Tip: Use the completed blackline master to assess how well students can make connections between sounds and the letters that stand for those sounds.

Spelling Assessment

Use the following procedure to assess students' spelling of the Unit 6 words.
• Say each spelling word and use it in a sentence.
• Have students write the word on a piece of paper.
• Continue with the next word on the list.
• When students have finished, collect their papers and analyze their spellings of misspelled words.
• Record their progress on a spelling record sheet, and provide extra practice as needed.

 # Small Group Activities

The following small group activities can be used to provide hands-on practice for students who need additional support. Assign blackline master 5 and Independent Activities for the rest of the class.

 ### PHONOLOGICAL AWARENESS

Initial Sounds Have students close their eyes. Then tell them that you are going to say a sentence; if they hear the /f/ sound, they should raise their hands. Say: *Fanny Fox fixed fans*. Say each word slowly, emphasizing the /f/ sound.

Poem Reread the poem with students. Have them clap when they hear the /f/ sound. Reread the poem and have students listen for words that rhyme. Have them tell you which words rhyme.

 ### SOUND/SYMBOL RELATIONSHIPS

Word Sort 1 Shuffle decodable word cards **man, sat, tan, fit, fat,** and **sit.** Ask volunteers to sort them by beginning sounds. After each sort is completed, have students read the words with you to make sure the words have been sorted correctly.

Word Sort 2 Have students sort the decodable word cards according to medial sounds. Have students read the words in each group to make sure they have been sorted correctly.

 ### BLENDING

Model Write the words *Sam, it, at, sit, fan, fin, tan, fit,* and *fat* on the board. Move your hand under each word and blend the sounds, then say the word. Have students sound out the words with you.

 ### SPELLING

Practice Have students use the "look, say, cover, write, and check" method to practice the spelling words.

Model Build a spelling word with letter cards. Ask a student to run his/her finger under the word and read it. Mix the cards, say the word, and ask another student to spell the word. Have another student run his or her fingers under the word and read it to check spelling. Repeat with another spelling word.

 ### SIGHT WORDS

Spell and Write Begin by giving each student in the group a half sheet of paper.
• Show students the word **is.** Read the word and have students spell the word aloud.
• Have students write the word on their papers.
• Have students construct the word with letter cards.

Student Name _____   Assessment Date _____

Phonological Awareness: Listening for Rhyme

Directions: Say the pair of words and ask the student if the words rhyme. If the student answers correctly, put a ✔. If the student's response is incorrect, put an **X**. **Example:** box/fox. *Yes.*

think/brink *(yes)*		bait/wait *(yes)*			
catch/couch *(no)*		toss/floss *(yes)*			
fog/fall *(no)*		cubs/cubes *(no)*		**Score**	**/6**

Phonemic Awareness: Differentiating Initial Sounds

Directions: Say each set of words. Then have the student say the two words that begin with the same sound. Put a ✔ if the student's response is correct. If not, record the words the student chooses. **Example:** milk/toe/money. *Milk, money.*

face/factory/tunnel *(face, factory)*			
neck/singer/supper *(singer, supper)*			
nails/tennis/note *(nails, note)*			
many/farm/mud *(many, mud)*			
nurse/tank/Tuesday *(tank, Tuesday)*			
faucet/four/sausage *(faucet, four)*		**Score**	**/6**

Phonics: Segmenting and Blending Sounds

Directions: Explain that these real and nonsense words use sounds the student has been learning. Have the student point to each word on the corresponding student sheet, say each sound, and then blend the sounds together. Put a ✔ if the student's response is correct. If the student misses the word, record the error. **Example:** Fim. /f/ /i/ /m/, fim.

nim *(/n/ /i/ /m/, nim)*		fis *(/f/ /i/ /s/, fis)*			
fam *(/f/ /a/ /m/, fam)*		mim *(/m/ /i/ /m/, mim)*			
nin *(/n/ /i/ /n/, nin)*		fas *(/f/ /a/ /s/, fas)*		**Score**	**/6**

Sight Word

Directions: Have the student point to the sight word on the corresponding student sheet and read it as quickly as possible. Put a ✔ if the student successfully reads the word and an **X** if the student hesitates more than a few seconds. If the student misses the word, record the error.

is		**Score**	**/1**

UNIT 7 Pp

Unit Objectives

Students will:

- Identify the sound /p/
- Associate the letter Pp with the /p/ sound
- Listen for words that rhyme and suggest pairs of words that rhyme
- Blend CVC words
- Read the sight words a, has
- Spell CVC words using p and letters previously learned

Day 1

 BLM 1

 BLM 6

 Letter Cards: **f, n, p, t**

Spelling Transparency

 Picture Word Cards: **fan, fish, fork, fox, pan, pen, plant, pumpkin, tent, tiger, top, tub,**

Day 2

 BLM 1

 BLM 7

 Sight Word Cards: **a, has**

 Decodable Word Cards: **at, fat, fit, it, mat, Nan, nap, Pam, pan, pat, pin, pit, set, tan, tin**

 Spelling Transparency

 Picture Word Cards: **fish, nut, pan, top**

Day 3

 BLM 1

 BLM 3

 BLM 8

 Spelling Transparency

Day 4

 BLM 1

 BLM 2

 BLM 4

Day 5

 BLM 5

 Letter Cards: **f, n, p, t**

 Sight Word Cards: **a, has, is**

 Quick-Check Student Sheet

 Picture Word Cards: **fish, fox, nest, nut, pan, pen, top, tub**

Poetry Poster

Student Workmat

Letter Frieze Card

Decodable Book

Poetry CD

Core Materials

All print resources can be downloaded from http://phonicsresources.benchmarkeducation.com.

DAY 1

Poetry Poster (Front)

PET PARADE

The pet parade
has just begun.
It's in the park
and will be fun!
Pandas and parrots,
pink bows on dogs,
and a big pot filled
with tiny frogs!

Letter Frieze Card

Picture Word Cards

Phonemic Awareness

Use the Poetry Poster
- Read aloud or play the recording of the poem *Pet Parade*.
- Say the sentence "The pet parade has just begun," emphasizing the /**p**/ sound.
- Have students say the sentence with you. Before each word that starts with /**p**/, say the phoneme first in isolation. Say: *The* /**p**/ *pet* /**p**/ *parade has just begun.*

Distribute blackline master 6 and instruct students to complete it at home.

Sound/Symbol Relationships

Model
- Display letter frieze card **Pp**. Explain that the letter **Pp** stands for the /**p**/ sound in the word **pumpkin**.
- Reread the poem *Pet Parade* and invite students to read along with you.
- Point to words in the poem that begin with the letter **p**. Say the words aloud, and ask students to say the words with you.

Practice with the Letter Cards
- Distribute letter cards **p**, **f**, and **n**. Have students line up the cards on their workmats.
- Have students pull down each letter card and say the letter name, then push it back up and say the letter sound.
- Ask them to pull down each letter card again, saying a word that starts with that sound.
- Have them push up the letter card that starts the word **pan**. (Repeat with the words **net** and **fit**.)

Practice with the Picture Cards
- Place letter cards **p**, **t**, and **f** in the pocket chart.
- Place picture cards **pan**, **top**, and **fish** under the corresponding letters while you say the name of the letter and the name of the object in the picture.
- Hold up picture card **pen** and have students say **pen** with you.
- Ask: *Does* **pen** *begin like* **pan, top,** *or* **fish***?*
- Place picture card **pen** under letter card **p**. Say: **Pen** *begins like* **pan**, *so I am putting picture card* **pen** *under the letter* **p**.
- Repeat with picture cards **pumpkin, tiger, tent, tub, fan, fox,** and **fork.**

Blending Sounds

Review
- Hold up letter frieze cards of previously taught words one at a time. Ask students to say the sound each letter stands for.

Model
- Write the word **pin** on the board. Sound out the word by moving your hand under each letter and blending the sounds. (/**piiiinnnn**/) Then say the word.
- Ask students to sound out the word with you.

Practice with the Word Lists
- Distribute blackline master 1.
- Have students point to the word **pin**. Ask them to sound out the word with you. Then ask them to say the word at regular speed.
- Repeat with **fat, tip,** and **if**. Then have students sound out the words in random order.

Spelling Words

Model

- Use the spelling transparency. Place counters under the second set of boxes.
- Say: *Today we are going to learn to spell* **tin** *and* **fat**. *Watch and listen as I say* **tin** *slowly:* /**tiiiinnnn**/. Remind students that the word has a stop sound at the beginning.
- As you say /**t**/, push a counter into the first box. Then say /**iiii**/ as you push a counter into the second box and /**nnnn**/ as you push a counter into the third box. Repeat the steps.
- Model recording the letters for the sounds on the transparency. Say: *The first sound is* /**t**/. *I know that the letter* **t** *stands for the* /**t**/ *sound. I'll write the letter* **t** *in the first box. Let's listen for the second sound:* /**tiiii**/. *I hear* /**i**/. *I know that the letter* **i** *stands for the* /**i**/ *sound, so I will write* **i** *in the second box. Let's listen for the last sound:* /**tinnnn**/. *I hear* /**n**/. *I know that the letter* **n** *stands for the* /**n**/ *sound, so I will write* **n** *in the last box.*
- Have students blend the sounds to check the spelling of the word.

Practice with the Workmat

- Instruct students to place counters under the second set of boxes on side 2 of the workmat.
- Ask students to slowly articulate the word *tin* as they push the counters into the boxes.
- Have students identify and record the letters that stand for the sounds they hear.
- Have students practice writing *tin* on their workmats.

Repeat the modeling and guided practice with the second spelling word, *fat*.

 # Sight Words

Review

- Write the word *is* on the board. Have students clap once for each letter as you spell the word together.
- Have students read the word.

Introduce

- Use the pocket chart and a letter card to model how the new word, *a,* looks in print. Say: *This is the word* **a**. *It is made up of the letter* **a**.
- Have students say the word as you point to it.
- Follow the same steps to introduce the word *has*.
- Write these sentences on the board: "Pam has a mat. It is tan." Read the sentences aloud.
- Have a volunteer find the word *is*. Underline the word. Repeat with the words *a* and *has*.

Write

- Have students write the words *a* and *has* three times on their workmats, using the models in the pocket chart.

Independent Activities

Phonemic Awareness

Make a Collage Provide magazines and scissors and invite students to cut out pictures of things that begin with */p/*.

Listen Have students listen to the recording of the poem *Pet Parade* in the listening center.

Sound/Symbol Relationships

Rhyming Sort Provide decodable word cards **it**, **pit**, **sit**, **in**, **pin**, **tin**, **pan**, **tan**, **at**, **pat**, and **mat**. Have students sort the words into sets of rhyming words.

Build Words Provide letter cards **m**, **a**, **s**, **t**, **n**, **i**, **f**, and **p**. Have students use the cards to make as many three-letter words as they can. Have them write the words they make.

**Poetry Poster
(Back)**

Phonemic Awareness

Use the Poetry Poster
• Show students the picture on the back of the poetry poster, and have them name all the objects in the picture.
• Point to a panda in the picture and say the word *panda*, stressing the beginning sound. Ask: *What sound do you hear at the beginning of the word?*
• Have students point to other objects that start with */p/*. Have them name the objects.

Sound/Symbol Relationships

Sort the Decodable Word Cards
• Place picture cards **pan**, **fish**, **nut**, and **top** in the pocket chart and have students say the name of the object on each card.
• Show students decodable word card **tan** and have them blend the word.
• Ask them if *tan* begins like *pan, fish, nut,* or *top*. Then place the word under picture card **top**.
• Repeat with decodable word cards **tin**, **pat**, **Pam**, **fat**, **fit**, **Nan**, and **nap**.

Distribute blackline master 7 and instruct students to complete it at home.

Assessment Tip: Note which students do not participate. Give these students word cards and ask them to place the cards under the correct picture cards. Assign Independent Activities for the rest of the class.

 ## Blending Sounds

• Have students blend the words *tap, pat, pan,* and *pin*.

 ## Spelling Words

• Review the words *tin* and *fat* by having students write the words several times.
• Follow the procedures for Day One to model and practice the words *tap* and *pat*.

Sight Words

Review
• Write the word *is* on the board and ask a volunteer to read it. Have students spell the word *is* in the air with their fingers.
• Place the sight word cards **a** and **has** in the pocket chart. Read the words aloud.
• Remove the words from the pocket chart, and encourage students to write the words without support. Make sure students read the word each time they write it.
• Return the words to the pocket chart and have students check their spelling.

Phonemic Awareness

Blend and Segment Onset and Rime

- Say the word **pan**, segmenting it into its onset and rime: **/p/ /an/**. Have students blend the sounds **/paaan/** and say the word.
- Continue with the words **fit, pit, man, fan, sit**, and **tan**.

 # Blending Sounds

- Have students blend the words **tan, nip, map**, and **sat**.

 # Spelling Words

- Review the words **tin, fat, tap**, and **pat** by having students write them several times on their papers or workmats.
- Follow the procedure for Day One to model and practice the words **pin** and **sip**.

Assessment Tip: Note students who do not slowly articulate the sounds when spelling a word.

 # Sight Words

- Write the words **is, a**, and **has** on the board. Read each word with students.
- Without students seeing, erase a letter in one of the words. Ask students which letter is missing. Replace the letter as students read the word. Repeat with the other two words.
- Ask volunteers to repeat this process.

Distribute blackline master 8 and instruct students to complete it at home.

Decodable Book

Work with small groups of students to read the decodable book *Pam Has a Map* on Days Three and Four. Assign blackline master 3 and Independent Activities for the rest of the class on Day Three.

Introduce the Book

- Show students the cover of the book. Point to the title, *Pam Has a Map*, and have them sound out the words as you run your finger under them.
- Ask: *What do you see in the picture? Who is Pam? What is a map?*

Read the Book

- Give each student a copy of the book and instruct them to turn to page 2. Have them run their fingers under the first word as they sound it out: **/Paaaammmm/**.
- Have students point to the next word. Remind them that this is a word they don't sound out and that they have been practicing during the week. Have them read the word **is**.
- Have students run their finger under the last word as they sound it out: **/ffffiiiit/**.
- Have students read the whole sentence at normal speed.
- Repeat with the other sentence on the page.
- If students are sounding out the words without difficulty, have them whisper-read the rest of the text.
- If students are having difficulty sounding out the words, continue to guide them page by page as they first sound out each word and then read the sentence at normal speed.

Discuss the Book

- When students have finished reading, involve them in a discussion about the book. Ask: *Why did Pam stick a pin in the map? Why did Pam and Tam sit?*

Decodable Book

 **SUPPORT TIPS**
for English Language Learners

Develop/Reinforce: past tense sat

- Before reading, play the game "Who sat in the chair?"
- Direct one student to sit in a special chair and then return to his/her own seat.
- Ask: *Who sat in the chair?* Accept a single-word response (name) but model the full sentence, emphasizing **sat** until the students respond using the full sentence.
- Students can extend the activity in pairs or small groups using dolls, puppets, or other manipulatives while matching their motions to the target response.

DAY 4

Independent Activities

Decodable Book

Independent Practice When students have had a chance to read the decodable book in the small group setting, have them read it independently or with a buddy for practice.

Fluency Practice Have students practice reading the story. Record their readings. Play the recordings so that students may review their readings.

Spelling

Independent Practice Write the week's spelling words on index cards and place them in the literacy center. Provide the letter cards needed to build the words and have students use the cards to spell the words.

Sight Words

Scrambled Words Write these scrambled sentences on index cards: "a man Tim is"; "is fit Pam"; "has a mat Nan"; "a map has Sam." Have students choose a card and rewrite the sentence correctly. Then have them circle the words *a, has,* and *is* in the sentences.

Phonological Awareness

Identify and Produce Rhyme

- Say *pan* and *man*. Remind students that these words rhyme because they have the same sounds at the end. Repeat the words.
- Reread the poem *Pet Parade* and have students listen for rhyming words.
- Say the following pairs of words and ask students to clap if the two words rhyme: *sat/mat, pan/pat, pin/tin, pot/hot, hop/stop, sit/sip, tap/cap*. Then repeat only the rhyming pairs and ask students to tell you what sounds are the same in both words.
- Have students tell you words that rhyme with *big, bow, pet,* and *tip*.

Assessment Tip: Note which students are clapping at the appropriate time. Call on individual students to listen for the rhyming words. Note which students can produce a rhyming word when asked.

Blending Sounds

- Have students blend the words *sap, pan, tin,* and *tap*.

Spelling Words

Review

- Have students write the spelling words several times on their workmats.
- Provide pairs of students with blackline master 2. While one student reads the words the other student writes the words.
- If the student spells a word correctly, the partner puts a check mark beside the word. If the student spells a word incorrectly, the partner prompts the student by sounding out the word slowly. If the student spells it correctly, the partner places a check mark in the "Second Try" column.

Assessment Tip: Collect students' completed blackline masters and note which words gave them difficulty.

Sight Words

Review

- Write the words *a, has,* and *is* on the board. Dim the lights in the room and shine a flashlight on the word *has*. Have a student read the word, spell it, and use it in a sentence. Repeat with *a* and *is*.

Decodable Book

- Read the decodable book *Pam Has a Map* with the remaining small groups of students. Assign blackline master 4 and Independent Activities for the rest of the class.

Assessment Tip: Use the completed blackline masters to assess how well students can identify rhyme.

Spelling Assessment

Use the following procedure to assess students' spelling of the Unit 7 words.

• Say each spelling word and use it in a sentence.
• Have students write the word on a piece of paper.
• Continue with the next word on the list.
• When students have finished, collect their papers and analyze their spellings of misspelled words.
• Record their progress on a spelling record sheet, and provide extra practice as needed.

Small Group Activities

The following small group activities can be used to provide hands-on practice for students who need additional support. Assign blackline master 5 and Independent Activities for the rest of the class.

PHONOLOGICAL AWARENESS

Practice Initial Sounds Display the picture on the back of the poster. Ask: *Do you see a panda with a pan? What words have /p/?* Have students take turns asking and answering similar questions about the poster.

Identify Onset and Rime Say the word *man* and ask: *What sound do you hear at the beginning of the word? What sounds do you hear at the end?* Have students say the onset and rime with you several times. Then blend the sounds and say *man*. Repeat this with the words *pan, tap*, and *tip*.

Work with Rhyme Repeat the word pairs used on Day Four. Ask students to identify the rhyming words. Then have them say a rhyming word for the following words from the poem: *park, fun, dog, pot*.

SOUND/SYMBOL RELATIONSHIPS

Read the Poem Display the poetry poster and provide each student with letter card **p.** Instruct students to hold up the letter card each time they hear a word in the poem that begins with /p/ as you read the poem.

Letter Match Place picture cards **pan, nut, fish,** and **top** in the pocket chart. Distribute letter cards **p, n, f,** and **t** and have students name the letters, say the sounds, and match them to the pictures. Repeat the activity with picture cards **nest, pen, tub,** and **fox.**

BLENDING

Blend Words Write the word *pan* on the board. Have students take turns running their fingers under the word as they blend the sounds. Then change the final letter to make the word *pat* and repeat the procedure.

SPELLING

Determine Missing Letters Write __*a*__ on the board and tell students that you want to make the word *pat*. Have one student write the letter for the beginning sound. Ask another student to write the letter for the ending sound. Have students say the word then repeat the procedure with the word *tap*.

Guess the Word Write the spelling words on the board. Have students guess which word you are thinking of. For example, say: *I'm thinking of a word that rhymes with* **tin**. *I'm thinking of a word that starts with* **t** *and ends with* **p**.

SIGHT WORDS

Search Write the words *a, has,* and *is* on the board and have students say each word as you point to it. Ask students to find the words *a, has,* and *is* in the decodable book.

Make a Sentence Model using the words *a, has,* and *is* in simple sentences. Place sight word cards **a, has,** and **is** in a box. Have students draw a card from the box, read the word, and use the word in an oral sentence.

Student Name _____   Assessment Date _____

Phonological Awareness: Identifying Rhyme

Directions: Say each set of words. Then have the student say the two words that rhyme. Put a ✔ if the student's response is correct. If not, record the words the student chooses. **Example:** mat/hat/lid. *Mat, hat.*

dog/fog/pen *(dog, fog)*		
lid/mad/rid *(lid, rid)*		
tap/let/sap *(tap, sap)*		
back/knock/sock *(knock, sock)*		
nod/net/bet *(net, bet)*		
fun/sun/den *(fun, sun)*		**Score /6**

Phonemic Awareness: Blending Onset and Rime

Directions: Say the first sound of the word followed by the rest of the word. Then have the student say the whole word. If the student says the word correctly, put a ✔. If the student misses the word, record the error. **Example:** /b/ /at/. *Bat.*

/p/ /in/ *(pin)*		/n/ /ap/ *(nap)*		
/m/ /at/ *(mat)*		/p/ /it/ *(pit)*		
/s/ /it/ *(sit)*		/m/ /an/ *(man)*		**Score /6**

Phonics: Segmenting and Blending Sounds

Directions: Explain that these nonsense words use sounds the student has been learning. Have the student point to each word on the corresponding student sheet, say each sound, and then blend the sounds together. Put a ✔ if the student's response is correct. If the student misses the word, record the error. **Example:** saf. /s/ /a/ /f/. *saf.*

paf *(/p/ /a/ /f/, paf)*		pim *(/p/ /i/ /m/, pim)*		
sif *(/s/ /i/ /f/, sif)*		taf *(/t/ /a/ /f/, taf)*		
naf *(/n/ /a/ /f/, naf)*		pif *(/p/ /i/ /f/, pif)*		**Score /6**

Sight Words

Directions: Have the student point to the first sight word on the corresponding student sheet and read across the line, saying each word as quickly as possible. Put a ✔ if the student successfully reads the word and an **X** if the student hesitates more than a few seconds. If the student misses the word, record the error.

a		has		**Score /2**

UNIT 8 Short Oo

Unit Objectives

Students will:

- Identify the sound /o/
- Associate the letter Oo with the /o/ sound
- Listen for medial sounds
- Listen for rhyme and suggest pairs of words that rhyme
- Blend CVC words
- Read the sight word the
- Spell CVC words using o and letters previously learned

Day 1

BLM 1

BLM 6

Letter Cards: **a, i, o**

Spelling Transparency

Picture Word Cards: **cap, dish, fan, fish, fox, hat, mop, quilt, sock, top**

Day 2

BLM 1

BLM 7

Decodable Word Cards: **fat, fin, man, mop, nap, not, Sam, sip, sit**

Sight Word Card: **the**

Spelling Transparency

Picture Word Cards: **fox, mop, nut**

Day 3

BLM 1

BLM 3

BLM 8

Spelling Transparency

Day 4

BLM 1

BLM 2

BLM 4

Sight Word Cards: **a, has, is, the**

Decodable Word Cards: **man, pan, Sam**

Spelling Transparency

Day 5

BLM 5

Letter Cards: **f, i, o, p, t**

Sight Word Cards: **a, has, is, the**

Quick-Check Student Sheet

Decodable Word Cards: **nip, on, top, mat**

Picture Word Cards: **fan, fox, map, mop, nest, nut, olive, ox**

Oo

Oliver and Dot

Oliver and Dot
go hop, hop, hop.
Dot says, "That's enough.
Let's stop, stop, stop."

Oliver and Dot
are ready to drop.
They fall on the ground
with a plop, plop, plop.

Poetry Poster

Student Workmat

Oo

Letter Frieze Card

Decodable Book

Poetry CD

Core Materials

All print resources can be downloaded from http://phonicsresources.benchmarkeducation.com

UNIT 8 Short Oo

**Poetry Poster
(Front)**

Letter Frieze Card

**Picture Word
Cards**

 # Phonemic Awareness

Use the Poetry Poster

- Read aloud or play the recording of the poem *Oliver and Dot.*
- Say the sentence "Oliver and Dot go hop, hop, hop," emphasizing the /o/ phoneme.
- Have students say the sentence with you.
- Reread the poem and have students clap when they hear a word that has the /o/ sound.

Distribute blackline master 6 and instruct students to complete it at home.

Sound/Symbol Relationships

Model

- Display letter frieze card **Oo.** Explain that the letter **Oo** stands for the /o/ sound at the beginning of *ostrich* and in the middle of *mop.*
- Reread the poem *Oliver and Dot.* Invite students to read along with you.
- Point to words in the poem that have the /o/ sound. Say the words, and ask students to say the words with you. Discuss whether the /o/ sound is at the beginning or in the middle.

Practice with the Letter Cards

- Distribute letter cards **o**, **i**, and **a.** Ask students to line up the cards on their workmats.
- Have students pull down each letter card and say the letter name, then push it back up and say the letter sound.
- Ask them to pull down each letter card again, saying a word that has that sound in the middle.
- Have them push up the letter card that stands for the middle sound in *mop.* (Repeat with *sit* and *man.*)

Practice with the Picture Cards

- Place letter cards **a**, **i**, and **o** in the pocket chart.
- Place picture cards **fan**, **fish**, and **sock** under the letter cards that have the same medial sounds. Say: *I hear /a/ in the middle of the word* **fan**. *I will place the picture of the fan under the letter* **a**.
- Hold up picture card **mop.** Have students say *mop* with you.
- Ask: *Is the middle sound in* **mop** *like the middle sound in* **fan**, **fish**, *or* **sock**?
- Place picture card **mop** under letter card **o.** Say: /**Moooop**/ *has the same middle sound as* /**sooook**/, *so I am putting picture card* **mop** *under the letter* **o**.
- Repeat with picture cards **top**, **dish**, **quilt**, **hat**, **fox**, and **cap**.

Blending Sounds

Review

- Hold up letter frieze cards of previously taught letter sounds. Ask students to say the sound each letter stands for.

Model

- Write the word *in* on the board. Sound out the word, moving your hand under each letter while blending the sounds. Then say the word.
- Ask students to sound out the word with you.

Practice with the Word Lists

- Distribute blackline master 1.
- Have students point to the word *in*. Ask them to sound out the word with you. Then ask them to say the word at regular speed.
- Repeat with the words *not*, *pan*, and *nap*. Then have students sound out the words in random order.

Spelling Words

Model

- Use the spelling transparency. Place counters under the second set of boxes.
- Say: *Today we are going to learn to spell* **nap** *and* **fit.** *Watch and listen as I say* **nap** *slowly:* /**nnnnaaaap**/.
- As you say /**nnnn**/, push a counter into the first box. Then say /***aaaa***/ as you push a counter into the second box and /***p***/ as you push a counter into the third box. Repeat the steps.
- Model recording the letters for the sounds on the transparency. Say: *The first sound is* /**n**/. *I know that the letter* **n** *stands for the* /**n**/ *sound. I'll write the letter* **n** *in the first box. Let's listen for the second sound:* /**naaaa**/. *I hear* /**a**/. *I know that the letter* **a** *stands for the* /**a**/ *sound, so I will write* **a** *in the second box. Let's listen for the last sound:* /**naaaap**/. *I hear* /**p**/. *I know that the letter* **p** *stands for the* /**p**/ *sound, so I will write* **p** *in the last box.*
- Have students blend the sounds to check the spelling of the word.

Practice with the Workmat

- Instruct students to place their counters under the second set of boxes on side 2 of the workmat.
- Ask students to slowly articulate the word ***nap*** as they push the counters into the boxes.
- Have students identify and record the letters that stand for the sounds they hear.
- Have students practice writing ***nap*** on side 1 of their workmats.

Repeat the modeling and guided practice with the second spelling word, ***fit.***

 ## Sight Words

Review

- Write the words ***a***, ***has***, and ***is*** on the board. Remind students that these are words they have been practicing so that they can read them quickly.
- Have students read the words aloud several times.
- Have volunteers use the words in oral sentences.

Introduce

- Write the word ***the*** on the board. Say: *This is the word* **the.** *It is made up of the letters* **t, h,** *and* **e.** *We will practice this word so that you can read it quickly.*
- Point to the word and say it again as students say it with you.
- Have students clap the letters as you spell the word together.

Write

- Have students write the word ***the*** on their workmats, using the model on the board.

DAY 2

Independent Activities

Phonemic Awareness

Picture Cards Provide picture cards in the literacy center. Students can:
- take a card, name the picture, and say another word that has the same medial sound
- separate the cards that have the /o/ sound
- match a card with another card that has the same medial sound

Sound Search Students can work with a partner to make a list of objects in and around the school that have the /o/ sound.

Listen Have students listen to the recording of the poem *Oliver and Dot* in the listening center.

Sound/Symbol Relationships

Word Sort Give students decodable word cards **Sam**, **man**, **fan**, **top**, **pop**, **not**, **sip**, **sit**, and **fit**. Have students sort the cards according to the medial sound.

Draw Display letter cards **m**, **s**, **t**, **n**, and **p**. Have students draw a picture of something that begins with each letter.

CVC Words Give students letter cards **a**, **i**, **o**, **t**, **n**, **f**, **m**, and **p**. Have them use the cards to make three-letter words. Then have students work with a partner to make lists of rhyming words.

Word Toss Write the letters *a*, *i*, and *o* on large paper squares. Put the squares on the floor. Students can:
- toss a beanbag onto a square and say the sound
- toss a beanbag onto a square and say a word that has that medial sound

 ## Phonemic Awareness

Use the Poetry Poster
- Show students the picture on the back of the poetry poster, and have them name all the objects in the picture.
- Point to a fox in the picture and say the word *fox*, emphasizing the /o/. Ask students to tell you what sound they hear in the middle of the word.
- Ask students to point to something in the picture that has /o/ in the middle. Have them say the name of the object, emphasizing the /o/.

Distribute blackline master 7 and instruct students to complete it at home.

 ## Sound/Symbol Relationships

Sort the Decodable Word Cards
- Place picture cards **mop**, **nut**, and **fox** in the pocket chart. Have students say the name of the object on each card.
- Show students decodable word card **fat** and have them blend the word.
- Ask students if *fat* begins like *mop*, *nut*, or *fox*. Place the card under the picture card **fox**.
- Repeat with decodable word cards **fin**, **man**, **mop**, **nap**, **not**, **Sam**, **sip**, and **sit.**

Assessment Tip: Note which letter/sound matches give students difficulty, and provide more practice with those letters and sounds. Assign Independent Activities for the rest of the class.

 ## Blending Sounds

- Have students sound out the words *nip*, *on*, *top*, and *map*, using the procedure for Day One.

 ## Spelling Words

- Review the words *nap* and *fit* by having students write the words several times.
- Follow the procedure for Day One to model and practice the words *on* and *pot*.

Sight Words

Review
- Write the words *the*, *a*, *has*, and *is* on the board and read them with students.
- Have students trace the words in the palm of their hands as they say the words.
- Hold up sight word card **the** and call on individual students to quickly read the word. Ask them to use the word in an oral sentence. The other students should clap when they hear the word *the*.

Phonemic Awareness

Discriminating Medial Sounds

- Tell students that you are going to say pairs of words. They are to give a "thumbs up" if the words have the same middle sound and a "thumbs down" if they do not.
- Say: **Stop, hot**. Have students repeat the words before they give their signal. Ask them to identify the middle sound in each word.
- Repeat with the word pairs **nap/not, Sam/Nan, Pop/pot, Tim/tan, sit/tin, mop/map**, and **top/tot**.

Assessment Tip: Select students whom you want to assess, give them a word, and ask them to identify the medial sound.

 # Blending Sounds

- Have students blend the words **sap, mop, tap**, and **not**, using the procedure for Day One.

Distribute blackline master 8 and instruct students to complete it at home.

 # Spelling Words

- Review the words **nap, fit, on**, and **pot** by having students write them several times.
- Follow the procedures for Day One to model and practice the words **mop** and **not**.

 # Sight Words

- Write the sight words on the board.
- Tell students that you are going to say some sentences and that they should raise their hands when they hear the words **a, has, is**, or **the**.
- Say: *My brother is funny. My grandpa has lots of friends. I like to go to the park. There is a fire station in town.*

 # Decodable Book

Work with small groups of students to read the decodable book *Pop* on Days Three and Four. Assign blackline master 3 and Independent Activities for the rest of the class on Day Three.

Introduce the Book

- Show students the cover of the book. Point to the title, *Pop*, and have them sound out the word as you run your finger under it.
- Ask: *What do you see in the picture?*

Read the Book

- Give each student a copy of the book. Ask them to turn to page 2. Have them run their fingers under the first word as they sound it out: /**Poooop**/.
- Have students point to the next word. Remind them that this is a word they don't sound out and that they have practiced. Have them say the word **is.**
- Have students run their fingers under the next word as they sound it out: /**iiiinnnn**/.
- Have students point to the next word. Remind them that this is a word they don't sound out. Have them say the word **the**.
- Have students run their fingers under the last word as they sound it out: /**piiiit**/.
- Have students read the whole sentence at normal speed. You might want to ask them what the pit is and point to it on the page.
- If students are sounding out the words without difficulty, have them whisper-read the rest of the text.
- If students have difficult, continue to guide them page by page.

Discuss the Book

- When students have finished reading, ask: *Why is the tot laughing? What is on top of the tot's head? What is Pop doing to help the tot?*

Poetry Poster
(Back)

Decodable Book

 **SUPPORT TIPS**
for English Language Learners

Develop/Reinforce Prepositions *in* and *on*

- Before reading, assess students in a one-on-one setting to find out how well they follow directions incorporating the prepositions in a situation.
- To teach or reinforce concepts, model and label the appropriate actions using real objects: *I put the pencil **in** the cup. I put the marker **on** the table.*
- Have students copy your actions as you describe the action: *Put the pencil **on** the table.*
- Have students work in pairs or small groups to play games requiring them to give and follow directions using the target prepositions.

Independent Activities

Decodable Book

Independent Practice When students have had a chance to read the decodable book in the small group setting, have them read it independently.

New Ending Have students use words from the book to write a new ending.

Dramatize Have students work in small groups to create a dramatization of the story. Students can take turns being the narrator and playing the parts of Pop and the tot.

Spelling

As words are introduced each day, write them on index cards and place them in the literacy center. Ensure that the letter cards needed to build the words are in the center. Students can use the following procedure to spell words.
• Choose a word card.
• Use their fingers and eyes to read the word.
• Turn over the card so that they can't see the word.
• Build the word using the letter cards.
• Turn over the card to check the word.
• Write the word.

Sight Words

Personal Dictionary Have students add *the* to their personal dictionaries.

Write a Sentence Have students write a sentence from the decodable book *Pop* and substitute their name for Pop's.

Letter Cards Have pairs of students use letter cards to make the words *a*, *has*, *is*, and *the*. After one partner makes the word, the other reads it.

 Phonological Awareness

Identify and Produce Rhyme
• Say the words *sit* and *fit*. Remind students that these words rhyme because they have the same sounds at the end. Repeat the words.
• Reread the poem *Oliver and Dot* and have students clap each time they hear a rhyming word.
• Say the following groups of words and ask students if the words rhyme: *tip/sip*, *can/cat*, *sap/sip*, *not/tot*, *hop/hip*, *Tim/tin*, *mop/top*.
• Tell students that you are going to say a word and that they are to say a word that rhymes. Use the words *cop*, *tap*, *in*, and *mat*.

 Blending Sounds

• Have students blend the words *sit*, *fat*, *Pop*, and *pan*, using the procedure for Day One.

 Spelling Words

Review
• Review the spelling words by having students write them several times on their workmats.
• Give blackline master 2 to pairs of students. While one student reads the words from the list, the other student writes each word.
• If a word is spelled correctly, the partner should put a check mark beside the word. If a word is spelled incorrectly, the partner may provide prompts. If the second spelling of the word is correct, the partner should place a check mark in the "Second Try" column.

Assessment Tip: Collect students' completed blackline masters and note which words gave them difficulty.

 Sight Words

Review
• Give seven students one of the following word cards each: **a**, **is**, **has**, **man**, **pan**, **Sam**, **the.**
• Have students line up in order and hold up the word cards to make one of these sentences as you say it. Say: *Sam is a man. The man is Sam. Sam has a pan. The man has a pan.*
• Have the rest of the group read the sentence to check that the students are in the right order.
• Repeat with the next sentence.

Decodable Book

• Read the decodable book *Pop* with the remaining small groups of students. Assign blackline master 4 and Independent Activities for the rest of the class.

Assessment Tip: Use the completed blackline master to assess how well students can identify rhyme.

Spelling Assessment

Use the following procedure to assess students' spelling of the Unit 8 words.
• Say each spelling word and use it in a sentence.
• Have students write the word on a piece of paper.
• Continue with the next word on the list.
• When students have finished, collect their papers and analyze their spellings of misspelled words.
• Record their progress on a spelling record sheet, and provide extra practice as needed.

Small Group Activities

The following small group activities can be used to provide hands-on practice for students who need additional support. Assign blackline master 5 and Independent Activities for the rest of the class.

PHONOLOGICAL AWARENESS

Medial Sounds Say the words *pot*, *fin*, *fox*, *bat*, *lock*, *cup*, *top*, *fat*, and *hop*. Tell students to stand when they hear words with the /o/ sound.

Initial Sounds Place picture cards **map**, **nut**, **ox**, **fox**, **mop**, **nest**, **olive**, and **fan** facedown. Have students turn over two cards at a time, say the names of the pictures, and identify the beginning sounds. If the pictures have the same beginning sound, the student makes a match and keeps the cards. Continue until all cards have been matched.

Rhyme Say these pairs of words: *tip/sip*, *can/cat*, *sap/sip*, *not/tot*, *hop/hip*, *Tim/tin*, *mop/top*. Have students identify the rhyming words. Then have students work with a partner to think of rhyming words for the words *lake*, *bed*, *bear*, and *go*.

SOUND/SYMBOL RELATIONSHIPS

Poem Reread the poem with students. Distribute letter card **o** to each student. Tell students to hold up the letter card each time you say a word that has the /o/ sound.

Build Words 1 Give students letter cards **p**, **o**, **t**, **f**, and **i**. Use letter cards to show students how to make the word *fit*. Say each sound as you make the word.

Build Words 2 Ask students to build the word on their workmats. Say the word *pit*. Have students choose the letter for the new beginning sound and make the word. Say the word *pot* and have students choose the letter for the new middle sound and make the word.

BLENDING

Model and Practice Provide more modeling in blending sounds in words, using the words *not*, *mop*, and *Tom*.
• Write the words one at a time on a workmat placed on the floor or on a desk so that students can easily see it. Move your hand under the sounds as you blend the sounds. Have students read the word with you, holding each sound, except for stop sounds, for one second. Check to make sure that each student is saying each sound and blending the sounds. Repeat with the rest of the words. Call on individual students to read the words.

• Say /nnnniiiip/. Ask: *What word is this?* Have students write the word on their workmats. Show them the word card and have them check their spelling, then have them blend the word again. Follow the same procedure with the words *on*, *top*, and *map*.

SPELLING

Scrambled Letters In a small group setting, write *anp* and *tfi* on the board. Have students unscramble the letters to make the words *nap* and *fit*.

Missing Letters Write the spelling words on the board, omitting the middle letter in each word. Say one of the words, and have students point to the word and name the missing letter. Write the letter, and have students read and spell the word. Repeat with the other spelling words.

 SIGHT WORDS

Guess the Word Divide the students into two teams, and give one team the sight word cards. Whisper a sight word to the other team and ask them to make up a sentence using the word. The other team must hold up the sight word card showing the word that was used. Continue the activity until all the students have an opportunity to practice making sentences and guessing the words.

Word Race Place sight word cards faceup on a table. Say a word and have students see how quickly they can find the word on a card and read it. Continue until all students have had several opportunities to recognize and read the words.

Student Name _____   Assessment Date _____

Phonological Awareness: Identifying Rhyme

Directions: Say each set of words. Then have the student say the two words that rhyme. Put a ✔ if the student's response is correct. If not, record the words the student chooses. **Example:** mat/hat/lid. *Mat, hat.*

cake/take/neck *(cake, take)*			
goat/get/boat *(goat, boat)*			
bell/call/sell *(bell, sell)*			
hood/good/head *(hood, good)*			
back/lick/sick *(lick/sick)*			
let/lot/spot *(lot, spot)*		**Score**	**/6**

Phonemic Awareness: Discriminating Medial Sounds

Directions: Say the word and ask the student to tell you the middle sound. If the student answers correctly, put a ✔. If the student misses the sound, record the error. **Example:** hat. /a/

knot *(/o/)*		snack *(/a/)*			
cliff *(/i/)*		plop *(/o/)*			
dock *(/o/)*		quit *(/i/)*		**Score**	**/6**

Phonics: Segmenting and Blending Sounds

Directions: Explain that these nonsense words use sounds the student has been learning. Have the student point to each word on the corresponding student sheet, say each sound, and then blend the sounds together. Put a ✔ if the student's response is correct. If the student misses the word, record the error. **Example:** fon. /f/ /o/ /n/, fon.

sof *(/s/ /o/ /f/, sof)*		nop *(/n/ /o/ /p/, nop)*			
fip *(/f/ /i/ /p/, fip)*		tam *(/t/ /a/ /m/, tam)*			
pom *(/p/ /o/ /m/, pom)*		sot *(/s/ /o/ /t/, sot)*		**Score**	**/6**

Sight Word

Directions: Have the student point to the sight word on the corresponding student sheet and read it as quickly as possible. Put a ✔ if the student successfully reads the word and an **X** if the student hesitates more than a few seconds. If the student misses the word, record the error.

the		**Score**	**/1**

Unit Objectives

Students will:

- Identify the sound /k/
- Associate the letter Cc with the sound /k/
- Listen for words that rhyme and suggest rhyming pairs
- Blend CVC words
- Read the sight words and, of
- Spell CVC words using c and letters previously learned

Day 1

BLM 1

BLM 6

Letter Cards:
c, f, p

Spelling Transparency

Picture Word Cards: **cap, car, cat, cup, fan, fork, fox, pan, pen, pumpkin**

Day 2

BLM 1

BLM 7

Decodable Word Cards: **cat, cot, Nan, nip, pat, pin, Sam, sat**

Spelling Transparency

Letter Cards:
c, f, p

Picture Word Cards: **car, nut, pen, sun**

Day 3

BLM 1

BLM 3

BLM 8

Letter Cards:
a, d, e, f, h, i, n, o, s, t,

Spelling Transparency

Day 4

BLM 1

BLM 2

BLM 4

Decodable Word Cards for Unit 9

Day 5

BLM 5

Letter Cards for Unit 9

Decodable Word Cards: **cat, cot, Nan, nip, pat, pin, Sam, sat**

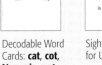
Sight Word Cards for Unit 9

Quick-Check Student Sheet

Poetry Poster

Student Workmat

Letter Frieze Card

Decodable Book

Poetry CD

Core Materials

All print resources can be downloaded from http://phonicsresources.benchmarkeducation.com.

Poetry Poster
(Front)

Letter Frieze Card

Picture Word
Cards

 Phonemic Awareness

Use the Poetry Poster

• Read aloud or play the recording of the poem *Camping*.
• Say the sentence "A cup of cocoa is very good for camping on a cold night," emphasizing the */k/* sound.
• Have students say the sentence with you. Before each of the words that start with */k/*, say the phoneme first in isolation. For example, say: *A /k/ cup of /k/ cocoa is very good for /k/ camping on a /k/ cold night*.
• Reread the poem and have students clap every time they hear a word that starts with */k/*.

Distribute blackline master 6 and instruct students to complete it at home.

Sound/Symbol Relationships

Model

• Display letter frieze card **Cc**. Explain that the letter **Cc** stands for the */k/* sound, as in the word *cat*.
• Reread the poem *Camping*. Invite students to read along with you.
• Point to words in the poem that begin with the letter **c**. Say each word aloud and ask students to say the words with you.

Practice with the Letter Cards

• Distribute letter cards **c**, **p**, and **f**. Ask students to line up the letter cards on their workmats.
• Have students pull down each letter card and say the letter name, then push it back up and say the letter sound.
• Ask them to pull down each letter card again, saying a word that starts with that sound.
• Have them push up the letter card that starts the word *cat*. (Repeat with the words *pan* and *fin*.)

Practice with the Picture Cards

• Place letter cards **c**, **p**, and **f** in the pocket chart.
• Place picture cards **car**, **pen**, and **fork** under the corresponding letters while you say the name of the letter and the name of the object in the picture.
• Hold up picture card **cup.** Have students say *cup* with you, emphasizing the initial sound.
• Ask: *Does* **cup** *begin like* **car**, **pen**, *or* **fork**?
• Place picture card **cup** under letter card **c**. Say: **Cup** *begins like* **car**, *so I am putting picture card* **cup** *under the letter* **c**.
• Repeat with picture cards **cat**, **cap**, **pumpkin**, **pan**, **fan**, and **fox**.

P + A + M   Blending Sounds

Review

• Hold up letter frieze cards of previously taught letter sounds. Ask students to say the sound each letter stands for.

Model

• Write the word *cat* on the board. Sound out the word by moving your hand under each letter while blending the sounds. Then say the word.
• Ask students to sound out the word with you.

Practice with the Word Lists

• Distribute blackline master 1.
• Have students point to the word *cat*. Ask them to sound out the word with you. Then ask them to say the word at regular speed.
• Repeat with the words *in*, *fan*, and *top.* Then have students sound out the words in random order.

Spelling Words

Model

- Use the spelling transparency. Place counters under the second set of boxes.
- Say: *Today we are going to learn to spell* **pit** *and* **top.** *Watch and listen as I say* **pit** *slowly:* /piiiit/. Remind students that the word has stop sounds at the beginning and the end.
- As you say /p/, push a counter into the first box. Then say /iiii/ as you push a counter into the second box and /t/ as you push a counter into the third. Repeat the steps.
- Model recording the letters for the sounds on the transparency. Say: *The first sound is* /p/. *I know that the letter* **p** *stands for the* /p/ *sound. I'll write the letter* **p** *in the first box. Let's listen for the second sound:* /piiii/. *I hear* /i/. *I know that the letter* **i** *stands for the* /i/ *sound, so I will write* **i** *in the second box. Let's listen for the last sound:* /piiiit/. *I hear* /t/. *I know that the letter* **t** *stands for the* /t/ *sound, so I will write* **t** *in the last box.*
- Have students blend the sounds to check the spelling.

Practice with the Workmat

- Instruct students to place counters under the second set of boxes on side 2 of their workmats.
- Ask students to slowly articulate the word *pit* as they push the counters into the boxes.
- Have students identify and record the letters that stand for the sounds they hear.
- Have students practice writing *pit* on side 1 of their workmats.

Repeat the modeling and guided practice with the second spelling word, *top*.

 # Sight Words

Review

- Write the words *a*, *has*, *is*, and *the* on the board.
- Have students write the words on their workmats and compare their spelling with the models on the board.

Introduce

- Write the word *and* on the board. Say: *This is the word* **and.** *Let's spell the word in the air with our fingers:* **a, n, d**.
- Follow the steps to introduce the word *of.*
- Write the following on the board: "Sam has a cat and a map." "The cat is on top of the map." Underline *and* and *of.* Have students read the underlined words and then the sentences.

Write

- Have students write *and* and *of* on side 1 of their workmats, using the models on the board.

DAY 2

Independent Activities

Phonological Awareness

Picture Cards Provide picture cards in the literacy center. Students can:
- take two picture cards, name the pictures, and tell if the words rhyme
- separate the cards that start with /k/
- match the picture card under the letter frieze card that has the same beginning sound

Art Have students use craft supplies to make a model of something that begins with /k/.

Listen Have students listen to the recording of the poem *Camping* in the listening center.

Sound/Symbol Relationships

Word Sort Provide decodable word cards from this lesson and previous lessons, and have students sort the cards into sets of words that have the same beginning sounds.

Letter Collage Display letter cards **c**, **p**, **f**, **n**, and **t**. Have students choose a letter and look in magazines or newspapers for pictures of objects that begin with that letter. Then students can make a collage of words.

Alliterative Sentences Place letter cards **c**, **p**, **f**, **n**, and **t** facedown. Have students pick a card. Then have them make up a sentence using only words that begin with that letter.

Letter Toss Write each of the letters *a, c, f, m, n, o, s,* and *t* on a small box. Students can:
- toss a ball into a box and say the letter's sound
- toss a ball into a box and say a word that begins with that letter's sound

Phonemic Awareness

Use the Poetry Poster
- Show students the picture on the back of the poetry poster and have them name all the objects in the picture.
- Point to the cake in the picture and say the word *cake*, emphasizing the /k/. Ask: *What sound do you hear at the beginning of the word?*
- Have students point to something in the picture that starts with /k/.

Sound/Symbol Relationships

Sort the Decodable Word Cards
- Place picture cards **car**, **pen**, **nut**, and **sun** in the pocket chart. Have students say the name of the object in each picture.
- Show students decodable word card **cat** and have them blend the word.
- Ask students if **cat** begins like **car**, **pen**, **nut**, or **sun**. Place the card under picture card **car**.
- Repeat with decodable word cards **cot**, **pat**, **pin**, **Nan**, **nip**, **Sam**, and **sat**.

Distribute blackline master 7 and instruct students to complete it at home.

Assessment Tip: Note which students have difficulty associating the sound with the appropriate letter. Give these students a word card and ask them to place the word under the correct picture card. Assign Independent Activities for the rest of the class.

Blending Sounds

- Have students blend the words **cap**, **can**, **tip**, and **cop**, using the procedure for Day One.

Spelling Words

- Review the words **pit** and **top** by having students write the words several times.
- Follow the procedure for Day One to model and practice the words **cat** and **can**.

👁 Sight Words

- Write the words **a**, **has**, **is**, **the**, **and**, and **of** on the board. Point to the words in random order and have students read them several times.
- Have volunteers choose a word to read and use in an oral sentence.

Phonemic Awareness

Discriminating Sounds
- Say: *I've been going grocery shopping. I bought corn and peas.* Ask students if the words **corn** and **peas** begin with the same sound.
- After students conclude that the words do not begin with the same sound, say the words again and ask students to identify the beginning sound in each word.
- Say: *I bought corn and carrots.* Ask students the same questions about **corn** and **carrots.**
- Repeat the procedure with the word pairs **cookies/meat**, **cabbage/cucumber**, **pizza/cupcake**, and **cauliflower/candy.**

 # Blending Sounds
- Have students blend the words **cop**, **cot**, **tap**, and **man**, using the procedure for Day One.

 # Spelling Words
- Review the words **pit**, **top**, **cat**, and **can** by having students write them several times.
- Follow the procedure for Day One to model and practice the words **cot** and **cap**.

 # Sight Words
- Write the words **and** and **of** on the board. Have students spell the words by tracing them on their palms with their fingers.
- Ask volunteers to use the words **and** and **of** in oral sentences.
- Place letter cards **a**, **n**, **d**, **o**, **f**, **t**, **h**, **e**, **s**, and **i** on a table. Say one of the words **and**, **of**, **the**, **a**, **has**, or **is.** Have volunteers come to the table and spell the word.

Distribute blackline master 8 and instruct students to complete it at home.

Decodable Book

Work with small groups of students to read the decodable book *Pop and the Fat Cat* on Days Three and Four. Assign blackline master 3 and Independent Activities for the rest of the class on Day Three.

Introduce the Book
- Display the cover of the book. Point to the title, *Pop and the Fat Cat*, and have students sound out the words as you run your finger under them.
- Ask: *What do you see in the picture? What is a nap? Who can take a nap?*

Read the Book
- Give each student a copy of the book. Have them turn to page 2. Instruct them to run their fingers under the first word as they sound it out: */Pooop/.*
- Have students point to the next word. Remind them that this is a word they don't sound out. Have them say the word **and**.
- Have students point to the next word. Remind them that this is also a word they don't sound out. Have them say the word **the**.
- Have students sound out each of the next five words as they run their fingers under the words. (*/ffffaaaat/, /taaaannnn/, /kaaaat/, /kaaaannnn/, /nnnnaaaap/*)
- Have students read the whole sentence at normal speed.
- If students are sounding out the words without difficulty, have them whisper-read the rest of the text.
- If students have difficulty, continue to guide them page by page.

Discuss the Book
- When students have finished reading, ask: *Where does Pop nap? Where does the cat nap? Why isn't Pop's cap fat?*

Poetry Poster (Back)

Decodable Book

 **SUPPORT TIPS** for English Language Learners

Develop/Reinforce the negative response to the question pattern *Is the…?*
- Before reading, revisit the preposition games introduced with *Pop*, but change the oral language to the question form ***Is the*** pencil in the cup?
- Begin by accepting simple yes/no responses. Model the complete sentences, *Yes, it is* and *No, it is not.*
- Elicit the complete sentences from the students.

DAY 4

Independent Activities

Decodable Book

Independent Practice When students have had a chance to read the decodable book in the small group setting, have them read it independently.

New Sentence Have students use decodable word cards to make a new sentence for a page in the book.

Spelling

As words are introduced each day, write them on index cards and place them in the literacy center. Ensure that the letter cards needed to build the words are in the center. Students can use the following procedure to spell words.
• Choose a word card.
• Use their fingers and eyes to read the word.
• Turn over the card so that they can't see the word.
• Build the word using the letter cards.
• Turn over the card to check the word.
• Write the word.

Sight Words

Personal Dictionary Have students write *and* and *of* in their personal dictionaries.

Build Words Have students build *and* and *of* using letter cards.

Find the Words Place sight word cards *and* and *of* in the center. Have students circle the words in a familiar poem, and write them several times on their workmats.

 ## Phonological Awareness

Identify and Produce Rhyme
• Say *bat* and *fat*. Say the words again and have students tell you what sounds are the same. Make sure they hear the */at/* sounds.
• Reread the poem *Camping* and have students listen for rhyming words. Have them snap their fingers when you say two rhyming words.
• Say the following groups of words and have students identify which two words rhyme: *bib/rib/fin*, *cup/cap/pup*, *tot/hit/hot*, *sled/snow/bed.* Then repeat the rhyming pairs and ask students to tell you what sounds they hear at the end of two words.
• Have students say words that rhyme with *an*, *it*, and *am*.

Assessment Tip: Observe which students are able to identify rhyming words but cannot identify the ending sounds of rhyming words. Provide practice in segmenting the words slowly to better hear the middle and ending sounds. Assign Independent Activities for the rest of the class.

P+A+M ## Blending Sounds

• Have students blend the words *nap*, *pit*, *can*, and *cat*, using the procedure for Day One.

 ## Spelling Words

Review
• Review the week's spelling words by having students write them several times on their workmats.
• Provide pairs of students with blackline master 2. One student reads the words from the list one at a time while the other student writes each word.
• The partner should put a check mark beside words spelled correctly. If a word is incorrect, the partner may provide prompts. If the second spelling of the word is correct, the partner places a check mark in the "Second Try" column.

Assessment Tip: Collect students' completed blackline masters and note which words gave them difficulty.

 ## Sight Words

Review
• Write *a*, *and*, *has*, *is*, *of*, *see*, *the*, *with*, and *for* on the board.
• Focusing on one word at a time, have students spell the word aloud as you point to each letter. Then erase the word, say the word, and have students spell it on their own.

 ## Decodable Book

• Read the decodable book *Pop and the Fat Cat* with the remaining small groups of students. Assign blackline master 4 and Independent Activities for the rest of the class.

Assessment Tip: Use the completed blackline masters to assess how well students can identify words that have the same ending sound.

Spelling Assessment

Use the following procedure to assess students' spelling of the Unit 9 words.
- Say each spelling word and use it in a sentence.
- Have students write the word on a piece of paper.
- Continue with the next word on the list.
- When students have finished, collect their papers and analyze their spellings of misspelled words.
- Record their progress on a spelling record sheet, and provide extra practice as needed.

 # Small Group Activities

The following small group activities can be used to provide hands-on practice for students who need additional support. Assign blackline master 5 and Independent Activities for the rest of the class.

 ### PHONOLOGICAL AWARENESS

Initial Sounds Explain to students that you are packing for a vacation and want to bring only things that begin like the word *cat*. Tell students that if they hear the */k/* sound in the word, they should raise their hands. Say the following words: *cap, towel, coat, sweater, mittens, camera, sweater, candy, pencils.* Say each word slowly, emphasizing the beginning sound. Repeat the words several times. Emphasize the beginning sound for students who are having difficulty identifying the */k/* phoneme.

Discriminating Sounds Say pairs of words and ask students to tell you if the words start with the same or different sounds.

Rhyme In a small group setting, repeat the pairs of words as students listen and identify the pairs that rhyme. Ask students to say a rhyming word for the words *bug, light,* and *tall*.

 ### SOUND/SYMBOL RELATIONSHIPS

Find a Word Reread the poem, emphasizing */k/* at the beginning of words. Have individual students find a word in the poem that starts with */k/*. Read each word that is found with students, emphasizing the */k/* sound.

Collect the Word Have students sit in a circle. Mix the decodable word cards **cat, cot, Nan, nip, pat, pin, Sam,** and **sat.** Give one card to each student. Have students hold up their cards for all to see. The first student reads the word on his or her card, then walks around the circle to find and collect a word that begins with the same sound. Continue the activity until all the cards have been collected. Then have students read the words with you.

 ### BLENDING

Modeled Practice Model blending each word on the word list first, then have students blend it with you. Finally, ask individual students to sound out a word. This may be a difficult task for some students. Repeat the blending process and be sure that each word is sounded out correctly before moving on to the next word.

Guided Practice Write the word *cap* on the board. Have students take turns running their fingers under the word as they blend the sounds. Then change the final letter to make the word *can* and repeat the process.

 ### SPELLING

Letter Cards Review the sounds the letters *a, c, p, n,* and *t* stand for. Using a set of letter cards, show students how to make the word *can.* Say each sound as you make the word. Give students the letter cards **a, c, p, n,** and **o.** Ask them to build the word *can* on their workmats. Have them say the sounds as they build the word. Then say the word *cap.* Have students choose the letter for the ending sound and make the word. Say the word *tap.* Have students choose the letter for the beginning sound and make the word. Make sure students read each word.

Guess the Word Write the spelling words on the board. Have students guess which of the words you're thinking of. Say: *I'm thinking of a word that rhymes with* **fat***. I'm thinking of a word that starts with* **c** *and ends with* **n***,* etc.

Build Spelling Words Write the spelling words *pit, top, cat, can, cot,* and *cap* on the board. Place the letter cards **a, c, i, n, o, p,** and **t** on a table. Point to a word on the board, read it, and have students take turns choosing a letter to build the spelling word. As each word is completed, ask a volunteer to read the word.

 ### SIGHT WORDS

Flashcards Make extra sets of the sight word cards **a, and, has, is, of,** and **the** to use as flash cards. Have student pairs use the flash cards to practice recognizing and reading the words quickly.

Find the Words Have students use their copies of the sight words to find and match the words in the decodable book *Pop and the Fat Cat.*

Student Name _____ Assessment Date _____

Phonological Awareness: Producing Rhyme

Directions: Say the rhyming pair. Then ask the student to say another real or nonsense word that rhymes with the pair. Record the student's response. **Example:** light/bite. *Kite.*

lick/stick		welt/pelt			
bought/caught		must/trust			
lake/make		dolls/falls		**Score**	**/6**

Phonemic Awareness: Differentiating Initial Sounds

Directions: Say each set of words. Then have the student say the two words that begin with the same sound. Put a ✔ if the student's response is correct. If not, record the words the student chooses. **Example:** milk/toe/money. *Milk, money.*

cabbage/cart/money *(cabbage, cart)*		
safety/pilot/salami *(safety, salami)*		
paint/family/pencil *(paint, pencil)*		
full/field/noise *(full, field)*		
cotton/tadpole/taxi *(tadpole, taxi)*		
piano/cane/cushion *(cane, cushion)*	**Score**	**/6**

Phonics: Segmenting and Blending Sounds

Directions: Explain that these nonsense words use sounds the student has been learning. Have the student point to each word on the corresponding student sheet, say each sound, and then blend the sounds together. Put a ✔ if the student's response is correct. If the student misses the word, record the error. **Example:** mot. /m/ /o/ /t/, mot.

pic (/p/ /i/ /k/, pic)		cos (/k/ /o/ /s/, cos)			
nof (/n/ /o/ /f/, nof)		som (/s/ /o/ /m/, som)			
maf (/m/ /a/ /f/, maf)		mic (/m/ /i/ /k/, mic)		**Score**	**/6**

Sight Words

Directions: Have the student point to the first sight word on the corresponding student sheet and read across the line, saying each word as quickly as possible. Put a ✔ if the student successfully reads the word and an **X** if the student hesitates more than a few seconds. If the student misses the word, record the error.

and		of		**Score**	**/2**

UNIT 10 Hh

Unit Objectives

Students will:

- Identify the sound /h/
- Associate the letter Hh with the /h/ sound
- Orally blend onset and rime
- Identify and produce rhyme
- Blend CVC words
- Read the sight words see, with
- Spell CVC words using h and letters previously learned

Day 1

BLM 1

BLM 6

Letter Cards **c, e, h, i, p, s, t, w**

Spelling Transparency

Picture Word Cards: **cap, car, cat, cup, hat, helicopter, hot dog, house, pan, pen, plant, pumpkin**

Day 2

BLM 1

BLM 7

Decodable Word Cards for Unit 10

Spelling Transparency

Picture Word Cards for Unit 10

Day 3

BLM 1

BLM 3

BLM 8

Spelling Transparency

Day 4

BLM 1

BLM 2

BLM 4

Sight Word Cards for Unit 10

Spelling Transparency

Day 5

BLM 5

Decodable Word Cards for Unit 10

Sight Word Cards for Unit 10

Quick-Check Student Sheet

Picture Word Cards: **cap, car, cat, cup, hat, helicopter, hot dog, house, pan, pen, plant, pumpkin, top**

Poetry Poster

Student Workmat

Letter Frieze Card

Decodable Book

Poetry CD

Core Materials

All print resources can be downloaded from http://phonicsresources.benchmarkeducation.com.

**Poetry Poster
(Front)**

Letter Frieze Card

**Picture Word
Cards**

Phonemic Awareness

Use the Poetry Poster

- Read aloud or play the recording of the poem *Happy Thoughts*.
- Read the sentence "But what really makes me happy is a humdinger hug from you!" Emphasize the */h/* sound.
- Have students say the sentence with you. Before each word that starts with */h/*, say the phoneme first in isolation. Say: *But what really makes me /**h**/ happy is a /**h**/ humdinger /**h**/ hug from you!*

Distribute blackline master 6 and instruct students to complete it at home.

Sound/Symbol Relationships

Model

- Display letter frieze card **Hh**. Explain that the letter **Hh** stands for the */h/* sound, as in the word ***house***.
- Reread *Happy Thoughts*. Have students read along with you.
- Point to words in the poem that have the */h/* sound, and have students read the words with you.

Practice with the Letter Cards

- Distribute letter cards **h**, **c**, and **t**. Ask students to line up the cards on their workmats.
- Have students pull down each letter card and say the letter name, then push it back up and say the letter sound.
- Ask them to pull down each letter card again, saying a word that starts with that sound.
- Have them push up the letter card that starts the word ***hall***. (Repeat with the words ***car*** and ***tip***.)

Practice with the Picture Cards

- Place letter cards **h**, **c**, and **p** in the pocket chart.
- Place picture cards **hat**, **cap**, and **pen** under the corresponding letters while you say the name of the letter and the name of the object in the picture.
- Hold up picture card **helicopter**. Have students say ***helicopter*** with you.
- Ask: *Does* **helicopter** *begin like* **hat**, **cap**, *or* **pen**?
- Place picture card **helicopter** under letter card **h**. Say: **Helicopter** *begins like* **hat**, *so I am putting picture card* **helicopter** *under the letter* **h**.
- Repeat with picture cards **house**, **hot dog**, **car**, **cup**, **cat**, **pan**, **plant**, and **pumpkin**.

Blending Sounds

Review

- Hold up letter frieze cards of previously taught sounds. Ask students to say the sound each letter stands for.

Model

- Write the word ***him*** on the board. Sound out the word by moving your hand under each letter while blending the sounds. (*/hiiiimmmm/*) Then say the word.
- Ask students to sound out the word with you.

Practice with the Word Lists

- Distribute blackline master 1.
- Have students point to the word ***him***. Ask them to sound out the word with you. Then ask them to say the word at regular speed.
- Repeat with the words ***sit***, ***fat***, and ***not***. Then have students sound out the words in random order.

Spelling Words

Model

- Use the spelling transparency. Place counters under the second set of boxes.
- Say: *Today we are going to learn to spell* **nip** *and* **can**. *Watch and listen as I say* **nip** *slowly:* /**nnnniiiip**/.
- As you say /**nnnn**/, push a counter into the first box. Then say /**iiii**/ as you push a counter into the second box and /**p**/ as you push a counter into the third. Repeat the steps.
- Model recording the letters for the sounds on the transparency. Say: *The first sound is* /**nnnn**/. *I know that the letter* **n** *stands for the* /**n**/ *sound. I'll write the letter* **n** *in the first box Let's listen for the middle sound:* /**niiii**/. *I hear* /**i**/. *I know that the letter* **i** *stands for the* /**i**/ *sound, so I will write* **i** *in the second box. Let's listen for the last sound:* /**niiiip**/. *I hear* /**p**/. *I know that the letter* **p** *stands for the* /**p**/ *sound, so I will write* **p** *in the last box.*
- Have students blend the sounds to check the spelling.

Practice with the Workmat

- Instruct students to place counters under the second set of boxes on side 2 of their workmats.
- Ask students to slowly articulate the word *nip* as they push the counters into the boxes.
- Have them identify and record the letters that stand for the sounds they hear.
- Have students practice writing *nip* on side 1 of their workmats.

Repeat the modeling and guided practice with the second spelling word, *can*.

Sight Words

Review

- Write the words *a*, *and*, *has*, *is*, *of*, and *the* on the board. Erase the *n* in *and*, say the word, and ask students which letter is missing. Continue to erase letters in the other words.

Introduce

- Place letter cards **s**, **e**, and **e** in the pocket chart. Say: *This is the word* **see**. *It is made up of the letters* **s, e,** *and* **e**.
- Point to the word and say it. Then have students say the word as you point to it.
- Follow the steps to introduce the word **with**.
- Write these sentences on the board: "Can Nan see a cat?" "Sam is with the fat cat." Read the sentences aloud. Have volunteers underline the words **see** and **with**. Repeat with the words *a*, *is*, and *the*.

Write

- Have students write the words **see** and **with**, using the models in the pocket chart.

Independent Activities

Phonemic Awareness

Picture Cards Provide **h, c,** and **p** picture cards in the literacy center. Students can:
• take two cards, name the pictures, and tell if the words begin with the same sound
• separate the cards that start with /**h**/
• choose a card and draw a picture of something that has the same beginning sound

Sound Collage Have students choose a picture card and look in magazines for pictures that start with the same sound as the picture on the card. Have them paste the pictures on posterboard to make a collage.

Listen Have students listen to the recording of the poem *Happy Thoughts* in the listening center.

Sound/Symbol Relationships

Word Sort Provide decodable word cards from this lesson and previous lessons in the literacy center. Students can:
• sort the cards into groups of rhyming words
• sort the cards into groups according to vowel sounds
• sort the cards into groups according to ending sounds

Letters and Sounds Write the letters **a, c, h, i, m, o, p,** and **t** on large cards. Attach the cards to a bulletin board. Students can:
• put a check mark by a letter and say the sound
• put a check mark by a letter and say a word that begins with the letter's sound

Phonemic Awareness

Use the Poetry Poster
• Show students the picture on the back of the poetry poster, and have them name all objects in the picture.
• Point to the horn in the picture and say the word **horn**. Ask: *What sound do you hear at the beginning of the word?*
• Ask students to point to something in the picture that starts with /**h**/. Have them say the name of the object.

Sound/Symbol Relationships

Sort the Decodable Word Cards
• Place picture cards **hot dog, cup,** and **top** in the pocket chart. Have students say the name of the objects in the pictures.
• Show students decodable word card **hot** and have them blend the word.
• Ask students if **hot** begins like **hot dog, cup,** or **top**. Place the card under picture card **hot dog**.
• Repeat with decodable word cards **hip, him, cat, cap, can, cot, tap, tan, tip,** and **Tim**.

Distribute blackline master 7 and instruct students to complete it at home.

Assessment Tip: Observe which students cannot match the word card to the appropriate picture card. Provide them with extra practice. Assign Independent Activities for the rest of the class.

Blending Sounds

• Have students blend the words **hat, cap, hot,** and **pin**, using the procedure for Day One.

Spelling Words

• Review the words **nip** and **can** by having students write the words several times.
• Follow the procedure for Day One to model and practice the words **hat** and **him**.

Sight Words

• Hold up the cards for previously taught sight words one at a time and have students read the words aloud.
• Have students trace the words on their palms as you read and spell the words together.
• Read the new words, **see** and **with**, several times.

Phonemic Awareness

Blend and Segment Onset and Rime
• Segment the word **hot** into its onset and rime: */h/ /ot/.* Have students blend the sounds and say the word.
• Repeat with the words **pot**, **hit**, and **mat**.
• Once students understand the concept of segmenting a word into its onset and rime, say the word **pin**. Ask: *What is the onset or beginning sound? What is the rest of the word?*
• Blend the sounds */p/* and */in/* and say the word with the class.
• Repeat with the words **fan**, **sit**, and **map**.

Assessment Tip: Assess students whom you feel are having difficulty by giving them a word and asking them to segment it into its onset and rime, and then blend it.

 Blending Sounds

• Have students blend the words **pot**, **hit**, and **mat**, using the procedure for Day One.

 Spelling Words

• Review the words **nip**, **can**, **hat**, and **him** by having students write them several times.
• Follow the procedure for Day One to model and practice the words **hit** and **hop**.

 Sight Words

• Write "I see a hot pot" on the board. Ask students which word is the word **see**.
• Have students write the word **see** on their papers several times.
• Write "Pam is with him" on the board. Ask students which word is the word **with**.
• Have students write the word **with** on their papers several times.

Distribute blackline master 8 and instruct students to complete it at home.

**Poetry Poster
(Back)**

📖 **Decodable Book**

Work with small groups of students to read the decodable book *The Hot Pan* on Days Three and Four. Assign blackline master 3 and Independent Activities for the rest of the class on Day Three.

Introduce the Book
• Show students the cover of the book. Point to the title, *The Hot Pan*, and have them sound out the words as you run your finger under them.
• Ask: *What do you see in the picture? Why do pans get hot?*

Read the Book
• Give each student a copy of the book and have them turn to page 2. Instruct students to run their fingers under the first word as they sound it out: */Poooop/.*
• Have students point to the next two words. Remind them that these are words they don't sound out. Have them say the words: **has**, **a**.
• Have students sound out the last word as they run their fingers under it: */paaaannnn/.*
• Have students read the sentence at normal speed.
• If students are sounding out the words without difficulty, have them whisper-read the rest of the text.
• If students have difficulty, continue to guide them page by page.

Discuss the Book
• When students have finished reading, ask: *Where is the pan? How does Pop get the cat away from the pan?*

Decodable Book

 **SUPPORT TIPS**
for English Language Learners

Develop/Reinforce: pronoun *him*
Develop/Reinforce: the question pattern *Can someone do something?*

• Before reading, ask a student if he/she can see a specific male student sitting in the class. Accept a single-word response, **Yes**.

• Ask another student, *Can _____ see him?* Model the complete response: *Yes, _____ can see him.*

• Encourage all students to respond to the question by repeating the second student's response, *_____ can see him.*

• Repeat the activity, using pictures of the different male characters from the stories.

DAY 4

Independent Activities

Decodable Book

Independent Practice After students have read the decodable book in a small group, have them read it independently.

Write a New Ending Have students use decodable words to write a new ending for the decodable book *The Hot Pan.*

Fluency Practice Tape-record the decodable book *The Hot Pan,* leaving pauses so that students can echo the reading as they follow along in the text.

Spelling

As words are introduced each day, write them on index cards and place them in the literacy center. Ensure that the letter cards needed to build the words are in the center. Students can use the following procedure to spell words.
• Choose a word card.
• Use their fingers and eyes to read the word.
• Turn over the card so that they can't see the word.
• Build the word using the letter cards.
• Turn over the card to check the word.
• Write the word.

Sight Words

Personal Dictionary Have students write *see* and *with* in their personal dictionaries.

Word Search Write *a, and, has, is, of, see, the,* and *with* on the board or chart paper. Give each student a page from a newspaper. Have them circle the word *a* in red crayon each time it appears and use different colors for the remaining words.

 Phonological Awareness

Identify and Produce Rhyme
• Say the words *hop* and *mop.* Remind students that these words rhyme because they have the same sound at the end. Repeat the words.
• Reread the poem *Happy Thoughts* and have students clap each time they hear a rhyming word.
• Say the following groups of words and ask students if the words rhyme: *cat/cot, pin/fin, run/fun, Pam/Tim, dog/frog.*
• Repeat the word pairs and ask students to tell you what sounds are the same in both words.

Assessment Tip: Note which students cannot produce rhyming words on their own. Say two rhyming words and ask students to provide a word that rhymes with the two words.

 Blending Sounds

• Have students blend the words *mop, sap, hip,* and *him,* using the procedure for Day One.

 Spelling Words

Review
• Review the week's spelling words by having students write them several times on their workmats.
• Provide pairs of students with blackline master 2. While one student reads the words, the other student writes them.
• If the student spells the word correctly, the partner should put a check mark beside the word. If a word is incorrect, the partner may provide prompts. If the second spelling of the word is correct, the partner places a check mark in the "Second Try" column.

Assessment Tip: Collect students' completed blackline masters and note which words gave them difficulty.

 Sight Words

Review
• Hold up sight word card **see.** Ask a student to read the word and use it in an oral sentence. The other students should clap when they hear the word **see.**
• Repeat with sight word cards **a, and, has, is, of,** and **the.**

 Decodable Book

• Read the decodable book *The Hot Pan* with the remaining small groups of students. Assign blackline master 4 and Independent Activities for the rest of the class.

Assessment Tip: Use the completed blackline master to assess how well students can make connections between sounds and the letters that stand for those sounds.

Spelling Assessment

Use the following procedure to assess students' spelling of the Unit 10 words.
• Say each spelling word and use it in a sentence.
• Have students write the word on a piece of paper.
• Continue with the next word on the list.
• When students have finished, collect their papers and analyze their spellings of misspelled words.
• Record their progress on a spelling record sheet and provide extra practice as needed.

 Small Group Activities

The following small group activities can be used to provide hands-on practice for students who need additional support. Assign blackline master 5 and Independent Activities for the rest of the class.

 PHONOLOGICAL AWARENESS

Initial Sounds Tell students that they are going to listen for words that have the /**h**/ sound. Ask students to stand. Tell them that you are going to say a sentence, one word at a time. If they hear the /**h**/ sound in a word, they should hop. Say: *Happy Harry hunted for hairy caterpillars and hungry worms.* Say each word of the sentence slowly, segmenting the beginning sound. (/**h**/ *happy*) Repeat several times. Then say the /**h**/ phoneme more naturally. Continue to segment the beginning sound for students who are having difficulty recognizing the /**h**/ phoneme.

Onset and Rime Ensure that students hear the onset and rime in a word. Say: *Listen to this word: tap. What is the beginning sound?* (/**t**/) *What are the other sounds?* (/**a**/ /**p**/) Have students say the onset and rime several times with you. Then blend the sounds and say the word. Continue with the words **hat**, **hop**, and **tip**.

Rhyme Make sure that students understand that rhyming words have the same sounds at the end. Say the following pairs of words and have students identify the ending sounds in each pair: **win/spin–/in/; cot/hot–/ot/; bet/pet–/et/; dim/Tim–/im/.**

 SOUND/SYMBOL RELATIONSHIPS

Picture Match Give each student one (or more) of the **c, h,** or **p** picture cards. Point to the letter **h** in the pocket chart, and ask students if their picture starts with /**h**/. Have the students holding **h** picture cards place their cards under the letter **h.** Continue with **c** and **p.**

Word Sort Have students put the decodable word cards into groups according to their ending sounds. First do this as a group activity. Then ask volunteers to sort the words on their own. When the words are sorted, have students read the words in each group with you and verify that the words in the group have the same ending sound.

 BLENDING

Guided Practice Sit holding a workmat so that all students in the group can easily see it. Write the word **hat** on the workmat. Have students take turns running their fingers under the word as they blend the sounds in the word. Then say one of the sounds in the word and ask students to point to the letter that stands for that sound. Repeat with the words **cap, hot,** and **pin.**

 SPELLING

Spelling Practice Guide students to look at the word, say it, cover it, write it, and check it as they practice spelling each word.

Word Patterns Have students write the word patterns __*i*__, __*a*__, and __*o*__ on their papers. Write the letters **c, h, m, n, p,** and **t** on the board. Tell students that they are going to spell words by adding letters at the beginning and end. Say the word **nip.** Ask: *What sound do you hear in the middle? Look at the word patterns. Which pattern has the letter that spells the /**i**/ sound?* Be sure students choose the __*i*__ pattern. Repeat the word **nip.** Say: *What sound do you hear at the beginning of* **nip**? *What letter spells that sound? Write the letter. What sound do you hear at the end of* **nip**? *Write the letter that spells that sound.* Have students read each word as they spell it.

 SIGHT WORDS

Match the Cards Create three sets of the sight words **a, and, has, is, of, see, the,** and **with.** Model how to look for and set aside matching words in your hand. Select a student and ask: *[Student's name], do you have the word card* **see**? If you receive a matching card, set aside the matching cards. Have students take turns asking for matching cards. Continue until one player has discarded all of his or her cards.

Word Search Using the decodable book *The Hot Pan*, have students look for examples of the words **see, with, and, has, is,** and **of.** Then provide pairs of students with another classroom book. Have them find the same words and mark them with self-stick notes. Let the pairs take turns showing the words they found.

Student Name _____ Assessment Date _____

Phonological Awareness: Producing Rhyme

Directions: Say the rhyming pair. Then ask the student to say another real or nonsense word that rhymes with the pair. Record the student's response.
Example: light/bite. *Kite.*

dad/glad		wrong/strong			
brick/thick		hatch/scratch			
speed/greed		strum/plum		**Score**	**/6**

Phonemic Awareness: Segmenting Onset and Rime

Directions: Say the word. Have the student say the first sound followed by the rest of the word and then say the whole word. If the student segments the word correctly, put a ✔. If the student's response is incorrect, record the error.
Example: bat. /b/ /at/, bat.

hot (/h/ /ot/, hot)		pop (/p/ /op/, pop)			
win (/w/ /in/, win)		hill (/h/ /ill/, hill)			
tap (/t/ /ap/, tap)		lack (/l/ /ack/, lack)		**Score**	**/6**

Phonics: Segmenting and Blending Sounds

Directions: Explain that these nonsense words use sounds the student has been learning. Have the student point to each word on the corresponding student sheet, say each sound, and then blend the sounds together. Put a ✔ if the student's response is correct. If the student misses the word, record the error.
Example: hos. /h/ /o/ /s/, hos.

hif (/h/ /i/ /f/, hif)		hom (/h/ /o/ /m/, hom)			
poc (/p/ /o/ /k/, poc)		tof (/t/ /o/ /f/, tof)			
hap (/h/ /a/ /p/, hap)		hin (/h/ /i/ /n/, hin)		**Score**	**/6**

Sight Words

Directions: Have the student point to the first sight word on the corresponding student sheet and read across the line, saying each word as quickly as possible. Put a ✔ if the student successfully reads the word and an **X** if the student hesitates more than a few seconds. If the student misses the word, record the error.

see		with		**Score**	**/2**

UNIT 11 Bb

Unit Objectives

Students will:

- Identify the sound /b/
- Associate the letter Bb with the /b/ sound
- Identify beginning and ending consonant sounds
- Identify and produce rhyme
- Blend CVC words
- Read the sight word for
- Spell CVC words using b and letters previously learned

Day 1

BLM 1

BLM 6

Letter Cards: **b, c, f, h, n, o, r**

Sight Word Cards for Unit 11

Spelling Transparency

Picture Word Cards: **bat, ball, bell, box, cap, car, cup, hat, hot dog, house**

Day 2

BLM 1

BLM 7

Decodable Word Cards for Unit 11

Sight Word Cards for Unit 11

Spelling Transparency

Letter Cards: **a, b, c, m, n, p, t**

Picture Word Cards: **ball, cat, house, pumpkin**

Day 3

BLM 1

BLM 3

BLM 8

Spelling Transparency

Day 4

BLM 1

BLM 2

BLM 4

Day 5

BLM 5

Sight Word Cards for Unit 11

Quick-Check Student Sheet

Poetry Poster

Student Workmat

Letter Frieze Card

Decodable Book

Poetry CD

Core Materials

All print resources can be downloaded from http://phonicsresources.benchmarkeducation.com

**Poetry Poster
(Front)**

Letter Frieze Card

**Picture Word
Cards**

 Phonemic Awareness

Use the Poetry Poster

- Read aloud or play the recording of the poem *Baby Bird*.
- Read the sentence "But Baby Bear was on his bike," emphasizing the /b/ sound.
- Have students say the sentence with you. Before each of the words that start with /b/, say the phoneme first in isolation. Say: /b/ *But* /b/ *Baby* /b/ *Bear was on his* /b/ *bike*.
- Reread the poem and have students give a "thumbs up" signal each time they hear the /b/ sound.

Distribute blackline master 6 and instruct students to complete it at home.

Sound/Symbol Relationships

Model

- Display letter frieze card **Bb**. Explain that the letter **Bb** stands for the /b/ sound in the word **ball**.
- Reread the poem *Baby Bird*. Invite students to read along with you.
- Point to words in the poem that begin with the letter **b**. Say the words aloud, then ask students to say the words with you.

Practice with the Letter Cards

- Distribute letter cards **b**, **c**, and **h**. Ask students to line up the cards on their workmats.
- Have students pull down each letter card and say the letter name, then push it back up and say the letter sound.
- Have them pull down each letter card again, saying a word that starts with that sound.
- Instruct them to push up the letter card that starts the word **bird**. (Repeat with the words **cot** and **hip**.)

Practice with the Picture Cards

- Place letter cards **b**, **c**, and **h** in the pocket chart.
- Place picture cards **ball**, **cup**, and **hat** under the corresponding letters while you say the name of the letter and the name of the object in the picture.
- Hold up the picture card **box**. Have students say **box** with you, emphasizing the initial sound.
- Ask: *Does* **box** *begin like* **ball**, **cup**, *or* **hat**?
- Place picture card **box** under letter card **b**. Say: **Box** *begins like* **ball**, *so I am putting picture card* **box** *under the letter* **b**.
- Repeat with picture cards **bat**, **bell**, **car**, **cap**, **house**, and **hot dog**.

P+A+M **Blending Sounds**

Review

- Hold up letter frieze cards of previously taught sounds. Ask students to say the sound each letter stands for.

Model

- Write the word **pot** on the board. Sound out the word by moving your hand under each letter while blending the sounds. (/**poooot**/) Then say the word.
- Ask students to sound out the word with you.

Practice with the Word Lists

- Distribute blackline master 1.
- Have students point to the word **pot**. Ask them to sound out the word with you. Then ask them to say the word at regular speed.
- Repeat with the words **hat**, **bat**, and **on**. Then have students sound out the words in random order.

Spelling Words

Model

- Use the spelling transparency. Place counters under the second set of boxes on the transparency.
- Say: *Today we are going to learn to spell* **hat** *and* **sap**. *Watch and listen as I say* **hat** *slowly:* /**haaaat**/.
- As you say /**h**/, push a counter into the first box. Then say /**aaaa**/ as you push a counter into the second box and /**t**/ as you push a counter into the third box. Repeat the steps.
- Model recording the letters for the sounds on the transparency. Say: *The first sound is* /**h**/. *I know that the letter* **h** *stands for the* /**h**/ *sound. I'll write the letter* **h** *in the first box. Let's listen for the second sound:* /**haaaa**/. *I hear* /**a**/. *I know that the letter* **a** *stands for the* /**a**/ *sound, so I will write* **a** *in the second box. Let's listen for the last sound:* /**hat**/. *I hear* /**t**/. *I know that the letter* **t** *stands for the* /**t**/ *sound, so I will write* **t** *in the last box.*
- Have students blend the sounds to check the spelling of the word.

Practice with the Workmat

- Instruct students to place their counters under the second set of boxes on side 2 of their workmats.
- Ask students to slowly articulate the word *hat* as they push the counters into the boxes.
- Have them identify and record the letters that stand for the sounds they hear.
- Have students practice writing *hat* on side 1 of their workmats.

Repeat the modeling and guided practice with the second spelling word, *sap*.

 **Sight Words**

Review

- Show students the review sight word cards one by one. Have them say the words as quickly as they can.
- Mix up the words and have students read them again.

Introduce

- Place letter cards **f, o, r,** and **n** in the pocket chart.
- Say: *This is the word* **for**. *It is made up of the letters* **f, o,** *and* **r**. Have students say the word as you point to it.
- Repeat the steps to introduce the word *no*.
- Write on the board: "No, cat. The hat is for Nan." Read the sentences and have volunteers identify the words *for* and *no*.
- Ask volunteers to point to the words *the* and *is*.

Write

- Have students write the words *for* and *no*, using the models in the pocket chart.

DAY 2

Independent Activities

Phonemic Awareness

Picture Cards Provide picture cards in the literacy center. Students can:
• take two cards, name the pictures, and tell if the words end with the same sound
• separate the cards that start with /b/
• sort picture cards according to their ending sounds
• choose a card and draw a picture of another object with the same ending sound

Rhyme Collage Paste a picture of an object at the top of a large sheet of paper. Have students find pictures in old magazines of objects whose names rhyme with the picture name.

Listen Have students listen to the recording of the poem *Baby Bird* in the listening center.

Sound/Symbol Relationships

Final Letters Display letter cards **n, m,** and **t**. Have students choose a letter and write a word that ends with the sound that letter stands for.

Picture Sorts Place picture cards from this unit and previous units for *Aa, Bb, Pp,* and *Nn*, along with letter cards **a, c, b, p,** and **n** from this lesson, in the literacy center. Have students group the pictures that start with the same sound, then place the letter card for the beginning sound with each group of pictures.

Scrambled Letters Write the words *nip, can, hat, him, hit,* and *hop* in scrambled form *(ipn, nac, tha, ihm, thi, oph)* on index cards. Have students write the words in their correct form, then read them aloud.

 ## Phonemic Awareness

Use the Poetry Poster
• Show students the picture on the back of the poetry poster, and have them name all the objects in the picture.
• Point to a bear in the picture and say the word *bear*, stressing the beginning sound. Ask: *What sound do you hear at the beginning of the word?*
• Ask students to point to something in the picture that starts with /b/. Have them say the name of the object.

 ## Sound/Symbol Relationships

Sort the Decodable Word Cards
• Place picture cards **cat, ball, house,** and **pumpkin** in the pocket chart. Have students say the name of the object on each card.
• Show students decodable word card **cot** and have them blend the word.
• Ask students if **cot** begins like **cat, ball, house,** or **pumpkin**. Then place the card under picture card **cat**.
• Repeat with decodable word cards **cap, Bob, bat, hat, hop, pit,** and **pin**.

Distribute blackline master 7 and instruct students to complete it at home.

Assessment Tip: Note which students have difficulty associating any sound with its letter. Give them extra practice with those sounds and letters. Assign Independent Activities for the rest of the class.

P+A+M Blending Sounds

• Have students sound out the words *bib, bop, nip,* and *nap,* using the procedure for Day One.

 ## Spelling Words

• Review the words *hat* and *sap* by having students write the words several times.
• Follow the procedure for Day One to model and practice the words *bat* and *bib*.

Sight Words

• Use sight word cards to review the words *a, and, has, is, of, see, the,* and *with* with students.
• Write these sentences on the board: "The pan is for Bob." "The bib is for Tam." "The mat is for Tim." "The bat is for Pop."
• Have students read each sentence with you. Have a volunteer come to the board, read a sentence aloud, and underline the word *for*.

Phonemic Awareness

Final Consonants

- Say the words **man**, **bin**, and **cob**. Have students repeat the words, then tell you if they hear the same sound at the end of each word. Ask them which word ends with a different sound.
- Repeat with the words **pot**, **hit**, and **pan**. After students recognize that two words end with the same sound, ask them what sound is the same in both words.
- Repeat with the words **tab/Bob/cap**, **sap/hat/nip**, **pit/Pam/him**.

 Blending Sounds

- Have students blend the words **Bob**, **tab**, **bin**, and **bit**, using the procedure for Day One.

 Spelling Words

- Review the words **hat**, **sap**, **bat**, and **bib** by having students write them several times.
- Follow the procedure for Day One to model and practice the words **bin** and **bit**.

 Sight Words

- Write the word **for** on the board. Have students read the word.
- Write the words **a**, **and**, **has**, **is**, **of**, **see**, **the**, and **with** on the board. Point to words randomly and have students read them. Repeat each word several times.
- Select a word and, without students seeing, erase a letter. Ask students which letter is missing. Replace the letter and have students read the word. Repeat with another word from the list.

Distribute blackline master 8 and instruct students to complete it at home.

Poetry Poster (Back)

Decodable Book

Work with small groups of students to read the decodable book *The Bib* on Days Three and Four. Assign blackline master 3 and Independent Activities for the rest of the class on Day Three.

Decodable Book

Introduce the Book

- Show students the cover of the book. Point to the title, *The Bib*, and have them sound out the words as you run your finger under them. Ask: *What do you see in the picture? What is a bib? When do you wear a bib?*

Read the Book

- Give each student a copy of the book. Have students turn to page 2 and put their fingers on the first word. Have them run their fingers under the word as they sound it out: **/Paaaammmm/**.
- Have students point to the next word. Remind them that this is a word they don't sound out and that they have practiced. Have them say the word **has**.
- Have students point to the next word, **the**. Remind them that this also is a word they don't sound out and that they have practiced. Have them say the word.
- Have students point to the last word and sound it out as they run their fingers under the word: **/coooob/**.
- Have students read the whole sentence at normal speed.
- If students can sound out the words without difficulty, have them whisper-read the rest of the text.
- If students have difficulty, continue to guide them page by page.

Discuss the Book

- When students have finished reading, ask: *Who eats the cob? Why does Bob fan the cob? What does Tim eat?*

 SUPPORT TIPS
for English Language Learners

Develop: background past tense bit

- Before reading, use puppets to act out simple activities, make sure to include biting. For example, the puppet could bite an apple.
- Model the past tense: The (puppet) bit the (apple).
- Ask students what the puppet did. Accept appropriate single words, phrases and/or sentences, and if necessary, model the target language structure: Noun bit the object.
- Give students the opportunity to manipulate the puppet and describe what the puppet did, or ask other students what the puppet did.
- Model the correct statement/ question as necessary.

DAY 4

Independent Activities

Decodable Book

Independent Practice After students have read the decodable book in a small group, have them read it independently.

Write a Sentence Have students choose a sentence from the book and write it, substituting their name for *Bob*.

Spelling

As words are introduced each day, write them on index cards and place them in the literacy center. Ensure that the letter cards needed to build the words are in the center. Students can use the following procedure to spell words.

• Choose a word card.
• Use their fingers and eyes to read the word.
• Turn over the card so that they can't see the word.
• Build the word using the letter cards.
• Turn over the card to check the word.
• Write the word.

Sight Words

Personal Dictionary Have students write *for* in their personal dictionaries.

Oral Sentences Make copies of sight word cards **a**, **and**, **has**, **is**, **of**, **see**, **the**, **with**, and **for**, and place them in a box. Students can take a card and use the word in an oral sentence.

Scrambled Letters Have student pairs use letter cards to make the words **a**, **and**, **has**, **is**, **of**, **see**, **the**, **with**, **no**, and **for**. After one partner makes a word, the other partner reads it. Then the partners scramble the cards and make a new word.

Phonological Awareness

Identify and Produce Rhyme
• Say the words **bat** and **fat**. Have students tell you what sounds are the same in the words.
• Reread the poem *Baby Bird* and have students listen for rhyming words. Have them snap their fingers each time you say two rhyming words.
• Say the following groups of words and have students identify which two words rhyme: **bib/rib/fin**, **cup/cap/pup**, **tot/hit/hot**, **sled/snow/bed**.
• Repeat the rhyming pairs and ask students to tell you what sounds they hear at the end of two words.
• Have students say words that rhyme with **an**, **it**, and **am**.

Assessment Tip: Observe which students are able to identify rhyming words but cannot identify the ending sounds of rhyming words. Provide practice in segmenting the words slowly to better hear the middle and ending sounds.

P+A+M Blending Sounds

• Have students blend the words **pit**, **cab**, **hip**, and **ban**, using the procedure for Day One.

Aa Spelling Words

Review
• Review the week's spelling words by having students write them several times on their workmats.
• Provide pairs of students with blackline master 2. One student reads the words from the list one at a time while the other student writes each word.
• The partner should put a check mark beside words spelled correctly. If a word is incorrect, the partner may provide prompts. If the second spelling of the word is correct, the partner places a check mark in the "Second Try" column.

Assessment Tip: Collect students' completed blackline masters and note which words gave them difficulty.

Sight Words

Review
• Write the words **a**, **and**, **has**, **is**, **of**, **see**, **the**, **with**, and **for** on the board.
• Focusing on one word at a time, have students spell the word aloud as you point to each letter. Then erase the word, say the word, and have students spell it on their own.

Decodable Book

• Read the decodable book *The Bib* with the remaining small groups of students. Assign blackline master 4 and Independent Activities for the rest of the class.

Assessment Tip: Use the completed blackline master to assess how well students can identify words that have the same ending sound.

Spelling Assessment

Use the following procedure to assess students' spelling of the Unit 11 words.
• Say each word and use it in a sentence.
• Have students write each word on a piece of paper.
• Collect students' papers and analyze their spellings of misspelled words.
• Record students' progress on a spelling record sheet, and provide extra practice as needed.

 Small Group Activities

The following small group activities can be used to provide hands-on practice for students who need additional support. Assign blackline master 5 and Independent Activities for the rest of the class.

 PHONOLOGICAL AWARENESS

Initial Sounds Provide extra practice in listening for words that have the /b/ sound. Say the following words slowly and repeat them if necessary: **bone**, **boot**, **pet**, **nap**, **bear**, **pup**, **band**, **cob**, **bug**, **fat**, **bib**. Ask students to give a "thumbs up" signal if the word starts with /b/ and a "thumbs down" if it doesn't.

Final Sounds Provide extra practice in listening for ending sounds. Have students identify the ending sounds they hear in these words: **cot**, **pup**, **Sam**, **bib**, **him**, **fit**, **tap**.

Rhyme Have each student fold a piece of paper in half. Have them draw pictures of two things whose names rhyme, such as a **bug** and a **rug**. Have them share their drawings and ask other students to say the rhyming words.

 SOUND/SYMBOL RELATIONSHIPS

Poem Read the poem again, displaying it so that a small group of students can see it as you read. Ask individual students to find a word in the poem that starts with /b/. Together read each word students find. Ask students what sound they hear at the beginning of the word.

Letter Review Give students extra practice in associating the sound with the symbol. Review the frieze cards for letters that are causing difficulty. Have students say the sound for each letter and then brainstorm words that start with that sound.

 BLENDING

Blending Practice 1 Provide students with more practice in blending. Gather students around a piece of chart paper. Write a word from a previous lesson on the chart and model how to sound it out by running your finger under the word. Then ask a student to come up and run his/her finger under the word and sound it out. Repeat with each student in the group. Then write a word that has the letter **b**, such as **bin**, on the chart paper and repeat the procedure.

Blending Practice 2 Have each student fold a piece of paper into three columns. Segment the word **bib**–/b/ /i/ /b/. Tell students to write the letter that stands for each sound in one column of their papers. Then have them say the word, blending the sounds as they move their fingers from letter to letter. Repeat the activity with the words **bop**, **nip**, and **nap**.

 SPELLING

Scrambled Letters Write the letters **t**, **h**, **a** and **s**, **p**, **a** on the board. Ask volunteers to unscramble the letters to make the words **hat** and **sap**.

What's Missing Write the words **hat**, **sap**, **bat**, and **bib** on the board. Together say and spell the words. Then erase one letter from each word. Ask volunteers to tell which letter is missing.

 SIGHT WORDS

Write Sentences Students need to be able to read these words quickly, without hesitation. Provide practice in using the words for spelling and reading. Write the words **a**, **and**, **has**, **is**, **of**, **see**, **the**, **with**, and **for** on the board. Have pairs of students write at least one sentence that uses some of the sight words and decodable words they know. Have the partners draw pictures to illustrate their sentences.

Pass the Card Take sight word cards **a**, **and**, **has**, **is**, **of**, **see**, **the**, and **with**. Hold up the **a** card and model using the word **a** in a sentence. Say: *I have a shiny new bike.* Pass the card to a student and have him or her make up a sentence using the word **a**. Have that student pass the card to the next student, and so on, until each student has had an opportunity to use the word **a** in a sentence. Repeat the activity with the other word cards.

Student Name _____ Assessment Date _____

Phonological Awareness: Identifying Rhyme

Directions: Say each set of words. Then have the student say the two words that rhyme. Put a ✔ if the student's response is correct. If not, record the words the student chooses. **Example:** mat/hat/lid. *Mat, hat.*

rail/nail/mile *(rail, nail)*			
sap/soap/cope *(soap, cope)*			
lied/deed/heed *(deed, heed)*			
why/tie/way *(why, tie)*			
wink/junk/pink *(wink, pink)*			
lot/gnat/dot *(lot, dot)*		**Score**	**/6**

Phonemic Awareness: Identifying Final Sounds

Directions: Say the word and ask the student to tell you the ending sound. If the student answers correctly, put a ✔. If the student misses the sound, record the error. **Example:** hat. /t/

bib (/b/)		night (/t/)			
lap (/p/)		moss (/s/)			
rain (/n/)		cram (/m/)		**Score**	**/6**

Phonics: Segmenting and Blending Sounds

Directions: Explain that these nonsense words use sounds the student has been learning. Have the student point to each word on the corresponding student sheet, say each sound, and then blend the sounds together. Put a ✔ if the student's response is correct. If the student misses the word, record the error. **Example:** nif. /n/ /i/ /f/, nif.

hof (/h/ /o/ /f/, hof)		baf (/b/ /a/ /f/, baf)			
boc (/b/ /o/ /k/, boc)		nom (/n/ /o/ /m/, nom)			
mip (/m/ /i/ /p/, mip)		bip (/b/ /i/ /p/, bip)		**Score**	**/6**

Sight Words

Directions: Have the student point to the first sight word on the corresponding student sheet and read across the line, saying each word as quickly as possible. Put a ✔ if the student successfully reads the word and an **X** if the student hesitates more than a few seconds. If the student misses the word, record the error.

for		no		**Score**	**/2**

UNIT 12 Short Uu

Unit Objectives

Students will:

- Identify the /u/ sound
- Associate the letter Uu with the /u/ sound
- Listen for medial sounds in words
- Identify onset and rime
- Identify and produce rhyming words
- Blend CVC words
- Review sight words a, and, for, has, is, of, see, the, with
- Spell CVC words using u and letters previously learned

Day 1

BLM 1

BLM 6

Letter Cards: **i, o, u**

Spelling Transparency

Picture Word Cards: **box, cup, dish, duck, fish, fox, king, mop, sun, tub**

Day 2

BLM 1

BLM 7

Letter Cards for Unit 12

Decodable Word Cards for Unit 12

Spelling Transparency

Picture Word Cards: **block, cat, duck, fish**

Day 3

BLM 1

BLM 3

BLM 8

Spelling Transparency

Day 4

BLM 1

BLM 2

BLM 4

Spelling Transparency

Day 5

BLM 5

Letter Cards for Unit 12

Decodable Word Cards for Unit 12

Sight Word Cards for Unit 12

Quick-Check Student Sheet

Picture Word Cards: **block, cat, cup, duck, fish, king, mop**

Poetry Poster

Student Workmat

Letter Frieze Card

Decodable Book

Poetry CD

Core Materials

All print resources can be downloaded from http://phonicsresources.benchmarkeducation.com

**Poetry Poster
(Front)**

Letter Frieze Card

**Picture Word
Cards**

 Phonemic Awareness

Use the Poetry Poster

- Read aloud or play the recording of the poem *Buddy* several times and encourage students to join in when they can.
- Say the sentence "Under my umbrella is my pug pup, Buddy."
- Point to each word that has the letter *u*. Ask: *Do you hear the /u/ sound at the beginning or the middle of the word?*
- Reread the poem. Have students raise their hands when they hear /u/ at the beginning of a word and clap if they hear /u/ in the middle of a word.

Distribute blackline master 6 and instruct students to complete it at home.

Sound/Symbol Relationships

Model

- Display letter frieze card **Uu**. Explain that the letter **Uu** stands for the /u/ sound at the beginning of **umbrella** and in the middle of **pug**.
- Reread the poem *Buddy*, encouraging students to read along with you.
- Point to words in the poem that contain the letter *u*. Say the words aloud and point out whether the /u/ is at the beginning or in the middle of the words.

Practice with the Letter Cards

- Distribute letter cards **i**, **o**, and **u**. Ask students to line up the cards on their workmats.
- Have students pull down each letter card and say the letter name, then push it back up and say the letter sound.
- Ask them to pull down each letter card again, saying a word that has that middle sound.
- Have them push up the letter card that has the middle sound in the word **pup**. (Repeat with the words **pin** and **tot**.)

Practice with the Picture Cards

- Place letter cards **i**, **o**, and **u** in the pocket chart.
- Place picture cards **dish**, **box**, and **tub** under the corresponding letters while you say the name of the letter and the name of the object in the picture.
- Hold up picture card **cup** and have students say **cup** with you, emphasizing the medial sound.
- Ask: *Is the middle sound in* **cup** *the same as the middle sound in* **dish**, **box**, *or* **tub**?
- Place picture card **cup** under letter card **u**. Say: **Cuuuup** *has a middle sound like* **tuuuub**, *so I am putting picture card* **cup** *under the letter* **u**.
- Repeat with picture cards **duck**, **fish**, **fox**, **king**, **mop**, and **sun**.

Blending Sounds

Review

- Hold up letter frieze cards of previously taught sounds. Ask students to say the sound each letter stands for.

Model

- Write the word **tab** on the board. Sound out the word, moving your hand under each letter while blending the sounds. (/**taaaab**/) Then say the word.
- Ask students to sound out the word with you.

Practice with the Word Lists

- Distribute blackline master 1.
- Have students point to the word **tab**. Ask them to sound out the word with you. Then ask them to say the word at regular speed.
- Repeat with the words **him**, **cut**, and **ban**. Then have students sound out the words in random order.

Spelling Words

Model

- Use the spelling transparency. Place counters under the second set of boxes.
- Say: *Today we are going to learn to spell* **bit** *and* **him.** *Watch and listen as I say* **bit** *slowly:* /**biiiit**/. Point out that the word has stop sounds at the beginning and the end.
- As you say /**b**/, push a counter into the first box. Then say /**iiii**/ as you push a counter into the second box and /**t**/ as you push a counter into the third box. Repeat the steps.
- Model recording the letters for the sounds on the transparency. Say: *The first sound is* /**b**/. *I know that the letter* **b** *stands for the* /**b**/ *sound. I'll write the letter* **b** *in the first box. Let's listen for the second sound:* /**biiii**/. *I hear* /**i**/. *I know that the letter* **i** *stands for the* /**i**/ *sound, so I will write* **i** *in the second box. Now let's listen for the last sound:* /**bit**/. *I hear* /**t**/. *I know that the letter* **t** *stands for the* /**t**/ *sound, so I will write* **t** *in the last box.*
- Have students blend the sounds to check the spelling of the word. Say: *Do the letters match the sounds in the word?*

Practice with the Workmat

- Instruct students to place their counters under the second set of boxes on side 2 of their workmats.
- Ask students to slowly articulate the word **bit** as they push the counters into the boxes.
- Have students identify and record the letters that stand for the sounds they hear.
- Have students practice writing **bit** on side 1 of their workmats. Make sure that as they write each word, they say it slowly and think about the sounds they hear.

Repeat the modeling and guided practice with the second spelling word, *him.*

Sight Words

Review

- Write the sight words on the board and have students read the words as you point to them in random order.

Introduce

- Write the word ***cannot*** on the board. Point out that this word is made up of two smaller words they already know: ***can*** and ***not***.
- Have students say the word.
- Ask volunteers to use the word in an oral sentence.

Write

Have students write the word three times on side 1 of their workmats, using the model on the board.

DAY 2

Independent Activities

Phonemic Awareness

Draw Pictures Provide two large sheets of paper. Have students draw pictures of things that begin with /u/ on one sheet and pictures of things that have /u/ in the middle on the other sheet.

Listen Have students listen to the recording of the poem *Buddy* in the listening center.

Sound/Symbol Relationships

Build Words Give letter cards **a**, **b**, **c**, **i**, **n**, **m**, **o**, **p**, and **t** to pairs of students. Have the partners work together to make as many three-letter words with the cards as they can. Point out that as they make the words, they should write them on paper.

Climb the Ladder Draw a ladder with five rungs on chart paper. Write the word *pat* on the bottom rung. Have students change one letter in the word to make a new word, for example, *sat*. Have them write the new word on the second rung. Have them continue changing one letter at a time to make new words until all the rungs are filled. Make other ladders with the words *can*, *hut*, *ten*, and *mop* on the bottom rungs.

Phonemic Awareness

Use the Poetry Poster
- Show students the picture on the back of the poster, and have them name all the objects in the picture.
- Point to a skunk in the picture and say the word *skunk*, emphasizing the /u/ sound. Ask: *Where do you hear the /u/ sound in the word?*
- Ask students to point to something in the picture that has /u/ in the middle.

Listen for Long Vowel Sounds
- Say: *Listen as I say the sounds that make up the word* **cube.** */k/ /ū/ /b/. The word* **cube** *has the long vowel sound. Listen again to the vowel sound. /k/ /ū/ /b/.*
- Repeat with the word *cute*.

Sound/Symbol Relationships

Sort the Decodable Word Cards
- Place picture cards **cat**, **fish**, **block**, and **duck** in the pocket chart and have students say the name of the object on each card.
- Show students decodable word card **cot.** Have them blend the word.
- Ask students if *cot* has a middle sound like *cat*, *fish*, *block*, or *duck*. Then place the card under picture card **block**.
- Repeat with decodable word cards **cub**, **fat**, **fit**, **jam**, **mop**, **nut**, and **tip**.

Distribute blackline master 7 and instruct students to complete it at home.

Assessment Tip: Observe which students have difficulty associating vowel sounds with the appropriate letters. Ask them to sort the decodable word cards into pairs according to the medial sounds. Assign Independent Activities for the rest of the class.

Compare/Contrast Long and Short Vowel Sounds
- Ask students to brainstorm a list of words that have the long **u** sound. Next ask students to brainstorm another list of words that have the short **u** sound.
- Discuss the two different sounds of the vowels.

Blending Sounds

- Have students blend the words *hut*, *cap*, *sun*, and *cup*, using the procedure from Day One.

Spelling Words

- Review the words *bit* and *him* by having students write the words several times.
- Follow the procedure for Day One to model and practice the words *cup* and *nut*.

Sight Words

- Place the cards of previously taught sight words in a box or hat. Have students take turns drawing a card and reading the word.
- Write several sight words on the board. Ask students to write the words on their workmats. Then erase the model and have students write the words without the model.

Phonemic Awareness

Blend and Segment Onset and Rime

- Say the word *cub*, segmenting it into its onset and rime: /**k**/ /**ub**/. Then have students blend the sounds and say the word.
- Continue with the words *cut*, *tub*, *not*, and *pop*.
- Play a guessing game by providing a clue to a word and then saying the word, separating it into its onset and rime. For example, say: *I'm thinking of something you can drink out of*: /**k**/ /**up**/. *What am I thinking of? I'm thinking of something a squirrel likes to eat*: /**n**/ /**ut**/.

 Blending Sounds

- Have students blend the words *tub*, *bun*, *pun*, and *nut*, using the procedure for Day One.

 Spelling Words

- Review the words *bit*, *him*, *cup*, and *nut* by having students write them several times.
- Follow the procedure for Day One to model and practice the words *sun* and *but*.

Assessment Tip: Note students who do not slowly articulate the sounds when spelling a word, and provide extra modeling.

 Sight Words

- Write the words *a*, *and*, *for*, *has*, *is*, *of*, *see*, *the*, and *with* on the board.
- Dim the lights in the room and shine a flashlight on a word.
- Ask individual students to read the word, spell it aloud, and use it in a sentence.
- Repeat the process for all the words.

Distribute blackline master 8 and instruct students to complete it at home.

Poetry Poster (Back)

Decodable Book

 **Decodable Book**

Work with small groups of students to read the decodable book *The Nut* on Days Three and Four. Assign blackline master 3 and Independent Activities for the rest of the class on Day Three.

Introduce the Book

- Display the cover of the book. Point to the title, *The Nut*, and have students sound out the words as you run your finger under them.
- Ask: *What do you see in the picture? What is a nut? Is the nut big or little?*

Read the Book

- Give each student a copy of the book and have them turn to page 2. Instruct them to put their fingers on the first word. Remind them that this is a word they don't sound out and that they have practiced. Have them say the word *The*.
- Have them run their fingers under the next word as they sound it out: /**nnnnuuuut**/.
- As students run their fingers under the next words, continue to distinguish between words they sound out and words they must recognize by sight.
- After students have completed the sentence once slowly, have them read the whole sentence at normal speed.
- If students are sounding out the words without difficulty, have them whisper-read the rest of the text.
- If students have difficulty, continue to guide them page by page.

Discuss the Book

- When students have finished reading, ask: *Who is Pat? Why can't Pat see the nut? Who gets the nut?*

SUPPORT TIPS for English Language Learners

Develop/reinforce: vocabulary *hut*

- Before reading, show students a picture of a doghouse and ask them to label it.
- Accept *doghouse* and other correct labels. Introduce the word *hut* if students do not spontaneously offer that label.

Develop/reinforce: prepositions *in* and *on*

- Have students play a barrier game using the target vocabulary from the book.
- Give pairs of students identical pictures of an empty doghouse. Create a visual barrier so students can't see one another's pictures.
- Have one student place a manipulative, such as a picture of a character or a unifix cube, on or in the hut. Have the student direct his/her partner to do the same with his/her manipulatives: *Put the dog on the hut*.
- Students can remove the visual barrier to compare and change roles. (Note: Providing a variety of pictures of the characters and other nouns used in the series will help develop and reinforce the vocabulary.)

DAY 4

Independent Activities

Decodable Book

Practice Reading Have students read the decodable book in small groups, independently, or with a buddy.

Write and Draw Have students choose a sentence from a page in the decodable book, write it on their papers, and draw a picture to go with the sentence.

Spelling

Independent Practice Write the week's spelling words on index cards and place them in the literacy center. Provide the letter cards needed to build the words and have students use the cards to spell the words.

Sight Words

Personal Dictionaries Ensure that students have the words *a*, *and*, *for*, *has*, *is*, *of*, *see*, *the*, and *with* in their personal dictionaries. Ask them to write a sentence using each word.

Phonological Awareness

Identify and Produce Rhyme
- Say *hut* and *cut*. Repeat the words and have students listen for the sounds that are the same. Ask: *Where do you hear these sounds?*
- Reread the poem *Buddy* and have students listen for rhyming words. Have them clap when you say two rhyming words.
- Say the following pairs of words and ask students if the words rhyme: *pug/tug*, *pup/tub*, *nut/not*, *must/just*, *in/pin*, *soak/poke*, *mud/cup*.
- Repeat the rhyming pairs and ask students to tell you what sounds they hear at the end of each pair.
- Have students tell you words that rhyme with *pup*, *tub*, and *mud*.

Assessment Tip: To check which students can or cannot identify rhyming words, call on them individually as you say a word pair.

Blending Sounds

- Have students blend the words *sub*, *cab*, *pad*, and *pup*, using the procedure for Day One.

Spelling Words

Review
- Review the week's spelling words by having students write them several times on their workmats.
- Provide pairs of students with blackline master 2. One student reads the words from the list while the other student writes each word.
- The partner should put a check mark beside words spelled correctly. If a word is incorrect, the partner may provide prompts. If the second spelling of the word is correct, the partner places a check mark in the "Second Try" column.

Assessment Tip: Collect students' completed blackline masters and note which words gave them difficulty.

Sight Words

Review
- Write the words *a*, *and*, *for*, *has*, *is*, *of*, *see*, *the*, and *with* on the board.
- Randomly point to the words and have students read them aloud.
- Erase a letter from one of the words and have students tell you which letter is missing. Replace the letter and have students read the word.

Decodable Book

- Read the decodable book *The Nut* with the remaining small groups of students. Assign blackline master 4 and Independent Activities for the rest of the class.

Assessment Tip: Use the completed blackline master to assess how well students can identify words that have the same medial sounds.

Spelling Assessment

Use the following procedure to assess students' spelling of the Unit 12 words.
• Say each spelling word and use it in a sentence.
• Have students write the word on a piece of paper.
• Continue with the next word on the list.
• When students have finished, collect their papers and analyze their spellings of misspelled words.
• Record their progress on a spelling record sheet, and provide extra practice as needed.

 # Small Group Activities

The following small group activities can be used to provide hands-on practice for students who need additional support. Assign blackline master 5 and Independent Activities for the rest of the class.

 ## PHONOLOGICAL AWARENESS

Practice Medial Sounds Say the words *jump*, *pot*, and *tin*, one at a time, emphasizing the middle sound. Have students identify the middle sound they hear in the word. Repeat the word and ask students to say another word that has the same middle sound.

Model Segmenting Onset and Rime Say: *Listen to the word* **cup**. *I hear* /k/ *at the beginning and* /**up**/ *at the end. Now you say* **cup** *and segment it into its onset and rime.* Repeat with *sum*, *him*, and *tap*. Then have students segment some words on their own.

Work with Rhyme Have students sit in a circle and provide them with a word. Working around the circle, ask students to say a word that rhymes with the assigned word. When students cannot come up with any new rhymes, provide them with a new word. Use the words *bat*, *pit*, *nut*, *tan*, and *mop*.

 ## SOUND/SYMBOL RELATIONSHIPS

Sort Picture Cards Place decodable word cards **cot**, **cub**, **fat**, and **tip** in the pocket chart. Have students read each word, focusing on the medial sound. Then give students picture cards **cat**, **fish**, **block**, **duck**, **king**, **mop**, and **cup**. Have students identify each picture and place it under the word card that has the same medial sound.

Medial Sounds Write *cap* on the board. Have students take turns running their fingers under the word as they blend the sounds. Then ask students what letter you need to change to make the word *cup*. Erase the *a* and replace it with *u*. Then ask them what letter they need to change to make the word *cop*.

 ## BLENDING

Model and Practice Sound out the word *tab*, moving your hand under the sounds and blending the word. (/*taaab*/) Have them repeat the sounds and then blend the sounds to say the whole word. Continue with *him*, *cut*, and *ban*.

Work With the /u/ Sound Write the words *bus*, *fun*, *hut*, *bun*, and *sub* on chart paper. Have volunteers take turns running their fingers under each word as they blend the sounds.

 ## SPELLING

Use Word Patterns Write the word patterns *b__t*, *h__m*, *c__p*, and *n__t* on the board. Say the word *bit* and use it in a sentence. Have a volunteer identify the word pattern for the word *bit* and fill in the missing letter. Have the student read the word aloud. Repeat the activity to complete the words *him*, *cup*, and *nut*.

Use the Letter Cards Write the spelling words *bit*, *him*, *cup*, *nut*, and *sun* on the board. Mix a set of letter cards. Have a student find the letters to spell the first word and place the cards in a row in the pocket chart. Return the cards to the set and ask another student to spell the next word.

 ## SIGHT WORDS

Word Search Provide texts other than the decodable book and have pairs of students look through the texts to find the words *a*, *and*, *for*, *has*, *is*, *of*, *see*, *the*, and *with*.

Student Name _____   Assessment Date _____

Phonological Awareness: Producing Rhyme

Directions: Say the rhyming pair. Then ask the student to say another real or nonsense word that rhymes with the pair. Record the student's response. **Example:** light/bite. *Kite.*

skunk/trunk		fret/set			
show/crow		store/snore			
thrill/chill		trash/smash		**Score**	**/6**

Phonemic Awareness: Blending Onset and Rime

Directions: Say the first sound of the word followed by the rest of the word. Then have the student say the whole word. If the student says the word correctly, put a ✔. If the student misses the word, record the error. **Example:** /b/ /at/. *Bat.*

/b/ /us/ (bus)		/m/ /ill/ (mill)			
/h/ /ot/ (hot)		/t/ /uck/ (tuck)			
/f/ /un/ (fun)		/s/ /ad/ (sad)		**Score**	**/6**

Phonics: Segmenting and Blending Sounds

Directions: Explain that these nonsense words use sounds the student has been learning. Have the student point to each word on the corresponding student sheet, say each sound, and then blend the sounds together. Put a ✔ if the student's response is correct. If the student misses the word, record the error. **Example:** pum. /p/ /u/ /m/, pum.

bof (/b/ /o/ /f/, bof)		mub (/m/ /u/ /b/, mub)			
nup (/n/ /u/ /p/, nup)		hab (/h/ /a/ /b/, hab)			
bic (/b/ /i/ /c/, bic)		rus (/r/ /u/ /s/, rus)		**Score**	**/6**

Sight Word

Directions: Have the student point to the sight word on the corresponding student sheet and read it as quickly as possible. Put a ✔ if the student successfully reads the word and an **X** if the student hesitates more than a few seconds. If the student misses the word, record the error.

cannot		**Score**	**/1**

UNIT 13 Rr

Unit Objectives
Students will:

- Identify the /r/ sound
- Associate the letter Rr with the /r/ sound
- Segment and blend onset and rime
- Identify initial and final consonant sounds
- Identify and produce rhyme
- Blend CVC words
- Read the sight words are, have
- Spell CVC words using r and letters previously learned

Day 1

BLM 1

BLM 6

Letter Cards: **a, b, e, h, r**

Spelling Transparency

Picture Word Cards:
bat, bell, box, hat, house, helicopter, rabbit, ring, rug

Day 2

BLM 1

BLM 7

Decodable Word Cards for Unit 13

Spelling Transparency

Picture Word Cards:
box, fan, rug

Day 3

BLM 1

BLM 3

BLM 8

Sight Word Cards for Unit 13: **are, have**

Spelling Transparency

Day 4

BLM 1

BLM 2

BLM 4

Day 5

BLM 5

Letter Cards: **a, b, c, h, i, o, p, r, t, u**

Decodable Word Cards for Unit 13

Sight Word Cards for Unit 13

Quick-Check Student Sheet

Picture Word Cards:
bell, box, cap, fan, hat, jam, rabbit, ring, tub

Poetry Poster

The Race
Ready, set, go!
Rooster ran a relay race
as fast as he could run.
Go, Rooster! Run, Rabbit!
A relay race is fun.

Student Workmat

Letter Frieze Card

Decodable Book

Poetry CD

Core Materials

All print resources can be downloaded from http://phonicsresources.benchmarkeducation.com

**Poetry Poster
(Front)**

Letter Frieze Card

**Picture Word
Cards**

 Phonemic Awareness

Use the Poetry Poster

- Read aloud or play the recording of the poem *The Race* several times.
- Say the sentence "Rooster ran a relay race as fast he could run," emphasizing the /**r**/ sound.
- Have students say the sentence with you, this time stretching the /**r**/ phoneme in the /**r**/ words.
- Reread the poem and have students raise their hands each time they hear /**r**/.

Distribute blackline master 6 and instruct students to complete it at home.

Sound/Symbol Relationships

Model

- Display letter frieze card **Rr**. Explain that the letter **Rr** stands for the /**r**/ sound in the word ***rabbit***.
- Reread the poem *The Race*. Invite students to read along with you.
- Point to words in the poem that begin with the letter **r**. Say the words aloud and ask students to say the words with you.

Practice with the Letter Cards

- Distribute letter cards **b**, **h**, and **r**. Have students line up the cards on their workmats.
- Have students pull down each letter card and say the letter name, then push it back up and say the letter sound.
- Ask them to pull down each letter card again, saying a word that starts with that sound.
- Have them push up the letter card that starts the word ***ring***. (Repeat with the words ***big*** and ***hat***.)

Practice with the Picture Cards

- Place letter cards **b**, **h**, and **r** in the pocket chart.
- Place picture cards **bell**, **hat**, and **ring** under the corresponding letters while you say the name of the letter and the name of the object in the picture.
- Hold up picture card **rug** and have students say ***rug*** with you.
- Ask: *Does* **rug** *begin like* **bell**, **hat**, *or* **ring**?
- Place picture card **rug** under letter card **r**. Say: **Rrrrug** *begins like* **rrrring**, *so I am putting picture card* **rug** *under the letter* **r**.
- Repeat with picture cards **bat**, **box**, **house**, **helicopter**, and **rabbit**.

Blending Sounds

Review

- Hold up letter frieze cards of previously taught sounds. Ask students to say the sound each letter stands for.

Model

- Write the word ***cup*** on the board. Sound out the word by moving your hand under each letter and blending the sounds. (/**kuuuup**/) Then say the word.
- Ask students to sound out the word with you.

Practice with the Word Lists

- Distribute blackline master 1.
- Have students point to the word ***cup***. Ask them to sound out the word with you. Then ask them to say the word at regular speed.
- Repeat with the words ***bat***, ***rug***, and ***run***. Then have students sound out the words in random order.

Spelling Words

Model

- Use the spelling transparency. Place counters under the second set of boxes on the transparency.
- Say: *Today we are going to learn to spell* **cup** *and* **hop.** *Watch and listen as I say* **cup** *slowly:* /**kuuuup**/. Remind students that the word has stop sounds at the beginning and at the end.
- As you say /**k**/, push a counter into the first box. Then say /**uuuu**/ as you push a counter into the second box and /**p**/ as you push a counter into the third box. Repeat the steps.
- Model recording the letters for the sounds on the transparency. Say: *The first sound is* /**k**/. *I know that the letter* **c** *stands for the* /**k**/ *sound. I'll write* **c** *in the first box. Let's listen for the second sound:* /**kuuuu**/. *I hear* /**u**/. *I know that the letter* **u** *stands for the* /**u**/ *sound, so I will write* **u** *in the second box. Let's listen for the last sound:* /**kup**/. *I hear* /**p**/. *I know that the letter* **p** *stands for the* /**p**/ *sound, so I will write* **p** *in the last box.*
- Have students blend the sounds to check the spelling of the word.

Practice with the Workmat

- Instruct students to place counters under the second set of boxes on side 2 of the workmat.
- Ask students to slowly articulate the word *cup* as they push the counters into the boxes.
- Have students identify and record the letters that stand for the sounds they hear.
- Have students practice writing *cup* on side 1 of their workmats.

Repeat the modeling and guided practice with the second spelling word, *hop*.

 Sight Words

Review

- Show students the sight word cards one at a time and have them read the words.
- Have volunteers select a card, read the word, and use the word in an oral sentence.

Introduce

- Use the pocket chart and letter cards to model how to spell the word *are*. Say: *This is the word* **are**. *It is made up of the letters* **a**, **r**, *and* **e.**
- Have students say the word as you point to it.
- Follow the same steps to introduce the word *have*.
- Take away a letter in the word *are* and ask students which letter is missing. Replace the letter and have them read the word with you. Repeat with the word *have*.

Write

- Have students write *are* and *have* on their workmats, using the models in the pocket chart.

DAY 2

Independent Activities

Phonological Awareness

Use Picture Cards Provide picture cards in the literacy center. Students can:
- take two picture cards, name the pictures, and tell if the words rhyme
- separate the cards that start with /r/
- match a picture card with another picture card that starts with the same sound
- choose a card and draw a picture of an object that ends with the same sound

Collage Have pairs of students work together to make a collage of pictures that start with /r/.

Listen Have students listen to the recording of the poem *The Race* in the listening center.

Sound/Symbol Relationships

Word Sort Using decodable word cards from this and previous units, have students sort the cards into groups according to their ending sounds.

Word Patterns Write the word patterns *ti__*, *ca__*, *ru__*, and *ho__* on cards. Have students add letters to make words, and then write and read the words.

Matching Sounds Make several copies of decodable words and place them in a small box. Students take cards and look for a student who has a card with the same medial sound.

Letter Search Have students choose a letter from a previous lesson and search in a magazine for words that begin with that letter.

 ## Phonemic Awareness

Use the Poetry Poster
- Show students the picture on the back of the poetry poster and have them name all the objects in the picture.
- Point to the raccoon in the picture and say the word *raccoon*, stressing the beginning sound. Ask: *What sound do you hear at the beginning of the word?*
- Have students point to other objects that start with /r/.

 ## Sound/Symbol Relationships

Sort the Decodable Word Cards
- Place picture cards **box**, **fan**, and **rug** in the pocket chart and have students say the name of the object on each card.
- Show students decodable word card **bat** and have them blend the word.
- Ask them if **bat** begins like **box**, **fan**, or **rug**. Then place the card under picture card **box**.
- Repeat with decodable word cards **bib**, **Bob**, **fat**, **fin**, **rap**, **rip**, and **rub**.

Distribute blackline master 7 and instruct students to complete it at home.

Assessment Tip: Note which students cannot correctly place the word cards, and work with them in a small group. Assign Independent Activities for the rest of the class.

 ## Blending Sounds

- Have students blend the words *ran*, *nap*, *run*, and *rap*, using the procedure for Day One.

 ## Spelling Words

- Review the words *cup* and *hop* by having students write them several times.
- Follow the procedure for Day One to model and practice the words *run* and *rub*.

Assessment Tip: Note students who do not slowly articulate the sounds when spelling a word, and provide extra modeling.

Sight Words

- Write *are*, *have*, *is*, *of*, *see*, *the*, and *with* on the board. Have volunteers read each word.
- Write "My cat _____ fat" on the board. Ask which word on the board completes the sentence.
- Continue with "Tam and Pam _____ a map"; "The cat is on top ___ the pan"; "Tim can _____ the cat"; "Bob is ____ Tim"; and "____ cat is fat."

Phonemic Awareness

Final Consonants

- Say the words **rap** and **hop**. Ask: *Do the words end with the same sound?*
- Continue with word pairs **ran/tin**, **map/bin**, **pop/pit**, **fan/sun**, **bib/rob**, and **tan/pot**.

 # Blending Sounds

P + A + M

- Have students blend the words **ram**, **hub**, **rip**, and **map**, using the procedure for Day One.

 # Spelling Words

- Review the words **cup**, **hop**, **run**, and **rub** by having students write them several times.
- Follow the procedure for Day One to model and practice the words **rub** and **rip**.

 # Sight Words

- Make several copies of sight word cards **are** and **have**. Distribute the cards and have each student use their word in an oral sentence.
- Divide a large sheet of chart paper into 10 squares. Write **are**, **cannot**, **for**, **has**, **have**, **no**, **of**, **see**, **the**, and **with** in the squares. Place the paper on the floor. Have two teams of students take turns throwing a beanbag onto a square. If the student can read the word in the square, the student's team scores one point.

Distribute blackline master 8 and instruct students to complete it at home.

Decodable Book

Work with small groups of students to read the decodable book *Rob* on Days Three and Four. Assign blackline master 3 and Independent Activities for the rest of the class on Day Three.

Introduce the Book

- Show students the cover of the book. Point to the title, *Rob*, and have them sound out the word as you run your finger under it.
- Ask: *What do you see in the picture? What is the rabbit doing?*

Read the Book

- Give each student a copy of the book and instruct them to turn to page 2. Have them run their fingers under the first word as they sound it out: */Paaaammmm/*.
- Have students point to the next word. Remind them that this is a word they don't sound out and that they have practiced. Have them say the word **and**.
- Continue distinguishing between words they sound out and words they don't sound out.
- Have students read the sentence at normal speed.
- Repeat with the rest of the sentences on the page.
- If students can sound out the words without difficulty, have them whisper-read the rest of the text.
- If students have difficulty, guide them page by page.

Discuss the Book

- When students have finished reading, ask: *Why does Rob run? What does the pup do? What happens at the end of the story?*

Poetry Poster (Back)

Decodable Book

 **SUPPORT TIPS**
for English Language Learners

Develop: background knowledge rabbit as a pet

- Before reading, bring a pet rabbit to class for the students to observe and discuss, making sure to identify the owner and what the owner likes to do with his/her pet rabbit.
- Throughout the day, ask students to tell you what the rabbit is doing, modeling the response *The **rabbit** is____* if students do not use the word **rabbit** when they respond.
- If you are unable to obtain a real rabbit, have students work in pairs or small groups to create lists/collages of pets they have or know about.
- If no one suggests a rabbit as a pet, challenge students to identify other animals that can be pets and suggest the idea that a rabbit can be a pet, pairing the word with a picture of a rabbit.
- Support the concept of a rabbit as a pet with photos of children playing with rabbits. Have students describe the pictures. Model the response, *The **rabbit** is____*, if students do not use the word **rabbit** when they respond.

DAY 4

Independent Activities

Decodable Book

Independent Reading After students have read the decodable book in a small group, have them read it independently or with a friend.

Write Have students select a sentence from the book that has the word **Pam** in it and write it on their papers. Have them substitute their name for **Pam**.

Book Words Write several words from the book on index cards. As one student reads the book aloud, another student holds up the appropriate card when the word is read.

Spelling

As words are introduced each day, write them on index cards and place them in the literacy center. Ensure that the letter cards needed to build the words are in the center. Students can use the following procedure to spell words.
- Choose a word card.
- Use their fingers and eyes to read the word.
- Turn over the card so that they can't see the word.
- Build the word using the letter cards.
- Turn over the card to check the word.
- Write the word.

Sight Words

Personal Dictionary Have students write **are** and **have** in their personal dictionaries.

Find the Words Write **and**, **has**, **for**, **is**, **see**, and **the** on strips of paper. Have students find and cut examples of the words from magazines, and tape the words on the correct strip.

 Phonological Awareness

Identify and Produce Rhyme
- Reread the poem *The Race* and have students listen for rhyming words.
- Say the following groups of words and have students identify the two words that rhyme: **rap/sap/tip**, **tub/pup/rub**, **bat/but/nut**, **bit/it/rip**.
- Repeat the rhyming pairs and ask students to tell you what sound they hear at the end of the two words.
- Have students say words that rhyme with **run**, **cot**, and **sip**.

Assessment Tip: Note which students cannot suggest words that rhyme, and provide additional support.

 Blending Sounds

- Have students blend the words **rob**, **rap**, **hip**, and **him**, using the procedure for Day One.

 Spelling Words

Review
- Review the week's words by having students write them several times on their workmats.
- Provide pairs of students with blackline master 2. While one student reads the words, the other student writes the words.
- If a word is spelled correctly, the partner puts a check mark beside it. If the student spells a word incorrectly, the partner may provide prompts. If the second spelling of the word is correct, the partner places a check mark in the "Second Try" column.

Assessment Tip: Collect students' completed blackline masters and note which words gave them difficulty.

 Sight Words

Review
- Write the words **a**, **are**, **and**, **for**, **no**, **has**, **have**, **is**, **of**, **see**, **the**, **cannot**, and **with** in random order in two columns on the board.
- Divide students into two teams. The first student on each team points to the first word in the column and reads it.
- If the word is read correctly, it is erased.
- The first team to erase all its words wins.

 Decodable Book

- Read the decodable book *Rob* with the remaining small groups of students. Assign blackline master 4 and Independent Activities for the rest of the class.

Assessment Tip: Use the completed blackline master to assess how well students can identify words that have the same ending sounds.

Spelling Assessment

Use the following procedure to assess students' spelling of the Unit 13 words.
• Say each word and use it in a sentence.
• Have students write each word on a piece of paper.
• Collect students' papers and analyze their spellings of misspelled words.
• Record students' progress on a spelling record sheet, and provide extra practice as needed.

 ## Small Group Activities

The following small group activities can be used to provide hands-on practice for students who need additional support. Assign blackline master 5 and Independent Activities for the rest of the class.

 ### PHONOLOGICAL AWARENESS

Initial Sounds 1 Say the following words slowly, and have students clap their hands when they hear the /r/ sound in a word: **red, road, raccoon, rooster, rice, rain**.

Initial Sounds 2 Display the picture on the back of the poetry poster. Ask: *Are the* **rrrrroses** *on the* **rrrrraft**? *Is the* **rrrrabbit** *in the* **rrrrocking** *chair*? Have students make up questions about the poster, stretching out the /r/ sounds.

Final Sounds Distribute picture cards **ring, cap, fan, jam**, and **tub**. Have students say the name of the picture and then say another word that has the same ending sound.

Rhyme Using the rhyming word pairs from Day Four, have students identify the sounds they hear at the end of each pair.

 ### SOUND/SYMBOL RELATIONSHIPS

Sound Search Give each student one of these picture cards: **bell, hat, ring, box**, or **rabbit**. Have students find objects in the classroom whose names begin with the same sound as the picture on their card.

Word Sort Have students sort the decodable word cards into four groups according to their ending sounds.

 ### BLENDING

Word Change Write the word **nap** on the board. Have students take turns blending the sounds. Then change **nap** to **rap**, **rap** to **ran**, and **ran** to **run**.

Blending Using decodable word cards **hum, rub, rap**, and **hip**, have students work with a partner to practice blending. One partner says the sounds of a word slowly, and the other partner blends the sounds to make the word.

 ### SPELLING

Spelling Practice Model saying and writing the spelling words while students say and write them with you.

Letter Lineup Give each student one of these letter cards: **c, u, p, h, o, r, a, t, b, i**. Ask students to line up to make the words **cup, hop, run, cat, rub**, and **rip**. Have each student say the name of the letter on his or her card and the sound the letter stands for. Then have students spell and say the whole word.

 ### SIGHT WORDS

Letter Scramble Write the words **are, have, is, of, see, the**, and **with** on the board. Mix up a set of letter cards. Have students choose a word, find the letters cards that spell the word, and arrange the letters in order on the board ledge.

Find the Words Write the words **a, are, and, have, see, cannot**, and **the** on the board. Then write the following sentences on the board: "Nan and Sam cannot have a cat"; "Pop and Tam are fit"; "See Pam rub the cat." Have students read the sentences aloud and find each sight word.

Student Name _____ Assessment Date _____

Phonological Awareness: Identifying Rhyme

Directions: Say each set of words. Then have the student say the two words that rhyme. Put a ✔ if the student's response is correct. If not, record the words the student chooses. **Example:** mat/hat/lid. *Mat, hat.*

lack/tack/sick *(lack, tack)*		
wig/jig/jag *(wig, jig)*		
gum/jam/sum *(gum, sum)*		
age/nudge/page *(age, page)*		
mind/mend/bend *(mend, bend)*		
hate/hoot/suit *(hoot, suit)*		**Score** /6

Phonemic Awareness: Identifying Final Sounds

Directions: Say the word and ask the student to tell you the ending sound. If the student answers correctly, put a ✔. If the student misses the sound, record the error. **Example:** hat. /t/

clam *(/m/)*		mine *(/n/)*	
quite *(/t/)*		flap *(/p/)*	
fuss *(/s/)*		fib *(/b/)*	**Score** /6

Phonics: Segmenting and Blending Sounds

Directions: Explain that these nonsense words use sounds the student has been learning. Have the student point to each word on the corresponding student sheet, say each sound, and then blend the sounds together. Put a ✔ if the student's response is correct. If the student misses the word, record the error. **Example:** rop. /r/ /o/ /p/, rop.

hun *(/h/ /u/ /n/, hun)*		ras *(/r/ /a/ /s/, ras)*	
rit *(/r/ /i/ /t/, rit)*		nuc *(/n/ /u/ /k/, nuc)*	
fub *(/f/ /u/ /b/, fub)*		rom *(/r/ /o/ /m/, rom)*	**Score** /6

Sight Words

Directions: Have the student point to the first sight word on the corresponding student sheet and read across the line, saying each word as quickly as possible. Put a ✔ if the student successfully reads the word and an **X** if the student hesitates more than a few seconds. If the student misses the word, record the error.

are		have	**Score** /2

UNIT 14 Short Ee

Unit Objectives

Students will:

- Identify the /e/ sound
- Associate the letter Ee with the /e/ sound
- Listen for medial sounds in words
- Segment and blend onset and rime
- Identify rhyme
- Blend CVC words
- Read the sight word said
- Spell CVC words using e and letters previously learned

Day 1

BLM 1

BLM 6

Letter Cards: **a, d, e, i, o, s, u**

Spelling Transparency

Picture Word Cards: **bell, dish, legs, mop, nest, ring, sock, stick, top, web**

Day 2

BLM 1

BLM 7

Decodable Word Cards for Unit 14

Letter Cards: **a, d, e, i, o, s, u**

Spelling Transparency

Picture Word Cards: **bell, cap, cup, sock, stick**

Day 3

BLM 1

BLM 3

BLM 8

Sight Word Cards for Unit 14

Spelling Transparency

Day 4

BLM 1

BLM 2

BLM 4

Sight Word Cards for Unit 14

Letter Cards for Unit 14

Day 5

BLM 5

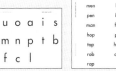

Letter Cards: **e, m, n, p, t**

Decodable Word Cards for Unit 14

Sight Word Cards for Unit 14

Quick-Check Student Sheet

Poetry Poster

Student Workmat

Letter Frieze Card

Decodable Book

Poetry CD

Core Materials

All print resources can be downloaded from http://phonicsresources.benchmarkeducation.com.

**Poetry Poster
(Front)**

Letter Frieze Card

**Picture Word
Cards**

Phonemic Awareness

Use the Poetry Poster
- Read aloud or play the recording of the poem *The Red Hen*.
- Read the sentence "Ted and Ed have a pet hen" and ask students to listen for the medial */e/* sound.
- Read the poem again and have students "cluck" each time they hear the */e/* sound.

Distribute blackline master 6 and instruct students to complete it at home.

Sound/Symbol Relationships

Model
- Display letter frieze card **Ee**. Explain that the letter **Ee** stands for the */e/* sound at the beginning of the word **elephant** and in the middle of the words **pet red hen**.
- Reread the poem *The Red Hen*. Invite students to read along with you.
- Point to words in the poem that have the */e/* sound. Say the words aloud and ask students to say them with you.

Practice with the Letter Cards
- Distribute letter cards **e**, **u**, and **o**. Ask students to line up the cards on their workmats.
- Ask them to pull down each letter card and say the letter name, then push it back up and say the letter sound.
- Have them pull down each letter card again, saying a word that has that middle sound.
- Ask them to push up the letter card that stands for the middle sound in the word **bed**. (Repeat with the words **cup** and **top**.)

Practice with the Picture Cards
- Place letter cards **e**, **i**, and **o** in the pocket chart.
- Place picture cards **legs**, **stick**, and **mop** under the corresponding letters while you say the name of the letter and the name of the object in the picture.
- Hold up picture card **nest** and have students say **nest** with you, emphasizing the middle sound.
- Ask: *Does* **nest** *have the same middle sound as* **legs, stick,** *or* **mop**?
- Place picture card **nest** under letter card **e**. Say: **Neeeest** *has the same middle sound as* **leeeegs,** *so I am putting picture card* **nest** *under the letter* **e**.
- Repeat with picture cards **bell**, **dish**, **ring**, **sock**, **top**, and **web**.

Blending Sounds

Review
- Hold up letter frieze cards of previously taught sounds. Ask students to say the sound each letter stands for.

Model
- Write the word **hut** on the board. Sound out the word by moving your hand under each letter while blending the sounds. (*/huuuut/*) Then say the word.
- Ask students to sound out the word with you.

Practice with the Word Lists
- Distribute blackline master 1.
- Have students point to the word **hut**. Ask them to sound out the word with you. Then ask them to say the word at regular speed.
- Repeat the modeling and guided practice with the words **met, rap,** and **hit**.

Spelling Words

Model

- Use the spelling transparency. Place counters under the second set of boxes.
- Say: *Today we are going to learn to spell* **rap** *and* **cab**. *Listen as I say* **rap** *slowly:* **/rrrraaaap/**. Remind students that the word has a stop sound at the end.
- As you say **/rrrr/**, push a counter into the first box. Then say **/aaaa/** as you push a counter into the second box and **/p/** as you push a counter into the third box. Repeat the steps.
- Model recording the letters for the sounds on the transparency. Say: *The first sound is* **/rrrr/**. *I know that the letter* **r** *stands for the* **/rrrr/** *sound. I'll write the letter* **r** *in the first box. Let's listen for the second sound:* **/raaaa/**. *I hear* **/a/**. *I know that the letter* **a** *stands for the* **/a/** *sound, so I will write* **a** *in the second box. Let's listen for the last sound:* **/rap/**. *I hear* **/p/**. *I know that the letter* **p** *stands for the* **/p/** *sound, so I will write* **p** *in the last box.*
- Have students blend the sounds to check the spelling of the word.

Practice with the Workmat

- Instruct students to place counters under the second set of boxes on side 2 of the workmat.
- Ask students to slowly articulate the word *rap* as they push the counters into the boxes.
- Have them identify and record the letters that stand for the sounds they hear.
- Have students practice writing *rap* on side 1 of their workmats.

Repeat the modeling and guided practice with the second spelling word, *cab*.

 ## Sight Words

Review

- Write the words *are*, *see*, *for*, and *have* on the board. Have students review the words by writing them on paper, reading them, and rewriting them.

Introduce

- Use the pocket chart and letter cards to model how to spell the new word, *said*. Say: *This is the word* **said**. *It isn't spelled the way it sounds. It is made up of the letters* **s**, **a**, **i**, *and* **d**.
- Point to the word and say it. Then have students say the word as you point to it.
- Have students spell the word in the air with their fingers.
- Remove one of the letters in the chart without students seeing, then ask them which letter is missing. Replace the letter and have students read the word.

Write

- Have students write the word *said* on side 1 of their workmats, using the word in the pocket chart as a model.

DAY 2

Independent Activities

Phonological Awareness

Use Picture Cards Provide picture cards in the literacy center. Students can:
- take two picture cards and tell if the words rhyme
- separate the cards that have the /e/ sound
- match a card with another with the same middle sound

Collage Have students choose a picture card and look in magazines for pictures whose names have the same middle sound. Have them cut out the pictures and make a collage.

Listen Have students listen to the recording of the poem *The Red Hen* in the listening center.

Sound/Symbol Relationships

Medial Sort Provide decodable word cards **cab**, **rap**, **set**, **men**, **pin**, **bit**, **hop**, **rob**, **hum**, and **fun**. Have students sort the cards into pairs that have the same middle sounds. Then have students write the words and highlight the middle sounds.

Sound Review Place decodable word cards **set**, **pin**, **rob**, and **fun** in the literacy center. Have students say the word name, build the word with letter cards, and write the word. Below the word, have them write:
- another word that begins with the same sound
- another word that has the same middle sound
- another word that ends with the same sound

Tongue Twisters Place letter cards **b**, **r**, and **f** facedown. Have students pick a letter and make up a tongue twister using words that begin with that letter.

 ## Phonemic Awareness

Use the Poetry Poster
- Display the picture on the back of the poetry poster and have students name all the objects in the picture.
- Point to the men in the picture and say the word *men*. Ask students to tell you where they hear the /e/ sound in the word.
- Ask students to point to something in the picture that has the /e/ sound. Have them say if the /e/ sound is in the beginning or the middle.

Listen for Long Vowel Sounds
- Say: *Listen as I say the sounds that make up the word* **free**. /f/ /r /ē/. *The word* **free** *has the long vowel sound. Listen again to the vowel sound.* /f/ /r/ /ē/.
- Repeat with the word *tie*.

 ## Sound/Symbol Relationships

Sort the Decodable Word Cards
- Place picture cards **bell**, **cup**, **sock**, **stick**, and **cap** in the pocket chart. Have students say the name of the object on each picture card.
- Show students decodable word card **man** and have them sound out the word.
- Ask: *Does* **man** *have the same middle sound as* **bell**, **cup**, **sock**, **stick**, *or* **cap**?
- Place word card **man** under picture card **cap**.
- Repeat with decodable word cards **let**, **bit**, **hop**, **fun**, **tip**, **ten**, **pin**, **rob**, and **hum**.

Distribute blackline master 7 and instruct students to complete it at home.

Assessment Tip: To assess a student, give the student a word card and ask him or her to place it under the correct picture card. Assign Independent Activities for the rest of the class.

 ## Blending Sounds

- Have students blend the words *net*, *ten*, *met*, and *Ben*, using the procedure for Day One.

 ## Spelling Words

- Review the words *rap* and *cab* by having students write the words several times.
- Follow the procedure for Day One to model and practice the words *met* and *pen*.

Assessment Tip: Note students who do not slowly articulate the sounds when spelling a word, and provide extra modeling.

Sight Words

- Write the words *and*, *for*, *said*, *cannot*, *with*, and *of* on the board. Have students clap and say each letter as you spell each word together.
- Say: *I want to write the words in alphabetical order. Do any of the words begin with* **a**? When students say *and*, write *and* at the top of the board. Go through the alphabet, having volunteers write the rest of the sight words in alphabetical order.
- When the list is finished, have students read through the list several times.

Compare/Contrast Long and Short Vowel Sounds
- Ask students to brainstorm a list of words that have the long *e* sound. Next, ask students to brainstorm another list of words that have the short *e* sound.
- Discuss the two different sounds of the vowels.

Phonemic Awareness

Segment and Blend Onset and Rime

- Say the word *mop*, segmenting it into its onset and rime: */m/ /op/*. Have students repeat the onset and rime with you several times.
- Say: *The beginning sound in* **mop** *is* /m/. *The middle and ending sounds are* /op/. *We can say these sounds separately:* /m/ /op/. *Then we can blend these sounds:* /**mop**/.
- Continue by having students segment the words *cab*, *ten*, *hit*, and *bus* into their onsets and rimes.

 # Blending Sounds

- Have students blend the words *cup*, *let*, *set*, and *ten*.

 # Spelling Words

- Review the words *rap*, *cab*, *met*, and *pen* by having students write them several times.
- Follow the procedure for Day One to model and practice the words *let* and *ten*.

 # Sight Words

- Write the word *said* on the board and read it aloud with students.
- Model using the word in an oral sentence and ask students to think of their own sentence using the word *said*.
- Have students say their sentences. Ask the listeners to clap when they hear the word *said*.
- Write the words *no*, *said*, *with*, *the*, *has*, *a*, and *is* in a row on the board and place the corresponding sight words in a box.
- Have students take turns drawing a card, saying the word, and placing the card on the board ledge under the matching word.

Distribute blackline master 8 and instruct students to complete it at home.

Poetry Poster (Back)

Decodable Book

Work with small groups of students to read the decodable book *Mem the Hen* on Days Three and Four. Assign blackline master 3 and Independent Activities for the rest of the class on Day Three.

Introduce the Book

- Display the cover of the book. Point to the title, *Mem the Hen*, and have students sound out the words as you run your finger under them.
- Ask: *What do you see in the picture? What color is Mem? Where is Mem?*

Read the Book

- Give each student a copy of the book and have them turn to page 2. Have them run their fingers under the first word as they sound it out: */Mmmmeeeemmmm/.*
- Have students point to the next two words. Remind them that these are words they don't sound out. Have them say the words *is* and *a*.
- Have students run their fingers under the next two words as they sound them out: */taaaannnn/, /heeeennnn/.*
- Have students read the sentence at normal speed.
- Repeat with the remaining sentences on the page.
- If students can sound out the words without difficulty, have them whisper-read the rest of the text.
- If students have difficulty, guide them page by page.

Discuss the Book

- When students have finished reading, ask: *Why can Mem get out of the pen? How does Ben catch Mem? Where is the pup at the end?*

Decodable Book

 **SUPPORT TIPS**
for English Language Learners

Develop/reinforce: past tense *ran*

- Before reading the book, read aloud a picture story that emphasizes the word *ran*, such as *The Gingerbread Man*.
- Have students join in whenever the text indicates that the character ran.
- Have students act out the running action themselves, or have them manipulate puppets to show the characters running and stopping.
- Have other students use simple sentences to describe the action.
- Model target sentence structure as necessary. Say: *The gingerbread man ran home. Tony ran to the door.*

Independent Activities

Decodable Book

Independent Reading Have students read the book independently or with a buddy.

Write and Draw Have students use decodable word cards to make a new sentence for a page in the book and draw a new picture to go with the sentence.

Drama Have students work in small groups to create a dramatization of the story.

Spelling

As words are introduced each day, write them on index cards and place them in the literacy center. Ensure that the letter cards needed to build the words are in the center. Students can use the following procedure to spell words.
- Choose a word card.
- Use their fingers and eyes to read the word.
- Turn over the card so that they can't see the word.
- Build the word using the letter cards.
- Turn over the card to check the word.
- Write the word.

Sight Words

Personal Dictionary Have students write *said* in their personal dictionaries.

ABC Order Select sight word cards and have students put the cards in alphabetical order.

Scrambled Words Write these scrambled sentences on cards: "hot pan The is not"; "Sam see the cat said"; "The pup for is Nan"; "cat The in is the hut"; "a net has Ben." Have students choose a card and rewrite a sentence.

Phonological Awareness

Identify and Produce Rhyme
- Say the words *net* and *pet*. Remind students that these words rhyme because they have the same sounds at the end. Repeat the words.
- Reread the poem *The Red Hen* and have students listen for rhyming words. Have them clap each time you say two rhyming words.
- Say the following pairs of words and ask students if the words rhyme: *set/pet*, *red/hen*, *pat/rat*, *pup/hut*, *wig/wag*, *chair/bear*, *Ben/pen*, *wish/dish.*
- Repeat the rhyming pairs and ask students to tell you what sounds they hear at the end of both words.

Assessment Tip: To assess individual students' ability to recognize rhyming words, call on them one at a time as you say a word pair.

Blending Sounds

- Have students blend the words *pen*, *rob*, *cup*, and *men*, using the procedure for Day One.

Spelling Words

Review
- Review the week's spelling words by having students write them several times.
- Provide pairs of students with blackline master 2. While one student reads the words, the other student writes each word.
- If a word is spelled correctly, the partner puts a check mark beside it. If a word is spelled incorrectly, the partner may provide prompts. If the second spelling of the word is correct, the partner places a check mark in the "Second Try" column.

Assessment Tip: Collect students' completed blackline masters and note which words gave them difficulty.

Sight Words

Review
- Write the words *are, have, a, and, for, has, is, no, of, said, see, the,* and **with** on the board.
- Write a story starter, such as "Pam has a cat," on the board. Read the sentence with the class as you point to each word.
- Ask students which words on the list appear in the sentence. Circle the words **has** and **a**.
- Have students continue the story by making up sentences, using the sight words and known decodable words.

Decodable Book

- Read the decodable book *Mem the Hen* with the remaining small groups of students. Assign blackline master 4 and Independent Activities for the rest of the class.

Assessment Tip: Use the completed blackline masters to assess how well students can identify the middle sounds in words.

Spelling Assessment

Use the following procedure to assess students' spelling of the Unit 14 words.
• Say each spelling word and use it in a sentence.
• Have students write the word on a piece of paper.
• Continue with the next word on the list.
• When students have finished, collect their papers.
• Record their progress on a spelling record sheet in the Assessment Guide.

 ## Small Group Activities

The following small group activities can be used to provide hands-on practice for students who need additional support. Assign blackline master 5 and Independent Activities for the rest if the class.

 ### PHONOLOGICAL AWARENESS

Medial /e/ Say the following words slowly: ***bell, can, nest, pan, dress, sled, wig, red, web.*** Have students hold up three fingers when they hear a word that has the ***/e/*** sound.

Rhyme Have students draw a cat on one side of a sheet of paper and a pot on the other side. Say the following words and have students show the cat for words that rhyme with ***cat*** and the pot for words that rhyme with ***pot: bat, not, cot, mat, dot, sat, fat, tot.***

 ### SOUND/SYMBOL RELATIONSHIPS

Sound Concentration Place decodable word cards **man, let, bit, hop, fun, tip, ten, pin, rob,** and **hum** facedown in rows on a table. Have a student turn over two cards and read the words. If the words have the same middle sound, the student keeps the cards and plays again. If the words do not have the same middle sound, the student turns the cards facedown, and the next student has a turn.

Word Building Using letter cards, show students how to make the word ***met***. Say each sound as you make the word. Give students letter cards **e, m, n, p,** and **t.** Ask them to build the word ***met*** on their workmats. Have students change a letter to make ***men***. Then have them change a letter to make ***ten***. Finally, have them change a letter to make ***pen***.

 ### BLENDING

Blending Practice 1 Use letter cards to make ***met***. Model for students how you sound out the word ***met***. Ask students to sound out the word with you.

 ### SPELLING

Tap and Spell Have students say the word ***rap*** with you and tap the number of sounds they hear. Then have them tap three times, once for each sound, and say the letter for the sound: [tap] ***r***, [tap] ***a***, [tap] ***p***. Continue with the week's spelling words.

Spell and Jump Select the spelling words from the decodable word cards. Have students read a word, squat, and start spelling the word. With each letter, they stand a little higher. When the word is said in its entirety, students jump.

 ### SIGHT WORDS

Read the Cards Select five sight word cards. Give each student a card and have him or her take turns reading their words. Then have students exchange cards.

Word Find Assign a sight word to pairs of students. Have them look in familiar books for sentences that have their words. Then have partners take turns reading their sentences aloud while the rest of the group identifies the sight words.

Student Name _____ Assessment Date _____

Phonological Awareness: Producing Rhyme

Directions: Say the rhyming pair. Then ask the student to say another real or nonsense word that rhymes with the pair. Record the student's response. **Example:** light/bite. *Kite.*

place/case		fluff/stuff			
check/speck		missed/wrist			
oak/stroke		please/bees		**Score**	**/6**

Phonemic Awareness: Segmenting Onset and Rime

Directions: Say the word. Have the student say the first sound followed by the rest of the word and then say the whole word. If the student segments the word correctly, put a ✔. If the student's response is incorrect, record the error. **Example:** bat. /b/ /at/, bat.

doll (/d/ /oll/, doll)		cup (/k/ /up/, cup)			
jet (/j/ /et/, jet)		miss (/m/ /iss/, miss)			
pat (/p/ /at/, pat)		neck (/n/ /eck/, neck)		**Score**	**/6**

Phonics: Segmenting and Blending Sounds

Directions: Explain that these nonsense words use sounds the student has been learning. Have the student point to each word on the corresponding student sheet, say each sound, and then blend the sounds together. Put a ✔ if the student's response is correct. If the student misses the word, record the error. **Example:** han. /h/ /a/ n/, han.

reb (/r/ /e/ /b/, reb)		fup (/f/ /u/ /p/, fup)			
com (/k/ /o/ /m/, com)		nep (/n/ /e/ /p/, nep)			
hes (/h/ /e/ /s/, hes)		rin (/r/ /i/ /n/, rin)		**Score**	**/6**

Sight Word

Directions: Have the student point to the sight word on the corresponding student sheet and read it as quickly as possible. Put a ✔ if the student successfully reads the word and an **X** if the student hesitates more than a few seconds. If the student misses the word, record the error.

said		**Score**	**/1**

UNIT 15 Gg

Unit Objectives

Students will:

- Identify the /g/ sound
- Associate the letter Gg with the /g/ sound
- Identify initial and final sounds
- Segment and blend onset and rime

- Identify and produce rhyme
- Blend CVC words
- Read the sight words I, me, you
- Spell CVC words using g and letters previously learned

Day 1

BLM 1

BLM 6

Letter Cards: **b, e, g, I, m, o, r, u, y**

Spelling Transparency

Picture Word Cards:
ball, bat, bell, gate, goat, goose, guitar, rabbit, ring, rug

Day 2

BLM 1

BLM 7

Decodable Word Cards for Unit 15

Sight Word Cards for Unit 15

Letter Cards: **b, g, h, p, r**

Spelling Transparency

Picture Word Cards:
goat, map, rug, tub

Day 3

BLM 1

BLM 3

BLM 8

Spelling Transparency

Day 4

BLM 1

BLM 2

BLM 4

Decodable Word Cards for Unit 15

Letter Cards for Unit 15

Day 5

BLM 5

Letter Cards for Unit 15

Decodable Word Cards for Unit 15

Sight Word Cards for Unit 15

Quick-Check Student Sheet

Picture Word Cards for Unit 15

UNIT 15 Gg

Poetry Poster

Student Workmat

Letter Frieze Card

Decodable Book

Poetry CD

Core Materials

All print resources can be downloaded from http://phonicsresources.benchmarkeducation.com.

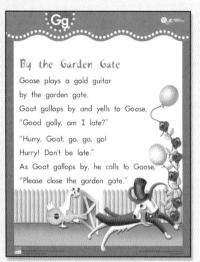

**Poetry Poster
(Front)**

Letter Frieze Card

**Picture Word
Cards**

 Phonemic Awareness

Use the Poetry Poster
- Read aloud or play the recording of the poem *By the Garden Gate*.
- Have students listen for words that begin with the /**g**/ sound as you read the sentence "Goose plays a gold guitar by the garden gate."
- Reread the poem and have students make the motion of strumming a guitar each time they hear the /**g**/ sound.

Distribute blackline master 6 and instruct students to complete it at home.

Sound/Symbol Relationships

Model
- Display letter frieze card **Gg**. Explain that the letter **Gg** stands for the /**g**/ sound, as in the word ***goose***.
- Reread the poem *By the Garden Gate*, and invite students to read along with you.
- Point to words in the poem that begin with the letter ***g***. Say each word aloud and ask students to say the word with you.

Practice with the Letter Cards
- Distribute letter cards **b**, **g**, and **r**. Ask students to line up the cards on their workmats.
- Ask students to pull down each letter card and say the letter name, then push it back up and say the letter sound.
- Have them pull down each letter card again, saying a word that starts with that sound.
- Ask them to push up the letter card that starts the word ***gas***. (Repeat with the words ***bird*** and ***rug***.)

Practice with the Picture Cards
- Place letter cards **b**, **g**, and **r** in the pocket chart.
- Place picture cards **ball**, **goat**, and **rug** under the corresponding letters while you say the name of the letter and the name of the object in the picture.
- Hold up picture card **gate**. Have students say ***gate*** with you.
- Ask: *Does* **gate** *begin like* **ball**, **goat**, *or* **rug**?
- Place picture card **gate** under letter card **g**. Say: **Gate** *begins like* **goat**, *so I am putting picture card* **gate** *under the letter* **g**.
- Repeat with picture cards **bell**, **bat**, **goose**, **guitar**, **rabbit**, and **ring**.

P+A+M **Blending Sounds**

Review
- Hold up letter frieze cards of previously taught sounds one at a time. Ask students to say the sound each letter stands for.

Model
- Write the word ***rim*** on the board. Sound out the word, moving your hand under each letter while blending the sounds. (/**rrrriiiimmmm**/) Then say the word.
- Ask students to sound out the word with you.

Practice with the Word Lists
- Distribute blackline master 1.
- Have students point to the word ***rim***. Ask them to sound out the word with you. Then ask them to say the word at regular speed.
- Repeat with the words ***bop***, ***map*** and ***tug***. Then have students sound out the words in random order.

 **Spelling Words**

Model
- Use the spelling transparency. Place counters under the second set of boxes on the transparency.
- Say: *Today we are going to learn to spell* **men** *and* **bin**. *Watch and listen as I say* **men** *slowly:* /**mmmmeeeennnn**/.
- As you say /**mmmm**/, push a counter into the first box. Then say /**eeee**/ as you push a counter into the second box and /**nnnn**/ as you push a counter into the third box. Repeat the steps.
- Model recording the letters for the sounds on the transparency. Say: *The first sound is* /**mmmm**/. *I know that the letter* **m** *stands for the* /**m**/ *sound. I'll write the letter* **m** *in the first box. Let's listen for the second sound:* /**meeee**/. *I hear* /**e**/. *I know that the letter* **e** *stands for the* /**e**/ *sound, so I will write* **e** *in the second box. Let's listen for the last sound:* /**mennnn**/. *I hear* /**n**/. *I know that the letter* **n** *stands for the* /**n**/ *sound, so I will write* **n** *in the last box.*
- Have students blend the sounds to check the spelling of the word.

Practice with the Workmat
- Instruct students to place counters under the second set of boxes on side 2 of their workmats.
- Ask students to slowly articulate the word *men* as they push the counters into the boxes.
- Have them identify and record the letters that stand for the sounds they hear.
- Have students practice writing *men* on side 1 of their workmats. .

Repeat the modeling and guided practice with the second spelling word, *bin*.

 Sight Words

Review
- Write the words *said*, *have*, *are*, *with*, *for*, *no*, and *cannot* on the board and read the words with students.
- Dim the lights and shine a flashlight on one of the words. Have students read the word together and spell it in the air with their fingers.
- Have volunteers shine the flashlight on words for the rest of the class to read and spell.

Introduce
- Use the pocket chart and letter cards to model how to spell the new word, *you*. Say: *This is the word* **you**. *It is made up of the letters* **y**, **o**, *and* **u**.
- Point to the word and say it. Then have students say the word.
- Follow the steps to introduce the words *I* and *me*.

Write
- Have students write the words *I*, *me*, and *you* on side 1 of their workmats, using the words in the pocket chart as models.

DAY 2

Independent Activities

Phonemic Awareness

Picture Cards Provide picture cards in the literacy center. Students can:
- take one card and find another with the same middle sound
- take two cards, name the pictures, and tell if the words begin with the same sound
- separate the cards that start with /g/
- sort picture cards according to their ending sounds

Collage Have students look in magazines for things that start with /g/. They can cut out the pictures and make a collage.

Listen Have students listen to the recording of the poem *By the Garden Gate* in the listening center.

Sound/Symbol Relationships

Pick, Read, and Write Make several copies of sight and decodable words and place them in a box. Students can take a card, and read and write the word.

Ending Sounds Display letter cards **g**, **b**, and **p**. Have students choose a letter and write a word that ends with the sound that letter stands for.

Initial Sounds Display letter cards **g**, **r**, **b**, and **h**. Have students draw a picture of something that begins with each letter.

Letter Toss Draw six large boxes on a large sheet of paper. Write **g**, **r**, **b**, **h**, **p**, and **f** in the boxes. Place the paper on the floor. Students can:
- throw a beanbag onto a box and say the sound the letter stands for
- throw a beanbag onto a box and say a word that begins with the sound the letter stands for

 Phonemic Awareness

Use the Poetry Poster
- Display the picture on the back of the poetry poster and have students name all the objects in the picture.
- Point to the girl in the picture and say the word **girl.** Ask: *What sound do you hear at the beginning of the word?*
- Ask students to point to other things in the picture whose names start with /g/.

 Sound/Symbol Relationships

Sort the Decodable Word Cards
- Place picture cards **goat**, **map**, **rug**, and **tub** in the pocket chart. Have students say the name of the object on each card.
- Show students decodable word card **gap** and have them blend the word.
- Ask students if **gap** begins like **goat**, **map**, **rug**, or **tub**. Then place the card under picture card **goat**.
- Repeat with decodable word cards **Gus**, **man**, **mop**, **ram**, **rub**, **tab**, and **tug**.

Distribute blackline master 7 and instruct students to complete it at home.

Assessment Tip: Select students whom you wish to assess and ask them to place the word cards according to initial or final sounds. Assign Independent Activities for the rest of the class.

 Blending Sounds

- Have students blend the words **bag**, **gum**, **tab**, and **get**.

 Spelling Words

- Review the words **men** and **bin** by having students write the words several times.
- Follow the procedure for Day One to model and practice the words ***tag*** and ***get***.

Assessment Tip: Note students who do not slowly articulate the sounds when spelling a word, and provide extra modeling.

Sight Words

Review
- Practice the sight words ***said***, ***have***, ***are***, ***with***, ***for***, ***no***, and ***cannot*** by showing students the sight word cards and having them read the words quickly.
- Line up the cards on the board ledge. Provide clues about a word and have students pick out the word to which you are referring. For example, say: *This word rhymes with* **door**. *This word ends with the letter* **r**.

Phonemic Awareness

Segment and Blend Onset and Rhyme
- Say the word **hot**, segmenting it into its onset and rime: **/h/ /ot/**. Have students repeat the onset and rime with you several times.
- Say: *The beginning sound in **hot** is /h/. The middle and ending sounds are /ot/. We can say these sounds separately: /h/ /ot/. Then we can blend these sounds: /hot/.*
- Have students say the word several times.
- Have students segment the following words into their onsets and rimes and then blend them to make the words: **bug**, **rag**, **gum**, **rip**.

 ## Blending Sounds

- Have students blend the words **hot**, **bag**, **rug**, and **gag**.

 ## Spelling Words

- Review the words **men**, **bin**, **tag**, and **get** by having students write them several times.
- Follow the procedure for Day One to model and practice the words **beg** and **rug**.

 ## Sight Words

- Write **I**, **has**, **me**, **see**, **the**, and **you** on the board. Read the words with students.
- Have students identify which words on the board they hear in the sentences as you say: *Does John **see** a clown? **The** dog barks loudly. **You** put your books away. Ken gave **me** an apple. **I** drew a picture. Liz **has** a brother and two sisters.*
- Have students write each word on their workmats, using the words on the board as models.

Distribute blackline master 8 and instruct students to complete it at home.

Decodable Book

Work with small groups of students to read the decodable book *Get the Gum* on Days Three and Four. Assign blackline master 3 and Independent Activities for the rest of the class on Day Three.

Introduce the Book
- Display the cover of the book. Point to the title, *Get the Gum*, and have students sound out the words as you run your finger under them.
- Ask: *What do you see in the picture? What do you do with gum? Do you like gum?*

Read the Book
- Give each student a copy of the book and have students turn to page 2. Instruct them to put their fingers on the first word and sound it out: */Kaaann/.*
- Have students point to the next word: **you**. Remind them that this is a word they learned this week.
- Have students continue pointing to each word in the sentence, sounding out decodable words and saying the sight words quickly.
- Have students read the whole sentence at normal speed.
- Point out the quotation marks and explain to students that these marks tell them what Gus said.
- If students can sound out the words without difficulty, have them whisper-read the rest of the text.
- If students have difficulty, continue to guide them page by page.

Discuss the Book
- When students have finished reading, ask: *Where is Gus? Why can't he get the gum? Where is Tam? Where is Ben? Who gets the gum for Gus?*

**Poetry Poster
(Back)**

Decodable Book

 **SUPPORT TIPS**
for English Language Learners

Develop/reinforce the response to a question *I cannot*
- Before reading, show students objects, or pictures of familiar objects. Ask: *Can you see the ____?*
- Accept the single-word response *Yes*, and model the complete response: *Yes, I can.*
- Cover or hide an object and ask question again.
- Accept the single-word response *No*, and model the complete response: *No, I **cannot**.*
- Put the object out of reach. Ask: *Can you get the ____?* Accept the single-word response *No*, and model the complete response: *No, I **cannot** get the ____.*
- Have students work in pairs or a small group to continue the activity.

DAY 4

Independent Activities

Decodable Book

Independent Practice After students have read the decodable book in a small group, have them read the book independently or with a friend.

Fluency Practice Have students practice reading the story. Record their readings. Play the recordings so that students may review the readings.

Write and Draw Have students use decodable word cards to make a new sentence for a page in the book.

Spelling

As words are introduced each day, write them on index cards and place them in the literacy center. Ensure that the letter cards needed to build the words are in the center. Students can use the following procedure to spell words.
• Choose a word card.
• Use their fingers and eyes to read the word.
• Turn over the card so that they can't see the word.
• Build the word using the letter cards.
• Turn over the card to check the word.
• Write the word.

Sight Words

Personal Dictionary Have students write *I*, *me*, and *you* in their personal dictionaries.

Word Search Give students self-stick notes and word cards **a, for, I, me, no, the, said,** and **you**. Have them look for the words in the room and mark the words with self-stick notes.

Phonological Awareness

Identify and Produce Rhyme
• Say the words *rag* and *sag*. Remind students that these words rhyme because they have the same sounds at the end.
• Reread the poem *By the Garden Gate* and have students clap each time you say a rhyming word.
• Ask students if these word pairs rhyme: *got/hot, goose/moose, play/plan, gold/cold, gate/late, yell/ball.*
• Repeat the rhyming pairs, and ask students to tell you what sounds they hear at the end of the words.
• Have students tell you rhyming words for the words *gag*, *big*, and *gab.*

Assessment Tip: To check which students can or cannot identify rhyming words, call on them individually as you say a word pair. Work with students who are having difficulty producing rhyme in a small group setting. Assign Independent Activities for the rest of the class.

 ## Blending Sounds

• Have students blend the words *let*, *ran*, *sag*, and *rag*, using the procedure for Day One.

Spelling Words

Review
• Review the week's words by having students write them several times on their workmats.
• Provide pairs of students with blackline master 2. While one student reads the spelling words, the other student writes each word.
• If a word is spelled correctly, the partner puts a check mark beside it. If a word is incorrect, the partner may provide prompts. If the second spelling is correct, the partner places a check mark in the "Second Try" column.

Assessment Tip: Collect students' completed blackline masters and note which words gave them difficulty.

 ## Sight Words

Review
• Write the words *have*, *said*, *no*, *I*, *me*, and *you* on the board.
• Focusing on one word at a time, have students spell the word aloud as you point to each letter. Then erase the word, say the word, and have students spell it on their own.

 ## Decodable Book

• Read the decodable book *Get the Gum* with the remaining small groups of students. Assign blackline master 4 and Independent Activities for the rest of the class.

Assessment Tip: Use the completed blackline master to assess how well students can make connections between sounds and the letters that stand for those sounds.

Spelling Assessment

Use the following procedure to assess students' spelling of the Unit 15 words.
• Say each spelling word and use it in a sentence.
• Have students write the word on a piece of paper.
• Continue with the next word on the list.
• When students have finished, collect their papers and analyze their spellings of misspelled words.
• Record their progress on a spelling record sheet and provide extra practice as needed.

 # Small Group Activities

The following small group activities can be used to provide hands-on practice for students who need additional support. Assign blackline master 5 and Independent Activities for the rest of the class.

 ### PHONOLOGICAL AWARENESS

Initial /g/ Ask students to tap their pencils on their desks if they hear the /g/ sound as you say these words: *Gus, gum, hen, get, gate, tub, got, go, cap, goat.*

Final Sounds Say: *Listen to this word:* **tap.** *I hear* /p/ *at the end. Listen again to see if you hear* /p/. Slowly say the following words and have students tell you the ending sound of each: *man, fat, am, hug, Bob, top, sit, nap.*

Rhyme Read aloud familiar poems and have students clap when they hear rhyming words. Ask students what the rhyming words are.

 ### SOUND/SYMBOL RELATIONSHIPS

Picture Sort Give each student one (or more) of the **b**, **g**, or **r** picture cards. Then point to the letter frieze card **Gg** and ask students if their picture starts with the sound that the letter stands for. Have the students holding **g** picture cards place their cards under the letters **Gg**. Continue with the **b** and **r** picture cards.

Word Sort Place decodable word cards **gap**, **man**, **ram**, and **tug** in the pocket chart. Have students read each word, focusing on the beginning sound. Then distribute picture cards **guitar**, **goat**, **mop**, **mitten**, **rabbit**, **ring**, **tiger**, and **tent**. Have students name each picture and place it under the word card that has the same beginning sound.

 ### BLENDING

Blending Practice Have students use letter cards to construct the words *fed*, *dab*, *bad*, and *had*, and then blend the words.

What's the Word? Say: */daaaad/*. Ask: *What word is this?* Have a volunteer write the word on the board. Follow the same procedure with the words *red*, *set*, and *dig.*

 ### SPELLING

Say and Spell Model saying and writing the spelling words. Have students say and write the words with you.

Spelling Patterns Write __*a*__ on chart paper. Tell students that you want to make the word *tag.* Have one student write the letter for the beginning sound and another write the letter for the ending sound. Have students use the pattern __*e*__ to make the words *men* and *get*, and the pattern __*i*__ to make the word *bin.*

Word Change Write the spelling words on the board. Have students write the answers to riddles. Say: *Start with* **bag.** *Change the* **a** *to* **e**. *What's the word? Start with* **bug**. *Change the* **b** *to* **r**. *What's the word?*

 ### SIGHT WORDS

Word Cards Place sight word cards **and**, **I**, **me**, **is**, **of**, **for**, **see**, and **you** faceup on a table. Say: *I will say a word. Point to the word I say, then repeat the word.* After a student correctly identifies and repeats your word, have him or her say a word and call on another student to respond.

Make Sentences Show one of sight word cards **I**, **has**, **me**, **see**, **the**, and **you** to a student. Say: *Read the word and make up an oral sentence using the word.* Then show the same card to another student. Say: *Make up a different sentence using this word.* Continue until all students have a chance to make a sentence.

Student Name _____ Assessment Date _____

Phonological Awareness: Identifying Rhyme

Directions: Say each set of words. Then have the student say the two words that rhyme. Put a ✔ if the student's response is correct. If not, record the words the student chooses.
Example: mat/hat/lid. *Mat, hat.*

bait/wait/sight (*bait, wait*)			
come/came/some (*come, some*)			
leg/tag/peg (*leg, peg*)			
meet/feet/rate (*meet, feet*)			
face/hiss/miss (*hiss, miss*)			
did/dude/rude (*dude, rude*)		**Score**	**/6**

Phonemic Awareness: Blending Onset and Rime

Directions: Say the first sound of the word followed by the rest of the word. Then have the student say the whole word. If the student says the word correctly, put a ✔. If the student misses the word, record the error.
Example: /b/ /at/. *Bat.*

/g/ /as/ (*gas*)		/s/ /ip/ (*sip*)		
/b/ /eg/ (*beg*)		/d/ /eck/ (*deck*)		
/k/ /ut/ (*cut*)		/g/ /ab/ (*gab*)		**Score** **/6**

Phonics: Segmenting and Blending Sounds

Directions: Explain that these nonsense words use sounds the student has been learning. Have the student point to each word on the corresponding student sheet, say each sound, and then blend the sounds together. Put a ✔ if the student's response is correct. If the student misses the word, record the error.
Example: ren. */r/ /e/ n/, ren.*

gos (*/g/ /o/ /s/, gos*)		pob (*/p/ /o/ /b/, pob*)		
fum (*/f/ /u/ /m/, fum*)		gac (*/g/ /a/ /k/, gac*)		
gif (*/g/ /i/ /f/, gif*)		rup (*/r/ /u/ /p/, rup*)		**Score** **/6**

Sight Words

Directions: Have the student point to the first sight word on the corresponding student sheet and read across the line, saying each word as quickly as possible. Put a ✔ if the student successfully reads the word and an **X** if the student hesitates more than a few seconds. If the student misses the word, record the error.

I		me	
you			**Score** **/3**

Unit Objectives

Students will:

- Identify the /d/ sound
- Associate the letter Dd with the /d/ sound
- Blend phonemes
- Identify and produce rhyme
- Decode CVC words
- Read the sight words come, here, to
- Spell CVC words using d and letters previously learned

Day 1

BLM 1

BLM 6

Letter Cards: **d, g, r**

Spelling Transparency

Picture Word Cards: **dinosaur, dish, dog, duck, gate, goat, guitar, rabbit, ring, rug**

Day 2

BLM 1

BLM 7

Decodable Word Cards for Unit 16

Letter Cards: **a, b, d, e, f, g, i, p, n, r, t**

Spelling Transparency

Picture Word Cards: **box, dinosaur, goat, ring**

Day 3

BLM 1

BLM 3

BLM 8

Spelling Transparency

Day 4

BLM 1

BLM 2

BLM 4

Day 5

 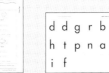

BLM 5

Letter Cards for Unit 16

Sight Word Cards for Unit 16

Quick-Check Student Sheet

Picture Word Cards: **dog, duck, gate, goat, rabbit, rug**

Poetry Posters

Student Workmat

Letter Frieze Card

Decodable Text

Poetry CD

Core Materials

All print resources can be downloaded from http://phonicsresources.benchmarkeducation.com

**Poetry Poster
(Front)**

Letter Frieze Card

**Picture Word
Cards**

Phonemic Awareness

Use the Poetry Poster

- Read aloud or play the recording of the poem *Dot.*
- Have students listen for the /*d*/ sound as you say the sentence "Dot likes to dig and dig."
- Reread the poem and have students make a digging motion whenever they hear the /*d*/ sound.

Distribute blackline master 6 and instruct students to complete it at home.

Sound/Symbol Relationships

Model

- Display letter frieze card **Dd.** Explain that the letter **Dd** stands for the /*d*/ sound at the beginning of **dog.**
- Reread the poem *Dot*, inviting students to read along with you.
- Point to words in the poem that begin with the letter **d.** Say each word aloud and ask students to say the words with you.

Practice with the Letter Cards

- Distribute letter cards **d**, **g**, and **r.** Ask students to line up the cards on their workmats.
- Have students pull down each letter card and say the letter name, then push it back up and say the letter sound.
- Ask them to pull down each letter card again, saying a word that starts with that sound.
- Have them push up the letter card that starts the word **deer.** (Repeat with the words **Gus** and **rabbit.**)

Practice with the Picture Cards

- Place letter cards **d**, **g**, and **r** in the pocket chart.
- Place picture cards **duck**, **goat**, and **rabbit** under the corresponding letters while you say the name of the letter and the name of the object in the picture.
- Hold up picture card **dog.** Have students say **dog** with you, emphasizing the initial sound.
- Ask: *Does* **dog** *begin like* **duck**, **goat**, *or* **rabbit**?
- Place picture card **dog** under letter card **d.** Say: **Dog** *begins like* **duck**, *so I am putting picture card* **dog** *under the letter* **d.**
- Repeat with picture cards **dish**, **dinosaur**, **gate**, **ring**, **guitar**, and **rug.**

Blending Sounds

Review

- Hold up letter frieze cards of previously taught sounds. Ask students to say the sound each letter stands for.

Model

- Write the word **net** on the board. Sound out the word, moving your hand under each letter while blending the sounds. (/*nnnneeeet*/) Then say the word.
- Ask students to sound out the word with you.

Practice with the Word Lists

- Distribute blackline master 1.
- Have students point to the word **net.** Ask them to sound out the word with you. Then ask them to say the word at regular speed.
- Repeat with the words **bag**, **fed**, and **bug.** Then have students sound out the words in random order.

Spelling Words

Model

- Use the spelling transparency. Place counters under the second set of boxes on the transparency.
- Say: *Today we are going to learn to spell* **bag** *and* **pen.** *Watch and listen as I say* **bag** *slowly:* /**baaaag**/.
- As you say /**b**/, push a counter into the first box. Then say /**aaaa**/ as you push a counter into the second box and /**g**/ as you push a counter into the third box. Repeat the steps.
- Model recording the letters for the sounds on the transparency. Say: *The first sound is* /**b**/. *I know that the letter* **b** *stands for the* /**b**/ *sound. I'll write the letter* **b** *in the first box. Let's listen for the second sound:* /**baaaa**/. *I hear* /**a**/. *I know that the letter* **a** *stands for the* /**a**/ *sound, so I will write* **a** *in the second box. Let's listen for the last sound:* /**bag**/. *I hear* /**g**/. *I know that the letter* **g** *stands for the* /**g**/ *sound, so I will write* **g** *in the last box.*
- Have students blend the sounds to check the spelling of the word.

Practice with the Workmat

- Instruct students to place counters under the second set of boxes on side 2 of their workmats.
- Ask students to slowly articulate the word *bag* as they push the counters into the boxes.
- Have them identify and record the letters that stand for the sounds they hear.
- Have students practice writing *bag* on side 1 of their workmats.

Repeat the modeling and guided practice with the second spelling word, *pen*.

 # Sight Words

Review

- Write the words *for*, *has*, *is*, *me*, *of*, *the*, and *you* on the board.
- Say the following sentences and have students raise their hand when they hear one of the words listed: *I will share my popcorn with* **you**. *Pedro* **has** *a swing in his yard. My apple* **is** *juicy. Will* **you** *call* **me** *tomorrow? Who* **is** *that gift* **for**? *I want a glass* **of** *water. Ben colored* **the** *picture.*

Introduce

- Write the words *come*, *here*, and *to* on the board. Read each word and have students repeat the words with you.
- Spell each word aloud while students spell the words in the air with their fingers.

Write

- Have students write the words *come*, *here*, and *to* on side 1 of their workmats, using the words on the board as models.

DAY 2

Independent Activities

Phonemic Awareness

Picture Cards Provide picture cards in the literacy center. Students can:
• separate the cards that start with /d/
• take two cards, name the pictures, and tell if the words have the same middle sound
• sort picture cards according to their ending sounds
• choose a card and draw a picture of another object that has the same ending sound.

Listen Have students listen to the recording of the poem *Dot* in the listening center.

Sound/Symbol Relationships

Ending Sounds Display letter cards **d**, **g**, **n**, and **b**. Have students choose a letter and write a word that ends with the sound that letter stands for.

Silly Stories Have students pick one of letter cards **d**, **g**, **n**, and **b**, and write a silly sentence using words that begin with the letter.

Scrambled Words Write the words *red*, *sad*, *dip*, *pug*, *tag*, *net*, *rub*, *hum*, and *tab* in scrambled form (*edr*, *dsa*, *ipd*, *ugp*, *gta*, *nte*, *urb*, *mhu*, *atb*) on index cards. Have students write the words correctly and then read them aloud.

Timed Words Give letter cards **a**, **b**, **d**, **e**, **f**, **g**, **i**, **p**, **n**, **r**, and **t** to students. Set a 10-minute time limit and have students make as many three-letter words as they can with the letter cards.

 ## Phonemic Awareness

Use the Poetry Poster
• Display the picture on the back of the poetry poster and have students name all the objects in the picture.
• Point to the duck in the picture and say the word *duck*, stressing the beginning sound. Ask: *What sound do you hear at the beginning of the word?*
• Ask students to point to something in the picture that starts with /d/.

 ## Sound/Symbol Relationships

Sort the Decodable Word Cards
• Place picture cards **box**, **dinosaur**, **goat**, and **ring** in the pocket chart. Have students say the name of the object on each card.
• Show students decodable word card **bit** and have them blend the word.
• Ask students if **bit** begins like **box**, **dinosaur**, **goat**, or **ring**. Then place the card under picture card **box**.
• Repeat with decodable word cards **bop**, **dim**, **dip**, **gab**, **gum**, **ram**, and **rob**.

Distribute blackline master 7 and instruct students to complete it at home.

Assessment Tip: Note which students have difficulty associating a sound with its letter. Provide extra practice with those sounds and letters. Assign Independent Activities for the rest of the class.

P+A+M Blending Sounds

• Have students blend the words *dad*, *red*, *set*, and *dig*, using the procedure for Day One.

 ## Spelling Words

• Review the words *bag* and *pen* by having students write the words several times.
• Follow the procedure for Day One to model and practice the words *dig* and *had*.

Assessment Tip: Note students who do not slowly articulate the sounds when spelling a word, and provide extra modeling.

 ## Sight Words

• Write the words *and*, *are*, *said*, and *see* on the board. Have students clap once for each letter as you spell the words together.
• Write the words *come*, *to*, and *here* on the board. Say the name of each letter as you write the words.
• Read the words aloud and have students trace the words on their palms with their fingers.
• Have students take turns telling something about their school using the words *and*, *are*, *said*, *see*, *come*, *to* and *here*.

Phonemic Awareness

Blend Phonemes
- Say: *I am going to slowly say the sounds that make up a word. I want you to tell me what the word is.* /**d**/ /**iiii**/ /**mmmm**/.
- Ask: *What is the word?*
- Repeat with the words *bad*, *run*, *bit*, *dot*, *map*, and *tin*.

 ## Blending Sounds

- Have students blend the words *rob*, *cut*, *bed*, and *did*, using the procedure for Day One.

 ## Spelling Words

- Review the words *bag*, *pen*, *dig*, and *had* by having students write them several times on side 1 of their workmats.
- Follow the procedure for Day One to model and practice the words *red* and *did*.

 ## Sight Words

- Write the words *come*, *here*, *I*, *me*, *no*, *of*, and *you* on the board.
- Point to each letter in one of the words and ask individual students to say the letter names as you point to them. Continue with the other words.

Distribute blackline master 8 and instruct students to complete it at home.

Decodable Book

Work with small groups of students to read the decodable book *The Red Pen* on days three and four. Assign blackline master 3 and Independent Activities for the rest of the class on Day Three.

Introduce the Book
- Display the cover of the book. Point to the title, *The Red Pen*, and have students sound out the words as you run your finger under them.
- Ask: *What do you see in the picture? What does Dan have? What do you do with a pen?*

Read the Book
- Give each student a copy of the book and have students turn to page 2. Ask them to put their fingers on the first word. Have them run their fingers under the word as they sound it out: /**Daaaannnn**/.
- Have students point to the next two words. Remind them that these are words they don't sound out. Have them say the words: *has*, *a*.
- Have students run their fingers under the next three words as they sound them out: /**ffffaaaat**/, /**rrrreeeed**/, /**peeeennnn**/.
- Have students read the whole sentence at normal speed.
- Repeat with the next sentence on the page.
- If students can sound out the words without difficulty, have them whisper-read the rest of the text.
- If students have difficulty, continue to guide them page by page.

Discuss the Book
- When students have finished reading, ask: *Who takes Dan's fat red pen? What does Tim do with the pen? Who finds Dan's pen?*

**Poetry Poster
(Back)**

Decodable Book

 **SUPPORT TIPS**
for English Language Learners

Develop/reinforce the adjective–noun pattern
- Before reading, give groups of students markers/crayons in a variety of colors and sizes (fat/thin, long/short, etc.).
- Model a request for a specific item: *Give me a **red crayon**.*
- Have students work in pairs to request color-specific items, using the target sentence pattern: *Give me the **adjective noun**.*
- Request an item using two descriptors: *Give me the **fat red marker**.*
- Have students request a specific item from you and model the target language structure: *Give me the **adjective adjective noun**.*
- Have students work in pairs again, this time requesting items using two descriptors.

Independent Activities

Decodable Book

Independent Reading After students have read the decodable book in a small group, have them read the book independently or with a friend.

Read and Draw Have students choose a sentence from the book that has the name **Dan** in it, substitute their name for **Dan**, and draw a picture to go with the sentence.

Spelling

As words are introduced each day, write them on index cards and place them in the literacy center. Ensure that the letter cards needed to build the words are in the center. Students can use the following procedure to spell words.
• Choose a word card.
• Use their fingers and eyes to read the word.
• Turn over the card so that they can't see the word.
• Build the word using the letter cards.
• Turn over the card to check the word.
• Write the word.

Sight Words

Personal Dictionary Have students write **come**, **to**, and **here** in their personal dictionaries.

Complete the Phrase Write words and phrases in columns as shown below.

of	a pan_____ me
and	the pup _____ the cat
for	_____ red cap
the	a tub _____ nuts
	a pad _____ Sam
	_____ tub in the sun
	top _____ the hat
	a rug ___ a bug

Have students copy the phrases and write one of the words to complete each phrase.

Phonological Awareness

Identify and Produce Rhyme

• Say the words **had** and **pad**. Ask students what sounds are the same in the words.
• Reread the poem *Dot* and have students listen for rhyming words. Have them clap each time you say two rhyming words.
• Say the following groups of words and have students identify which two words rhyme: **Dan/Dad/man**, **Ben/net/pen**, **dig/dog/big**, **time/dime/dim.**
• Repeat the rhyming pairs and ask students to tell you what sounds they hear at the end of the words.
• Have students say words that rhyme with **Tim**, **Bob**, and **Pam.**

Assessment Tip: Note which students can produce rhyme when asked.

Blending Sounds

• Have students blend the words **fed**, **dab**, **bad**, and **had**, using the procedure for Day One.

Spelling Words

Review

• Review the week's spelling words by having students write them several times on their workmats.
• Provide pairs of students with blackline master 2. While one student reads the words from the list, the other student writes each word.
• If a word is spelled correctly, the partner puts a check mark beside it. If a word is incorrect, the partner may provide prompts. If the second spelling of the word is correct, the partner places a check mark in the "Second Try" column.

Assessment Tip: Collect students' completed blackline masters and note which words gave them difficulty.

Sight Words

Review

• Write the words **a**, **and**, **come**, **has**, **here**, **is**, **said**, **see**, **the**, and **with** on the board.
• Focusing on one word at a time, have students spell the word aloud as you point to each letter.
• Erase one word, say the word, and have students spell it on their own.
• Repeat with the remaining words.

Decodable Book

• Read the decodable book *The Red Pen* with the remaining small groups of students. Assign blackline master 4 and Independent Activities for the rest of the class.

Assessment Tip: Use the completed blackline master to assess how well students can identify words that have the same beginning sound.

Spelling Assessment

Use the following procedure to assess students' spelling of the Unit 16 words.
• Say each spelling word and use it in a sentence.
• Have students write the word on a piece of paper.
• Continue with the next word on the list.
• When students have finished, collect their papers and analyze their spellings of misspelled words.
• Record their progress on a spelling record sheet, and provide extra practice as needed.

 ## Small Group Activities

The following small group activities can be used to provide hands-on practice for students who need additional support. Assign blackline master 5 and Independent Activities for the rest of the class.

 ### PHONOLOGICAL AWARENESS

Initial Sounds 1 Ask students to stand if they hear a word that has the /d/ sound. Say these words: *Dan, dog, goat, door, deer, ring, dime, doll, rug, dish, gorilla.*

Initial Sounds 2 Hold up picture cards **duck, goat, rabbit, dog, gate,** and **rug,** one at a time. Ask students to identify the picture and the beginning sound in the picture name. Then ask them to say another word that has the same beginning sound.

Rhyme Using the word groups from the whole group lesson, ask students to identify the rhyming words. Then have them say a rhyming word for the words *dog, name, hide,* and *duck.*

 ### SOUND/SYMBOL RELATIONSHIPS

Letter Cards Display letter cards **b, d, g,** and **r** in the pocket chart. Say the words *dark, doll,* and *dime.* Point out that these words start with /d/. Point to the letter *d* and remind students that *d* stands for the /d/ sound. Have students listen to the following sets of words and identify the beginning sound and the letter that stands for the sound: *dip/dollar/Dan; Bob/bag/bug; goose/Gus/Game; rice/rag/roof.*

 ### BLENDING

Blending Practice Have students use letter cards to construct the words *fed, dab, bad,* and *had,* and then blend the words.

What's the Word? Say: /daaaad/. Ask: *What word is this?* Have a volunteer write the word on the board. Follow the same procedure with the words *red, set,* and *dig.*

 ### SPELLING

Letter Cards Distribute letter cards **b, a, g, p, e, n, d, d, i, h,** and **r.** Tell students that you are going to say the sounds in the spelling words. After you say each sound, have students hold up the letter that spells the sound.

Guess the Word Write the spelling words on the board. Provide clues and have students guess which word you are thinking of. Say: *I'm thinking of two words that have the same beginning sound. I'm thinking of a word that rhymes with* **tag.**

 ### SIGHT WORDS

Hold up sight word cards **and, are, come, here, see,** and **said** one at a time. Say: *I like to hike* **and** *swim.* Pass sight word card **and** to a student and have him or her make up a sentence using the word. Have students pass the card until each student has had an opportunity to use the word *and* in a sentence. Repeat with the other word cards.

Read the Cards Using sight word cards **come, here, I, me, no, of,** and **you,** choose a card and show it to students. The first student to recognize and say the word collects the card, then draws a card to show. Continue until all cards have been used.

Student Name _____ Assessment Date _____

Phonological Awareness: Producing Rhyme

Directions: Say the rhyming pair. Then ask the student to say another real or nonsense word that rhymes with the pair. Record the student's response. **Example:** light/bite. *Kite.*

snug/plug		blame/frame			
trot/plot		stole/pole			
sweep/sleep		skip/ship		**Score**	**/6**

Phonemic Awareness: Blending Phonemes

Directions: Say the word sound by sound. Then have the student say the word. Put a ✔ if the student's response is correct. If the student misses the word, record the error. **Example:** /d/ /o/ /g/. *Dog.*

/d/ /u/ /g/ (dug)		/s/ /a/ /p/ (sap)			
/m/ /e/ /t/ (met)		/k/ /o/ /b/ (cob)			
/p/ /i/ /n/ (pin)		/d/ /e/ /n/ (den)		**Score**	**/6**

Phonics: Segmenting and Blending Sounds

Directions: Explain that these nonsense words use sounds the student has been learning. Have the student point to each word on the corresponding student sheet, say each sound, and then blend the sounds together. Put a ✔ if the student's response is correct. If the student misses the word, record the error. **Example:** tum. /t/ /u/ m/, *tum.*

dac (/d/ /a/ /k/, dac)		nib (/n/ /i/ /b/, nib)			
pof (/p/ /o/ /f/, pof)		dag (/d/ /a/ /g/, dag)			
dut (/d/ /u/ /t/, dut)		hus (/h/ /u/ /s/, hus)		**Score**	**/6**

Sight Words

Directions: Have the student point to the first sight word on the corresponding student sheet and read across the line, saying each word as quickly as possible. Put a ✔ if the student successfully reads the word and an **X** if the student hesitates more than a few seconds. If the student misses the word, record the error.

come		to			
here				**Score**	**/3**

UNIT 17 Ww

Unit Objectives

Students will:

- Identify the /w/ sound
- Associate the letter Ww with the /w/ sound
- Identify initial /w/
- Segment and blend onset and rime
- Orally blend phonemes
- Blend CVC words
- Read the sight words he, look, my
- Spell CVC words using w and letters previously learned

Day 1

BLM 1

BLM 6

Letter Cards: **d**, **g**, **w**

Spelling Transparency

Picture Word Cards: **dinosaur**, **dog**, **duck**, **gate**, **goat**, **guitar**, **wagon**, **wasp**, **watch**, **web**

Day 2

BLM 1

BLM 7

Decodable Word Cards for Unit 17

Spelling Transparency

Picture Word Cards: **dinosaur**, **guitar**, **ring**, **web**

Day 3

BLM 1

BLM 3

BLM 8

Sight Word Cards for Unit 17

Spelling Transparency

Day 4

BLM 1

BLM 2

BLM 4

Sight Word Cards for Unit 17

Day 5

BLM 5

Letter Cards for Unit 17

Decodable Word Cards for Unit 17

Sight Word Cards for Unit 17

Quick-Check Student Sheet

Poetry Poster

Student Workmat

Letter Frieze Card

Decodable Book

Poetry CD

Core Materials

All print resources can be downloaded from http://phonicsresources.benchmarkeducation.com

Poetry Poster
(Front)

Letter Frieze Card

Picture Word
Cards

Phonemic Awareness

Use the Poetry Poster

• Read aloud or play the recording of the poem *Worm*.
• Say the sentence "Worm lives in a windmill." Have students tell you where they hear /**w**/ in the sentence.
• Reread the poem and have students snap their fingers every time they hear the /**w**/ sound.

Distribute blackline master 6 and instruct students to complete it at home.

Sound/Symbol Relationships

Model

• Display letter frieze card **Ww**. Explain to students that the letter *Ww* stands for the /**w**/ sound, as in the word *watch*.
• Reread the poem *Worm*. Invite students to read along with you.
• Point to words in the poem that begin with /**w**/. Say each word aloud, emphasizing the /**w**/ sound, and ask students to say the words with you.

Practice with the Letter Cards

• Distribute letter cards **d**, **g**, and **w**. Ask students to line up the cards on their workmats.
• Ask students to pull down each letter card and say the letter name, then push it back up and say the letter sound.
• Have them pull down each letter card again, saying a word that has that middle sound.
• Ask students to push up the letter card that starts the word *wag*. (Repeat with the words *dab* and *gap*.)

Practice with the Picture Cards

• Place letter cards **d**, **g**, and **w** in the pocket chart.
• Place picture cards **dog**, **gate**, and **watch** under the corresponding letters while you say the name of the letter and the name of the object in the picture.
• Hold up picture card **web**. Have students say *web* with you, emphasizing the beginning sound.
• Ask: *Does* **web** *begin like* **dog**, **gate**, *or* **watch**?
• Place picture card **web** under letter card **w**. Say: **Web** *begins like* **watch**, *so I am putting picture card* **web** *under the letter* **w**.
• Repeat with picture cards **duck**, **dinosaur**, **goat**, **guitar**, **wagon**, and **wasp**.

Blending Sounds

Review

• Hold up letter frieze cards of previously taught sounds one at a time. Ask students to say the sound each letter stands for.

Model

• Write the word *did* on the board. Sound out the word, moving your hand under each letter while blending the sounds. (/*diiiid*/) Then say the word.
• Ask students to sound out the word with you.

Practice with the Word Lists

• Distribute blackline master 1.
• Have students point to the word *did*. Ask them to sound out the word with you. Then ask them to say the word at regular speed.
• Repeat with the words *sun*, *tag*, and *had*. Then have students sound out the words in random order.

Spelling Words

Model

- Use the spelling transparency. Place counters under the second set of boxes on the transparency.
- Say: *Today we are going to learn to spell* **bed** *and* **pat**. *Watch and listen as I say* **bed** *slowly:* /**beeeed**/. Point out that the word has stop sounds at the beginning and the end.
- As you say /**b**/, push a counter into the first box. Then say /**eeee**/ as you push a counter into the second box and /**d**/ as you push a counter into the third box. Repeat the steps.
- Model recording the letters for the sounds on the transparency. Say: *The first sound is* /**b**/. *I know that the letter* **b** *stands for the* /**b**/ *sound. I'll write the letter* **b** *in the first box. Let's listen for the second sound:* /**beeee**/. *I hear* /**e**/. *I know that the letter* **e** *stands for the* /**e**/ *sound, so I will write* **e** *in the second box. Let's listen for the last sound:* /**bed**/. *I hear* /**d**/. *I know that the letter* **d** *stands for the* /**d**/ *sound, so I will write* **d** *in the last box.*
- Have students blend the sounds to check the spelling of the word.

Practice with the Workmat

- Instruct students to place counters under the second set of boxes on side 2 of their workmats.
- Ask students to slowly articulate the word ***bed*** as they push the counters into the boxes.
- Have students identify and record the letters that stand for the sounds they hear.
- Have students practice writing ***bed*** on side 1 of their workmats.

Repeat the modeling and guided practice with the second spelling word: pat.

Sight Words

Review

- Write the words ***come***, ***for***, ***here***, ***is***, ***no***, ***said***, and ***with*** on the board and ask volunteers to read the words aloud.
- Have students write the letters in the air as you spell the words aloud.
- Have volunteers use the words in an oral sentence.

Introduce

- Write the word ***he*** on the board. Point to the word and say it. Then have students say the word as you point to it.
- Follow the steps to introduce the words ***look*** and ***my***.
- Write these sentences on the board and read them aloud:
  "He can pat the cat."; "My cat has a red rug."; "Look at the cat nap."
- Have volunteers underline the words ***he***, ***my***, and ***look***.

Write

- Have students write the words ***he***, ***look***, and ***my*** on side 1 of their workmats, using the words on the board as models.

Independent Activities

Phonological Awareness

Picture Sorts Provide picture cards in the literacy center. Students can:
- take two picture cards, name the pictures, and tell if the words rhyme
- separate the cards that start with /**w**/
- take a picture card and name a word that has the same middle sound
- match a card with another picture card that has the same beginning sound

Draw Have students fold a sheet of paper in half. On the left side, they can draw pictures of things that have the same beginning sounds. On the right side, they can draw pictures of things that have different beginning sounds.

Listen Have students listen to the recording of the poem *Worm* in the listening center.

Sound/Symbol Relationships

Build Words Place picture cards **cat**, **dog**, **map**, **pan**, **sun**, **tub**, and **web** in the literacy center. Have students choose a card, say the name of the object in the picture, and build the word with letter cards.

Letter Patterns Write the following word patterns on a sheet of paper, three times each: *p___t*, *___un*, *pi___*, *b___g*. Provide copies of the paper. Have students add letters to make words.

Letter Toss Write the letters *c*, *h*, *b*, *r*, *g*, *d*, and *w* on a cup, one cup for each letter. Students can:
- toss a button into a cup and say the sound for the letter
- toss a button into a cup and say a word that begins with the letter's sound

Phonemic Awareness

Use the Poetry Poster
- Show students the picture on the back of the poetry poster and have them name all the objects in the picture.
- Point to the window in the picture and say the word **window**, emphasizing the /**w**/ sound. Ask: *What sound do you hear at the beginning of the word?*
- Ask students to point to something in the picture that starts with /**w**/.

Sound/Symbol Relationships

Sort the Decodable Word Cards
- Place picture cards **dinosaur**, **guitar**, **ring**, and **web** in the pocket chart. Have students say the name of the object on each card.
- Show students decodable word card **dab** and have them blend the word.
- Ask: *Does **dab** begin like **dinosaur**, **guitar**, **ring**, or **web**?* Then place decodable word card **dab** under picture card **dinosaur**.
- Repeat with decodable word cards **dip**, **gab**, **get**, **rap**, **rug**, **wet**, and **wag**.

Assessment Tip: Note which students have difficulty with auditory discrimination and provide additional support in a small group setting. Assign Independent Activities for the rest of the class.

Distribute blackline master 7 and instruct students to complete it at home.

 ## Blending Sounds

- Have students blend the words **win**, **wet**, **hit**, and **gag**, using the procedure for Day One.

Spelling Words

- Review the words **bed** and **pat** by having students write the words several times.
- Follow the procedure for Day One to model and practice the words **wet** and **win**.

Assessment Tip: Note students who do not slowly articulate the sounds when spelling a word, and provide extra modeling.

 ## Sight Words

- Write the words **and**, **come**, **here**, **I**, **me**, **said**, **see**, **the**, and **you** on the board. Say the words one at a time.
- Have pairs of students work together to write a sentence using at least two of the words.
- Have the pairs take turns reading their sentences to the group. Ask the rest of the class to raise their hands when they hear one of the words on the board.

Phonemic Awareness

Blend Phonemes
- Say: *I am going to say the sounds that make up a word. I want you to tell me what the word is:* /**rrrr**/ /**oooo**/ /**b**/.
- Repeat with the words **web**, **wag**, **dip**, **get**, and **fun**.

 Blending Sounds

- Have students blend the words **rob**, **cut**, **wed**, and **wit**.

 Spelling Words

- Review the words **bed**, **pat**, **wet**, and **win** by having students write them several times.
- Follow the procedure for Day One to model and practice the words **wig** and **wed**.

 Sight Words

- Make extra sets of the sight word cards by reproducing the blackline master several times.
- Place students in small groups and give each group a set of sight words. Have students take turns drawing a card, reading it, and placing it facedown at the bottom of the pile.

Distribute blackline master 8 and instruct students to complete it at home.

 Decodable Book

Work with small groups of students to read the decodable book *The Wig* on Days Three and Four. Assign blackline master 3 and Independent Activities for the rest of the class on Day Three.

Introduce the Book
- Display the cover of the book. Point to the title, *The Wig*, and have students read the first word quickly and sound out the second word as you run your finger under it.
- Ask: *What do you see in the picture? What does the boy have on his head? Why do you think he is wearing a wig?*

Read the Book
- Give each student a copy of the book and have them turn to page 2. Have them run their fingers under the first two words as they sound them out: /**Daaaannnn**/, /**Taaaammmm**/.
- Have students point to and read the next word, **and**. Remind them that this is a word they don't sound out.
- Have students continue pointing to the words in the sentence, sounding out the decodable words and saying the sight words quickly.
- Have students read the whole sentence at normal speed.
- Repeat with the rest of the sentences on the page.
- If students are sounding out the words without difficulty, have them whisper-read the rest of the text.
- If students have difficulty, continue to guide them page by page.

Discuss the Book
- When students have finished reading, ask: *What happens to Gus's wig? What does Dan give to Gus? What does Tam give to Gus?*

Poetry Poster (Back)

Decodable Book

ell SUPPORT TIPS
for English Language Learners

Develop/reinforce concept of costume competition
- Before reading, probe for and elicit students' previous experiences with costumes.
- Show a picture of a child in costume. Have students describe the picture and tell about when they wore costumes.
- Have students create their own costumes by using classroom items. Include a mop-head and other props students could use as a wig. You may need to model putting the items on your own head to introduce the idea of a wig.
- While still in costumes, have students describe what the others used to create their costumes. Accept one-word responses, such as **coat** and **hat**, and model the target sentence structure: *Maria has a hat.*
- Have students tell which costume they like best (accept a one-word response). Tally the responses and give the winner a blue ribbon.

Independent Activities

Decodable Book

Independent Reading Have students read the decodable book independently.

Write Have students use words from the book to write a new ending.

Fluency Practice Have students practice reading the story. Then record them. Play the recordings so that students can review their readings.

Spelling

As words are introduced each day, write them on index cards and place them in the literacy center. Ensure that the letter cards needed to build the words are in the center. Students can use the following procedure to spell words.
- Choose a word card.
- Use their fingers and eyes to read the word.
- Turn over the card so that they can't see the word.
- Build the word using the letter cards.
- Turn over the card to check the word.
- Write the word.

Sight Words

Personal Dictionary Have students write *the*, *my*, and *look* in their personal dictionaries.

Sight Word Tally Have students write *and*, *has*, *he*, *is*, *me*, *my*, and *you* in a column on a sheet of paper. Then have them search through decodable books for the words. Each time they find a word, they make a mark next to it on the paper.

 ## Phonemic Awareness

Blend and Segment Onset and Rime
- Model how to segment the word *wet* into its onset and rime. Say: *I hear the /w/ sound in the beginning of the word* **wet**. *I hear /et/ in the middle and end of the word. I can blend the sounds to make the word /wet/.* Have students say the word several times.
- Have students segment the following words into their onsets and rimes and then blend the sounds to make the words: *fig*, *pep*, *rub*, *hum*.

Assessment Tip: Note which students cannot identify the onset and rime of a word. Provide extra practice in segmenting words into their onsets and rimes.

 ## Blending Sounds

- Have students blend the words *wet*, *dab*, *wig*, and *dig*.

 ## Spelling Words

Review
- Review the week's words by having students write them several times on their workmats.
- Provide pairs of students with blackline master 2. While one student reads the spelling words, the other student writes each word.
- If a word is spelled correctly, the partner puts a check mark beside it. If a word is incorrect, the partner may provide prompts. If the second spelling is correct, the partner places a check mark in the "Second Try" column.

Assessment Tip: Collect students' completed blackline masters and note which words gave them difficulty.

 ## Sight Words

Review
- Write *I*, *for*, *go*, *is*, *look*, *me*, *my*, *said*, and *the* on the board. Read the words with students.
- Ask several students to read and clap the spellings.
- Provide clues for the words and have students guess which words you are referring to. For example, say: *This word rhymes with* **bed**. *This word has two* **O**s *in the middle. This word starts with* **t**.

Decodable Book

- Read the decodable book *The Wig* with the remaining small groups of students. Assign blackline master 4 and Independent Activities to the rest of the class.

Assessment Tip: Use the completed blackline master to assess how well students can make connections between letters and the sounds they make.

Spelling Assessment

Use the following procedure to assess students' spelling of the Unit 17 words.
- Say each spelling word and use it in a sentence.
- Have students write the word on a piece of paper.
- Continue with the next word on the list.
- When students have finished, collect their papers and analyze their spellings of misspelled words.
- Record their progress on a spelling record sheet, and provide extra practice as needed.

 # Small Group Activities

The following small group activities can be used to provide hands-on practice for students who need additional support. Assign blackline master 5 and Independent Activities for the rest of the class.

 ### PHONOLOGICAL AWARENESS

Initial /w/ Make up a sentence using words from the poster, making sure to emphasize the /w/ sound. Say: **Wendy** is in a **wagon**. Can you hear /w/? Listen again: **Wwwwendy**, **wwwwagon.** Ask students to make up other sentences about objects in the picture that begin with the /w/ sound.

Onset and Rime Using the words **win**, **red**, **pug**, **had**, and **cob**, have one student segment the word into its onset and rime and another blend the onset and rime to make the word.

 ### SOUND/SYMBOL RELATIONSHIPS

Poem Give each student letter card **w**. Read the poem and ask students to hold up the letter card each time you say a word that begins with /w/.

Word Sort Have students sort the decodable word cards into four groups according to their beginning sounds. As a group, go through the whole set, identifying the beginning sound in each word. Then ask students which cards belong together. After the cards are sorted, have students read the words in a group to check that their beginning sounds are the same. Repeat the process, this time sorting the cards according to the ending sounds.

 ### BLENDING

Blending Practice 1 Distribute letter cards **a**, **d**, **g**, **h**, **i**, **n**, **t**, and **u.** Segment the sounds in the words **did**, **gun**, **tag**, and **had** one at a time. As you say each sound, have students find the letter and say the sound with you. Gradually have them build the word by hearing the sounds and matching the letters. After students build each word, have them run their fingers under the words as they blend the sounds.

Blending Practice 2 Write the word **win** on a workmat. Have students take turns running their fingers under the word as they blend the sounds. Then say one of the sounds in the word and ask students to point to the letter that stands for that sound. Repeat with the words **wet**, **hit**, and **gag.**

Blending Practice 3 Have pairs of students work together to practice blending the words **web**, **dab**, **wig**, and **dig.** One partner says the sounds of the words slowly, and the other partner blends the sounds to make the word.

 ### SPELLING

Scrambled Words Write the spelling words on the board in scrambled order. Say one of the words, then ask a volunteer to unscramble the letters to spell the word.

Word Patterns Write the word patterns **b__d**, **p__t**, **w__t**, **w__n**, **w__g**, and **w__d** on the board. Say the word **bed** and use it in a sentence. Have a volunteer identify the word pattern for the word **bed** and fill in the missing letter. Have the student read the word **bed** aloud. Repeat with the words **pat**, **wet**, **win**, **wig**, and **wed.**

 ### SIGHT WORDS

Word Search Assign three of the words **come**, **for**, **he**, **here**, **is**, **look**, **my**, **no**, **said**, and **with** to pairs of students. Have partners write their words on sticky notes and use the sticky notes to mark the words in a familiar book. Ask students to copy one sentence for each word and then read the sentence to the group.

Student Name _____ Assessment Date _____

Phonemic Awareness: Blending Phonemes

Directions: Say the word sound by sound. Then have the student say the word. Put a ✔ if the student's response is correct. If the student misses the word, record the error. **Example:** /d/ /o/ /g/. Dog.

/p/ /o/ /d/ (pod)		/p/ /u/ /f/ (puff)			
/r/ /a/ /p/ (rap)		/d/ /i/ /d/ (did)			
/w/ /i/ /g/ (wig)		/w/ /e/ /t/ (wet)		**Score**	/6

Phonemic Awareness: Segmenting Onset and Rime

Directions: Say the word. Have the student say the first sound followed by the rest of the word and then say the whole word. If the student segments the word correctly, put a ✔. If the student's response is incorrect, record the error. **Example:** bat. /b/ /at/, bat.

got (/g/ /ot/, got)		dot (/d/ /ot/, dot)			
well (/w/ /ell/, bell)		wag (/w/ /ag/, wag)			
pad (/p/ /ad/, pad)		fed (/f/ /ed/, fed)		**Score**	/6

Phonics: Segmenting and Blending Sounds

Directions: Explain that these nonsense words use sounds the student has been learning. Have the student point to each word on the corresponding student sheet, say each sound, and then blend the sounds together. Put a ✔ if the student's response is correct. If the student misses the word, record the error. **Example:** nof. /n/ /o/ /f/, nof.

wab (/w/ /a/ /b/, wab)		hep (/h/ /e/ /p/, hep)			
buc (/b/ /u/ /c/, buc)		wut (/w/ /u/ /t/, wut)			
wob (/w/ /o/ /b/, wob)		dus (/d/ /u/ /s/, dus)		**Score**	/6

Sight Words

Directions: Have the student point to the first sight word on the corresponding student sheet and read across the line, saying each word as quickly as possible. Put a ✔ if the student successfully reads the word and an **X** if the student hesitates more than a few seconds. If the student misses the word, record the error.

he		my			
look				**Score**	/3

Unit Objectives

Students will:

- Identify the sound /l/
- Associate the letter Ll with the /l/ sound
- Listen for initial and final consonant sounds

- Segment and blend onset and rime
- Blend CVC words
- Read the sight word go
- Spell CVC words using l and letters previously learned

Day 1

BLM 1

BLM 6

Letter Cards: **d, g, l, o, w**

Spelling Transparency

Picture Word Cards: **dinosaur, dog, duck, lamp, leaf, legs, lunchbox, wagon, wasp, watch**

Day 2

BLM 1

BLM 7

Letter Cards: **b, l, n, r**

Decodable Word Cards for Unit 18

Sight Word Cards for Unit 18

Spelling Transparency

Picture Word Cards for Unit 18

Day 3

BLM 1

BLM 3

BLM 8

Decodable Word Cards for Unit 18

Sight Word Cards for Unit 18

Spelling Transparency

Picture Word Cards: **ball, cat, fan, rug**

Day 4

BLM 1

BLM 2

BLM 4

Decodable Word Cards for Unit 18

Letter Cards for Unit 18

Day 5

BLM 5

Letter Cards: **a, b, d, e, g, i, l, l, p, t, w**

Decodable Word Cards for Unit 18

Sight Word Cards for Unit 18

Quick-Check Student Sheet

Picture Word Cards: **dinosaur, dog, goat, guitar, lamp, legs, wagon, web**

Poetry Poster

Student Workmat

Letter Frieze Card

Decodable Book

Poetry CD

Core Materials

All print resources can be downloaded from http://phonicsresources.benchmarkeducation.com.

**Poetry Poster
(Front)**

Letter Frieze Card

**Picture Word
Cards**

Phonemic Awareness

Use the Poetry Poster
- Read aloud or play the recording of the poem *Lenny Lion*, and encourage students to join in when they can.
- Say the sentence "Lenny Lion just loves to leap over bushes and rocks and logs." Emphasize the /l/ phoneme.
- Reread the poem. Ask students to clap every time they hear a word that starts with the /l/ sound.

Distribute blackline master 6 and instruct students to complete it at home.

Sound/Symbol Relationships

Model
- Display letter frieze card **Ll.** Explain that the letter *Ll* stands for the /l/ sound, as in the word *leaf*.
- Reread the poem *Lenny Lion*. Invite students to read along with you.
- Point to words in the poem that begin with /l/. Say the words aloud.

Practice with the Letter Cards
- Distribute letter cards **d**, **l**, and **w.** Ask students to line up the cards on their workmats.
- Have students pull down each letter card and say the letter name, then push it back up and say the letter sound.
- Ask them to pull down each letter card again, saying a word that starts with that sound.
- Have them push up the letter card that starts the word *lion*. (Repeat with the words *doll* and *watch*.)

Practice with the Picture Cards
- Place letter cards **d**, **l**, and **w** in the pocket chart.
- Place picture cards **dog**, **leaf**, and **wasp** under the corresponding letters while you say the name of the letter and the name of the object in the picture.
- Hold up picture card **lunchbox** and have students say *lunchbox* with you.
- Ask: *Does* **lunchbox** *begin like* **dog**, **leaf**, *or* **wasp**?
- Place picture card **lunchbox** under letter card **l** and picture card **leaf**. Say: /Llllunchbox/ *begins like* /lllleaf/, *so I am putting picture card* **lunchbox** *under the letter* **l**.
- Repeat with picture cards **dinosaur**, **duck**, **legs**, **lamp**, **wagon**, and **watch.**

Blending Sounds

Review
- Hold up letter frieze cards of previously taught sounds. Ask students to say the sound each letter stands for.

Model
- Write the word *will* on the board. Sound out the word by moving your hand under each letter while blending the sounds. (/wwwwiiiillll/) Then say the word. Point out that the two letter *ll*s stand for one sound.

Practice with the Word Lists
- Distribute blackline master 1.
- Have students point to the word *will*. Ask them to sound out the word with you. Then ask them to say the word at regular speed.
- Repeat with the words *did*, *hub*, and *nap*. Then have students sound out the words in random order.

Spelling Words

Model

- Use the spelling transparency. Place counters under the second set of boxes.
- Say: *Today we are going to learn to spell* **bag** *and* **dad**. *Watch and listen as I say* **bag** *slowly:* **/baaaag/.** Point out that the word has stop sounds at the beginning and the end.
- As you say **/b/,** push a counter into the first box. Then say **/aaaa/** as you push a counter into the second box and **/g/** as you push a counter into the third box. Repeat the steps.
- Model recording the letters for the sounds on the transparency. Say: *The first sound is* **/b/.** *I know that the letter* **b** *stands for the* **/b/** *sound. I'll write the letter* **b** *in the first box. Let's listen for the second sound:* **/baaaa/.** *I hear* **/a/.** *I know that the letter* **a** *stands for the* **/a/** *sound, so I will write* **a** *in the second box. Let's listen for the last sound:* **/bag/.** *I hear* **/g/.** *I know that the letter* **g** *stands for the* **/g/** *sound, so I will write* **g** *in the last box.*
- Have students blend the sounds to check the spelling of the word.

Practice with the Workmat

- Instruct students to place their counters under the second set of boxes on side 2 of their workmats.
- Ask students to slowly articulate the word **bag** as they push the counters into the boxes.
- Have them identify and record the letters that stand for the sounds they hear.
- Have students practice writing **bag** on side 1 of their workmats.

Repeat the modeling and practice with the second spelling word, *dad*.

Sight Words

Review

- Write **and**, **he**, **look**, **me**, **my**, and **with** on the board. Erase the **a** in **and**, say the word, and ask students which letter is missing. Repeat with the other words.

Introduce

- Use the pocket chart and letter cards to model how to spell the word **go**. Point to the word and say it.
- Have students say the word as you point to it.
- Write this sentence on the board: "He will go with me." Have a volunteer underline the word **go**. Ask other volunteers to underline **He**, **with**, and **me**.

Write

- Have students write **go** on side 1 of their workmats, using the model in the pocket chart.

DAY 2

Independent Activities

Phonological Awareness

Picture Cards Provide picture cards in the literacy center. Students can:
• take a card, name the picture, and say another word that has the same ending sound
• separate cards that start with the /w/ sound
• match a card with another that has the same middle sound

Collage Have students look through magazines for things that start with /l/. They can cut out the pictures and make a collage.

Listen Have students listen to the recording of the poem *Lenny Lion* in the listening center.

Sound/Symbol Relationships

Letter Toss Write the letters *d, g, m, l, p,* and *w* on paper squares. Place the squares on the floor. Students can:
• toss a beanbag onto a square and say the sound for that letter
• toss a beanbag onto a square and say a word that has that letter's sound

Read and Draw Make several copies of sight and decodable words, and place them in a box. Students can take a card, and read and write the word.

Draw Pictures Display letter cards **b, l, n,** and **r**. Have students draw a picture of something that begins with each letter.

 ## Phonemic Awareness

Use the Poetry Poster
• Show students the picture on the back of the poetry poster and have them name all the objects in the picture.
• Point to the lamp in the picture and say the word *lamp*, emphasizing the /l/. Ask: *What sound do you hear at the beginning of the word?*
• Ask students to point to something in the picture that starts with /l/.

 ## Sound/Symbol Relationships

Sort the Decodable Word Cards
• Place picture cards **dinosaur**, **goat**, **lamp**, and **wagon** in the pocket chart and have students say the name of the object on each card.
• Show students decodable word card **dim** and have them blend the word.
• Ask students if *dim* begins like *dinosaur*, *goat*, *lamp*, or *wagon*. Then place the card under picture card **dinosaur**.
• Repeat with decodable word cards **dot**, **gas**, **Gus**, **Len**, **lab**, **wag**, and **wed.**

Distribute blackline master 7 and instruct students to complete it at home.

Assessment Tip: Observe which students have difficulty associating sounds with letters, and provide extra support in a small group setting. Assign Independent Activities to the rest of the class.

 ## Blending Sounds

• Have students blend the words *let*, *lug*, *rug*, and *rap*, using the procedure for Day One.

 ## Spelling Words

• Review the words *bag* and *dad* by having students write the words several times.
• Follow the procedure for Day One to model and practice the words *let* and *lap*.

Assessment Tip: Note students who do not slowly articulate the sounds when spelling a word, and provide extra modeling.

Sight Words

• Write the word *go* on the board. Ask a volunteer to read it.
• Have students spell *go* in the air with their fingers.
• Have students read the sight word cards as you hold them up.

Phonemic Awareness

Final Consonants

- Place picture cards **cat**, **fan**, **ball**, and **rug** in the pocket chart. Write the numbers 1, 2, 3, and 4 on index cards, and place the cards above the pictures.
- Say the name of each picture card, stressing the ending sound. Instruct students to hold up one finger if a word ends with /t/, two fingers if it ends in /n/, three fingers if it ends in /l/, and four fingers if it ends in /g/.
- Repeat with the words **pool**, **wet**, **leg**, **rainy**, **yell**, **spoon**, **foot**, and **tag**.

 # Blending Sounds

- Have students blend the words **lab**, **bib**, **nut**, and **lid**.

 # Spelling Words

- Review the words **bag**, **dad**, **let**, and **lap** by having students write them several times.
- Follow the procedure for Day One to model and practice the words **lid** and **lip**.

 # Sight Words

- Write this sentence on the board and underline the word **go**: "Pop can go in the lab." Ask students to read the sentence.
- Have students use decodable words to write a sentence using **go**.
- Write **no, are, go, has, have, here, and,** and **said** on the board. Hold up a sight word card and have students read it. Ask a volunteer to match the card to the word on the board. Repeat with all the words.

Distribute blackline master 8 and instruct students to complete it at home.

Poetry Poster (Back)

Decodable Book

Work with small groups of students to read the decodable book *Pop and Len* on Days Three and Four. Assign blackline master 3 and Independent Activities for the rest of the class on Day Three.

Introduce the Book

- Display the cover of the book. Point to the title, *Pop and Len*, and have students sound out the decodable words **Pop** and **Len** as you run your finger under them. Have them read the word **and** quickly.
- Ask: *What do you see in the picture?*

Read the Book

- Give each student a copy of the book and have them turn to page 2. Instruct them to run their fingers under the first word, **Can**, as they sound it out.
- Have students point to the next word. Remind them that this is a word they don't sound out and that they have practiced. Have them say the word **I**.
- Have students continue pointing to the words in the sentence, sounding out decodable words and saying sight words quickly.
- Have students read the whole sentence at normal speed.
- Repeat with the next sentence, sounding out decodable words and reading sight words quickly. Point out the quotation marks and explain that these denote what the characters are saying.
- If students can sound out the words without difficulty, have them whisper-read the rest of the text.
- If students have difficulty, continue to guide them page by page.

Discuss the Book

- When students have finished reading, ask: *What does Len do in the lab? What does Len do with the cat? What does Pop say that Len can do?*

Decodable Book

 **SUPPORT TIPS** for English Language Learners

Develop/reinforce concept and vocabulary: *lab*

- Before reading, show a picture of white-coated scientists working in a lab, and ask students to identify whom they see and where they work. Accept generic labels (man, boy, girl, doctor) if students do not know the word **scientist**.
- Introduce the word **lab** to describe where the people work. Model the target language: *He works in a lab.*
- Show pictures of people in different places, including a picture of someone working in a lab, to pairs of students. Have students tell where the people are. (at school, in the bus)
- Model the target language structure and vocabulary **in the**.

Independent Activities

Decodable Book

Independent Reading After students have read the decodable book in a small group, have them read the book independently or with a friend.

Dramatize Have students work in small groups to create a dramatization of the story.

Write a Sentence Have students use decodable word cards to make a new sentence for a page in the book.

Listen for Words Write several words from *Pop and Len* on index cards, and distribute the cards. Have one student read the book aloud. The other students hold up their card whenever their word is read.

Spelling

As words are introduced each day, write them on index cards and place them in the literacy center. Ensure that the letter cards needed to build the words are in the center. Students can use the following procedure to spell words.
• Choose a word card.
• Use their fingers and eyes to read the word.
• Turn over the card so that they can't see the word.
• Build the word using the letter cards.
• Turn over the card to check the word.
• Write the word.

Sight Words

Personal Dictionary Have students write *go* in their personal dictionaries.

Word Search Write *a*, *for*, *I*, *me*, *no*, *the*, *said*, and *you* on the board. Have students look for the words in the classroom and mark the words with sticky notes.

 Phonemic Awareness

Blend and Segment Onset and Rime
• Segment the word *lab* into its onset and rime: /l/ /ab/. Have students repeat the onset and rime with you several times.
• Ask: *What is the beginning sound in* **lab?** *What are the middle and ending sounds in* **lab***?*
• Continue, with students segmenting the following words into their onsets and rimes and then blending them to make the words: **Len**, **lap**, **lip**.

Assessment Tip: Note students who cannot segment onsets and rimes. Ask them to segment the onsets and rimes in the words **log**, **win**, and **sad**.

 Blending Sounds

• Have students blend the words **met**, **cub**, **ran**, and **lip**, using the procedure for Day One.

 Spelling Words

Review
• Review the week's words by having students write them several times on their workmats.
• Provide pairs of students with blackline master 2. While one student reads the words from the list, the other writes each word.
• If a word is spelled correctly, the partner puts a check mark beside it. If a word is incorrect, the partner may provide prompts. If the second spelling of the word is correct, the partner places a check mark in the "Second Try" column.

Assessment Tip: Collect students' completed blackline masters and note which words gave them difficulty.

 Sight Words

Review
• Write *I*, *for*, *go*, *is*, *look*, *me*, *my*, *said*, and *the* on the board. Read the words with students.
• Ask several students to read and clap the spellings.
• Provide clues for the words and have students guess which words you are referring to. For example, say: *This word rhymes with* **bed***. This word has two* **o***s in the middle. This word starts with* **t***.*

 Decodable Book

• Read the decodable book *Pop and Len* with the remaining small groups of students. Assign blackline master 4 and Independent Activities for the rest of the class.

Assessment Tip: Use the completed blackline masters to assess how well students can make connections between sounds and the letters that stand for those sounds.

Spelling Assessment

Use the following procedure to assess students' spelling of the Unit 18 words.
• Say each spelling word and use it in a sentence.
• Have students write the word on a piece of paper.
• Continue with the next word on the list.
• When students have finished, collect their papers and analyze their spellings of misspelled words.
• Record their progress on a spelling record sheet, and provide extra practice as needed.

 # Small Group Activities

The following small group activities can be used to provide hands-on practice for students who need additional support. Assign blackline master 5 and Independent Activities for the rest of the class.

 ## PHONOLOGICAL AWARENESS

Initial /l/ Ask a volunteer to hold picture card **lamp.** Say the words **web, line, lean, goat, list, land, bike, card, lot, lad,** and **laugh.** Tell students that if they hear the /l/ sound at the beginning of a word, they should line up behind the volunteer.

Final Consonants Say the following groups of words and ask which words in each group end with the same sound: **cool/flag/doll, sat/ pet/mug, pan/bib/bun, nag/pug/nip.**

Onset and Rime Model how to segment the onset and rimes in the words **let, tag, big,** and **dog.**

 ## SOUND/SYMBOL RELATIONSHIPS

Reread the Poem Reread the poem and have students find words in the poem that start with /l/.

Word and Picture Sort Place decodable word cards **dim, Gus, Len,** and **wag** in the pocket chart. Then distribute picture cards **dinosaur, dog, goat, guitar, lamp, legs, wagon,** and **web.** Have students name each picture and place it under the word card that has the same beginning sound.

 ## BLENDING

Model Use letter cards **i, l, l,** and **w** to build the word **will** on a workmat. Say the word. Then mix the letters and have a student remake the word on the workmat. Repeat with the words **lot** and **lid.**

 ## SPELLING

Write Model saying and writing the spelling words one at a time. Have students say and write the words with you on their workmats.

Guess What's Missing Write **bag, dad, let, lap, lid,** and **lip** on the board. Then erase one letter from each word and ask volunteers to tell which letters are missing.

Letter Cards Write **bag, dad, let, lap, lid,** and **lip** on the board. Mix a set of letter cards **a, b, d, e, i, g, l, p,** and **t.** Have a student find the letters to spell a word and place the cards in the pocket chart.

 ## SIGHT WORDS

Word Draw Place sight word cards **and, go, he, look, me, my,** and **with** in a box. Have students draw a card, read the word, and use the word in a sentence.

Make Up Sentences Display one of the following sight word cards: **are, go, has, have, here, no, said.** Have a student make up a sentence using the word. Then show the same card to another student and have them make up a different sentence.

Student Name _____   Assessment Date _____

Phonemic Awareness: Differentiating Final Sounds

Directions: Say each set of words. Then have the student say the two words that end with the same sound. Put a ✔ if the student's response is correct. If not, record the words the student chooses.
Example: dig/peg/mad. *Dig, peg.*

pan/fin/pop (*pan, fin*)		log/nod/wig (*log, wig*)			
led/leg/did (*led, did*)		rib/top/dip (*top, dip*)			
got/pal/fall (*pal, fall*)		wet/mitt/miss (*wet, mitt*)		**Score**	**/6**

Phonemic Awareness: Blending Onset and Rime

Directions: Say the first sound of the word followed by the rest of the word. Then have the student say the whole word. If the student says the word correctly, put a ✔. If the student misses the word, record the error.
Example: /b/ /at/. *Bat.*

/l/ /ick/ (*lick*)		/l/ /ess/ (*less*)			
/d/ /uck/ (*duck*)		/b/ /ud/ (*bud*)			
/p/ /an/ (*pan*)		/f/ /og/ (*fog*)		**Score**	**/6**

Phonics: Segmenting and Blending Sounds

Directions: Explain that these nonsense words use sounds the student has been learning. Have the student point to each word on the corresponding student sheet, say each sound, and then blend the sounds together. Put a ✔ if the student's response is correct. If the student misses the word, record the error.
Example: wof. */w/ /o/ /f/, wof.*

lem (*/l/ /e/ /m/, lem*)		hon (*/h/ /o/ /n/, hon*)			
bap (*/b/ /a/ /p/, bap*)		lus (*/l/ /u/ /s/, lus*)			
lif (*/l/ /i/ /f/, lif*)		wid (*/w/ /i/ /d/, wid*)		**Score**	**/6**

Sight Word

Directions: Have the student point to the sight word on the corresponding student sheet and read it as quickly as possible. Put a ✔ if the student successfully reads the word and an **X** if the student hesitates more than a few seconds. If the student misses the word, record the error.

go		**Score**	**/1**

Unit Objectives

Students will:

- Identify the sound /j/
- Associate the letter Jj with the /j/ sound
- Listen for initial /j/
- Substitute initial sounds
- Segment and blend phonemes
- Blend CVC words
- Read the sight words put, want
- Spell CVC words using j and letters previously learned

Day 1

BLM 1

BLM 6

Letter Cards: j, l, w

Spelling Transparency

Picture Word Cards: jacks, jam, jar, jump rope, lamp, leaf, lunchbox, wagon, wasp, web

---

Day 2

BLM 1

BLM 7

Decodable Word Cards for Unit 19

Sight Word Cards for Unit 19

Spelling Transparency

Picture Word Cards: cup, dog, duck, fish, jacks, jam, lamp, nut, wasp

---

Day 3

BLM 1

BLM 3

BLM 8

Sight Word Cards for Unit 19

Spelling Transparency

Day 4

BLM 1

BLM 2

BLM 4

Letter Cards for Unit 19

Day 5

BLM 5

Decodable Word Cards for Unit 19

Sight Word Cards for Unit 19

Quick-Check Student Sheet

Poetry Poster

Student Workmat

Letter Frieze Card

Decodable Book

Poetry CD

Core Materials

All print resources can be downloaded from http://phonicsresources.benchmarkeducation.com.

**Poetry Poster
(Front)**

Letter Frieze Card

**Picture Word
Cards**

 # Phonemic Awareness

Use the Poetry Poster

- Read aloud or play the recording of the poem *Jumping.*
- Have students listen for the */j/* sound at the beginning of the sentence "Johnny, Jane, and Jellybean jumping on a trampoline."
- Reread the poem. Have students clap when they hear */j/.*

Distribute blackline master 6 and instruct students to complete it at home.

Sound/Symbol Relationships

Model

- Display letter frieze card **Jj.** Explain that the letter *Jj* stands for the */j/* sound, as in **jump rope**.
- Reread the poem *Jumping,* encouraging students to read along with you.
- Point to words in the poem that begin with the letter *j.* Say the words aloud.

Practice with the Letter Cards

- Distribute letter cards **j, l,** and **w.** Ask students to line up the cards on their workmats.
- Have students pull down each letter card and say the letter name, then push it back up and say the letter sound.
- Ask them to pull down each letter card again, saying a word that starts with that sound.
- Have students push up the letter card that starts the word **jog.** (Repeat with **win** and **lad.**)

Practice with the Picture Cards

- Place letter cards **j, l,** and **w** in the pocket chart.
- Place picture cards **jam, lunchbox,** and **wagon** under the corresponding letters while you say the name of the letter and the name of the object in the picture.
- Hold up picture card **jar** and have students say **jar** with you.
- Ask: *Does* **jar** *begin like* **jam, lunchbox,** *or* **wagon**?
- Place picture card **jar** under letter card **j.** Say: **Jar** *begins like* **jam,** *so I am putting picture card* **jar** *under the letter* **j**.
- Repeat with picture cards **jacks, jump rope, lamp, leaf, wasp,** and **web.**

P+A+M Blending Sounds

Review

- Hold up letter frieze cards of previously taught sounds. Have students say the sound each letter stands for.

Model

- Write the word **wet** on the board. Sound out the word by moving your hand under each letter while blending the sounds. (*/wwwweeeet/*) Then say the word. Remind students that **wet** has a stop sound at the end.
- Ask students to sound out the word with you.

Practice with the Word Lists

- Distribute blackline master 1.
- Have students point to the word **wet.** Ask them to sound out the word with you. Then ask them to say the word at regular speed.
- Repeat with the words **bog, jet,** and **Len.** Then have students sound out the words in random order.

Spelling Words

Model

- Use the spelling transparency. Place counters under the second set of boxes on the transparency.
- Say: *Today we are going to learn to spell* **lab** *and* **bin.** *Watch and listen as I say* **lab** *slowly:* /llllaaaab/.
- As you say */llll/*, push a counter into the first box. Then say */aaaa/* as you push a counter into the second box and */b/* as you push a counter into the third box. Repeat the steps.
- Model recording the letters for the sounds on the transparency. Say: *The first sound is* /llll/. *I know that the letter* l *stands for the* /l/ *sound. I'll write the letter* l *in the first box. Let's listen for the second sound:* /laaaa/. *I hear* /a/. *I know that the letter* a *stands for the* /a/ *sound, so I will write* a *in the second box. Let's listen for the last sound:* /lab/. *I hear* /b/. *I know that the letter* b *stands for the* /b/ *sound, so I will write* b *in the last box.*
- Have students blend the sounds to check the spelling of the word.

Practice with the Workmat

- Instruct students to place their counters under the second set of boxes on side 2 of their workmats.
- Ask students to slowly articulate the word *lab* as they push the counters into the boxes.
- Have students identify and record the letters that stand for the sounds they hear.
- Have students practice writing *lab* on side 1 of their workmats.

Repeat the modeling and practice with the second spelling word, *bin*.

 Sight Words

Review

- Write the sight words *is, for, see, the,* and *you* on the board. Have students write them with a colored pencil, read them, and rewrite them in a different color.

Introduce

- Write the word *put* on the board.
- Point to the word and say: *This is the word* **put***. It is made up of the letters* **p**, **u**, *and* **t***.*
- Have students say the word.
- Follow the same steps to introduce the word *want*.

Write

Have students write *put* and *want* on side 1 of their workmats, using the models on the board.

Independent Activities

Phonemic Awareness

Picture Cards Provide picture cards in the literacy center. Students can:
- sort the cards into those that start with /j/ and those that don't
- take a card and find another that has the same middle sound
- sort picture cards according to their ending sounds

Beginning Sounds Have students fold a sheet of paper in half and choose one of picture cards **cup, dog, fish, jam,** and **nut.** Students then draw pictures of things that have the same beginning sound as the card on the top of the paper and things that have the same ending sound on the bottom.

Listen Have students listen to the recording of the poem *Jumping* in the listening center.

Sound/Symbol Relationships

Rhyming Words Provide a sheet of paper with these pairs of words: ***pin/fin, lit/sit, jug/bug, pen/hen, tot/cot.*** Have students copy the words, write a word that rhymes with each pair, and circle the letters that spell the rhyming sounds.

Word Toss Draw six boxes on a sheet of paper. Place the paper on the floor. Write ***jug, red, web, leg, hum,*** and ***cot*** in the boxes. Students can:
- throw a beanbag onto a box, read the word, and say a word that has the same beginning sound
- throw a beanbag onto a box, read the word, and say a word that has the same ending sound

 ## Phonemic Awareness

Use the Poetry Poster
- Show students the picture on the back of the poetry poster and have them name all the objects in the picture.
- Point to the jet in the picture and say the word *jet*, stressing the /j/. Ask: *What sound do you hear at the beginning of the word?*
- Ask students to point to something in the picture that starts with /j/.

 ## Sound/Symbol Relationships

Sort the Decodable Word Cards
- Place picture cards **duck, jacks, lamp,** and **wasp** in the pocket chart and have students say the name of the object on each picture card.
- Show students the decodable word cards one at a time, and have them blend each word.
- Ask students if the word begins like ***duck, jacks, lamp,*** or ***wasp***. Place the card under the correct picture card.

Distribute blackline master 7 and instruct students to complete it at home.

Assessment Tip: In a small group, ask students who do not seem to be responding to place the card under the correct picture card. Assign Independent Activities for the rest of the class.

P+A+M Blending Sounds

- Have students sound out the words ***job, jam, can,*** and ***win,*** using the procedure for Day One.

Aa Spelling Words

- Review the words ***lab*** and ***bin*** by having students write the words several times.
- Follow the procedure for Day One to model and practice the words ***job*** and ***jam***.

 ## Sight Words

- Hold up the sight word cards one at a time. Cover the card and have students spell the word.
- Write the words on the board. Say: *I am going to say some sentences. When you hear a word from the list, raise your hand. If I call on you, come to the board, circle the word, and read it aloud.*
- Say: *I want a horn for my bike. Did you put your shoes away? I see a picture of my family. Sal and Pat want to go. Is that gift for me?*

Phonemic Awareness

Initial Sound Substitution

- Say the word *jet*. Ask students what sound they hear at the beginning of the word.
- Segment the sounds: */j/ /e/ /t/*. Then say: *I want to change /j/ to /m/. What word will I have?*
- Together segment the sounds in the new word: */m/ /e/ /t/*. Then say the new word, *met*.
- Continue with these word pairs, changing the first word into the second: *jig/wig, jab/cab, Jim/Tim, lad/pad, wet/get, mad/bad, hot/not.*

 # Blending Sounds

- Have students blend the words *set, top, jet,* and *Jim*, using the procedure for Day One.

 # Spelling Words

- Review the words *lab, bin, job,* and *jam* by having students write them several times.
- Follow the procedure for Day One to model and practice the words *Jim* and *Jen*.

 # Sight Words

- Write the words *put* and *want* on the board. Have students chant the letters with you.
- Write these sentences on the board: "I _____ a cat." "_____ the pup here."
- Have students write the sentences on their papers and put the words *put* and *want* in the correct places.
- Give students sight word cards **a, I, has, have, look, me, my, put,** and **want**. Have students place the words faceup on their desks. Say the following sentences slowly, and have students hold up their cards for the sight words they hear. Say: *I have a red jacket. It has two pockets. I want to play outside. I put on my jacket. Look at me. I have blue mittens.*

Distribute blackline master 8 and instruct students to complete it at home.

 # Decodable Book

Work with small groups of students to read the decodable book *The Job* on Days Three and Four. Assign blackline master 3 and Independent Activities for the rest of the class on Day Three.

Introduce the Book
- Display the cover of the book. Point to the title, *The Job*, and have students sound out the words as you run your fingers under them.
- Ask: *What do you see in the picture? What is a job? What jobs can you do?*

Read the Book
- Give each student a copy of the book and have them turn to page 2.
- Instruct students to point to each of the first three words. Remind them that these are words they don't sound out.
- Have students point to the next word and sound it out: */jjjoooob/*.
- As students run their fingers under the next words, continue to distinguish between words they sound out and words they must recognize by sight.
- Have students read the sentence at normal speed.
- Point out the quotation marks, which let students know what Dan said.
- If students can sound out the words without difficulty, have them whisper-read the rest of the text.
- If students are having difficulty, continue to guide them page by page.

Discuss the Book
- When students have finished reading, ask: *What is Dan's job? What do Jen and Jim see? Who gets the jam?*

Poetry Poster (Back)

Decodable Book

 **SUPPORT TIPS**
for English Language Learners

Develop/reinforce idiomatic language: *in a jiff*

- Before reading, direct students to complete a common task, such as putting their names on a paper, but do not put pencils or markers on the table.
- When students request the necessary materials, respond by saying, *In a jiff*, and give them the materials after a short delay.
- Pass out the materials necessary to complete the task, giving all of one item, such as the glue, to one student.
- Have students take turns requesting the items needed to complete the assigned task.
- Model the target response so that the student who has the needed item responds *In a jiff* before handing over the materials.
- Use the phrase as often as possible throughout the day. For example, as students are picking up after an activity, give specific directions: *Marcos, put the crayon in the box.*
- Model the response—*Yes, teacher, in a jiff*—if the student does not follow the direction immediately.

DAY 4

Independent Activities

Decodable Book

Independent Reading After students have read the book in a small group, have them read it with a friend.

Write a New Ending Have students use words from the book to write a new ending.

Fluency Practice Record students reading the book. Play the recordings so students may review their readings.

Spelling

As words are introduced each day, write them on index cards and place them in the literacy center. Ensure that the letter cards needed to build the words are in the center. Students can use the following procedure to spell words.

- Choose a word card.
- Use their fingers and eyes to read the word.
- Turn over the card so that they can't see the word.
- Build the word using the letter cards.
- Turn over the card to check the word.
- Write the word.

Sight Words

Personal Dictionary Have students write **put** and **want** in their personal dictionaries.

Scrambled Sentences Write these scrambled sentences on index cards: "to the hut Go"; "the in pot I put the lab"; "the mat and The are ram on rat"; "is bug a in jar The." Have students choose a card and rewrite the sentence.

 ## Phonemic Awareness

Segment and Blend Phonemes
- Say the word **jam**, segmenting the phonemes: /j/ /a/ /m/. Then have students say the sounds slowly several times.
- Ask students to blend the sounds. Ask: *What word do you hear?*
- Explain that you are going to say other sets of sounds. They are to repeat the sounds, then blend them. Say these sets of sounds: /t/ /i/ /n/, /l/ /u/ /g/, /m/ /a/ /d/.
- Tell students that you are going to say a word. They are to repeat the word, then segment it into its sounds. Use the words **jug, lip, had,** and **set**.

 ## Blending Sounds

- Have students blend the words **job, tin, map,** and **Jen**.

 ## Spelling Words

Review
- Review the week's spelling words by having students write them several times on their workmats.
- Provide pairs of students with blackline master 2. While one student reads the words from the list, the other student writes each word.
- If a word is spelled correctly, the partner puts a check mark beside it. If a word is incorrect, the partner may provide prompts. If the second spelling of the word is correct, the partner places a check mark in the "Second Try" column.

Assessment Tip: Collect students' completed blackline masters and note which words gave them difficulty.

 ## Sight Words

Review
- Write the words **and, are, come, go, of, put, see, want,** and **with** on the board.
- Have students clap once for each letter as you spell the words together. Then have them tell about places in their community, using the words.

Decodable Book

- Read the decodable book *The Job* with the remaining small groups of students. Assign blackline master 4 and Independent Activities for the rest of the class.

Assessment Tip: Use the completed blackline master to assess how well students can match beginning sounds with the letters that stand for those sounds.

Spelling Assessment

Use the following procedure to assess students' spelling of the Unit 19 words.
- Say each spelling word and use it in a sentence.
- Have students write the word on a piece of paper.
- Continue with the next word on the list.
- When students have finished, collect their papers and analyze their spellings of misspelled words.
- Record their progress on a spelling record sheet, and provide extra practice as needed.

 Small Group Activities

The following small group activities can be used to provide hands-on practice for students who need additional support. Assign blackline master 5 and Independent Activities for the rest of the class.

 PHONOLOGICAL AWARENESS

Initial /j/ Display the picture on the back of the poetry poster. Say: *This is Jolly Jim. Jolly Jim likes to jump.* Ask students to tell about things they like that start with */j/*, substituting their names for Jolly Jim's.

Manipulating Sounds Say: /j/ /et/: jet. *The first sound is* /j/. *I can change* /j/ *to* /m/ *and to make* /m/ /et/, met. *The first sound in* **met** *is* /m/. *If I change the* /m/ *to* /l/, *what word will I have?* Repeat the activity, starting with **pan** and making **fan, can, tan,** and **van**.

Segmenting and Blending Model how to segment the sounds in **jet** and **lap**. Have students blend the sounds. Then have them segment and blend the sounds in **pep** and **sun**.

 SOUND/SYMBOL RELATIONSHIPS

Sound Concentration Place the decodable word cards facedown in rows on a table. Have a student turn over two cards and read the words. If the words have the same beginning sound, the student keeps the cards and turns over two more. If the words do not have the same beginning sound, the student turns the cards facedown again and the next student has a turn. Continue until all the cards have been matched.

 BLENDING

Blending Practice Write the word **wet** on a workmat. Model sounding out the word by moving your hand under the letters as you say the sounds. Ask students to sound out the word with you. Continue with the words **Jen, jig, jab,** and **jug**.

 SPELLING

Spelling Patterns Write __*a*__ on chart paper. Tell students that you want to make the word **lab**. Have one student write the letter for the beginning sound. Ask another student to write the letter for the ending sound. Use the same pattern to make the word **jam,** the pattern __*o*__ to make the word **job**, and the pattern __*u*__ to make the word **hut**.

Scrambled Words Write the spelling words in scrambled form in a row on the board: **bla, uth, bjo, maj, enJ, mJi**. Have volunteers write the word correctly below each scrambled form.

 SIGHT WORDS

Read Around the Circle 1 Have students sit in a circle and pass the Unit 19 sight word cards, one at a time. Have each student read the word and use it in an oral sentence before passing the card.

Read Around the Circle 2 Place sight word cards in a stack on the floor. Have students sit in a circle around the cards. Choose a card and quickly show it to the students. The first student who correctly reads the word collects the card. Continue until all cards have been used.

Student Name _____ Assessment Date _____

Phonemic Awareness: Segmenting Phonemes

Directions: Say the word. Have the student say the word sound by sound and then say the whole word. If the student segments the word correctly, put a ✔. If the student's response is incorrect, record the error. **Example:** sip. /s/ /i/ /p/, *sip.*

jig (/j/ /i/ /g/, *jig*)		den (/d/ /e/ /n/, *den*)			
rub (/r/ /u/ /b/, *rub*)		bag (/b/ /a/ /g/, *bag*)			
pep (/p/ /e/ /p/, *pep*)		pod (/p/ /o/ /d/, *pod*)		**Score**	**/6**

Phonemic Awareness: Initial Sound Substitution

Directions: Say the word, and then segment it sound by sound. Ask the student to replace the first sound in the word with the new sound while segmenting sound by sound and then say the new word. Put a ✔ if the student's response is correct. If the student misses the word, record the error. **Example:** man, /m/ /a/ /n/. Change /m/ to /p/. /p/ /a/ /n/, *pan.*

jug, /j/ /u/ /g/. Change /j/ to /t/. (/t/ /u/ /g/, *tug*)	
bed, /b/ /e/ /d/. Change /b/ to /f/. (/f/ /e/ /d/, *fed*)	
sap, /s/ /a/ /p/. Change /s/ to /n/. (/n/ /a/ /p/, *nap*)	
hip, /h/ /i/ /p/. Change /h/ to /l/. (/l/ /i/ /p/, *lip*)	
rod, /r/ /o/ /d/. Change /r/ to /p/. (/p/ /o/ /d/, *pod*)	
cut, /k/ /u/ /t/. Change /k/ to /n/. (/n/ /u/ /t/, *nut*) **Score** **/6**	

Phonics: Segmenting and Blending Sounds

Directions: Explain that these nonsense words use sounds the student has been learning. Have the student point to each word on the corresponding student sheet, say each sound, and then blend the sounds together. Put a ✔ if the student's response is correct. If the student misses the word, record the error. **Example:** wob. /w/ /o/ /b/, *wob.*

tof (/t/ /o/ /f/, *tof*)		jun (/j/ /u/ /n/, *jun*)			
jid (/j/ /i/ /d/, *jid*)		lat (/l/ /a/ /t/, *lat*)			
rem (/r/ /e/ /m/, *rem*)		jop (/j/ /o/ /p/, *jop*)		**Score**	**/6**

Sight Words

Directions: Have the student point to the first sight word on the corresponding student sheet and read across the line, saying each word as quickly as possible. Put a ✔ if the student successfully reads the word and an **X** if the student hesitates more than a few seconds. If the student misses the word, record the error.

put		want		**Score**	**/2**

UNIT 20 Kk

Unit Objectives

Students will:

- Identify the sound /k/
- Associate the letter Kk with the /k/ sound
- Listen for /k/
- Orally substitute initial sounds

- Segment and blend phonemes
- Blend CVC words
- Read the sight words saw, she, this
- Spell CVC words using k and letters previously learned

Day 1

BLM 1

BLM 6

Letter Cards: **j, k, l**

Spelling Transparency

Picture Word Cards: **jacks, jam, jump rope, kangaroo, king, kite, kitten, leaf, legs, lunchbox**

Day 2

BLM 1

BLM 7

Decodable Word Cards for Unit 20

Sight Word Cards for Unit 20

Spelling Transparency

Picture Word Cards: **house, jam, kangaroo, leaf, mitten, watch, web**

Day 3

BLM 1

BLM 3

BLM 8

Sight Word Cards for Unit 20

Spelling Transparency

Day 4

BLM 1

BLM 2

BLM 4

Spelling Transparency

Day 5

BLM 5

Letter Cards for Unit 20

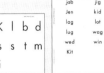
Decodable Word Cards for Unit 20

Sight Word Cards for Unit 20

Quick-Check Student Sheet

Picture Word Cards for Letters **j, k, l**

Poetry Poster

Student Workmat

Letter Frieze Card

Decodable Book

Poetry CD

Core Materials

All print resources can be downloaded from http://phonicsresources.benchmarkeducation.com.

**Poetry Poster
(Front)**

Letter Frieze Card

**Picture Word
Cards**

Phonemic Awareness

Use the Poetry Poster

- Read aloud or play the recording of the poem *King Karl's Kangaroo.*
- Say the sentence "'Have you seen my kangaroo?' King Karl asked of me." Have students listen for the /*k*/ sound.
- Reread the poem. Have students clap each time they hear /*k*/ in the poem.

Distribute blackline master 6 and instruct students to complete it at home.

Sound/Symbol Relationships

Model

- Display letter frieze card **Kk.** Explain that the letter *Kk* stands for the /*k*/ sound, as in *kite.*
- Reread the poem *King Karl's Kangaroo,* encouraging students to read along with you.
- Point to words in the poem that have the /*k*/ sound. Say each word aloud.

Practice with the Letter Cards

- Distribute letter cards **j**, **l**, and **k.** Ask students to line up the cards on their workmats.
- Have students pull down each letter card and say the letter name, then push it back up and say the letter sound.
- Ask them to pull down each letter card again, saying a word that starts with that sound.
- Have students push up the letter card that starts the word *kite.* (Repeat with *jam* and *lap.*)

Practice with the Picture Cards

- Place letter cards **j**, **k**, and **l** in the pocket chart.
- Place picture cards **jacks**, **kite**, and **lunchbox** under the corresponding letters while you say the name of the letter and the name of the object in the picture.
- Hold up picture card **kitten** and have students say *kitten* with you.
- Ask: *Does* **kitten** *begin like* **jacks**, **kite**, *or* **lunchbox**?
- Place picture card **kitten** under letter card **k.** Say: **Kitten** *begins like* **kite**, *so I am putting picture card* **kitten** *under the letter* **k.**
- Repeat with picture cards **jump rope**, **jam**, **kangaroo**, **king**, **leaf**, and **legs.**

Blending Sounds

Review

- Hold up letter frieze cards of previously taught sounds. Ask students to say the sound each letter stands for.

Model

- Write the word *ten* on the board. Sound out the word by moving your hand under each letter while blending the sounds. (/*teeeennnn*/) Point out that *ten* has a stop sound at the beginning.
- Say the word at normal speed, then ask students to sound out the word with you.

Practice with the Word Lists

- Distribute blackline master 1.
- Have students point to the word *ten.* Ask them to sound out the word with you. Then ask them to say the word at regular speed.
- Repeat with the words *jet*, *will*, and *Kit.* Then have students sound out the words in random order.

Spelling Words

Model

- Use the spelling transparency. Place counters under the second set of boxes on the transparency.
- Say: *Today we are going to learn to spell* **led** *and* **bad.** *Watch and listen as I say* **led** *slowly:* /**lllleeeed**/.
- As you say /**llll**/, push a counter into the first box. Then say /**eeee**/ as you push a counter into the second box and /**d**/ as you push a counter into the third box. Repeat the steps.
- Model recording the letters for the sounds on the transparency. Say: *The first sound is* /**llll**/. *I know that the letter* **l** *stands for the* /**l**/ *sound. I'll write the letter* **l** *in the first box. Let's listen for the second sound:* /**leeee**/. *I hear* /**e**/. *I know that the letter* **e** *stands for the* /**e**/ *sound, so I will write* **e** *in the second box. Let's listen for the last sound:* /**led**/. *I hear* /**d**/. *I know that the letter* **d** *stands for the* /**d**/ *sound, so I will write* **d** *in the last box.*
- Have students blend the sounds to check the spelling of the word.

Practice with the Workmat

- Instruct students to place their counters under the second set of boxes on side 2 of their workmats.
- Ask students to slowly articulate the word **led** as they push the counters into the boxes.
- Have students identify and record the letters that stand for the sounds they hear.
- Have students practice writing **led** on side 1 of their workmats.

Repeat the modeling and practice with the second spelling word, *bad.*

Sight Words

- Write the sight words on the board and have students read the words as you point to them in random order.

Introduce

- Write the word **saw** on the board.
- Say: *This is the word* **saw**. *It is made up of the letters* **s**, **a**, *and* **w**.
- Have students say the word as you point to it.
- Follow the same steps to introduce the words **she** and **this**.
- Write these sentences on the board: "I_____ Kim." "_____ has a fat pup." "_____ pup is my pal." Read the sentences aloud together.
- Say the words **saw**, **she**, and **this.** Ask students which word completes which sentence. Have volunteers write the words in the sentences.

Write

Have students write the words **saw**, **she**, and **this** three times on side 1 of their workmats, using the models on the board.

DAY 2

Independent Activities

Phonemic Awareness

Picture Cards Provide picture cards in the literacy center. Students can:
- take two cards, name the pictures, and tell if the words begin with the same sound
- sort the word cards into those that start with /k/ and those that don't
- take a picture card and find another picture card that has the same middle sound
- match each card to something in the classroom that starts with the same sound

Ending Sounds Have students choose one of the picture cards **mitten**, **web**, and **house**, and look in magazines for pictures that have the same ending sound as their word.

Listen Have students listen to the recording of the poem *King Karl's Kangaroo* in the listening center.

Sound/Symbol Relationships

Letter Toss Write the letters *a*, *e*, *i*, *o*, and *u* on large paper squares. Place the squares on the floor. Students can:
- toss a beanbag onto a square and say the sound that letter stands for
- toss a beanbag onto a square and say a word that has the sound that letter stands for

Letter Spin Provide a spinner that has the letters *f*, *j*, *k*, *p*, *t*, and *w* written in the sections. Students can:
- spin the spinner and say the sound for the letter
- spin the spinner and say a word that begins with that letter's sound

Phonemic Awareness

Use the Poetry Poster
- Show students the picture on the back of the poetry poster, and have them name all the objects in the picture.
- Point to the kittens in the picture and say the word ***kittens***, stressing the beginning sound.
- Ask: *What sound do you hear at the beginning of the word?*
- Ask students to point to something in the picture that starts with /**k**/.

 ## Sound/Symbol Relationships

Sort the Decodable Word Cards
- Place picture cards **jam**, **kangaroo**, **leaf**, and **watch** in the pocket chart. Have students say the name of the object on each picture card.
- Show students decodable word card **jab** and have them blend the word.
- Ask students if ***jab*** begins like ***jam***, ***kangaroo***, ***leaf***, or ***watch***. Then place the card under picture card **jam**.
- Repeat with decodable words cards **Jen**, **jig**, **kid**, **Kit**, **lag**, **lot**, **lug**, **wag**, **wed**, and **win**.

Distribute blackline master 7 and instruct students to complete it at home.

Assessment Tip: Note which letter/sound matches give students difficulty, and provide more practice with those letters and sounds in a small group. Assign Independent Activities for the rest of the class.

P+A+M ## Blending Sounds
- Have students blend the words ***but***, ***ran***, ***let***, and ***kiss***, using the procedure for Day One.

 ## Spelling Words
- Review the words ***led*** and ***bad*** by having students write the words several times.
- Follow the procedure for Day One to model and practice the words ***kiss*** and ***Kit***.

Assessment Tip: Note students who do not slowly articulate the sounds when spelling a word, and provide extra modeling.

Sight Words
- Place the Unit 20 sight word cards in a hat or box. Have students take turns drawing a card and reading the word.

Phonological Awareness

Initial Sound Substitution

- Say the word *kit*. Ask: *What sound do you hear at the beginning of the word?*
- Tell students that you want to make a new word. Say: *I want to change /k/ to /p/. What word will I have?* Segment the sounds in the new word: */p/ /i/ /t/*. Then say the word.
- Have students say what word rhymes with *Tim* and starts the same as *kangaroo*, *sit* and starts the same as *fish*, *pet* and starts the same as *monkey*, *rug* and starts the same as *bear*, *hen* and starts the same as *parrot*.

 Blending Sounds

- Have students blend the words *rid*, *led*, *Kim*, and *kid*.

 Spelling Words

- Review the words *led*, *bad*, *kiss*, and *Kit* by having students write them several times.
- Follow the procedure for Day One to model and practice the words *jam* and *Kim*.

 Sight Words

- Write the words *and*, *are*, *come*, *go*, *I*, *is*, *here*, and *with* on the board. Read them aloud with students.
- Using the following sentences, one at a time, have students cross out the words on the board that they hear in the sentences. Say: *Can Tim go? She stayed with Pop. Gus is my pal. Nan and Gus went home. They are over there. Come see me. I have a red cap. Here comes Kim.*

Distribute blackline master 8 and instruct students to complete it at home.

 Decodable Book

Work with small groups of students to read the decodable book *Kit and Kim* on Days Three and Four. Assign blackline master 3 and Independent Activities for the rest of the class on Day Three.

Introduce the Book

- Display the cover of the book. Point to the title, *Kit and Kim*, and have students sound out the words as you run your finger under them.
- Ask: *What do you see in the picture? Is the pet big or small? Do you have a pet?*

Read the Book

- Give each student a copy of the book and have them turn to page 2. Instruct them to sound out the first word as they run their fingers under it: */JJJeeennnn/*.
- Have students point to the next word. Remind them that this is a word they don't sound out and that they have practiced. Have them say the word *has*.
- Have students run their fingers under the last word as they sound it out: */Kiiiit/*.
- Have students read the whole sentence at normal speed.
- Repeat with the next sentence on the page.
- If students can sound out the words without difficulty, have them whisper-read the rest of the text.
- If students have difficulty, continue guiding them page by page.

Discuss the Book

- When students have finished reading, ask: *Who chases Kit? Who picks up the kitten? How do you know Kit is happy?*

Poetry Poster (Back)

Decodable Book

 **SUPPORT TIPS** for English Language Learners

Develop/reinforce past tense: *saw*

- Before reading, show students objects or pictures. Ask one student: *What did you see?* Accept one-word answers. Model the target language: *(Student's name) saw ____.* Have students repeat the target response: *(Student's name) saw ____.*
- Have students work in pairs as they look at pictures. Have one student describe what he/she sees: *I see/saw a ____.* The other student tells the teacher or another student what the first student saw: *____ saw ____.*
- Alternatively, have students view a common experience, such as a recess activity, and tell the group what they saw. Using students' responses, model the target language structure: *____ saw a ____.*

DAY 4

Independent Activities

Decodable Book

Independent Reading After students have read the decodable book in a small group, have them read the book independently or with a friend.

Dramatize Have students create a dramatization of the story.

Fluency Practice Have students practice reading the story. Videotape the student readings and encourage students to self-monitor their reading progress.

Spelling

As words are introduced each day, write them on index cards and place them in the literacy center. Ensure that the letter cards needed to build the words are in the center. Students can use the following procedure to spell words.
- Choose a word card.
- Use their fingers and eyes to read the word.
- Turn over the card so that they can't see the word.
- Build the word using the letter cards.
- Turn over the card to check the word.
- Write the word.

Sight Words

Personal Dictionary Have students write *saw*, *she*, and *this* in their personal dictionaries.

Word Collage Write *come*, *has*, *have*, *here*, *he*, *is*, *me*, *my*, and *with* on long strips of paper. Have students cut the words from old magazines and tape the words on the correct strip.

 ## Phonemic Awareness

Blend and Segment Sounds

- Model segmenting and blending the word *Kim*. Say: *Listen to these sounds:* /k/ /i/ /m/.
- Have students say the sounds several times. Then have them blend the sounds and say the word.
- Explain that you are going to say another set of sounds. They are to repeat the sounds, then blend them. Use these sound sets: /r/ /a/ /p/, /b/ /i/ /b/, /k/ /i/ /s/.
- Say the word *win* and have students segment it into its individual sounds. Continue with the words *gum*, *dot*, and *jet*.

Assessment Tip: Note which students are having difficulty blending and segmenting sounds, and work with them individually or in a small group.

 ## Blending Sounds

Have students blend the words *kid*, *dug*, *job*, and *kin*, using the procedure for Day One.

 ## Spelling Words

- Review the week's words by having students write them several times on their workmats.
- Provide pairs of students with blackline master 2. While one student reads the words from the list, the other student writes each word.
- If a word is spelled correctly, the partner puts a check mark beside it. If a word is incorrect, the partner may provide prompts. If the second spelling of the word is correct, the partner places a check mark in the "Second Try" column.

Assessment Tip: Collect students' completed blackline masters and note which words gave them difficulty.

Sight Words

Review

- Write the words *and*, *come*, *for*, *here*, *is*, *look*, *said*, *saw*, *she*, *the*, and *this* on the board.
- Erase a letter from one of the words and ask students which letter is missing. Replace the letter and have students read the word.

Decodable Book

- Read the decodable book *Kit and Kim* with the remaining small groups of students. Assign blackline master 4 and Independent Activities for the rest of the class.

Assessment Tip: Use the completed blackline master to assess how well students can match beginning sounds with the letters that stand for those sounds.

Spelling Assessment

Use the following procedure to assess students' spelling of the Unit 20 words.
• Say each spelling word and use it in a sentence.
• Have students write the word on a piece of paper.
• Continue with the next word on the list.
• When students have finished, collect their papers and analyze their spellings of misspelled words.
• Record their progress on a spelling record sheet, and provide extra practice as needed.

 ## Small Group Activities

The following small group activities can be used to provide hands-on practice for students who need additional support. Assign blackline master 5 and Independent Activities for the rest of the class.

 PHONOLOGICAL AWARENESS

Initial /k/ Say: *The king saw a kitten sitting by the kettle. Kim drew a kangaroo on her kite.* Have students tell you which words have the /**k**/ sound.

Initial /k/ Display the back of the poetry poster. Have students make up a phrase about the picture, using at least one /**k**/ word.

Substituting Initial Sounds Have students make a new word by changing the beginning sound in a word to /**b**/. Use the words **hand**, **look**, **sit**, **mat**. Repeat using the words **mad**, **cat**, **fun**, **rub**, and the /**s**/ sound.

Segmenting and Blending Have one student segment the words **Sam**, **tap**, **hip**, and **nut**, and another student blend the sounds.

 SOUND/SYMBOL RELATIONSHIPS

Poem Distribute letter card **k** to each student. Read the poem and have students hold up the card each time you say a word that begins with /**k**/.

Picture Match Place decodable word cards **jab**, **kid**, **lot**, and **wag** in the pocket chart. Have students read each word. Then give each student one (or all) of the picture cards for the letters **k**, **j**, and **l**. Have students name each picture and place it under the appropriate word card.

 BLENDING

Model Write the word **jet** on a workmat. Sound out the word, running your finger under it. Then say the word. Have students do the same. Repeat with the words **kit**, **Kim**, **let**, and **hill**.

 SPELLING

Model and Practice Using a workmat, model saying the sounds and writing the letters in the word **led**. Have students say and write the word on their workmats. Continue with the rest of the spelling words.

Letter Cards Write the spelling words on the board. Mix a set of letter cards. Have a student find the letters of the first word and place the cards on the board ledge.

 **SIGHT WORDS**

Word and Picture Show students sight word cards **for**, **has**, **he**, **me**, **my**, **no**, **saw**, **she**, and **this**. Have them read the words. Hold up a picture card from a previous lesson and have students take turns making up sentences that use the sight word and the picture word.

Say and Spell Show students three or four sight word cards and have them read each word. Then have them clap its spelling and write the word on their papers.

Student Name _____ Assessment Date _____

Phonemic Awareness: Blending Phonemes

Directions: Say the word sound by sound. Then have the student say the word. Put a ✔ if the student's response is correct. If the student misses the word, record the error. **Example:** /d/ /o/ /g/. Dog.

/p/ /o/ /p/ (pop)		/w/ /a/ /g/ (wag)			
/k /i/ /s/ (kiss)		/d/ /i/ /p/ (dip)			
/r/ /e/ /d/ (red)		/m/ /o/ /m/ (mom)		**Score**	/6

Phonemic Awareness: Initial Sound Substitution

Directions: Say the word, and then segment it sound by sound. Ask the student to replace the first sound in the word with the new sound while segmenting sound by sound and then say the new word. Put a ✔ if the student's response is correct. If the student misses the word, record the error. **Example:** man, /m/ /a/ /n/. Change /m/ to /p/. /p/ /a/ /n/, pan.

fin, /f/ /i/ /n/. Change /f/ to /w/. (/w/ /i/ /n/, win)	
bug, /b/ /u/ /g/. Change /b/ to /t/. (/t/ /u/ /g/, tug)	
dot, /d/ /o/ /t/. Change /d/ to /k/. (/k/ /o/ /t/, cot)	
jog, /j/ /o/ /g/. Change /j/ to /l/. (/l/ /o/ /g/, log)	
den, /d/ /e/ /n/. Change /d/ to /t/. (/t/ /e/ /n/, ten)	
can, /k/ /a/ /n/. Change /k/ to /r/. (/r/ /a/ /n/, ran)	**Score** /6

Phonics: Segmenting and Blending Sounds

Directions: Explain that these nonsense words use sounds the student has been learning. Have the student point to each word on the corresponding student sheet, say each sound, and then blend the sounds together. Put a ✔ if the student's response is correct. If the student misses the word, record the error. **Example:** hib. /h/ /i/ /b/, hib.

mec (/m/ /e/ /c/, mec)		ked (/k/ /e/ /d/, ked)			
kig (/k/ /i/ /g/, kig)		tof (/t/ /o/ /f/, tof)			
sup (/s/ /u/ /p/, sup)		kaj (/k/ /a/ /j/, kaj)		**Score**	/6

Sight Words

Directions: Have the student point to the first sight word on the corresponding student sheet and read across the line, saying each word as quickly as possible. Put a ✔ if the student successfully reads the word and an **X** if the student hesitates more than a few seconds. If the student misses the word, record the error.

saw		this			
she				**Score**	/3

UNIT 21 Yy

Unit Objectives
Students will:

- Identify the sound /y/
- Associate the letter Yy with the /y/ sound
- Listen for initial /y/
- Segment and blend phonemes
- Orally substitute medial sounds
- Blend CVC words
- Read the sight words do, like, now
- Spell CVC words using y and letters previously learned

Day 1

BLM 1

BLM 6

Letter Cards: **j, k, y**

Sight Word Cards for Unit 21

Spelling Transparency

Picture Word Cards: **jacks, jam, jar, jump rope, kangaroo, king, kite, kitten, yak, yarn, yolk, yo-yo**

Day 2

BLM 1

BLM 7

Decodable Word Cards for Unit 21

Spelling Transparency

Picture Word Cards: **jam, jar, kangaroo, lamp, rug, sub, sun, web, yak, yo-yo**

Day 3

BLM 1

BLM 3

BLM 8

Sight Word Cards for Unit 21

Spelling Transparency

Day 4

BLM 1

BLM 2

BLM 4

Day 5

BLM 5

Letter Cards for Unit 21

Sight Word Cards for Unit 21

Quick-Check Student Sheet

Poetry Poster

Student Workmat

Letter Frieze Card

Decodable Book

Poetry CD

Core Materials
All print resources can be downloaded from http://phonicsresources.benchmarkeducation.com.

**Poetry Poster
(Front)**

Letter Frieze Card

**Picture Word
Cards**

Phonemic Awareness

Use the Poetry Poster

- Read aloud or play the recording of the poem *Yellow,* and encourage students to join in when they can.
- Say the sentence "I did yard work in my sweater made of yellow yarn." Have students listen for words that have the /y/ sound.
- Reread the poem. Have students clap when they hear words that have the /y/ sound.

Distribute blackline master 6 and instruct students to complete it at home.

Sound/Symbol Relationships

Model

- Display letter frieze card **Yy.** Explain that the letter *Yy* stands for the /y/ sound, as in *yo-yo.*
- Reread the poem *Yellow* and invite students to read along with you.
- Point to words in the poem that begin with the letter **y.** Say the words aloud.

Practice with the Letter Cards

- Distribute letter cards **j, k,** and **y.** Ask students to line up the cards on their workmats.
- Have students pull down each letter card and say the letter name, then push it back up and say the letter sound.
- Ask them to pull down each letter card again, saying a word that starts with that sound.
- Have students push up the letter card that starts the word *yes.* (Repeat with *joke* and *key.*)

Practice with the Picture Cards

- Place letter cards **j, k,** and **y** in the pocket chart.
- Place picture cards **jam, king,** and **yarn** under the corresponding letters while you say the name of the letter and the name of the object in the picture.
- Hold up picture card **yak** and have students say *yak* with you.
- Ask: *Does* **yak** *begin like* **jam, king,** *or* **yarn**?
- Place picture card **yak** under letter card **y.** Say: **Yak** *begins like* **yarn,** *so I am putting picture card* **yak** *under the letter* **y.**
- Repeat with picture cards **jacks, jar, jump rope, kangaroo, kitten, kite, yolk,** and **yo-yo.**

Blending Sounds

Review

- Hold up letter frieze cards of previously taught sounds. Ask students to say the sound each letter stands for.

Model

- Write the word *jog* on the board. Sound out the word by moving your hand under each letter while blending the sounds. (*/joooog/*) Point out that *jog* has stop sounds at the beginning and the end. Then say the word.

Practice with the Word Lists

- Distribute blackline master 1.
- Have students point to the word *jog.* Ask them to sound out the word with you. Then ask them to say the word at regular speed.
- Repeat with the words *kiss, did,* and *yap.* Then have students sound out the words in random order.

Spelling Words

Model

- Use the spelling transparency. Place counters under the second set of boxes on the transparency.
- Say: *Today we are going to learn to spell* **jog** *and* **but***. Watch and listen as I say* **jog** *slowly:* /**joooog**/.
- As you say /**jj**/, push a counter into the first box. Then say /**oooo**/ as you push a counter into the second box and /**g**/ as you push a counter into the third box. Repeat the steps.
- Model recording the letters for the sounds on the transparency. Say: *The first sound is* /**j**/. *I know that the letter* **j** *stands for the* /**j**/ *sound. I'll write the letter* **j** *in the first box. Let's listen for the second sound:* /**joooo**/. *I hear* /**o**/. *I know that the letter* **o** *stands for the* /**o**/ *sound, so I will write* **o** *in the second box. Let's listen for the last sound:* /**jog**/. *I hear* /**g**/. *I know that the letter* **g** *stands for the* /**g**/ *sound, so I will write* **g** *in the last box.*
- Have students blend the sounds to check the spelling of the word.

Practice with the Workmat

- Instruct students to place their counters under the second set of boxes on side 2 of their workmats.
- Ask students to slowly articulate the word *jog* as they push the counters into the boxes.
- Have students identify and record the letters that stand for the sounds they hear.
- Have students practice writing *jog* on side 1 of their workmats.

Repeat the modeling and practice with the second spelling word, *but***.**

 # Sight Words

Review

- Write the sight words on the board. Have students say each word and clap its spelling.

Introduce

- Write the word *do* on the board. Say: *This is the word* **do***. It is made up of the letters* **d** *and* **o***.* Have students say the word.
- Follow the steps to introduce the words *like* and *now*.
- Write these sentences on the board: "Do you pat the pup?" "I like to jog with a pal." "I want the jam now."
- Have volunteers underline the words *Do, like,* and *now*.

Write

- Have students write the words *do, like* and *now* on side 1 of their workmats, using the words on the board as a model.

Independent Activities

Phonological Awareness

Picture Cards Provide picture cards in the literacy center. Students can:
- sort the cards into those that start with the /y/ sound and those that don't
- take two picture cards, name the pictures, and tell if the words end with the same sound
- match a picture card with another card that has the same middle sound

Draw Give students a large sheet of paper and have them fold it into fourths. Have them draw pictures of things that begin with /y/, /j/, /l/, and /w/ in each of the sections.

Listen Have students listen to the recording of the poem *Yellow* in the listening center.

Sound/Symbol Relationships

Pick a Picture Place picture cards **jam, sun, sub, web, rug,** and **yak** in the literacy center. Have students choose a card and name the object in the picture. Then have them build the word with letter cards and write the word.

Vowel Pictures Write the letters *a, e, i, o,* and *u* on separate sheets of chart paper. Have students cut pictures from magazines of objects that have the vowel sound each letter stands for and paste the pictures on the appropriate paper.

Letter Search Have students choose a letter from a previous lesson and search in decodable books for words that begin with that letter.

Phonemic Awareness

Use the Poetry Poster
- Show students the picture on the back of the poetry poster and have them name all the objects in the picture.
- Point to the yo-yo in the picture and say the word *yo-yo*, emphasizing the /y/. Ask: *What sound do you hear at the beginning of the word?*
- Ask students to point to something in the picture that starts with /y/.

Sound/Symbol Relationships

Sort the Decodable Word Cards
- Place picture cards **jar, kangaroo, lamp,** and **yo-yo** in the pocket chart. Have students say the name of the object on each picture card.
- Show students decodable word card **jab.** Have them blend the word.
- Ask students if the word begins like *jar, kangaroo, lamp,* or *yo-yo.* Then place the card under picture card **jar**.
- Repeat with decodable word cards **Jim, job, Kit, kid, lag, leg, lot, yam, yes,** and **yet.**

Distribute blackline master 7 and instruct students to complete it at home.

Assessment Tip: Note which students have difficulty associating any sound with its letter. In a small group, provide extra practice with these sounds and letters. Assign Independent Activities for the rest of the class.

Blending Sounds

- Have students blend the words **yes, yip, set,** and **hub,** using the procedure for Day One.

Spelling Words

- Review the words *jog* and *but* by having students write the words several times.
- Follow the procedure for Day One to model and practice the words *yes* and *yap.*

Assessment Tip: Note students who do not slowly articulate the sounds when spelling a word, and provide extra modeling.

Sight Words

- Write "Do you have a pet?" on the board. Read the sentence with students.
- Ask students to write a sentence using the word *do.* Display the sight word cards in the pocket chart for students to use as models.
- Repeat with the words *like* and *now.*

Phonemic Awareness

Vowel Substitution

- Say the word **bat**, segmenting the sounds: **/b/ /a/ /t/.** Ask: *What sound do you hear in the middle of the word?*
- Say: *I want to change* /a/ *to* /e/. *What word will I have?* Together segment the sounds in the new word and say the word.
- Continue with the following word pairs: **leg/lag, pit/pot, tug/tag, lad/lid, mud/mad, cot/hut.**

 Blending Sounds

- Have students blend the words **ten, mop, yet,** and **yell.**

 Spelling Words

- Review the words **jog, but, yes,** and **yap** by having students write them several times.
- Follow the procedure for Day One to model and practice the words **yell** and **yet.**

 Sight Words

- Write several sight words on the board. Randomly point to words and have students read them with you.
- Erase a letter in one of the words and have students tell you which letter is missing. Replace the letter and have students read the word. Repeat with another sight word.

Distribute blackline master 8 and instruct students to complete it at home.

Poetry Poster (Back)

Decodable Book

Work with small groups of students to read the decodable book *Yip and Yap* on Days Three and Four. Assign blackline master 3 and Independent Activities for the rest of the class on Day Three.

Introduce the Book
- Display the cover of the book. Point to the title, *Yip and Yap*, and have students sound out the words as you run your finger under them.
- Ask: *What do you see in the picture? What is the dog doing? Why is the dog doing that?*

Read the Book
- Give each student a copy of the book and have them turn to page 2. Instruct them to put their fingers on the first word. Remind them that this is a word they don't sound out and that they have practiced. Have them say the word **The.**
- Have them run their fingers under the next word as they sound it out: **/puuuup/.**
- Have students sound out the other words in the sentence: **/kaaaannnn/, /rrrruuuunnnn/, /aaaat/, /Kiiit/.**
- Have students read the whole sentence at normal speed.
- Repeat with the remaining sentences on the page.
- If students can sound out the words without difficulty, have them whisper-read the rest of the text.
- If students have difficulty sounding out the words, continue to guide them page by page.

Discuss the Book
- When students have finished reading, ask: *What does the pup say? What does Pam want? What is Bob doing? Why does the pup stop saying "yip" and "yap"?*

Decodable Book

 **SUPPORT TIPS**
for English Language Learners

Develop/reinforce future tense: will
(Note: This is a late-learned verb tense that requires significant experience with, and exposure to, the structure.)

- Before reading and before recess, ask: *What will you do at recess?* Accept a single-word response, such as **swing**, and model the target response: ___ *will swing.*

- Ask other students what a particular student will do. Accept one-word responses and model the complete target response: *Hui will* ____.

- Ask students what they will do over the upcoming weekend. Accept a single-word response, such as *basketball*, and model the target sentence: ___ *will play basketball.*

DAY 4

Independent Activities

Decodable Book

Independent Reading After students have read the decodable book in a small group, have them read the book independently or with a friend.

Create a Sentence Have students use decodable word cards to make a new sentence for a page in the book.

Spelling

As words are introduced each day, write them on index cards and place them in the literacy center. Ensure that the letter cards needed to build the words are in the center. Students can use the following procedure to spell words.
- Choose a word card.
- Use their fingers and eyes to read the word.
- Turn over the card so that they can't see the word.
- Build the word using the letter cards.
- Turn over the card to check the word.
- Write the word.

Sight Words

Personal Dictionary Have students write *do, like,* and *now* in their personal dictionaries.

Write Sentences Write the following sentences on a sheet of paper, with space below each. Underline words as indicated. Have students read each sentence and then write their own sentence using one or more underlined words.

    <u>I</u> <u>like</u> to pet <u>the</u> pup.
    <u>Put a</u> cup in <u>my</u> lab.
    <u>See</u> him <u>go</u> in <u>the</u> hut <u>with</u> Sam.
    <u>A</u> nut <u>is</u> in <u>the</u> tub.

 ## Phonemic Awareness

Blend and Segment Sounds
- Say the word *yes* by segmenting it into its sounds: */y/ /e/ /s/.* Have students say the sounds.
- Say the following sets of sounds: */p/ /a/ /n/, /j/ /u/ /g/, /y/ /a/ /m/.* Students are to repeat the sounds and blend them to say the words.
- Say the word *yet*. Students should segment it into its individual sounds. Repeat with the words *kin, jag,* and *log.*

Assessment Tip: Note which students are having difficulty segmenting and blending sounds in words, and provide extra practice.

 ## Blending Sounds

- Have students blend the words *pun, lid, yes,* and *yet,* using the procedure for Day One.

 ## Spelling Words

Review
- Review the week's words by having students write them several times on their workmats.
- Provide pairs of students with blackline master 2. While one student reads the words from the list, the other student writes each word.
- If a word is spelled correctly, the partner puts a check mark beside it. If a word is incorrect, the partner may provide prompts. If the second spelling of the word is correct, the partner places a check mark in the "Second Try" column.

Assessment Tip: Collect students' completed blackline masters and note which words gave them difficulty.

Sight Words

Review
- Write the words *do, he, like, look, now,* and *she* on the board.
- Say each word. Ask a volunteer to trace the letters with their finger.

 ## Decodable Book

- Read the decodable book *Yip and Yap* with the remaining small groups of students. Assign blackline master 4 and Independent Activities for the rest of the class.

Assessment Tip: Use the completed blackline master to assess how well students can match beginning sounds with the letters that stand for these sounds.

Spelling Assessment

Use the following procedure to assess students' spelling of the Unit 21 words.
• Say each spelling word and use it in a sentence.
• Have students write the word on a piece of paper.
• Continue with the next word on the list.
• When students have finished, collect their papers and analyze their spellings of misspelled words.
• Record their progress on a spelling record sheet, and provide extra practice as needed.

 ## Small Group Activities

The following small group activities can be used to provide hands-on practice for students who need additional support. Assign blackline master 5 and Independent Activities for the rest of the class.

 ### PHONOLOGICAL AWARENESS

Initial /y/ Display the back of the poetry poster. Ask: *Do you have a yak in your yard? What words have /y/?* Have students take turns using the sentence pattern "Do you have a _____ in your yard?" to ask questions about **y** objects in the poster.

Medial Substitution Have students change the vowel sound in each of the following words to /i/: *tap, set, hot, hum.* Repeat with /o/ and the words *jab, net, rib,* and *cut.*

Blending and Segmenting Say the words *bag, beg, big, bog,* and *bug* one at a time. Have one student segment the word into its sounds and another student blend the sounds.

 ### SOUND/SYMBOL RELATIONSHIPS

Poem Give each student letter card **y.** Reread the poem and have students hold up the card each time you say a word that begins with /y/.

Initial Sounds Place letter cards **j, k, l,** and **y** in the pocket chart. Say the words *yawn, yip,* and *year.* Point to the letter **y** and remind students that **y** stands for the /y/ sound. Repeat with *January/June/July, keep/keg/kitten, lake/log/lick,* and *yip/yap/yo-yo.*

 ### BLENDING

Blending Practice 1 Say the sounds in each word on the word list, and let each student blend the sounds to make the word.

Blending Practice 2 Write the words *yak, yes, yip,* and *yum* on chart paper. Have students take turns running their fingers under each word as they blend the sounds.

 ### SPELLING

Letter Cards Write the spelling words on the board. Place letter cards **a, b, e, g, j, o, p, s, t, u, l, l,** and **y** on a table. Have students take turns choosing a word and the letters to build the word.

Missing Vowels Write spelling words *jog, but, yes, yap, yell,* and *yet* on the board, with the vowel missing in each word. Say one of the words. Have students name the missing letter. Continue with the other words.

 ### SIGHT WORDS

Read the Cards Hold up sight word cards **a, are, come, do, is, like, now, put, said, saw,** and **this,** one at a time. Have students read each word.

Spotlight Write the words *and, do, for, has, have, here, I, like, my, no, now,* and *see* on the board. Dim the lights in the room. Have students take turns shining a flashlight on a word, reading it, spelling it, and using it in a sentence.

Student Name _____ Assessment Date _____

Phonemic Awareness: Segmenting Phonemes

Directions: Say the word. Have the student say the word sound by sound and then say the whole word. If the student segments the word correctly, put a ✔. If the student's response is incorrect, record the error. **Example:** sip. /s/ /i/ /p/, sip.

yet (/y/ /e/ /t/, yet)		him (/h/ /i/ /m/, him)			
bun (/b/ /u/ /n/, bun)		yell (/y/ /e/ /l/, yell)			
peg (/p/ /e/ /g/, peg)		lip (/l/ /i/ /p/, lip)		**Score**	**/6**

Phonemic Awareness: Medial Sound Substitution

Directions: Say the word, and then segment it sound by sound. Ask the student to replace the middle sound in the word with the new sound while segmenting sound by sound and then say the new word. Put a ✔ if the student's response is correct. If the student misses the word, record the error. **Example:** man, /m/ /a/ /n/. Change /a/ to /e/. /m/ /e/ /n/, men.

tin, /t/ /i/ /n/. Change /i/ to /a/. (/t/ /a/ /n/, tan)			
big, /b/ /i/ /g/. Change /i/ to /e/. (/b/ /e/ /g/, beg)			
not, /n/ /o/ /t/. Change /o/ to /e/. (/n/ /e/ /t/, net)			
lock, /l/ /o/ /k/. Change /o/ to /u/. (/l/ /u/ /k/, luck)			
hem, /h/ /e/ /m/. Change /e/ to /i/. (/h/ /i/ /m/, him)			
cub, /k/ /u/ /b/. Change /u/ to /o/. (/k/ /o/ /b/, cob)		**Score**	**/6**

Phonics: Segmenting and Blending Sounds

Directions: Explain that these nonsense words use sounds the student has been learning. Have the student point to each word on the corresponding student sheet, say each sound, and then blend the sounds together. Put a ✔ if the student's response is correct. If the student misses the word, record the error. **Example:** nem. /n/ /e/ /m/, nem.

yag (/y/ /a/ /g/, yag)		bic (/b/ /i/ /k/, bic)			
pof (/p/ /o/ /f/, pof)		yok (/y/ /o/ /k/, yok)			
yed (/y/ /e/ /d/, yed)		sut (/s/ /u/ /t/, sut)		**Score**	**/6**

Sight Words

Directions: Have the student point to the first sight word on the corresponding student sheet and read across the line, saying each word as quickly as possible. Put a ✔ if the student successfully reads the word and an **X** if the student hesitates more than a few seconds. If the student misses the word, record the error.

do		now			
like				**Score**	**/3**

UNIT 22 Vv

Unit Objectives

Students will:

- Identify the sound /v/
- Associate the letter Vv with the /v/ sound
- Listen for initial /v/
- Listen for medial sounds
- Segment and blend phonemes
- Blend CVC words
- Read the sight words home, they, went
- Spell CVC words using v and letters previously learned

UNIT 22 Vv

Day 1

BLM 1

BLM 6

Letter Cards: **v, y, l, w**

Spelling Transparency

Picture Word Cards: **lamp, leaf, legs, van, vase, vegetables, vest, wasp, watch, web**

Day 2

BLM 1

BLM 7

Decodable Word Cards for Unit 22

Spelling Transparency

Picture Word Cards: **box, mop, pen, vase**

Day 3

BLM 1

BLM 3

BLM 8

Spelling Transparency

Day 4

BLM 1

BLM 2

BLM 4

Day 5

BLM 5

Letter Cards for Unit 22

Quick-Check Student Sheet

Poetry Poster

Student Workmat

Letter Frieze Card

Decodable Book

Poetry CD

Core Materials

All print resources can be downloaded from http://phonicsresources.benchmarkeducation.com.

**Poetry Poster
(Front)**

Letter Frieze Card

**Picture Word
Cards**

Phonemic Awareness

Use the Poetry Poster

- Read aloud or play the recording of the poem *Violins and Violets,* and encourage students to join in when they can.
- Say the sentence "I really love my violin and my velvet vest." Have students listen for */v/.*
- Reread the poem. Have students clap each time they hear */v/.*

Distribute blackline master 6 and instruct students to complete it at home.

Sound/Symbol Relationships

Model

- Display letter frieze card **Vv.** Explain that the letter **Vv** stands for the */v/* sound, as in **vest.**
- Reread the poem *Violins and Violets,* inviting students to read along with you.
- Point to words in the poem that begin with the letter **v.** Say the words aloud and ask students to say the words with you.

Practice with the Letter Cards

- Distribute letter cards **v, y,** and **l.** Ask students to line up the cards on their workmats.
- Have students pull down each letter card and say the letter name, then push it back up and say the letter sound.
- Ask them to pull down each letter card again, saying a word that starts with that sound.
- Have students push up the letter card that starts the word **vest.** (Repeat with **year** and **lamp.**)

Practice with the Picture Cards

- Place letter cards **v, l,** and **w** in the pocket chart.
- Place picture cards **van, leaf,** and **web** under the corresponding letters while you say the name of the letter and the name of the object in the picture.
- Hold up picture card **vest** and have students say **vest** with you.
- Ask: *Does* **vest** *begin like* **van, leaf,** *or* **web***?*
- Place picture card **vest** under letter card **v.** Say: *Vvvvest begins like* **vvvvan,** *so I am putting picture card* **vest** *under the letter* **v.**
- Repeat with picture cards **vegetables, vase, lamp, legs, watch,** and **wasp.**

Blending Sounds

Review

- Hold up letter frieze cards of previously taught sounds. Ask students to say the sound each letter stands for.

Model

- Write the word **tip** on the board. Sound out the word by moving your hand under each letter while blending the sounds. (*/tiiiip/*) Then say the word.

Practice with the Word Lists

- Distribute blackline master 1.
- Have students point to the word **tip.** Ask them to sound out the word with you. Then ask them to say the word at regular speed.
- Repeat with the words **cup, yet,** and **but.** Then have students sound out the words in random order.

Spelling Words

Model

- Use the spelling transparency. Place counters under the second set of boxes on the transparency.
- Say: *Today we are going to learn to spell* **yet** *and* **tip.** *Watch and listen as I say* **yet** *slowly:* /**yyyyeeeet**/. Remind students that the word has a stop sound at the end.
- As you say /**yyyy**/, push a counter into the first box. Then say /**eeee**/ as you push a counter into the second box and /**t**/ as you push a counter into the third box. Repeat the steps.
- Model recording the letters for the sounds on the transparency. Say: *The first sound is* /**yyyy**/. *I know that the letter* **y** *stands for the* /**y**/ *sound. I'll write the letter* **y** *in the first box. Let's listen for the second sound:* /**yeeee**/. *I hear* /**e**/. *I know that the letter* **e** *stands for the* /**e**/ *sound, so I will write* **e** *in the second box. Let's listen for the last sound:* /**yet**/. *I hear* /**t**/. *I know that the letter* **t** *stands for the* /**t**/ *sound, so I will write* **t** *in the last box.*
- Have students blend the sounds to check the spelling of the word.

Practice with the Workmat

- Instruct students to place their counters under the second set of boxes on side 2 of their workmats.
- Ask students to slowly articulate the word *yet* as they push the counters into the boxes.
- Have students identify and record the letters that stand for the sounds they hear.
- Have students practice writing *yet* on side 1 of their workmats.

Repeat the modeling and practice with the second spelling word, *tip.*

Sight Words

Review

- Write the words *now, like, do, this, she,* and *saw* on the board. As a group, read the words aloud, then spell them aloud. Ask volunteers to use each word in a sentence.

Introduce

- Write the word *home* on the board.
- Say: *This is the word* **home.** *It is made up of the letters* **h, o, m,** *and* **e.**
- Have students say the word and spell it in the air with their fingers.
- Follow the same steps for the words *they* and *went.*

Write

Have students write the words *home, they,* and *went* on side 1 of their workmats, using the words on the board as a model.

DAY 2

Independent Activities

Phonological Awareness

Picture Cards Provide picture cards in the literacy center. Students can:
- place the picture cards facedown, turn over a card, say the picture name, and tell if it starts with /v/
- sort the cards into piles according to beginning sounds
- pick two pictures that start with the same sound and make up a sentence about the pictures

Draw Tape a sheet of paper to a wall. Let students draw things that start with /v/.

Listen Have students listen to the recording of the poem *Violins and Violets* in the listening center.

Sound/Symbol Relationships

Vowel Sort Provide decodable word cards and have students sort them according to vowel sound.

Letter Cards Place letter cards for the words *van, vet, nap, pug, run, set, hop,* and *tip* in an envelope, one envelope per word. Have students take an envelope and build the word using the letter cards.

Poetry Poster (Back)

Phonemic Awareness

Use the Poetry Poster
- Show students the picture on the back of the poetry poster, and have them name all the objects in the picture.
- Point to the violin in the picture and say the word *violin*. Ask: *What sound do you hear at the beginning of the word?*
- Have students take turns naming objects to put in the van that start with /v/. Model by saying: *I can put* **violets** *in the van.*

Sound/Symbol Relationships

Sort the Decodable Word Cards
- Place picture cards **vase, box, mop,** and **pen** in the pocket chart and have students say the name of the object on each picture card.
- Show students decodable word card **van** and have them blend the word.
- Ask students if **van** begins like **vase, box, mop,** or **pen.** Then place the card under picture card **vase**.
- Repeat with decodable word cards **vet, bun, bag, man, map, pen,** and **pot.**

Distribute blackline master 7 and instruct students to complete it at home.

Assessment Tip: Note which students cannot match the words and the pictures. Give them extra practice with identifying the beginning sounds of the picture names, then the words. Assign Independent Activities for the rest of the class.

Blending Sounds

- Have students blend the words **van, vet, pan,** and **pet,** using the procedure for Day One.

Spelling Words

- Review the words **yet** and **tip** by having students write the words several times.
- Follow the procedure for Day One to model and practice the words **vet** and **van.**

Sight Words

- Write the words **home, they,** and **went** on the board. Have students write the letters in the air with their fingers.
- Write **put, want, go,** and **my** on the board. Erase one word, then say the word and have students write it on side 1 of their workmats. Write the word on the board and have students check their spelling. Continue with the other words.

Phonemic Awareness

Vowel Substitution

• Say the word **vet**. Ask: *What sound do you hear in the middle of* **vet**?
• Tell students that you are going to change the */e/* to */a/*. Ask what word you will have.
• Continue in the same way, changing **tip** to **top**, then to **tap**.

Blending Sounds

• Have students blend the words **bid, ram, Val,** and **wit**.

Spelling Words

• Review the words **yet, tip, vet,** and **van** by having students write them several times.
• Follow the procedure for Day One to model and practice the words **Val** and **hug.**

Sight Words

• Write **home, they,** and **went** on the board. Say sentences that each contain one of these words. Students are to raise their hands when they hear a word from the board. For example, say: *Who* **went** *with you?* **They** *are my sisters. Is your mother at* **home**?
• Write **look, here, come, home, they,** and **went** on the board, leaving out one letter in each word. Have volunteers write the missing letter.

Distribute blackline master 8 and instruct students to complete it at home.

Decodable Book

Work with small groups of students to read the decodable book *The Vet* on Days Three and Four. Assign blackline master 3 and Independent Activities for the rest of the class on Day Three.

Introduce the Book

• Display the cover of the book. Point to the title, *The Vet*, and have students sound out the words as you run your finger under them.
• Ask: *What do you see in the picture? What is a vet? What does a vet do?*

Read the Book

• Give each student a copy of the book and have them turn to page 2. Instruct them to run their fingers under the first word as they sound it out: */SSSaaammm/*.
• Have students point to the next word. Remind them that this is a word they don't sound out and that they have practiced. Have them say the word **said.**
• As students run their fingers under the next words, continue to distinguish between words they sound out and words they must recognize by sight.
• Have students read the whole sentence at normal speed.
• If students can sound out the words without difficulty, have them whisper-read the rest of the text.
• If students have difficulty sounding out the words, continue to guide them page by page.

Discuss the Book

• When students have finished reading, ask: *Why did Sam and Pop go to the vet? Who went to the vet with Sam and Pop? Why was the cat fat?*

Decodable Book

SUPPORT TIPS
for English Language Learners

Develop/reinforce future tense: *will*

(Note: This is a late-learned verb tense that requires significant experience with, and exposure to, the structure.)

• Before lunch, ask: *What* **will** *you eat for lunch?* Accept single-word responses, such as *pizza*, and model the target response: ___ **will** *eat pizza.*

• Ask other students what a particular student will eat. Accept single-word responses and model the target response: *Maria* **will** *eat pizza.*

• Ask students what they will do over the upcoming weekend. Accept single-word responses, such as *skate*, and model the target response: ___ **will** *skate.*

• Ask other students what a particular student will do. Accept single-word responses and model the target response: *Maria* **will** *skate.*

Independent Activities

Decodable Book

Independent Reading Have students read the book independently or with a buddy for practice.

What Comes Next? Have students draw a picture showing what happens after the last page in the book.

Dramatize Have students read the story as a play. Provide time for students to practice, then have them present the story to the class.

Spelling

As words are introduced each day, write them on index cards and place them in the literacy center. Ensure that the letter cards needed to build the words are in the center. Students can use the following procedure to spell words.
• Choose a word card.
• Use their fingers and eyes to read the word.
• Turn over the card so that they can't see the word.
• Build the word using the letter cards.
• Turn over the card to check the word.
• Write the word.

Sight Words

Personal Dictionary Have students write the words **home, they,** and **went** in their personal dictionaries.

Construct Ask students to build the words **home, they,** and **went** by cutting letters from a newspaper and pasting them on construction paper.

Word Draw Place sight word cards in a bowl. Have each student draw a card, read the word, and write a sentence with the word.

 ## Phonemic Awareness

Blend and Segment Sounds
• Segment and blend the sounds in the word **vet**: */vvvv/ /eeee/ /t/, /vet/*. Have students do the same.
• Say: */vvvv/ /aaaa/ /nnnn/*. Ask students to tell you what the word is.
• Repeat for the words **pick, vest,** and **will.**

Assessment Tip: Note students who have difficulty blending the sounds, and provide more practice.

 ## Blending Sounds

• Have students blend the words **van, cut, hot,** and **rid,** using the procedure for Day One.

 ## Spelling Words

Review
• Review the week's words by having students write them several times on their workmats.
• Provide pairs of students with blackline master 2. While one student reads the words from the list, the other student writes each word.
• If a word is spelled correctly, the partner puts a check mark beside it. If a word is incorrect, the partner may provide prompts. If the second spelling of the word is correct, the partner places a check mark in the "Second Try" column.

Assessment Tip: Collect students' completed blackline masters and note which words gave them difficulty.

 ## Sight Words

Review
• Write the words **home, they, went, now, this, want, she,** and **come** on the board.
• Pair students and have them think of a sentence in which they use two or more of the words on the list. Have pairs write their sentences on the board.

Decodable Book

• Read the decodable book *The Vet* with the remaining small groups of students. Assign blackline master 4 and Independent Activities for the rest of the class.

Assessment Tip: Use the completed blackline master to assess how well students can make connections between beginning sounds and the letters that stand for those sounds.

Spelling Assessment

Use the following procedure to assess students' spelling of the Unit 22 words.
• Say each spelling word and use it in a sentence.
• Have students write the word on a piece of paper.
• Continue with the next word on the list.
• When students have finished, collect their papers and analyze their spellings of misspelled words.
• Record their progress on a spelling record sheet, and provide extra practice as needed.

 # Small Group Activities

The following small group activities can be used to provide hands-on practice for students who need additional support. Assign blackline master 5 and Independent Activities for the rest of the class.

 ### PHONOLOGICAL AWARENESS

Initial Sounds Say the words *vase, vet,* and *van*. Have students tell you what sound is the same in all the words. Repeat the activity, using *web/want/wagon, yellow/yes/your,* and *king/ketchup/kite.*

Vowel Substitution Say the words *pan* and *pin*. Ask students what sound is different in the words. Then ask what word could be made from *pin* by changing the middle sound to /e/.

 ### SOUND/SYMBOL RELATIONSHIPS

Poem Distribute letter card **v.** Reread the poem, emphasizing words with /v/. Have students take turns holding their card under each word that begins with /v/.

Segmenting Sounds Write the words *cut, hot, rid,* and *van* on the board. Let students take turns separating the words into their sounds.

 ### BLENDING

Modeling Write the word *van* on a workmat. Sound out the word by moving your hand under each letter as you blend the sounds. Then say the word and have students sound it out with you. Have the student point to each letter and say each sound.

 ### SPELLING

Letter Cards Distribute letter cards **y, e, t, i, p, v, V, a, h, u, g,** and **n.** Say the word *yet* and ask students to make the word with their letters. Then have them change letters to make the words *vet, van,* and *Val.* (Remind them to use the capital letter for the name.)

 ### SIGHT WORDS

Make a Sentence Write the words *home, they, went, now, like, do, this, she,* and *saw* on the board. Ask students to use a word in a sentence and draw a picture based on the sentence.

Oral Cloze Write the words *home, went,* and *they* on the board. Tell a story that is missing some words. Students are to tell you which word on the board goes in each place. Say: *School was over. Laura and Alex were going ___. Then ___ saw a little kitten. It ___ up a tree.*

Student Name _____ Assessment Date _____

Phonemic Awareness: Blending Phonemes

Directions: Say the word sound by sound. Then have the student say the word.
Put a ✓ if the student's response is correct. If the student misses the word, record the error.
Example: /d/ /o/ /g/. *Dog.*

/v/ /a/ /n/ (van)		/h/ /i/ /l/ (hill)			
/b/ /u/ /s/ (bus)		/j/ /e/ /t/ (jet)			
/w/ /e/ /b/ (web)		/m/ /o/ /s/ (moss)		Score	/6

Phonemic Awareness: Medial Sound Substitution

Directions: Say the word, and then segment it sound by sound. Ask the student
to replace the middle sound in the word with the new sound while segmenting
sound by sound and then say the new word. Put a ✓ if the student's response is
correct. If the student misses the word, record the error.
Example: man, /m/ /a/ /n/. Change /a/ to /e/. /m/ /e/ /n/, men.

vat, /v/ /a/ /t. Change /a/ to /e/. (/v/ /e/ /t/, vet)	
lot, /l/ /o/ /t/. Change /o/ to /e/. (/l/ /e/ /t/, let)	
dill, /d/ /i/ /l/. Change /i/ to /o/. (/d/ /o/ /l/, doll)	
tub, /t/ /u/ /b/. Change /u/ to /a/. (/t/ /a/ /b/, tab)	
net, /n/ /e/ /t/. Change /e/ to /o/. (/n/ /o/ /t/, not)	
sock, /s/ /o/ /k/. Change /o/ to /i/. (/s/ /i/ /k/, sick)	Score /6

Phonics: Segmenting and Blending Sounds

Directions: Explain that these nonsense words use sounds the student has been
learning. Have the student point to each word on the corresponding student sheet,
say each sound, and then blend the sounds together. Put a ✓ if the student's response
is correct. If the student misses the word, record the error.
Example: mof. /m/ /o/ /f/, mof.

sab (/s/ /a/ /b/, sab)		vel (/v/ /e/ /l/, vel)			
vig (/v/ /i/ /g/, vig)		tup (/t/ /u/ /p/, tup)			
wen (/w/ /e/ /n/, wen)		vak (/v/ /a/ /k/, vak)		Score	/6

Sight Words

Directions: Have the student point to the first sight word on the corresponding
student sheet and read across the line, saying each word as quickly as possible.
Put a ✓ if the student successfully reads the word and an **X** if the student hesitates
more than a few seconds. If the student misses the word, record the error.

home		went			
they				Score	/3

Unit Objectives

Students will:

- Identify the sound /kw/
- Associate the letter Qq with the /kw/ sound
- Listen for /kw/ in words
- Segment and blend phonemes
- Orally substitute medial sounds
- Blend CVC words
- Read the sight word good
- Spell CVC words using q and letters previously learned

Day 1

BLM 1   BLM 6   Letter Cards: **q, v, y**   Sight Word Cards for Unit 23   Spelling Transparency   Picture Word Cards: **quail, quarter, queen, quilt, van, vase, vegetables, vest, yak, yarn, yolk, yo-yo**

Day 2

BLM 1   BLM 7   Decodable Word Cards for Unit 23   Spelling Transparency   Picture Word Cards: **jacks, king, queen, quilt, vegetables, vest, yak, yarn**

Day 3

BLM 1   BLM 3   BLM 8   Spelling Transparency

Day 4

BLM 1   BLM 2   BLM 4   Sight Word Cards for Unit 23   Letter Cards for Unit 23

Day 5

BLM 1   BLM 5   Decodable Word Cards for Unit 23   Sight Word Cards for Unit 23   Quick-Check Student Sheet   Picture Word Cards: **king, queen, vest, yarn**

Poetry Poster

Student Workmat

Letter Frieze Cards

Decodable Book

Poetry CD

Core Materials

All print resources can be downloaded from http://phonicsresources.benchmarkeducation.com.

**Poetry Poster
(Front)**

**Letter Frieze
Cards**

**Picture Word
Cards**

 ## Phonemic Awareness

Use the Poetry Poster

- Read aloud or play the recording of the poem *The Queen's Nap.*
- Say the sentence "'Quiet now,' said the Queen." Have students listen for the */kw/* sound.
- Reread the poem. Have students clap each time they hear a word that starts with */kw/*.

Distribute blackline master 6 and instruct students to complete it at home.

Sound/Symbol Relationships

Model

- Display letter frieze cards **Qq** and **Uu.** Explain that together the letters **Qq** and **Uu** stand for the */kw/* sound, as in the word **queen.**
- Reread the poem and have students read along with you.
- Point to words in the poem that begin with the letter **q.** Say the words aloud and ask students to say the words with you.

Practice with the Letter Cards

- Distribute letter cards **q, v,** and **y.** Ask students to line up the cards on their workmats.
- Have students pull down each letter card and say the letter name, then push it back up and say the letter sound.
- Ask them to pull down each letter card again, saying a word that starts with that sound.
- Have students push up the letter card that starts the word **queen.** (Repeat with **van** and **yet.**)

Practice with the Picture Cards

- Place letter cards **q, v,** and **y** in the pocket chart.
- Place picture cards **queen, van,** and **yarn** under the corresponding letters while you say the name of the letter and the name of the object in the picture.
- Hold up picture card **quilt** and have students say **quilt** with you.
- Ask: *Does* **quilt** *begin like* **queen, van,** *or* **yarn***?*
- Place picture card **quilt** under letter card **q.** Say: **Quilt** *begins like* **queen,** *so I am putting picture card* **quilt** *under the letter* **q.**
- Repeat with picture cards **quail, quarter, vase, vest, vegetables, yo-yo, yak,** and **yolk.**

Blending Sounds

Review

- Hold up letter frieze cards of previously taught sounds. Ask students to say the sound each letter stands for.

Model

- Write the word **vet** on the board. Sound out the word by moving your hand under each letter while blending the sounds. (*/vvvveeeet/*) Then say the word.
- Ask students to sound out the word with you. Point out that **vet** has a stop sound at the end.

Practice with the Word Lists

- Distribute blackline master 1.
- Have students point to the word **vet.** Ask them to sound out the word with you. Then ask them to say the word at regular speed.
- Repeat with the words **yes, jam,** and **kiss.** Then have students sound out the words in random order.

Spelling Words

Model
- Use the spelling transparency. Place counters under the second set of boxes on the transparency.
- Say: *Today we are going to learn to spell* **jam** *and* **bad***. Watch and listen as I say* **jam** *slowly:* /jjjjaaaammmm/***.**
- As you say **/jjjj/,** push a counter into the first box. Then say **/aaaa/** as you push a counter into the second box and **/mmmm/** as you push a counter into the third box. Repeat the steps.
- Model recording the letters for the sounds on the transparency. Say: *The first sound is* /jjjj/*. I know that the letter* **j** *stands for the* /**j**/ *sound. I'll write the letter* **j** *in the first box. Let's listen for the second sound:* /j**aaaa**/*. I hear* /**a**/*. I know that the letter* **a** *stands for the* /**a**/ *sound, so I will write* **a** *in the second box. Let's listen for the last sound:* /jam**mmm**/*. I hear* /**m**/*. I know that the letter* **m** *stands for the* /**m**/ *sound, so I will write* **m** *in the last box.*
- Have students blend the sounds to check the spelling of the word.

Practice with the Workmat
- Instruct students to place their counters under the second set of boxes on side 2 of their workmats.
- Ask students to slowly articulate the word **jam** as they push the counters into the boxes.
- Have students identify and record the letters that stand for the sounds they hear.
- Have students practice writing **jam** on side 1 of their workmats.

Repeat the modeling and practice with the second spelling word, *bad*.

 # Sight Words

Review
- Show students the sight word cards and have them say the words.

Introduce
- Write the word **good** on the board.
- Have students say the word.
- Write "This jam is good" on the board. Read the sentence and ask students which word is the word **good**. Have volunteers make up oral sentences using the word **good**. Have the rest of the students clap when they hear the word.

Write
Have students write the word **good** three times on side 1 of their workmats, using the word on the board as a model.

DAY 2

Independent Activities

Phonemic Awareness

Picture Cards Provide picture cards in the literacy center. Students can:
- match a picture with an object in the room that has the same beginning sound
- sort the pictures according to beginning sound
- show a picture to a partner and have the partner name words that have the same beginning sound
- find a picture in a magazine that has the same beginning sound as a picture card

Sound Quilt Draw large squares on mural paper. Display picture cards **quilt, vegetables, yak,** and **jacks.** Have students draw pictures in the squares that begin with the same sounds.

Listen Have students listen to the recording of the poem *The Queen's Nap* in the listening center.

Sound/Symbol Relationships

Q Words Have students make a crown out of construction paper and write words that begin with *qu* on it.

Match Have students place decodable word cards **yet, yes, van, vet, quip, quill, job,** and **jet** facedown. Students take turns choosing a card and reading the word. They keep the card. When a word comes up that has the same beginning sound as a previously used word, either player may say "Match," read the words, and tell what letter stands for the beginning sound.

 Phonemic Awareness

Use the Poetry Poster
- Show students the picture on the back of the poetry poster and have them name all the objects in the picture.
- Point to the queen in the picture and say the word **queen.** Ask: *What sound do you hear at the beginning of the word?*
- Ask students to point to something in the picture that starts with */kw/.*

 Sound/Symbol Relationships

Sort the Decodable Word Cards
- Place picture cards **queen, vest, yarn,** and **king** in the pocket chart and have students say the name of the object on each picture card.
- Show students decodable word card **quit** and have them blend the word.
- Ask students if **quit** begins like **queen, vest, yarn,** or **king.** Then place the card under picture card **queen.**
- Repeat with decodable word cards **quill, vet, van, yet, yes, kit,** and **kid.**

Distribute blackline master 7 and instruct students to complete it at home.

Assessment Tip: Note which students have difficulty associating any sound with its letter. In a small group, provide extra practice with these sounds and letters. Assign Independent Activities for the rest of the class.

P+A+M **Blending Sounds**

- Have students blend the words **quit, quip, bin,** and **had,** using the procedure for Day One.

 Spelling Words

- Review the words **jam** and **bad** by having students write the words several times.
- Follow the procedure for Day One to model and practice the words **quit** and **yet.**

Assessment Tip: Note students who do not slowly articulate the sounds when spelling a word, and provide extra modeling.

 Sight Words

- Write the word **good** on the board. Read and spell the word with students. Then erase the word and have students write it.
- Provide clues to various words and have students make guesses. For example, say: *This word ends with* **d.**

Phonological Awareness

Initial Sound Substitution

- Say the word *quit*. Ask: *What sound do you hear at the beginning of the word? If I change /kw/ to /h/, what word will I have?*
- Ask students for the answers to some riddles. For example, ask: *What word rhymes with* **back** *and starts with the /kw/ sound? What word rhymes with* **get** *and starts with the /v/ sound? What word rhymes with* **sick** *and starts with the /kw/ sound? What word rhymes with* **Pam** *and starts with the /y/ sound? What word rhymes with* **hill** *and starts with the /kw/ sound?*

 ## Blending Sounds

- Have students blend the words *quill, yell, will,* and *pad.*

 ## Spelling Words

- Review the words *jam, bad, quit,* and *yet* by having students write them several times.
- Follow the procedure for Day One to model and practice the words *quip* and *quill*.

 ## Sight Words

- Write the word *good* on the board. Have students take turns using the word in oral sentences.
- Write *come, here, said, have, want, this,* and *like* under *good,* then draw a row of boxes. Say: *I'm thinking of one of these words.* Write one letter of the word in one box as a clue. Students should say the word *come.* Continue in the same way with the remaining words.

Distribute blackline master 8 and instruct students to complete it at home.

 ## Decodable Book

Work with small groups of students to read the decodable book *Quinn* on Days Three and Four. Assign blackline master 3 and Independent Activities for the rest of the class on Day Three.

Introduce the Book

- Display the cover of the book. Point to the title, *Quinn,* and have students sound out the word as you run your finger under it. Ask: *What do you see in the picture? Who is Quinn? What do you think will happen?*

Read the Book

- Give each student a copy of the book and have them turn to page 2. Instruct them to put their fingers on the first word and sound it out: */JJJJiiiimmmm/.*
- Have students point to the next word. Remind them that this is a word they don't sound out and that they have practiced. Have them say the word *and.*
- Have students point to the other words in the sentence and sound out each one as they run their fingers under them: */JJJJeeeennnn/, /haaaad/, /Kiiiit/.*
- Have students read the whole sentence at normal speed.
- If students can sound out the words without difficulty, have them whisper-read the rest of the text.
- If students are having difficulty, continue to guide them page by page.

Discuss the Book

- When students have finished reading, ask: *Why were people in the contest unhappy with Quinn? What did Len say to Quinn? Why? Who won the contest? Why?*

Poetry Poster (Back)

Decodable Book

 **SUPPORT TIPS** for English Language Learners

Develop/reinforce past tense: *had*

- Before reading, give three or four students different classroom items or pictures of characters. Have students show the class their items/pictures.
- Collect the items and ask: *Who had the ____?*
- Accept single-word responses, but model the target past tense verb sentence, *Daniel had the ____,* and have students chime in.
- Repeat the activity, having individual students ask the question and choosing a student to respond. Model the target response as necessary.
- Assign students to small groups to repeat the activity, using the question and the complete sentence to respond.

Independent Activities

Decodable Book

Independent Practice After students have read the decodable book in the small group setting, have them read the book independently or with a buddy for practice.

Dialogue Ask students to make up a dialogue between Len and another pet owner. Have them perform their dialogue.

Spelling

As words are introduced each day, write them on index cards and place them in the literacy center. Ensure that the letter cards needed to build the words are in the center. Students can use the following procedure to spell words.

- Choose a word card.
- Use their fingers and eyes to read the word.
- Turn over the card so that they can't see the word.
- Build the word using the letter cards.
- Turn over the card to check the word.
- Write the word.

Sight Words

Personal Dictionary Have students write the word **good** in their personal dictionaries.

Complete the Sentence Write this sentence pattern on chart paper: "A ___ is good." Have students draw a picture or write a word to complete the sentence.

Phonemic Awareness

Blend and Segment Sounds

- Say **quit**, segmenting and then blending the sounds: **/kw/ /i/ /t/, /kwit/**. Have students say the word.
- Reread the first two lines of the poem, but instead of saying the word **nap**, segment the sounds. Have students repeat the segmented sounds and blend them. Repeat with the words **Duck, sat,** and **lap**.
- Segment the sounds in the words **quip, van,** and **yes,** and have students say the words.

Assessment Tip: Have individual students segment and blend sounds. Note those who are having difficulty.

 ## Blending Sounds

- Have students blend the words **kid, quit, quip,** and **can,** using the procedure for Day One.

Spelling Words

Review

- Review the week's words by having students write them several times on their workmats.
- Provide pairs of students with blackline master 2. While one student reads the words from the list, the other student writes each word.
- If a word is spelled correctly, the partner puts a check mark beside it. If a word is incorrect, the partner may provide prompts. If the second spelling of the word is correct, the partner places a check mark in the "Second Try" column.

Assessment Tip: Collect students' completed blackline masters and note which words gave them difficulty.

Sight Words

Review

- Select sight word cards and place them in the pocket chart. Have students say and spell each word aloud.
- Turn a card around and have students spell the word in the air with their fingers. Turn the card back around and have students say the word. Repeat with the other cards.

 ## Decodable Book

- Read the decodable book *Quinn* with the remaining small groups of students. Assign blackline master 4 and Independent Activities for the rest of the class.

Assessment Tip: Use the completed blackline master to assess how well students can match beginning sounds with the letters that stand for those sounds.

Spelling Assessment

Use the following procedure to assess students' spelling of the Unit 23 words.
• Say each spelling word and use it in a sentence.
• Have students write the word on a piece of paper.
• Continue with the next word on the list.
• When students have finished, collect their papers and analyze their spellings of misspelled words.
• Record their progress on a spelling record sheet, and provide extra practice as needed.

 Small Group Activities

The following small group activities can be used to provide hands-on practice for students who need additional support. Assign blackline master 5 and Independent Activities for the rest of the class.

 PHONOLOGICAL AWARENESS

Initial /kw/ Say the words *queen, fish, quilt, duck,* and *quit.* Students are to say the word *quack* if a word begins with the /kw/ sound.

Segment and Blend Phonemes Using the word lists, say a word by segmenting its sounds. Have students tell you the word. Then have students segment sounds and blend them.

Sound Substitution Say the word *jet* and ask students what the word would be if the beginning sound was changed to /m/. Continue, making the words *bet, let,* and *set.* Then say the word *sad* and have students change the beginning sound to make the words *bad, dad, had,* and *pad.*

 SOUND/SYMBOL RELATIONSHIPS

Initial /kw/ Distribute letter card **q** to each student. Read the poem *The Queen's Nap.* Have students hold up their card each time you say a word that begins with /kw/.

Word Match Place picture cards **queen, vest, yarn,** and **king** in the pocket chart. Place word cards **quit, quill, vet, van, yet, yes, kit,** and **kid** in a stack. Students take turns choosing a word card, sounding out the word, and placing the card under the picture card that has the same beginning sound.

 BLENDING

Model Write the word *quit* on the board. Sound out the word by moving your hand under the letters as you blend the sounds. Ask students to sound out the word with you. Repeat with the words *vet, quack, yes,* and *dad.*

 SPELLING

Spelling Practice 1 Using the spelling words *jam, bad, quit, yet, quip,* and *quill,* have a student write a word on the board. If the student spells the word correctly, he or she chooses a spelling word for another student to spell.

Spelling Practice 2 Using the same spelling words, ask a student to say the first letter of a word. Write the letter on a workmat. Go around the group, having students add letters while you write them on the workmat.

 SIGHT WORDS

Read a Word Show sight word cards to students and have them read the words aloud. Then place the cards facedown. Have students take turns choosing a card, reading the word, and using the word in an oral sentence.

Pass the Word Have students sit in a circle and give each one a sight word card. Ask them to pass the cards to the right until you say "Stop." Then each student reads their word.

Student Name _____ Assessment Date _____

Phonemic Awareness: Segmenting Phonemes

Directions: Say the word. Have the student say the word sound by sound and then say the whole word. If the student segments the word correctly, put a ✔. If the student's response is incorrect, record the error. **Example:** sip. /s/ /i/ /p/, *sip*.

well (/w/ /e/ /l/, *well*)		quack (/kw/ /a/ /k/, *quack*)			
cup (/k/ /u/ /p/, *cup*)		get (/g/ /e/ /t/, *get*)			
knob (/n/ /o/ /b/, *knob*)		hip (/h/ /i/ /p/, *hip*)		**Score**	**/6**

Phonemic Awareness: Initial Sound Substitution

Directions: Say the word, and then segment it sound by sound. Ask the student to replace the first sound in the word with the new sound while segmenting sound by sound and then say the new word. Put a ✔ if the student's response is correct. If the student misses the word, record the error. **Example:** man, /m/ /a/ /n/. Change /m/ to /p/. /p/ /a/ /n/, *pan*.

quit, /kw/ /i/ /t/. Change /kw/ to /h/. (/h/ /i/ /t/, *hit*)	
mug, /m/ /u/ /g/. Change /m/ to /r/. (/r/ /u/ /g/, *rug*)	
loss, /l/ /o/ /s/. Change /l/ to /b/. (/b/ /o/ /s/, *boss*)	
sop, /s/ /o/ /p/. Change /s/ to /m/. (/m/ /o/ /p/, *mop*)	
pet, /p/ /e/ /t/. Change /p/ to /w/. (/w/ /e/ /t/, *wet*)	
bad, /b/ /a/ /d/. Change /b/ to /d/. (/d/ /a/ /d/, *dad*) **Score** **/6**	

Phonics: Segmenting and Blending Sounds

Directions: Explain that these nonsense words use sounds the student has been learning. Have the student point to each word on the corresponding student sheet, say each sound, and then blend the sounds together. Put a ✔ if the student's response is correct. If the student misses the word, record the error. **Example:** bup. /b/ /u/ /p/, *bup*.

mif (/m/ /i/ /f/, *mif*)		quet (/kw/ /e/ /t/, *quet*)			
quan (/kw/ /a/ /n/, *quan*)		vad (/v/ /a/ /d/, *vad*)			
ruc (/r/ /u/ /k/, *ruc*)		quok (/kw/ /o/ /k/, *quok*)		**Score**	**/6**

Sight Word

Directions: Have the student point to the sight word on the corresponding student sheet and read it as quickly as possible. Put a ✔ if the student successfully reads the word and an **X** if the student hesitates more than a few seconds. If the student misses the word, record the error.

good		**Score**	**/1**

UNIT 24 Xx

Unit Objectives

Students will:

- Identify the sound /ks/
- Associate the letter Xx with the /ks/ sound
- Orally blend and segment phonemes
- Orally substitute medial sounds
- Listen for the sound /ks/
- Listen for ending sounds
- Blend CVC words
- Read the sight words be, was, we
- Spell CVC words using x and letters previously learned

Day 1

BLM 1

BLM 6

Letter Cards: **g, t, x**

Spelling Transparency

Picture Word Cards: **ax, bat, box, dog, egg, fox, frog, goat, hat, nut, ox, rug**

Day 2

BLM 1

BLM 7

Decodable Word Cards for Unit 24

Letter Cards: **a, b, f, i, m, o, s, t, w, x**

Spelling Transparency

Picture Word Cards: **ax, bat, box, dog, egg, fox, frog, goat, hat, nut, ox, rug**

Day 3

BLM 1

BLM 3

BLM 8

Spelling Transparency

Day 4

BLM 1

BLM 2

BLM 4

Sight Word Cards for Unit 24

Letter Cards for Unit 24

Day 5

BLM 5

Letter Cards for Unit 24

Sight Word Cards for Unit 24

Decodable Word Cards for Unit 24

Quick-Check Student Sheet

Poetry Poster

Student Workmat

Letter Frieze Card

Decodable Book

Poetry CD

Core Materials

All print resources can be downloaded from http://phonicsresources.benchmarkeducation.com.

**Poetry Poster
(Front)**

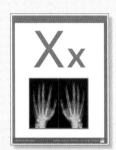

Letter Frieze Card

**Picture Word
Cards**

Phonemic Awareness

Use the Poetry Poster

- Read aloud or play the recording of the poem *Max,* and encourage students to join in when they can.
- Say the sentence "I'll have to fix the bone you broke by falling on a box," emphasizing the */ks/* sound.
- Reread the poem. Have students raise their hands when they hear */ks/.*

Distribute blackline master 6 and instruct students to complete it at home.

Sound/Symbol Relationships

Model

- Display letter frieze card **Xx.** Explain that the letter **Xx** stands for the */ks/* sound at the beginning of **X ray** and the end of **Max.**
- Reread the poem *Max,* inviting students to read along with you.
- Point to words in the poem that end with the letter **x.** Say the words aloud and ask students to say them with you.

Practice with the Letter Cards

- Distribute letter cards **x, g,** and **t.** Ask students to line up the cards on their workmats.
- Have students pull down each letter card and say the letter name, then push it back up and say the letter sound.
- Ask them to pull down each letter card again, saying a word that ends with that sound.
- Have them push up the letter card that ends the word **mix.** (Repeat with the words **pig** and **cat.**)

Practice with the Picture Cards

- Place letter cards **x, t,** and **g** in the pocket chart.
- Place picture cards **fox, bat,** and **dog** under the corresponding letters while you say the name of the letter and the name of the object in the picture.
- Hold up picture card **ax** and have students say **ax** with you. Ask: *Does* **ax** *end like* **fox, bat,** *or* **dog**?
- Place picture card **ax** under letter card **x.** Say: **Ax** *ends like* **fox,** *so I am putting picture card* **fox** *under the letter* **x.**
- Repeat with picture cards **box, ox, goat, hat, nut, frog, egg,** and **rug.**

Blending Sounds

Review

- Hold up letter frieze cards of previously taught sounds. Ask students to say the sound each letter stands for.

Model

- Write the word **quit** on the board. Sound out the word by moving your hand under each letter while blending the sounds. (*/kwiiit/*) Point out that **quit** has stop sounds at the beginning and the end. Then say the word.
- Ask students to sound out the word with you.

Practice with the Word Lists

- Distribute blackline master 1.
- Have students point to the word **quit.** Ask them to sound out the word with you. Then ask them to say the word at regular speed.
- Repeat with the words **nab, sip,** and **ox.** Then have students sound out the words in random order.

Spelling Words

Model

- Use the spelling transparency. Place counters under the second set of boxes on the transparency.
- Say: *Today we are going to learn to spell* **sip** *and* **did***. Watch and listen as I say* **sip** *slowly: /ssssiiiip/.*
- As you say **/ssss/,** push a counter into the first box. Then say **/iiii/** as you push a counter into the second box and **/p/** as you push a counter into the third box. Repeat the steps.
- Model recording the letters for the sounds on the transparency. Say: *The first sound is* **/ssss/***. I know that the letter* **s** *stands for the* **/ssss/** *sound. I'll write the letter* **s** *in the first box. Let's listen for the second sound:* **/siiii/***. I hear* **/i/***. I know that the letter* **i** *stands for the* **/i/** *sound, so I will write* **i** *in the second box. Let's listen for the last sound:* **/sip/***. I hear* **/p/***. I know that the letter* **p** *stands for the* **/p/** *sound, so I will write* **p** *in the last box.*
- Have students blend the sounds to check the spelling of the word.

Practice with the Workmat

- Instruct students to place their counters under the second set of boxes on side 2 of the workmat.
- Ask students to slowly articulate the word **sip** as they push the counters into the boxes.
- Have students identify and record the letters that stand for the sounds they hear.
- Have students practice writing **sip** on side 1 of their workmats.

Repeat the modeling and practice with the second spelling word, *did*.

 # Sight Words

Review

- Write the words **good, with, for, saw**, and **want** on the board. Have students read and spell the words together.

Introduce

- Write the words **was, be,** and **we** on the board**.** Point to each word and say it. Then have students say and spell the words as you point to them.
- Write these sentences on the board: "We will be here." "The pot was in the box." Have volunteers underline the words **be, We,** and **was**.

Write

Have students write the words **be, we,** and **was** on side 1 of their workmats, using the models on the board.

DAY 2

Independent Activities

Phonological Awareness

Picture Cards Provide picture cards in the literacy center. Students can:
- choose a card and name words that begin with the same sound as the picture name
- look for pictures that end with the /ks/ sound
- say words that rhyme with each picture name
- sort cards according to their ending sounds

Draw Provide sheets of paper and ask students to draw things that end with /ks/.

Listen Have students listen to the recording of the poem *Max* in the listening center.

Sound/Symbol Relationships

Words with X Distribute letter cards **a, i, o, x, b, f, s, m, t,** and **w.** Have students build words that end with /ks/.

On Target On a large sheet of paper, draw a target made up of four concentric circles. Write *p, t,* and *g* in the three outer circles and *x* in the center circle. Students can:
- toss a beanbag and say the sound for the letter
- toss a beanbag and say a word that ends with the sound the letter stands for

Similar Words Place decodable word cards in an envelope. Pair students and have one partner choose two words that are alike in some way. That student reads the words and shows them to his or her partner. The partner then reads the words and tells how they are alike.

Phonemic Awareness

Use the Poetry Poster
- Show students the picture on the back of the poetry poster and have them name all the objects in the picture.
- Point to the fox in the picture and say the word *fox*, emphasizing the /ks/ sound. Ask: *What sound do you hear at the end of the word?*
- Ask students to point to something in the picture that ends with /ks/.

Sound/Symbol Relationships

Sort the Decodable Word Cards
- Place picture cards **fox, dog, cup,** and **bat** in the pocket chart and have students say the name of the object on each card.
- Show students decodable word card **ox.** Have them blend the word.
- Ask students if **ox** ends like **fox, dog, cup,** or **bat.** Then place the card under picture card **fox.**
- Repeat with decodable word cards **fix, tax, big, tug, rag, gap, hop, sip, fat, get,** and **pot.**

Distribute blackline master 7 and instruct students to complete it at home.

Assessment Tip: Note which students are not able to match words with pictures. Let them work with one picture at a time and identify the words that go with that picture. Assign Independent Activities for the rest of the class.

Blending Sounds

- Have students blend the words *mix, box, van,* and *cot.*

Spelling Words

- Review the words *sip* and *did* by having students write the words several times.
- Follow the procedure for Day One to model and practice the words *mix* and *box.*

Assessment Tip: Note students who do not slowly articulate the sounds when spelling a word, and provide extra modeling.

Sight Words

- Write *be, we,* and *was* on the board. Ask students to suggest sentences for each word. Record the sentences on the board and have volunteers underline the words *be, we,* and *was.*
- Write selected sight words on the board. Provide clues to each word and have students guess the word.

Phonemic Awareness

Vowel Substitution

- Say the word **fox**. Ask: *What sound do you hear in the middle of* **fox**? *If I take out the /o/ and put in /i/, what word do I make?*
- Continue, changing **fix** to **fax**.
- Let students suggest ways to change **cob, big**, and **fan**.

 # Blending Sounds

- Have students blend the words **fox, sax, fix,** and **ax**.

 # Spelling Words

- Review the words **sip, did, mix**, and **box** by having students write them several times.
- Follow the procedure for Day One to model and practice the words **fox** and **wax**.

 # Sight Words

- Write the words **we, be, was, want, have, put, here, you,** and **has** on the board.
- Erase the **n** in **want**, say the word, and ask students which letter is missing. Have a volunteer write the missing letter.
- Continue, erasing and replacing letters in the other words.

Distribute blackline master 8 and instruct students to complete it at home.

Poetry Poster (Back)

Decodable Book

Work with small groups of students to read the decodable book *The Sax* on Days Three and Four. Assign blackline master 3 and Independent Activities for the rest of the class on Day Three.

Introduce the Book

- Display the cover of the book. Point to the title, *The Sax,* and have students sound out the words as you run your finger under them.
- Ask: *What do you see in the picture? What is a sax? How do you play a sax?*

Read the Book

- Give each student a copy of the book and have them turn to page 2. Instruct them to run their fingers under the first word as they sound it out: */Beeeennnn/*.
- Have students point to the next two words. Remind them that these are words they don't sound out and that they have practiced. Have them say the words **saw** and **the**.
- Have students point to the last word and sound it out: */ssssaaaaks/*.
- Have students read the whole sentence at normal speed.
- Repeat with the remaining sentences.
- If students can sound out the words without difficulty, have them whisper-read the rest of the text.
- If students have difficulty, continue to guide them page by page.

Discuss the Book

- When students have finished reading, ask: *Why did Ben go to see Max and Rex? What did Max and Rex do for Ben? What will Ben do next?*

Decodable Book

 **SUPPORT TIPS for English Language Learners**

Develop/reinforce vocabulary word: *sax*

- Before reading, borrow a few instruments from the music teacher and/or collect pictures of a few instruments, including a sax, to show students.
- Ask individual students to identify and pantomime how to play an instrument they recognize.
- If students recognize the sax as a saxophone, accept the response and ask if anyone knows another name for it. Provide **sax** if no one knows the word.
- Have all students repeat the name of each instrument and copy the pantomimed actions.
- Ask individual students to pantomime playing one of the instruments while the other students try to guess the name of the instrument. Model and reinforce **sax** as often as possible during the activity.

DAY 4

Independent Activities

Decodable Book

Independent Practice After students have read the decodable book in a small group, have them read the book independently or with a friend.

Take Home Let students take the decodable book home and read it to a family member.

Write a Letter Have students pretend they are Ben and write a thank-you note to Max and Rex.

Spelling

As words are introduced each day, write them on index cards and place them in the literacy center. Ensure that the letter cards needed to build the words are in the center. Students can use the following procedure to spell words.
• Choose a word card.
• Use their fingers and eyes to read the word.
• Turn over the card so that they can't see the word.
• Build the word using the letter cards.
• Turn over the card to check the word.
• Write the word.

Sight Words

Personal Dictionary Have students write *we, be* and *was* in their personal dictionaries.

Spell the Words Place the sight word cards in an envelope. Pair students and have one partner take out the cards, one at a time, and read the word while the other partner writes the word.

Phonemic Awareness

Blend and Segment Sounds
• Say the word *sax*, segmenting and blending the sounds: */s/ /a/ /ks/, /saks/.* Have students imitate you.
• Segment the sounds in some words and have students tell you what the words are. Use the words *quit, vet,* and *yam.*

Assessment Tip: Ask individual students to segment and blend sounds. Note those who are having difficulty.

Blending Sounds

• Have students blend the words *quit, kin, ax,* and *lox,* using the procedure for Day One.

Spelling Words

Review
• Review the week's words by having students write them several times on their workmats.
• Provide pairs of students with blackline master 2. While one student reads the words from the list, the other student writes each word.
• If a word is spelled correctly, the partner puts a check mark beside it. If a word is incorrect, the partner may provide prompts. If the second spelling of the word is correct, the partner places a check mark in the "Second Try" column.

Assessment Tip: Collect students' completed blackline masters and note which words gave them difficulty.

Sight Words

Review
• Write the words *be, was, home, now, this, have, and, to,* and *and* on the board. Have students take turns circling a word, reading it, and using it in a sentence.

Decodable Book

• Read the decodable book *The Sax* with the remaining small groups of students. Assign blackline master 4 and Independent Activities for the rest of the class.

Assessment Tip: Use the completed blackline master to assess how well students can match beginning sounds with the letters that stand for these sounds.

Spelling Assessment

Use the following procedure to assess students' spelling of the Unit 24 words.
• Say each spelling word and use it in a sentence.
• Have students write the word on a piece of paper.
• Continue with the next word on the list.
• When students have finished, collect their papers and analyze their spellings of misspelled words.
• Record their progress on a spelling record sheet, and provide extra practice as needed.

 # Small Group Activities

The following small group activities can be used to provide hands-on practice for students who need additional support. Assign blackline master 5 and Independent Activities for the rest of the class.

 PHONOLOGICAL AWARENESS

Final /ks/ Say a series of words and have students raise their hands if they hear a word that ends with the /ks/ sound. Use the words **box, tax, van, sip, mix, wax, did,** and **fox.**

Sound Substitution Say the words **bed** and **bad** and have students sound them out. Ask what sound is different in the two words. Have students substitute /i/, then /u/ to make the words **bid** and **bud.**

 SOUND/SYMBOL RELATIONSHIPS

Ending Sounds 1 Distribute letter cards **x, t, g, p, n,** and **b.** Say the following words and have students hold up the letter card for the sound they hear at the end of the word: **pet, rob, dog, fun, box, top, fox, dig, tub, tan, man, ox, jig, hat.**

Ending Sounds 2 Show students the decodable word cards one at a time. Have them read the words, identify the ending sounds, and sort the cards according to their ending sounds.

 BLENDING

Group Practice 1 Distribute letter cards **m, i, x, b, o, a, n, c,** and **t,** one per student. Say the word **mix.** Have students holding **m, i,** and **x** stand in a row and say the sound his or her letter stands for. Repeat with the words **cot, man, can, tab, box,** and **not.**

Group Practice 2 Distribute word cards **fox, tax, fix,** and **ax** to four students and ask all the students to stand in a circle. Have students pass the cards to the right. When you say "Stop," the students holding cards sound out the words.

 SPELLING

Spelling Practice Write the letters **s, d, m, b, f,** and **w** in a column on chart paper. Say the spelling words **sip, did, mix, box, fox,** and **wax,** one at a time. Have volunteers identify the letter that starts the spelling word and then write the rest of the word on the chart paper.

 SIGHT WORDS

Partner Practice Have students practice reading the sight word cards with a partner. They can time themselves to see how fast they can read the words.

Draw a Card Have students draw a sight word card, read the word, and use it in a sentence.

Student Name _____ Assessment Date _____

Phonemic Awareness: Blending Phonemes

Directions: Say the word sound by sound. Then have the student say the word. Put a ✔ if the student's response is correct. If the student misses the word, record the error. **Example:** /d/ /o/ /g/. Dog.

/t/ /a/ /ks/ (tax)		/t/ /a/ /b/ (tab)			
/s/ /u/ /n/ (sun)		/m/ /i/ /ks/ (mix)			
/f/ /e/ /l/ (fell)		/t/ /o/ /t/ (tot)		**Score**	**/6**

Phonemic Awareness: Medial Sound Substitution

Directions: Say the word, and then segment it sound by sound. Ask the student to replace the middle sound in the word with the new sound while segmenting sound by sound and then say the new word. Put a ✔ if the student's response is correct. If the student misses the word, record the error. **Example:** man, /m/ /a/ /n/. Change /a/ to /e/. /m/ /e/ /n/, men.

fix, /f/ /i/ /ks/. Change /i/ to /o/. (/f/ /o/ /ks/, fox)		
bit, /b/ /i/ /t/. Change /i/ to /e/. (/b/ /e/ /t/, bet)		
mop, /m/ /o/ /p/. Change /o/ to /a/. (/m/ /a/ /p/, map)		
rag, /r/ /a/ /g/. Change /a/ to /i/. (/r/ /i/ /g/, rig)		
pen, /p/ /e/ /n/. Change /e/ to /i/. (/p/ /i/ /n/, pin)		
bud, /b/ /u/ /d/. Change /u/ to /e/. (/b/ /e/ /d/, bed)		**Score** /6

Phonics: Segmenting and Blending Sounds

Directions: Explain that these nonsense words use sounds the student has been learning. Have the student point to each word on the corresponding student sheet, say each sound, and then blend the sounds together. Put a ✔ if the student's response is correct. If the student misses the word, record the error. **Example:** fac. /f/ /a/ /k/, fac.

tib (/t/ /i/ /b/, tib)		vax (/v/ /a/ /ks/, vax)			
quox (/kw/ /o/ /ks/, quox)		nes (/n/ /e/ /s/, nes)			
mup (/m/ /u/ /p/, mup)		yix (/y/ /i/ /ks/, yix)		**Score**	**/6**

Sight Words

Directions: Have the student point to the first sight word on the corresponding student sheet and read across the line, saying each word as quickly as possible. Put a ✔ if the student successfully reads the word and an **X** if the student hesitates more than a few seconds. If the student misses the word, record the error.

be		we			
was				**Score**	**/3**

UNIT **25Zz**

Unit Objectives

Students will:

- Identify the sound /z/
- Associate the letter Zz with the /z/ sound
- Listen for initial and final /z/
- Orally substitute final sounds
- Orally blend and segment phonemes
- Blend CVC words
- Read the sight words there, then, out
- Spell CVC words using z and letters previously learned

Day 1

 BLM 1

 BLM 6

 Letter Cards: **q, v, x, z**

 Spelling Transparency

 Picture Word Cards: **quail, quarter, queen, quilt, van, vase, vegetables, vest, zebra, zero, zipper, zoo**

Day 2

 BLM 1

 BLM 7

 Decodable Word Cards for Unit 25

 Letter Cards: **a, e, i, n, o, p, t, u, v, w, z**

 Spelling Transparency

 Picture Word Cards: **quail, quarter, queen, quilt, van, vase, vegetables, vest, zebra, zero, zipper, zoo**

Day 3

 BLM 1

 BLM 3

 BLM 8

 Sight Word Cards for Unit 25

 Spelling Transparency

Day 4

 BLM 1

 BLM 2

 BLM 4

 Sight Word Cards for Unit 25

 Letter Cards for Unit 25

Day 5

 BLM 5

 Decodable Word Cards for Unit 25

 Sight Word Cards for Unit 25

 Quick-Check Student Sheet

 **Poetry Poster**

 **Student Workmat**

 Letter Frieze Card

 Decodable Book

 Poetry CD

Core Materials

All print resources can be downloaded from http://phonicsresources.benchmarkeducation.com.

**Poetry Poster
(Front)**

Letter Frieze Card

**Picture Word
Cards**

Phonemic Awareness

Use the Poetry Poster
• Read aloud or play the recording of the poem *Baby Zigzag* several times, and encourage students to join in when they can.
• Say the sentence "Zelda Zebra is a mommy." Stretch the **/z/** phoneme in the **/z/** words.
• Reread the poem. Have students clap when they hear the **/z/** sound.

Distribute blackline master 6 and instruct students to complete it at home.

Sound/Symbol Relationships

Model
• Display letter frieze card **Zz.** Explain that the letter **Zz** stands for the **/z/** sound, as in *zebra*.
• Reread the poem *Baby Zigzag*, inviting students to read along with you.
• Point to words in the poem that begin with the letter **z.** Say the words aloud and ask students to say them with you.

Practice with the Letter Cards
• Distribute letter cards **z** and **x.** Ask students to line up the cards on their workmats.
• Have students pull down each letter card and say the letter name, then push it back up and say the letter sound.
• Ask them to pull down a letter card again, saying a word that ends with that sound.
• Have students push up the letter card that ends the word *buzz*. (Repeat with *fox*.)

Practice with the Picture Cards
• Place letter cards **z, q,** and **v** in the pocket chart.
• Place picture cards **zebra, queen,** and **vase** under the corresponding letters while you say the name of the letter and the name of the object in the picture.
• Hold up picture card **zoo** and have students say **zoo** with you.
• Ask: *Does* **zoo** *begin like* **zebra, queen,** *or* **vase**?
• Place picture card **zoo** under letter card **z.** Say: **Zzzzoo** *begins like* **zzzzebra,** *so I am putting picture card* **zoo** *under the letter* **z.**
• Repeat with picture cards **zipper, zero, quilt, quail, quarter, vest, vegetables,** and **van.**

Blending Sounds

Review
• Hold up letter frieze cards of previously taught sounds. Ask students to say the sound each letter stands for.

Model
• Write the word *fox* on the board. Sound out the word by moving your hand under each letter while blending the sounds. (**/ffffooooks/**) Point out that *fox* has a stop sound at the end.
• Ask students to sound out the word with you.

Practice with the Word Lists
• Distribute blackline master 1. Have students point to the word *fox*. Ask them to sound out the word with you. Then ask them to say the word at regular speed.
• Repeat with the words *bag, pun,* and *wet.* Then have students sound out the words in random order.

 # Spelling Words

Model
- Use the spelling transparency. Place counters under the second set of boxes on the transparency.
- Say: *Today we are going to learn to spell* **fox** *and* **quiz.** *Watch and listen as I say* **fox** *slowly: /ffffooooks/.* Point out that the word has a stop sound at the end.
- As you say */ffff/,* push a counter into the first box. Then say */oooo/* as you push a counter into the second box and */ks/* as you push a counter into the third box. Repeat the steps.
- Model recording the letters for the sounds on the transparency. Say: *The first sound is /ffff/. I know that the letter* **f** *stands for the /ffff/ sound. I'll write the letter* **f** *in the first box. Let's listen for the second sound: /foooo/. I hear /o/. I know that the letter* **o** *stands for the /o/ sound, so I will write* **o** *in the second box. Let's listen for the last sound: /foks/. I hear /ks/. I know that the letter* **x** *stands for the /ks/ sound, so I will write* **x** *in the last box.*
- Have students blend the sounds to check the spelling of the word.

Practice with the Workmat
- Instruct students to place their counters under the second set of boxes on side 2 of their workmats.
- Ask students to slowly articulate the word *fox* as they push the counters into the boxes.
- Have students identify and record the letters that stand for the sounds they hear.
- Have students practice writing *fox* on side 1 of their workmats.

Repeat the modeling and practice with the second spelling word, *quiz.*

 # Sight Words

Review
- Numerically list the words ***want, is, put, has, go, the, look, and, he,*** and ***of*** on the board. Have volunteers say a number from 1 to 10, read the word that has that number, and erase the word.

Introduce
- Write the word ***there*** on the board. Have students say the word as you point to it.
- Repeat with the words ***then*** and ***out.***
- Write the following sentences on the board: "He put the cup out there." "Then she got it." Ask volunteers to underline the words ***there, out,*** and ***then.***

Write
- Have students write the words ***there, out,*** and ***then*** on side 1 of their workmats, using the words on the board as a model.

Independent Activities

Phonological Awareness

Picture Sort Provide picture cards in the literacy center. Students can:

- sort the cards into groups according to beginning sounds
- take two cards and tell if the picture names rhyme
- sort the cards into those that start with /z/ and those that don't
- show a partner two pictures that have the same beginning sound and have the partner tell what the sound is

Sound Mural Attach a sheet of paper to a wall. Divide it into three columns. Place picture card **zebra** in the first column, picture card **queen** in the second, and picture card **van** in the third. Have students draw or cut out pictures of things that begin with the same sound as the pictures.

Listen Have students listen to the poem *Baby Zigzag* at the listening center.

Sound/Symbol Relationships

CVC Words Give letter cards **u, e, w, t, z, p, i, o, v, a,** and **n** to pairs of students. Have pairs make three-letter words.

Letter Toss Write the letters *z, q, y, k, j, l,* and *w* on cups, one letter per cup. Students can:

- toss a button into a cup and say the sound for the letter
- toss a button into a cup and say a word that starts with the sound of the letter

Picture/Letter Match Provide picture cards and the letter cards that stand for the beginning sounds of the pictures. Place each set of cards facedown. Have students turn over a picture and a letter, trying to match the picture and its beginning letter.

 Phonemic Awareness

Use the Poetry Poster

- Show students the picture on the back of the poetry poster and have them name all the objects in the picture.
- Point to a zebra in the picture and say the word *zebra*. Ask: *Where do you hear the /z/ sound in this word?*
- Ask students to point to something in the picture that has the /z/ sound.

 Sound/Symbol Relationships

Sort the Decodable Word Cards

- Place picture cards **zebra, queen,** and **van** in the pocket chart and have students say the name of the object on each picture card.
- Show students decodable word card **zip** and have them blend the word.
- Ask students if **zip** begins like **zebra, queen,** or **van**. Then place the card under picture card **zebra**.
- Repeat with decodable word cards **zap, Zak, quit, quiz, quill, van, vet,** and **Val.**

Distribute blackline master 7 and instruct students to complete it at home.

Assessment Tip: Note which students cannot match words with pictures. Have them work with one picture at a time and identify the words that go with that picture. Assign Independent Activities for the rest of the class.

 Blending Sounds

- Have students blend the words **zip, buzz, zap,** and **fuzz,** using the procedure for Day One.

 Spelling Words

- Review the words **fox** and **quiz** by having students write the words several times.
- Follow the procedure for Day One to model and practice the words **zip** and **buzz.** Highlight the double consonants at the end of the word **buzz.**

Assessment Tip: Note students who do not slowly articulate the sounds when spelling a word, and provide extra modeling.

Sight Words

Review

- Write **want, is, there, no, has, he, of,** and **look** in one column on the board, and **here, then, put, go, the, and, then,** and **said** in another. Divide the group into two teams. The first player on each team reads the first word in a column and, if correct, erases it. If incorrect, the next player tries to read the word. Play until one team has erased all its words.

Phonemic Awareness

Final Sound Substitution
- Say the word **buzz**. Ask: *What sound do you hear at the end of the word?*
- Say: *I want to change /z/ to /g/. What word will I have?*
- Continue, changing **pin** to **pit, map** to **man, hot** to **hop, bet** to **bed,** and **him** to **hid.**

 # Blending Sounds

- Have students blend the words **fix, buzz, zip,** and **net.**

 # Spelling Words

- Review the words **fox, quiz, zip,** and **buzz** by having students write them several times.
- Follow the procedure for Day One to model and practice the words **zap** and **fuzz.**

 # Sight Words

- Display sight word cards in the pocket chart.
- Ask a student to say a sentence with one of the words, saying "blank" instead of the word.
- Have a volunteer remove the word that correctly completes the sentence and repeat the sentence with the word.

Distribute blackline master 8 and instruct students to complete it at home.

Decodable Book

Work with small groups of students to read the decodable book *Buzz, Buzz* on Days Three and Four. Assign blackline master 3 and Independent Activities for the rest of the class on Day Three.

Introduce the Book
- Display the cover of the book. Point to the title, *Buzz, Buzz,* and have students sound out the words as you run your finger under them.
- Ask: *What do you see in the picture? What might go "buzz, buzz"?*

Read the Book
- Give each student a copy of the book and have them turn to page 2. Instruct them to run their fingers under the words as they sound them out: */buuuuzzzz/, /buuuuzzzz/.*
- Have students point to the next word. Remind them that this is a word they don't sound out and that they have practiced. Have them say the word **went.**
- Have students point to the last word and sound it out as they run their fingers under it: */Zzzzaaaak/.*
- Have students read the whole sentence at normal speed.
- Repeat with the rest of the page.
- If students can sound out the words without difficulty, have them whisper-read the rest of the text.
- If students have difficulty sounding out the words, continue to guide them page by page.

Discuss the Book
- When students have finished reading, ask: *What did the pup do? What did Zak do to the pup? Why? How did Ben help the pup?*

**Poetry Poster
(Back)**

Decodable Book

 **SUPPORT TIPS**
for English Language Learners

**Develop/reinforce the concepts:
in and *out***
- Before reading, distribute cups and small manipulatives, such as unifix cubes.
- Model putting an item in your cup while directing the students to put the item in their cups. Have students tell you their item is in the cup.
- Model taking the item out of the cup while directing students to do the same. Create a visual barrier so that students cannot see where you put your item as you tell them where the item is. Have students place their item according to your description. Say: *The block is in the cup.*
- Remove the visual barrier so that all can compare their efforts with your model. Model the sentence that describes the placement and have students repeat the sentence.
- Repeat this as often as necessary to develop the vocabulary.
- Divide students into pairs or small groups to continue the activity. Create a visual barrier so that students cannot see each other's materials.
- One student places the manipulative in or out of the cup and directs his/her partner(s) to do the same.
- Have students use the target prepositions as they describe their placement and the original placement after the barrier is removed: *The block is in the cup.*

DAY 4

Independent Activities

Decodable Book

Independent Practice When students have read the decodable book in the small group setting, have them read the book independently.

Dramatize Have students present the book as a play. Tell one group to be the actors and another group the readers. Each reader should read one page.

Spelling

As words are introduced each day, write them on index cards and place them in the literacy center. Ensure that the letter cards needed to build the words are in the center. Students can use the following procedure to spell words.
- Choose a word card.
- Use their fingers and eyes to read the word.
- Turn over the card so that they can't see the word.
- Build the word using the letter cards.
- Turn over the card to check the word.
- Write the word.

Sight Words

Personal Dictionary Have students write *there, out,* and *then* in their dictionaries.

Word Draw Let pairs of students draw sight word cards from a paper bag and read the words.

Word Collage Give students some newspaper pages. Have them select a sight word and look for examples of the word in the paper. Have them cut out the words and paste them on a sheet of paper.

Word Concentration Place two identical sets of sight word cards in the center. Students should place the cards facedown. Have students turn over two cards at a time, trying to match the words.

 ## Phonemic Awareness

Blend and Segment Sounds
- Say the word *zap*, segmenting and blending the sounds. Have students say the sounds slowly and then blend the sounds.
- Segment the following words and have students blend them to tell you the words: *zip, buzz, fox, quit.*
- Say the words *zig, fuzz, mix,* and *quack,* and have students segment them into their individual sounds.

Assessment Tip: Note which students are having difficulty segmenting and blending sounds in words, and provide more practice.

 ## Blending Sounds

- Have students blend the words *mix, van, lip,* and *fuzz,* using the procedure for Day One.

 ## Spelling Words

Review
- Review the week's words by having students write them several times on their workmats.
- Provide pairs of students with blackline master 2. While one student reads the words from the list, the other student writes each word.
- If a word is spelled correctly, the partner puts a check mark beside it. If a word is incorrect, the partner may provide prompts. If the second spelling is correct, the partner places a check mark in the "Second Try" column.

Assessment Tip: Collect students' completed blackline masters and note which words gave them difficulty.

 ## Sight Words

Review
- Show students the sight word cards, one at a time, and have them read them quickly.
- Place the cards on a table. Have students take a card, read it, and use it in an oral sentence.

Decodable Book

- Read the decodable book *Buzz, Buzz* with the remaining small groups of students. Assign blackline master 4 and Independent Activities for the rest of the class.

Assessment Tip: Use the completed blackline masters to assess how well students can make connections between ending sounds and the letters that stand for these sounds.

Spelling Assessment

Use the following procedure to assess students' spelling of the Unit 25 words.
• Say each spelling word and use it in a sentence.
• Have students write the word on a piece of paper.
• Continue with the next word on the list.
• When students have finished, collect their papers and analyze their spellings of misspelled words.
• Record their progress on a spelling record sheet, and provide extra practice as needed.

 Small Group Activities

The following small group activities can be used to provide hands-on practice for students who need additional support. Assign blackline master 5 and Independent Activities for the rest of the class.

 PHONOLOGICAL AWARENESS

Initial and Final /z/ Say *zebra, zip, fox, bag, zoo, net, lag,* and *zero.* If a word begins with /z/, students are to make a buzzing sound. Then say *buzz, fuzz, van, box, yard,* and *fizz,* with students making a buzzing sound when they hear /z/ at the end of a word.

Substitute Final Sounds Say *hit* and *hip.* Ask which sounds are different. Then say *pan, cap, sip,* and *hug.* Have students change the final sounds to make *pat, cab, sit,* and *hut.*

Segment and Blend Using the words *Zak, fizz, quick,* and *tax,* have one student segment a word and another student blend the sounds.

 SOUND/SYMBOL RELATIONSHIPS

Card Sorts Have students sort the decodable word cards according to initial, final, and medial sounds.

 BLENDING

Blending Practice Write words on the board and have a student run his or her fingers under a word while the group says each sound.

 SPELLING

Double Consonants Write *fuzz* and *buzz* on the board. Have students tell where they hear /z/ in each word and what letter or letters stand for /z/.

Spelling Patterns Write *zip/zap* and *buzz/fuzz* on the board. Have students tell how the words are alike and different. Then ask them to write each pair of words on their workmats.

Practice Write *fox, quip, zip, buzz, zap,* and *fuzz* on the board. Have students practice spelling the words, then erase the words. Say each word and ask students to write it on their workmats. Then have a student read aloud his or her spelling.

 SIGHT WORDS

Word Search Give one or two sight word cards to students. Have them look for the words in familiar books. Then have them take turns sharing the sentences with the group.

Word Flash Pair students and give each pair some sight word cards. One partner shows the cards, and the other partner reads the words.

Student Name _____ Assessment Date _____

Phonemic Awareness: Segmenting Phonemes

Directions: Say the word. Have the student say the word sound by sound and then say the whole word. If the student segments the word correctly, put a ✔. If the student's response is incorrect, record the error. **Example:** sip. /s/ /i/ /p/, sip.

zap (/z/ /a/ /p/, zap)		tag (/t/ /a/ /g/, tag)			
sub (/s/ /u/ /b/, sub)		pen (/p/ /e/ /n/, pen)			
box (/b/ /o/ /ks/, box)		zip (/z/ /i/ /p/, zip)		**Score**	**/6**

Phonemic Awareness: Final Sound Substitution

Directions: Say the word, and then segment it sound by sound. Ask the student to replace the last sound in the word with the new sound while segmenting sound by sound and then say the new word. Put a ✔ if the student's response is correct. If the student misses the word, record the error.
Example: man, /m/ /a/ /n/. Change /n/ to /d/. /m/ /a/ /d/, mad.

fill, /f/ /i/ /l/. Change /l/ to /z/. (/f/ /i/ /z/, fizz)			
tug, /t/ /u/ /g/. Change /g/ to /b/. (/t/ /u/ /b/, tub)			
dog, /d/ /o/ /g/. Change /g/ to /t/. (/d/ /o/ /t/)			
knot, /n/ /o/ /t/. Change /t/ to /b/. (/n/ /o/ /b/, knob)			
pen, /p/ /e/ /n/. Change /n/ to /k/. (/p/ /e/ /k/, peck)			
bass, /b/ /a/ /s/. Change /s/ to /t/. (/b/ /a/ /t/, bat)		**Score**	**/6**

Phonics: Segmenting and Blending Sounds

Directions: Explain that these nonsense words use sounds the student has been learning. Have the student point to each word on the corresponding student sheet, say each sound, and then blend the sounds together. Put a ✔ if the student's response is correct. If the student misses the word, record the error. **Example:** kad. /k/ /a/ /d/, kad.

ziv (/z/ /i/ /v/, ziv)		zox (/z/ /o/ /ks/, zox)			
heb (/h/ /e/ /b/, heb)		fic (/f/ /i/ /c/, fic)			
yuz (/y/ /u/ /z/, yuz)		quaz (/kw/ /a/ /z/, quaz)		**Score**	**/6**

Sight Words

Directions: Have the student point to the first sight word on the corresponding student sheet and read across the line, saying each word as quickly as possible. Put a ✔ if the student successfully reads the word and an **X** if the student hesitates more than a few seconds. If the student misses the word, record the error.

there		out			
then				**Score**	**/3**

Pre/Post Assessment Instructions

Step 1

☐ Make a copy of the teacher record for each student and place it in his or her file.

Teacher Record

Step 2

☐ Administer tests on a one-to-one basis. Use the examples provided with the directions to ensure students understand what to do.

Student Sheet

Step 3

☐ Analyze results to determine where to place students in the kit and how to group them for small-group instruction. If students lack phonological and letter awareness skills, you may wish to review these by completing the Level 1 lessons before moving on to the Level 2 phonics units.

Letter Recognition Pre- and Post-Tests

Student: _____

Directions: Ask the student to point to each letter, moving across the page, and name each one. If the student comes to a letter he or she doesn't know, say the letter name, put an X next to the letter in the column, and have the student continue. If the student says an incorrect letter name, record what he or she says in the column.

	Pre-Test Date _____	Post-Test Date _____		Pre-Test Date _____	Post-Test Date _____		Pre-Test Date _____	Post-Test Date _____		Pre-Test Date _____	Post-Test Date _____
e			f			L			B		
h			l			U			K		
m			g			N			J		
c			z			T			X		
o			j			A			P		
a			p			D			M		
y			k			V			G		
b			q			Z			C		
x			r			R			Y		
i			v			F			Q		
d			s			O			E		
n			w			W			I		
u			H			S					
t											

Letter Recognition

e h m c o a y b x

i d n u t f l g z

j p k q r v s w

H L U N T A D V Z

R F O W S B K J X

P M G C Y Q E I

Student Name: _____

Word Awareness

Directions: Say the sentence. Have the student repeat the sentence and tell you the number of words. **Example:** *This is my dog. I can hear four words in this sentence.*

	Pre-Test Date _____	Post-Test Date _____
I see my cat.	/4	/4
Can you do this?	/4	/4
This book is fun to read.	/6	/6
Please sit on the chair.	/5	/5
Where do you live?	/4	/4
Score	/23	/23

Observations: _____
_____
_____

Identify Rhyme

Directions: Say the word pairs and ask the student if the words rhyme. **Example:** Roast/toast. *Yes, these words rhyme.* Roast/ran. *No, these words don't rhyme.*

	Pre-Test Date _____	Post-Test Date _____
bug/rug		
pink/sink		
big/box		
hop/hip		
jump/pump		
Score	/5	/5

Observations: _____
_____
_____

Syllable Awareness

Directions: Say the word. Have the student repeat the word and clap for the number of syllables. **Example:** Engine. *I hear two syllables in* engine.

	Pre-Test Date _____	Post-Test Date _____
happy	/2	/2
Saturday	/3	/3
book	/1	/1
sunshine	/2	/2
experiment	/4	/4
Score	/12	/12

Initial Sounds

Directions: Say the word. Have the student repeat the word and tell you the sound at the beginning. **Example:** Hat. *I hear /h/ at the beginning of the word* hat.

	Pre-Test Date _____	Post-Test Date _____
turtle		
man		
sink		
pudding		
leg		
Score	/5	/5

Student Name: _____

Final Sounds

Directions: Say the word. Have the student repeat the word and tell you the sound at the end. **Example:** Hat. *I hear /t/ at the end of the word* hat.

	Pre-Test Date _____	Post-Test Date _____
park		
noise		
rabbit		
trap		
head		
Score	/5	/5

Observations: _____
_____
_____

Differentiating Sounds

Directions: Say the words. Have the student repeat the words and say which word starts with a different sound. **Example:** Mix, man, nose. Nose *starts with a different sound.*

	Pre-Test Date _____	Post-Test Date _____
bag, bug, cup		
table, nut, tent		
cup, cat, bat		
fish, pan, pin		
sun, sit, man		
Score	/5	/5

Observations: _____
_____
_____

Medial Sounds

Directions: Say the word. Have the student repeat the word and tell you the sound in the middle. **Example:** Hat. *I hear /a/ in the middle of the word* hat.

	Pre-Test Date _____	Post-Test Date _____
pet		
sack		
hit		
stop		
cut		
Score	/5	/5

Onset and Rime

Directions: Say the word. Have the student repeat the word, say the first sound in the word, and then say the rest of the word. **Example:** dig: /d/ /ig/.

	Pre-Test Date _____	Post-Test Date _____
cat: /k/ /at/		
run: /r/ /un/		
pop: /p/ /op/		
hen: /h/ /en/		
rid: /r/ /id/		
Score	/5	/5

Student Name: _____

Phoneme Segmentation

Directions: Say the word. Have the student tell you all the sounds in the word. **Example:** *If I say* run, *you will say* /r/ /u/ /n/.

	Pre-Test Date _____	Post-Test Date _____
cat: /k/ /a/ /t/	/3	/3
top: /t/ /o/ /p/	/3	/3
said: /s/ /e/ /d/	/3	/3
jumps: /j/ /u/ /m/ /p/ /s/	/5	/5
rugs: /r/ /u/ /g/ /z/	/4	/4
Score	**/18**	**/18**

Observations: _____
_____
_____

Blending Phonemes

Directions: Say the word sound by sound. Then have the student say the word. **Example:** *I will say the sounds of some words. I want you to blend the sounds and say the words: for example,* /r/ /u/ /t/: rut.

	Pre-Test Date _____	Post-Test Date _____
/n/ /u/ /t/ : nut		
/j/ /e/ /t/: jet		
/w/ /i/ /g/: wig		
/s/ /a/ /t/: sat		
/m/ /o/ /p/: mop		
Score	**/5**	**/5**

Observations: _____
_____
_____

Initial Sound Substitution

Directions: Say the word. Ask the student to replace the first sound in the word with the new sound. **Example:** *I can change the* /b/ *in* bat *to* /k/ *to make the word* cat.

	Pre-Test Date _____	Post-Test Date _____
tin: change /t/ to /b/ [bin]		
mug: change /m/ to /r/ [rug]		
hop: change /h/ to /b/ [bop]		
pen: change /p/ to /t/ [ten]		
lake: change /l/ to /k/ [cake]		
Score	**/5**	**/5**

Student Name: _____

Consonant Sounds Assessment

Directions: Have students point to each letter and tell you the sound each consonant stands for. Some letters stand for more than one sound. Note whether students say both sounds. Circle any letters they miss on the recording sheet.

	Pre-Test Date _____	Post-Test Date _____
m: /m/		
s: /s/, /z/		
c: /k/, /s/		
v: /v/		
l: /l/		
g: /g/, /j/		
n: /n/		
d: /d/		
t: /t/		
j: /j/		
w: /w/		
p: /p/		
r: /r/		
b: /b/		
q: /kw/		
h: /h/		
z: /z/		
f: /f/		
k: /k/		
x: /ks/		
n: /n/		
Score	**/21**	**/21**

Vowel Sounds Assessment

Directions: Have the student point to each word and tell you the sound each vowel stands for in the word. Record the student's responses in the column.

	Pre-Test Date _____	Post-Test Date _____
mat		
rub		
get		
hot		
fit		
Score	**/5**	**/5**

Blending Sounds Assessment

Student Name: _____

Directions: Explain to the student that these are nonsense words that you want him or her to sound out. Have the student put his or her finger on the example word on the student sheet. **Say:** *I can sound out this nonsense word:* /m/ /i/ /n/: min. Have the student say each sound in the nonsense word and then blend the sounds.

	Pre-Test Date _____	Post-Test Date _____		Pre-Test Date _____	Post-Test Date _____
fam: /f/ /a/ /m/			yad: /y/ /a/ /d/		
tif: /t/ /i/ /f/			hep: /h/ /e/ /p/		
wug: /w/ /u/ /g/			bab: /b/ /a/ /b/		
pof: /p/ /o/ /f/			ven: /v/ /e/ /n/		
rac: /r/ /a/ /k/			sut: /s/ /u/ /t/		
zot: /z/ /o/ /t/			gom: /g/ /o/ /m/		
jun: /j/ /u/ /n/			dat: /d/ /a/ /t/		
sot: /s/ /o/ /t/			nex: /n/ /e/ /ks/		
rog : /r/ /o/ /g/			leb: /l/ /e/ /b/		
mic: /m/ /i/ /k/			quet: /kw/ /e/ /t/		
pum: /p/ /u/ /m/			sil: /s/ /i/ /l/		
cof: /k/ /o/ /f/			kif: /k/ /i/ /f/		

Score   _____ /24   _____ /24

Observations: _____

_____

Consonant Sounds

m   s   c   v   l

g   n   d   t   j

w   p   r   b   q

h   z   f   k   x

n

Vowel Sounds

mat   rub   get   hot   fit

Blending Sounds

Example: min /m/ /i/ /n/

fam	tif	wug	pof
rac	zot	jun	sot
rog	mic	pum	cof
yad	hep	bab	ven
sut	gom	dat	nex
leb	quet	sil	kif

Benchmark Phonics • StartUp Level 2 • Short Vowels and Consonants

©2012 Benchmark Education Company, LL

Sight Words

Student Name: _____

Directions: Have the student put his or her finger on the first word on the student sheet and then read across the line, saying the words as quickly as possible. Count as incorrect any word the student misses or hesitates on before reading.

	Pre-Test Date _____	Post-Test Date _____		Pre-Test Date _____	Post-Test Date _____
is			look		
a			he		
the			go		
has			put		
and			want		
of			this		
with			she		
see			saw		
for			now		
no			like		
cannot			do		
have			home		
are			they		
said			went		
I			good		
you			was		
me			be		
come			we		
here			there		
to			then		
my			out		
			Score	_____/42	_____/42

Observations: _____

Sight Words

is	a	the	has	and
of	with	see	for	no
cannot	have	are	said	I
you	me	come	here	to
my	look	he	go	put
want	this	she	saw	now
like	do	home	they	went
good	was	be	we	there
then	out			

1

2

3

Dear Parent/Guardian,

This year your child will learn all about sounds, letters, and words. There are many ways you can help your child learn to read. In class we will read many stories. I will send copies of these books home. Please listen to and help your child read the books to you. I will also send home some fun activities and games for your family to enjoy together.

I look forward to an exciting year of learning. Thank you in advance for the important part you play in helping your child learn to read.

Sincerely,

_____

Estimado padre de familia:

En el curso de este año escolar, su hijo aprenderá sobre sonidos, letras y palabras. Hay muchas maneras en que usted puede ayudar a su hijo a aprender a leer. En el aula leeremos muchos cuentos. Enviaré copias de los textos a su casa. Tenga la amabilidad de escuchar y ayudar a su hijo a leer los libros. También enviaré algunos juegos y actividades divertidas a su casa para que los disfruten juntos.

Será un año de aprendizaje emocionante. Le agradezco de antemano el apoyo que aportará al ayudar a su hijo a aprender a leer. Sin más por el momento, me despido cordialmente.

Atentamente,

_____

Closed Syllable	a syllable or morpheme that precedes one or more consonants, as in /a/ in hat
Diphthong	a vowel sound produced when the tongue moves or glides from one vowel sound to another vowel or semivowel sound in the same syllable. Example: bee, bay, boo, boy, and bough
Formal Assessments	the collection of data using standardized tests or procedures under controlled conditions
Formal Assessment	an assessment that is both an instructional tool that a teacher and student use while learning is occurring and an accountability tool to determine if learning has occurred. Note: Benchmark Literacy Formal Assessments include Comprehension Strategy Assessment Handbooks for grades K-6.
Grapheme	a written or printed representation of a phoneme, as b for /b/ and oy for /oi/ in boy
High-frequency Word	a word that appears many more times than most other words in spoken or written language
Homonym	a word with different origin and meaning but the same oral or written form as one or more other words, as bear (an animal) vs. bear (to support) vs. bare (exposed)
Homophone	a word with different origin and meaning, but the same pronunciation as another word, whether or not spelled alike, as hare and hair
Homograph	a word with the same spelling as another word whether or not pronounced alike, as pen (a writing instrument) vs. pen (enclosure).
Informal Assessments	evaluations by casual observation or by other nonstandardized procedures. Note: Benchmark Literacy Informal Assessments include Informal Assessment Handbooks for reading comprehension, writing, spelling, fluency, vocabulary and English Language development provide teacher observation checklists, forms, and rubrics for ongoing assessment.
Initial Blend	the joining of two or more consonant sounds, represented by letters that begin a word without losing the identity of the sounds, as /bl/ in black, /skr/ in scramble.
Listening Center	a place where a student can use a headset to listen to recorded instructional material
Miscue	a term to describe a deviation from text during oral reading or a shift in comprehension of a passage

Modeling	teacher's use of clear demonstrations and explicit language
Open Syllable	a syllable ending in a vowel sound rather than a consonant
Oral Reading	the process of reading aloud to communicate to another or to an audience
Phonological Awareness	awareness of the constituent sounds of words in learning to read and spell (by syllables, onsets and rimes, and phonemes)
Print Awareness	a learner's growing recognition of conventions and characteristics of a written language, including directionality, spaces between words, etc.
Sight Word	a word that is immediately recognized as a whole and does not require word analysis for identification
Teacher Resource Web Site	a free Benchmark Education Web site that provides a searchable database of titles, levels, subject areas, themes, and comprehension strategies; the site contains downloadable resources including literacy texts and teacher's guides, comprehension question cards, oral reading records, take-home books, and assessment resources
Teacher Resource System	the analysis of the structural characteristics of the text, coherence, organization, concept load, etc.

Baumann, J. F., E. C. Edwards, G. Font, C. A. Tereshinksi, E. J. Kame'enui, and S. Olejnik. "Teaching Morphemic and Contextual Analysis to Fifth-Grade Students." Reading Research Quarterly: 37 (2), pp. 150–176. 2002.

Bear, D. R., M. Invernizzi,, S. Templeton, and F. Johnston. Words Their Way: Word Study for Phonics, Vocabulary, and Spelling Instruction. Columbus, OH: Merrill Publishing Company, 1995.

Blevins, W. Teaching Phonics & Word Study in the Intermediate Grades. New York: Scholastic, 2001.

Cunningham, Patricia M. Phonics They Use: Words for Reading and Writing. Boston: Allyn & Bacon. 2005.

Cunningham, Patricia M., and Dorothy P. Hall. Making Words. Torrance, CA: Good Apple, 1994.

Ganske, K. Mindful of Words: Spelling and Vocabulary Explorations 4-8. New York: Guilford Press, 2008.

Ganske, K. Word Journeys: Assessment-guided Phonics, Spelling, and Vocabulary Instruction. New York: Guilford Press, 2000.

Ganske, K. Word Sorts and More: Sound, Pattern, and Meaning Explorations K–3. New York: Guilford Press, 2006.

Gill, S. "Teaching Rimes with Shared Reading." The Reading Teacher 60, pp. 191–193. 2006.

Moats, L. "How Spelling Supports Reading—And Why It Is More Regular and Predictable than You May Think." American Educator, pp. 12-16, 20-22, 42-43. Winter 2005/2006.

Moats, L. C. "Teaching Decoding." American Educator, pp. 42–49. Spring/Summer 1998.

Schreiber, P. A., and C. Read. "Children's Use of Phonetic Cues in Spelling, Parsing, and–Maybe–Reading." Bulletin of the Orton Society, 30, pp. 209–224. 1980.

Tunmer, W. E. and Nesdale, A. R. "Phonemic Segmentation Skill and Beginning Reading." Journal of Educational Psychology, 77, pp. 417–427. 1985.

Zutell, J. "Word Sorting: A Developmental Spelling Approach to Word Study for Delayed Readers." Reading & Writing Quarterly, 14, pp. 219–238. 1998.